Pippa Roscoe lives in Nor[...] and makes daily promises [...] day she'll leave her compu[...] in the countryside. She can[...]remember a time when she wasn't dreaming about handsome heroes and innocent heroines. Totally her mother's fault, of course—she gave Pippa her first romance to read at the age of seven! She is inconceivably happy that she gets to share those daydreams with you. Follow her on X, @PippaRoscoe.

Millie Adams is the very dramatic pseudonym of *New York Times* bestselling author Maisey Yates. Happiest surrounded by yarn, her family and the small woodland creatures she calls pets, she lives in a small house on the edge of the woods, which allows her to escape in the way she loves best—in the pages of a book. She loves intense alpha heroes and the women who dare to go toe-to-toe with them.

AN ENEMY'S CONSEQUENCE

PIPPA ROSCOE

MILLIE ADAMS

MILLS & BOON

First published in Great Britain 2026
by Mills & Boon, an imprint of HarperCollins*Publishers* Ltd,
1 London Bridge Street, London, SE1 9GF

www.harpercollins.co.uk

HarperCollins*Publishers*, Macken House, 39/40 Mayor Street Upper, Dublin 1, D01 C9W8, Ireland

An Enemy's Consequence © 2026 Harlequin Enterprises ULC

Their Boardroom Baby © 2026 Pippa Roscoe

Heir of Scandal © 2026 Millie Adams

ISBN: 978-0-263-41765-4

01/26

This book contains FSC™ certified paper and other controlled sources to ensure responsible forest management.

For more information visit www.harpercollins.co.uk/green.

Printed and Bound in the UK using 100% Renewable Electricity at CPI Group (UK) Ltd, Croydon, CR0 4YY

THEIR BOARDROOM BABY

PIPPA ROSCOE

MILLS & BOON

PROLOGUE

HE HAD TO find Maria. He… Micha could barely pull his thoughts together. They'd scattered like the marbles he'd seen other children play with on the streets. He couldn't… He didn't…

Gio Gallo, the man he'd had the temerity—and desperation—to try and steal from, the man who had plucked Micha and his mother from the streets, given him a job, an education, a place to live, a future, the man to whom he owed *everything*, had just broken his heart.

Ask her. Ask her and see what she says.

Micha was a few days from his eighteenth birthday. And he'd been happy. He'd been pinch-me-hard-because-this-didn't-happen-to-people-like-me happy. Gio had been his fairy godfather far beyond the time when Micha had believed in fairytales—if he ever had.

He'd grown up hard and quick, forced to do and see things most adults never did. Not that he'd ever lay the blame at his mother's feet. She'd done the best she could. She'd done *whatever* she could and he forced his thoughts away from the darkness that filled his mind when memories of the past came calling. His father had run off before he was born, leaving his mother saddled with debts she had no hope of paying, and debtors who had plenty of ideas. He'd been on edge, hovering between desperation and hopelessness when he'd run across Gio.

Gio, who had given him everything.

Gio, who wanted to send him away.

Gio had brought him into his business, his family and his sprawling family estate in Tuscany, and Micha had thrived. As for the rest of his family? They were not all like Gio, who had seen in him what no money could have bought—an intelligence that matched his own and a determination that would achieve great things, given half the chance. No, instead, most of the Gallos simply saw a half Italian and half Russian illegitimate street urchin who would never amount to anything.

Maria hadn't thought that though. She and Antonio had never treated him as anything but an equal. They had befriended him, and they became inseparable. The Three Musketeers, that's what they had been called. He hadn't understood the reference at first and had to look it up, but he liked it. Three friends who would do anything for each other.

Ask her and see what she says.

Micha had genuinely thought he and Maria had been careful enough that no one had known about their relationship. He stumbled over the word *love*. He felt it, but could still hardly believe that someone like Maria could feel that way for him. But he *adored* her. She filled his every thought. She made his heart ache just at the sight of her.

But Gio wanted to send him away.

Micha had always wanted to work for Gio. He'd wanted to repay the man who had changed his and his mother's entire lives. He was going to work for Gio and so was Maria. Because Maria wanted to run Gallo Group—the international conglomerate that Gio ruled with an iron fist.

But the only way that Gio would allow that to happen was if she married Antonio—her adopted cousin. Gio Gallo was *fixated* on the union of his two grandchildren, having given up fully on his own, useless children.

Micha had thought that if he could just prove himself, if he could show the old man just how good he was, Gio might eventually change his mind. He'd thought he would have time.

'I'm sending you to Paris,' Gio had announced that morning.

'That's…kind of you, Mr Gallo, but I'd rather stay here. To be near—' *Maria* '—my mother.' The guilt at the lie twisted in his soul.

'This is no problem. I will be providing you both with accommodation.'

'I have—' *friends* '—colleagues here. And I was just beginning to grow—'

From behind his desk, Gio had pulled up to his full height, the black-eyed glare stopping Micha's words so much so that he nearly bit his tongue.

'It's just that—' Micha had tried again.

'No,' Gio said. The word a bullet. 'It's not your mother, it's not your friends or your career prospects. What it *is*,' he said, stressing the word, 'is an impossibility.'

'Sir, I—'

'She is not meant for you,' Gio spat, the poison dropping into Micha's skin. 'You know my feelings on this.'

Micha clenched his jaw.

'But, really, it's not *my* feelings you have to worry about. You know how much she wants to lead this company. At seventeen, she already has a better business head than my children do at twice her age. She was born for this. She wants this. And she *will* choose this over you, Micha.'

Micha huffed out a disbelieving breath.

She wouldn't.

'Ask her, Micha. Ask her and see what she says.'

He couldn't say it was sadness that he'd seen in the old man's eyes. Pity and such things were far beyond Gio's emotional capabilities. But it didn't matter, Micha thought to himself. She would choose him.

Micha found her lounging on the large verdant lawn of Gio's Tuscan villa laughing with Antonio and for a moment a vicious splinter of jealousy cut through his heart. They *did* look good together. Together they could run Gallo Group and life would be easy and rich and…

'Micha!' Maria called when she caught sight of him, her gaze happy and her face bright.

His heart shuddered and he forced a smile to his lips.

'*Ciao bella,*' Micha called as he drew closer.

Antonio raised a hand to clap him on the back when he arrived.

'Good, take this one off my hands, please. She's driving me round the bend. I have to go, Mama is waiting,' he said easily, dropping a kiss to Maria's cheek and another slap to Micha's back. 'Look after her,' Antonio called as he loped back up to the estate.

Maria smiled up at him and patted the ground beside her, Micha dropping to his knees strangely out of breath.

'I have to ask you something,' he said, focusing on the tumble of dark curls that surrounded her like a halo.

'Hello, how are you? Well, thank you, and you?' Maria said on a laugh which petered out when she saw the look on his face. 'Of course, you can ask me whatever you like,' she said, placing a hand on his forearm.

'What would…?' Micha swallowed.

Tell her.

No.

Tell her why you're asking.

'What would you do to become head of this company? If Gio offered it to you? What would you do?' The words rushed out of Micha's mouth, his heart thudding painfully, as if already he was running from her answer, as if already he was rushing to pack his bags for Paris.

Would you do it? Would you marry Antonio if Gio asked?

Maria blinked at him, pulling a strand of her curls that the wind had blown across her face. Her smile bright and her eyes gleaming.

'Anything,' she said, enthusiastically. 'Anything. You know that.'

And then she leaned forward and pressed a kiss against his lips, not knowing that her declaration had broken him forever.

CHAPTER ONE

Eleven years later...

THE SOUND OF her heels against the marble flooring of the foyer of Gallo Group headquarters in France made Maria Aurora Guilia Gallo feel like a *boss*. The boss that she would be within *months*.

Some may have found it petty that she had taken the Gallo Group jet from Italy to France for the sole purpose of rubbing that very fact into Micha Rufina's face, but she didn't care.

The receptionist looked at her warily and Maria realised that it was a very real possibility that she had just growled. Out loud.

She shook it off, sending a ripple across the billowing cream silk button-up shirt, tucked into the camel-coloured cashmere trousers pressed to perfection with a flawless crease down the centre of each leg. The patent leather cream one-of-a-kind Louboutins—the ones clicking *so* satisfyingly towards the private elevator that only family and board members had access to—were her favourite pair.

Every single item of clothing, down to the lace basque, had been intentionally chosen. They were pieces of her armour. The armour she would wear to the final battle she ever had with Micha Rufina—her nemesis. Her enemy. And if he had been anything before that, anything more, she had forced herself to burn it from her memory until all that remained was a jagged scar, hidden so deep, her heart could barely remember it.

She arrived at the lift, swiped her key card and waited.

A woman came hurrying up to her.

'Mademoiselle Gallo, it's so lovely...' she trailed off when Maria cut her a glare. 'Does Mr Rufina know you're here?' The pitch of the poor woman's voice rose into the stratosphere.

'No,' Maria replied, turning back to the lift, ending any and all hopes of further conversation the receptionist may have had.

To her right was the bank of public lifts that would take the building's staff to whatever floor they worked on. She was aware of a few of the staff casting surreptitious glances her way as they left for the evening. Or trying to at least.

At first, Maria had bemoaned the way that she drew the male gaze.

'They'll never take me seriously,' she'd complained to her cousin Antonio. 'All they see is this,' she'd said, yanking on the thick tumble of long black curls. 'And these,' she'd said, pushing out her chest. Antonio had barked out a laugh and pushed her out of his face, telling her to 'get those things away from me.' They'd both ended up crying with laughter. 'Then, *mi amor*,' he'd said, 'make them take you seriously in spite of it.'

He'd been right. As always. Her cousin, her favourite family member in the whole wide world, and not just because the rest of them were worse than a den of poisonous vipers out for whatever cent they could get their greedy little hands on. No, Antonio had always been there supporting her, cheering her on, even when her own parents wouldn't. And so what if, for the last six years, Antonio had been a little distracted by his company, and avoiding the wrath of their grandfather. He was *still* the only person she could rely on to help her.

And so—despite having worked for longer, and harder, than most of the family members there—she had always used her clothing with near deadly intent.

Dress the part, act the part, get the part.

And today she had dressed *rich. Expensive.* She had dressed with the kind of class that went beyond money. And she'd done it for one reason and one reason only. She wanted Micha to know that she was so far beyond his reach they may as well be on different planets.

She wanted the boy she'd all but grown up with to know that this was the last time he would ever see her, no matter what he'd meant to her grandfather. The grandfather she had looked up to, had loved with everything she had in her, but who had never once seen her as worthy. The grandfather who had been a complex, deeply difficult man, but who sometimes she'd thought she understood. Until he had passed away and his last will and testament had been read. The shock waves that had rippled out had been catastrophic for some, but for her and Antonio? Life changing.

Because Gio's last will and testament revealed that no matter what they had done in the last six years—Antonio marrying someone else, Maria working every hour god sent to prove her worth—Gio Gallo had never given up on his eccentric and utterly irrational plan for her and Antonio to marry and together produce the perfect heir to inherit and run his empire.

It didn't matter that they were already Gallos. Antonio was adopted and she was female, these two things marring them in some way for their grandfather. But a child from the two of them? *That* was what Gio had wanted from the beginning. And if they didn't marry and fulfil the terms of the will? The entire company would be handed over to Micha Rufina—something Maria would *never* allow to happen while she still had breath in her lungs.

Antonio felt the same, which was why he had agreed to marry her in name only, to fulfil the terms of the will. Once Antonio got a divorce from the woman he'd married for convenience six years ago, he would then be free to marry *her.* And once they were married, once they had inherited the company, he would sign over his share of the company that he had absolutely no interest in and they would go their separate ways. Him to his business, Alessina International, and her to Gallo Group. And no one would ever look down on her again.

Ding.

The elevator doors opened and she entered a small cubicle big enough for three people at a push. The rose gold mirrored glass threw her image back at her in soft reflections and she counted the floors down as she rose higher up the building, all the way to the penthouse.

She had been to the Paris office of Gallo Group several times over the past six years, but made sure to do so when Micha wasn't there. She, unlike many others, had *not* been surprised by the meteoric rise of the boy Gio had taken under his wing all those years ago. No, she knew something of Micha's mettle.

And it was cold, hard and impenetrable.

But still, even she had to begrudgingly respect the man's business acumen. And where others in the family had snidely remarked about the 'transferable skills' of begging and thieving on the streets of Roma, she had only seen survival and determination, her sympathy for the boy she had once known refusing to budge on that instance. But she had also learned at her cost not to underestimate him.

Maria arrived at the penthouse floor with a ding and the lift doors parted to an exquisite reception area, continuing the use of the Gallo Group's brand colours of rose gold and cream, she saw with no small sense of satisfaction.

She had been integral to the rebranding three years before and while the board had raised objections Gio had seen the sense in her plan. Gallo Group's global perception skewed towards older males and while that had worked in the past, women were the future. And it was time for the Gallos to damn well catch up.

Frowning when she realised that the receptionist was not at her desk, she checked her watch. It was, she realised, after six in the evening, but it was strange that Micha's secretary would have left already.

She made her way on thickly piled carpet towards the regional CEO's office. The doors were wide open and unable to help herself, she entered and—just like the previous times she'd been here—immediately gravitated over to the window that stretched from floor to ceiling across one entire side of the huge office.

Many others might have boasted three-hundred-and-sixty-degree views. But what did that matter, when the one window of this office showed the Eiffel Tower in its entirety? Even as a little girl, she'd loved Paris. And her heart sighed just to see the most famed image of France stretched out before her.

For a moment, she wondered what it would have been like to be here under different circumstances, but before that half-formed fantasy could even take hold, she felt the hairs on the back of her neck raise.

'What are you doing here, *cara*?'

'You don't get to call me that,' she said, her words filled with the poison she wished she could use to hurt him the way that he'd hurt her.

Micha saw her flinch at his words, at how the muscles tightened all the way across her shoulders and back. He clenched his jaw, instantly regretting the word that had slipped past his usually ruthless self-control.

'How did you get in here?' he demanded, raising the armour that had broken at her shocking and surprising appearance in his office. He stalked over to his desk to put down the folder he had in his hands. And to buy himself some time to get over the impact of the sudden and perturbing sight of Maria Gallo.

He had seen her only a few weeks before at Alessina Gallo's party. Antonio's mother was trying her best to keep the disparate threads of the family together in her father's absence. The man's will had left more than the company without leadership, and both the family and the business were at risk of breaking apart because of it.

'I walked.'

'Oh really? I thought you might have flown in on your broomstick,' he muttered under his breath.

'How original, Micha. Calling me a witch.'

Maria's words lashed across his skin and he winced. He knew how often she was belittled by family members who were half outraged that she dared to be more than just a pretty face. And while she and he had a somewhat fractious—okay, downright toxic—relationship, he was nothing like those who called her names like the one he had just used.

'You know I meant it differently,' he growled.

And her lack of response told him that she *did* know it. Otherwise, she would have nailed his balls to the wall.

'Where is your secretary?' she asked and he looked up to find her standing behind the chair opposite his desk, her hands gripping onto the back.

'Why? Afraid to be alone with me?' he couldn't help but taunt.

'From what I remember, there is little to be afraid of,' she bit back.

Ouch. How could he have forgotten that her tongue was quick and that her wit was harsh?

He locked his jaw before he could say anything that would take them further down a road neither of them wanted to travel. Frankly he didn't have time for this, for *her*. While the rest of the Gallos were playing games he seemed to be the only person with sense trying to keep the ship afloat, rather than deciding—or caring—who steered her.

'She's at a training seminar,' he said, lying about his secretary's whereabouts. The poor woman had been driven to the edge by the hounding the various outliers of the Gallo family were giving her, so he had let her go home early. Not everyone was privy to the contents of the will and it was causing problems.

Not that Maria would have cared about that. Oh no. All she probably cared about was that she would finally get her hands on the company that she—in all honesty—deserved. And if she did? She'd probably sack him. Perhaps that's why she was here. Perhaps—

That pulled him up short.

So much so that she caught him staring at her.

'What?' she asked.

Micha shook his head, not willing to put the idea in her head if it wasn't already. Which he doubted. He cursed under his breath.

'Out with it, Maria. I have things to do. Contracts to secure.'

She laughed, as if it were genuinely amusing to her that he actually worked here. He wanted to pinch the bridge of his nose, but that would give away his frustration. And it pleased him no end that it was her inability to ruffle him that caused her the greatest irritation.

'Sure. Why not. The last act of a drowning man. Have at it, Rufina.'

He nodded, shooing her away with his hand, until he realised the subtext beneath her words.

Last act.

Why not.

Cristo, she was going to do it. She was going to marry Antonio to get her hands on the company.

His hands, fists, pressed into the table, concealing the white knuckles betraying his feelings, and for one single heartbeat—nothing but blind fury, masked, leashed and utterly denied by the next pump of blood around his body.

Slowly, he raised his gaze to hers, inch by inch, covering the cream shirt and trousers she wore, luxurious, rich, expensive. The pearls at her neck, the free-falling thick curls that dropped over one shoulder. She'd probably dressed just to remind him that he'd once been nothing more than a street urchin, while she'd always been an heiress.

By the time he'd reached her face, her expression told him that his guess had been true. The gleam of satisfaction shone like a north star that would never point to a home for him. He thought…*minchia!* He didn't know what he thought.

Unlike the rest of the family, who had never even heard of Ivy McKellen, Micha knew all about the convenient marriage that took place six years ago between Ivy and Antonio, meant solely to circumvent the pressure piled on by Gio

Gallo for Antonio to marry Maria. But their relationship was a lot more complicated than Maria knew.

Micha had met Ivy. He'd seen the grit and determination that drove her, even in her darkest hours. And more than that, Micha had liked her. Whether Antonio knew it or not, Ivy was a near perfect match for him and *Cristo*, if he had even an ounce of intellect, he wouldn't let her slip away. Certainly not for the sake of a damn company—no matter how many billions it was worth.

And it was most definitely worth billions.

'What have you done, *cara*?' he demanded, his voice low to his own ears with a warning that he knew she wouldn't heed.

'What I had to do,' she shot back just as hard and just as low, and damn it if it didn't turn him on.

As a girl, she'd been all soft curves and sighs, giggles and curiosity. As a woman? She would be something else altogether. For a moment, the apocryphal sight of her entwined in Antonio's embrace rose in his mind, making him nearly want to retch.

'Antonio and I will be married by the end of the month,' she declared.

He barked out a laugh. 'That's ridiculous. He doesn't love you like that.'

'Who said anything about love?'

'*Dio mio*, are you so desperate for this company that marriage means nothing to you?' he accused. 'Vows before god, your family, your *mother*?'

Maria felt her cheeks heat with anger and her pulse pick up beneath her skin.

'My mother?' Maria scoffed. How dare he talk about her mother? About marriage. About *vows*. 'I'm surprised you managed to say all that with a straight face, Micha. Or is this just another little ploy to shame me, to manipulate me, *distract me*? "Look over here, Maria," all the while, you're over there...playing another game entirely.'

Bitterness dripped like poison between them.

'Well, I won't fall for it. Not this time,' she said, ignoring the way dark red slashes appeared on cheekbones she'd known both women *and* men to swoon over. 'My marriage to Antonio *will* happen,' she insisted. 'The company *will* be mine. And you *will* be gone.'

Micha's only response was the slight narrowing of his eyes.

Oh, damn this man! She was trying to have an epic, victorious moment and he wasn't doing what she'd spent years, a near decade, imagining. He was supposed to be on his knees, begging for mercy.

She turned away from him, wanting to hide her reaction to his words. He knew. He *knew* what her parents' marriage had been like. How distant and cold, and unbearable it had been for her. The endless sniping and degrading, demeaning and belittling from her father—the near horrific silence of her mother. She'd once begged and pleaded with them to get a divorce, hoping that perhaps then she might be able to find space to breathe from the suffocation she had grown up with. And ironically, it had been the one single thing in their entire marriage that they agreed on.

There would be no divorce.

Throughout her childhood she had sought sanctuary with Antonio and, yes, even at one point, Micha. At many points even—but she refused to dwell on those times. Together the three of them had run amok throughout Tuscany and it had felt as if the entire world was at their feet. They had been the only family her age or near enough—distant cousins removed more than once were either older or not yet born. As for siblings, for her father, her mother's inability to bear a second child only furthered the distance between the wife who had failed him and the daughter who would always be a disappointment instead of the heir apparent he'd always wanted.

Antonio and Micha had been her salvation. They had protected her, distracted her. Antonio's mother had called them the Three Musketeers, and they had imagined playing with swords, attacking their enemies and cutting down their foes.

Well, she was still doing that. Only now, her weapon of choice was marriage. Marriage to Antonio. Not marriage to the boy she had once given her sovery-precious heart to. She braced herself before turning back to where Micha was riffling through some pages on his desk, still standing.

And oddly, she knew that he would stand for as long as she did. Something gentlemanly that he had inherited from her grandfather. He might not have been related to her by blood, but Micha carried some things from Gio Gallo that were instinctive. The way he held himself. His manners. It was perhaps a goddamn relief that he hadn't inherited the man's morals. Micha was ruthless enough by himself. He didn't need that in his blood too.

'It will, perhaps, be a little harder than you think to get rid of me,' he said, without bothering to look at her. It made her feel small. It made her feel dismissed. But she was done allowing Micha Rufina to make her feel those things. She'd had enough of that when she was sixteen.

'On the contrary. I think you'll find it quite expeditiously done with two little words. You're fired.'

'You underestimate how much I do for this company, Maria.'

'And you overestimate how much I care,' she shot back,

recklessly. Because no matter what had passed between them, no matter where in the world they were, he had *always* made her reckless.

'You'd do it, wouldn't you? You'd fire me, and damn the consequences?' he asked, a strange light in his eye.

'Absolutely.'

'No questions?'

'None.'

'I have one,' he said, surprising her a little.

'Shoot.'

'Do you really believe that you hate me?'

She stilled, sensing the danger in his question.

'Your arrogance is truly exceptional, Micha,' she fired back.

'Answer the question.'

'Believe? I don't *believe*. I *know* how much I hate you, Micha. Much as that might shock you. If the rumours are true, you've built quite the dance card from the women here in Paris.'

'Careful, Maria. Sounds a little like jealousy to me.'

Maria scoffed. 'It's not jealousy, Micha,' she said sweeping her gaze over him, 'it's disgust.'

He threw his head back and barked a laugh, dismissing her put-down. The long column of his neck was stubbled with the shadow of a beard she knew he'd shaved that morning.

Dressed in a three-piece suit, he should have looked all business and boring. But damn it, he looked anything but. The grey superfine wool of the suit was cut to fit him perfectly, with a white shirt made from Egyptian cotton. He filled it all out to perfection.

'See, I don't think that you hate me,' he said circling back round to his earlier question, his tongue sweeping out for barely a second before his teeth plunged into his bottom lip, as he looked at her in a very dominant and utterly unbusinesslike way.

No. This? Here? Right now? He was pure alpha male. A predator stalking its prey.

And she was the prey.

He shrugged off his suit jacket and hung it on the back of his chair, before coming around from behind the large ornate table that had once been used by her grandfather. He came to stand in front of her as he unhooked his cufflinks and pocketed them, before rolling back the sleeves of his shirt, something she found inexplicably fascinating.

He leaned back against the desk, arms folded across his chest—pulling the shirt tight across his chest and biceps beneath the matching grey waistcoat—his gaze running up and down the length of her body insolently, *carelessly*, heating every single place it touched.

And he knew it too.

Micha took his time, and his fill. Oh, he was aware how crass it was, but at this point he realised that he had very little to lose.

For years, he'd behaved himself. He'd done as Gio wanted, confined himself to the little box that Gio Gallo had put him in, safely away from the proximity of his favourite *female* grandchild. The gender qualifier wasn't important to him, but it had been to Gio. Gio, who had all but been near maniacal about who his business empire went to after his death.

Gio had been obsessed with it going to a male of the family—but Antonio wasn't a Gallo by blood, his adoption by Alessina apparently not enough to satisfy the old man. But a marriage between Antonio and Maria—an adopted grandchild and a female grandchild?—that had seemed just about enough in Gio Gallo's mind.

And Micha? Oh, he'd been used as the stick to beat or threaten the Gallos with for years and Gio's death had not changed that. Micha would inherit the entire company, lock, stock and barrel, if Antonio and Maria didn't marry.

No one, not even the two people he'd once considered friends, *more* even, had ever once thought that he might actually be good at what he did here. That he might actually have added to the wealth of the Gallos—heaven forbid, that he might actually even deserve it. But then…not even Gio Gallo had truly thought that of Micha.

'I *do* hate you,' she ground out from between perfect white teeth, bared at him in a silent growl. 'And this? This is the last time you'll ever see me,' she announced with a flourish.

He smirked, unable to help himself.

'What's so funny?' she demanded, furious that her threat hadn't been met with trembling knees and chattering teeth.

She must have forgotten that he was built differently than the simpering, pathetic members of the Gallo clan on whom her ire would have worked.

'You. Threatening me.'

'It's not a threat, it's a promise.'

'Mmm,' he said, closing the distance between them in just a few short strides.

'What are you doing?' she asked, backing up, startled when her legs hit the back of the chair behind her.

'Whatever I want,' he replied, unable to take his gaze from her. His eyes searched, scored, imprinted every single moment of her onto his soul. The way that the silk of her shirt shivered when she breathed, the superbly fitting palazzo trousers, pressing against skin and curves he'd never once forgotten.

Oh, they'd not done much as teenagers, no matter what Gio Gallo had thought. No matter what anyone had thought. Heavy petting, the Americans might have called it. But it hadn't mattered. He'd know her in one hundred years. Blind, deaf and unable to speak, he'd *know* her.

But she'd never really known him, had she?

'Stop it,' she said, trying to back up again.

'Why?' he asked, cocking his head to one side. 'What are you going to do? Fire me?' he taunted.

He pressed closer to her, knowing that he was invading her space, obsessively hunting the flush that started from the sliver of skin he could see in the V of her shirt and crept up her throat. The pulse that flickered at the base of her jaw. The tremble to her lips she tried to stop by pinning one beneath her teeth.

'Maria,' he warned.

'Yes?'

'That is not helping.' His voice was a growl.

She clenched her teeth together.

'You can't do this,' she said, putting her hands on him. His heart thundered at the press of her palm over it, and he finally gave in to the need that was coursing through his veins. The one he had spent years hiding, denying, destroying.

He'd been fooled into thinking he had it under control. But he was wrong. So wrong.

Maria looked up at him with huge dark brown eyes, her hair cascading in tumbled curls down her back, her lips parted as if on a gasp.

'Then stop me,' he commanded.

He waited.

He waited for the hands on his chest to push him away in disgust, the way he'd imagined her doing time and time and time again in the deepest, darkest dreams of half-formed memories and damaged desires.

He waited for her to turn her head to the side, to snub him as she so often did in public, their hostilities as much a spectator sport for the families as not.

He waited for her to hiss and spit and curse his name, to damn him to hell and back.

But she didn't. She did none of those things. Instead, she seemed as enthralled to this madness as he was. Her gaze, licking at him like flames that would devour. Hot, harsh, *demanding*.

'Stop me,' he half begged, himself no longer sure whether this was madness or mistake.

Her lush lips parted, but nothing came out.

He'd given her warning. She was certainly bold enough to refuse him if she wanted.

He claimed her mouth, already half open beneath his, no timid greeting of soft gentle touches. This was a clash, powerful, brash, possessive and demanding, consuming to the point of insanity. It was like coming home and leaving home all at once. Something earthily familiar and completely unknowable. Déjà vu and *jamais vu*, together at the same time.

They both pulled back, shocked, confused, glaring accusations at each other, breaths heaving, lips tingling.

'You—'

Micha cut her off before she could ruin it and claimed her once more. His hands thrust into her hair, shaping her head with his fingers, and she groaned her pleasure into his mouth and sank against his chest in wanton abandonment.

Dio mio.

CHAPTER TWO

MARIA WAS UTTERLY LOST. Completely and without question. She felt as if she was made up of pure sensual delight, every place she could feel, delicious, every pulse a throb so perfectly pleasurable, it was near inconceivable.

From just a kiss.

Per dio!

She indulged the moan of sheer want creeping up the back of her throat, her mouth opening just a little wider, which Micha took full advantage of. The thrust of his tongue carnal, sending thousands of little shivers across her skin until she trembled from the weight of them.

Her hands fisted in his shirt, pulling it taut across his chest. She wanted it gone. She wanted the barrier between their skin incinerated. With shaking fingers, she slipped the buttons of his waistcoat free, her hands stretching out beneath the silk lining, and not so gently scratching the sides of his torso through the cotton of his shirt.

The growl of pleasure against her lips only spurred her on.

Mirroring her hands, his palms moved from her head to her hips, dragging her against him, against the hard ridge of his arousal. The noise she made, primal, instinctive, spun out from her mouth into him, and he turned them, walking her backwards until her backside met the large office table.

He lifted her, effortlessly, up onto the table and pushed

his way between her legs in a move that was both possessive and domineering at the same time.

Oh, why was it *this* man? Why him?

Why was it only Micha who had ever made her this way?
This crazy, this aroused, this hedonistic, this wanton?

She closed her eyes, her head falling back as his lips tra-
versed the column of her throat and across her collarbone.
Delight fanned out in sparks across her skin, sinking into
her blood, her bones, her soul.

If she thought he'd stop, if she thought he'd lift the shirt
from the waist of her trousers, she'd been wrong. Instead,
with a near ruthless efficiency, he simply hooked his finger around the front of her basque and pulled, exposing her
breasts to his sight and her nipples to his tongue.

Wet heat pooled instantly between her thighs and where
she would have pulled her legs closed, she instead clamped
around Micha's hips, securing him in place, so that he could
tease every single erogenous zone she knew of.

She leaned back to give him more access, his mouth closing over one nipple, over the silk of her shirt, his tongue
leaving a damp stain on her breast, cooling to tease the taut
flesh as he turned his attention to the other.

Until, he returned hungrily to her mouth. With one hand
on her jaw, and the other swept around her backside, pulling her hard against him, she felt devoured. Completely and
utterly. There was no escape and she wanted none. Pleasure
and pressure were building in her, the restlessness frustrat-
ing as what she wanted ebbed and flowed from her reach.

'Maria.'

Her name, half plea, half promise, on his lips, in his
voice…it was as if it had travelled back through the years,
drenched from the depths of her memories. She opened her
eyes, and saw him gazing back.

Him.

Micha.

The boy who had broken her heart.

She shouldn't be doing this. She couldn't. Not again.

She pulled back from his hold, and she saw the moment the shutters came down, cutting her off from the savage heat of the previous moment.

'This was a mistake,' she said, scrabbling for the broken shards of her armour and pulling them about her defensively.

'Don't do that,' he warned, with a thread of darkness she'd not heard before.

'Don't what?'

'Don't demean this,' he commanded.

'Why? You did,' she threw at him as she pushed past him with her shoulder.

Micha reached out and clasped her wrist, stopping her when she would have left, spinning her back to face him. He had been talking about their kiss, but she was talking about the past. Her fury sparked gold shards of lightning in the depths of her chestnut-coloured eyes. He'd always been fascinated by the colour, as if one wasn't enough for her, she needed as many as she could get: browns, golds, some flashes of something near green.

The rest of her family had brown eyes so dark they appeared nearly black. But Maria had inherited her eyes from her mother, who had married into the Gallos. And now, they displayed fury in multicoloured hues.

'I went where your grandfather sent me,' Micha ground out. He refused to think back to that day, that time, when she'd severed his heart, gleefully telling him that she'd do anything to run Gallo Group, knowing that Gio had wanted her to marry Antonio. *Cristo*, here she was, exactly eleven years later, ready to do just that. He'd made the right decision then to leave. To protect himself and his mother. Because no one else would.

'You could have said no to him,' she accused.

This time he did laugh out loud. 'Yes, *cara*. Because we all know that Gio would have taken no for an answer.'

'You *could* have. You might have been the only one able to do it out of all of us,' she said, and he wondered whether he saw hurt there in her gaze or whether he was just so desperate to see it that he was imagining it.

'What about you?' he returned. 'When did you ever say no to your grandfather?'

She was shaking her head, sending the tumble of her curls swaying across her shoulders, when he let go of her wrist. Her obtuse denial infuriated him.

'You deny it? Even now you're rushing to do his bidding,' Micha pointed out. 'You feel nothing more for Antonio than familial love, yet you are going to marry him just as Gio wanted.'

'I'm going to marry Antonio because I want the company,' Maria insisted.

'Why that company? Why not any other company in the entire world? You're an incredible businesswoman. Your reputation is stellar. You're respected, financially solvent. *Cristo*, if you wanted to sell your shares in Gallo Group you would have millions at your disposal.'

You'd be free, he thought internally, the words sounding like an accusation and a plea at the same time.

'I don't want another company. I want this one. I want the one that I should have inherited all along, without having to do some silly tap dance. I want the one that, had I been born a man, would have been mine without question. I want the one that I have worked for my entire professional

life. I want,' she said, her breathing harsh with the fury
of her sense of injustice, 'the company that I have helped
grow, whose wealth I have helped increase. I want what I've
earned, Micha. I've earned Gallo Group. Far more than Antonio, who hasn't worked in it since he was twenty-one. Far
more than any of the uncles that have sat on the board and
done nothing but voted with their wallets.'

'Far more than me?' Micha asked finally when she paused
to take a breath.

Maria glared at him, unable to say anything back. Because out of everyone, he was the only other person who
had held a candle to what she'd given to Gallo Group. The
only other person who could stand at the helm without ruining it—no matter what her family might think of him.

'Or have you become like the rest of your family and decided that I am far from your equal?' he said, finally ready
to face the truth.

If they were burning bridges, then so be it. He would
burn them all.

'I am not like them,' she hotly denied.

'But you don't think we are equals, do you?'

'You aren't family, Micha.'

The punch of air that fell from his lips was the only sign
of the way she had cut him off at his knees. He'd always
thought it, but never really wanted to believe it. But she'd
never thought he was good enough. He wasn't like Antonio,
who'd had the good graces to get himself adopted. No, no
matter what he did, how hard he worked, he'd never shake
the stigma of his humble origins, or the depths of what he'd
been driven to do for his mother, for himself.

He looked down at her, seeing Maria in a new light. Beautiful, but cruelly removed.

She might think herself better than him, but that didn't

stop her wanting him. And it certainly didn't stop him wanting her.

'You might not like me, Maria. Or think me good enough. But you still desire me, don't you?' he bit out. 'That must *really* sting,' he said, satisfied by the sight of the flare in her gaze.

'I don't know what you're talking about,' she tried to dismiss.

But he wasn't letting her get away with it. Not this time. If she'd come to kick him out on his backside once she took over the company, then he was going to make her work for it. She was going to have to admit a few things and he wasn't going to let her go until she had.

'Oh really? That's not what those breathy little moans you were making in my ear only moments ago suggested,' he taunted in a cruel whisper.

He knew how much that would hurt. Because it hurt him too. To want her so much, to be driven to almost demented lengths by the memory of what had been, the knowledge of what could have been and the awareness of what never would be.

'Go on, tell me how much you hated my kiss,' he demanded, pressing into her personal space, forcing her back a step.

'I—' She searched his gaze, knowing and understanding morphing into frustration. She couldn't lie, but she wouldn't admit it either.

'Tell me, Maria, how much you hated the feel of my mouth on your breast,' he said, his gaze dropping to her mouth. 'My touch on your skin.'

'Micha—'

'Tell me,' he said dropping his lips to the shell of her ear, as she hit the wall of the office and had nowhere else to go, 'how you hated me so much you haven't fantasised about this for *years*.'

Her breath poured in and out of her, raising her chest to his again and again, the flush on her cheeks, the pink of her lips so recently kissed, a warning, a flare.

'I…' She swallowed, her head leaning up to look at him, her eyes glowing and her skin flushed. 'I can't.'

'Because you *didn't* hate it?' he pushed. 'Because you *have* fantasised about this? Because…' He swallowed, daring her, daring himself to go as far as this would take them. 'Because you *do* want this?'

She nodded her head slowly, not once taking her eyes off him. As if she were as bound to this madness as he was. And in that moment, he wasn't sure who had just won the battle, because it might have required his own surrender.

Maria stared at the man who had just bared her deepest secret to the light of day. That no matter how much she hated him, for leaving her, for walking away as if she were nothing, as if what they had shared was nothing, she still wanted him. Needed him like an addiction that wouldn't quit.

'Yes,' she said, the confession wrenched from her lips. 'Are you happy now?' she demanded, breath heaving in her chest, lust clashing with injustice, with the near ache of misery.

But when she looked into his eyes, the rich swirls of a bitter chocolate that had once danced with laughter—so long ago she thought she might have made it up—she didn't see happiness. She didn't see victory. She saw the same frustrated need that she felt.

'Not at all, *cara*,' he said, finally answering her question.

Frantic energy sparked and hissed in the air between them as they edged closer and closer to a line that had been drawn between them years before. As if they both knew that once they crossed it, there would be no going back. And there would be no going forward either.

But she couldn't take it any more. She couldn't live like this—in this half-life, stuck in the middle of what had been and what could never be.

'You understand? What you're doing?' she asked, lips trembling, from desire or fear she didn't know. Not fear of *him*. No matter what had passed between them, no matter how angry they had been with each other, she had never *feared* him.

But he was pushing them. Though, she had—she admitted to herself—started it by coming here. Perhaps she'd known that all along. Perhaps, in fact, that was what had brought her here. The truth of what had brought her here. Maybe all along she'd hoped that he would push her, that she would rile him enough to finally call her on it, in a way he'd never have dared to do while her grandfather was alive.

'Do you?' he asked her in return.

She nodded.

'I need to hear it, *mi amor.*'

The affectionate endearment made her want to growl, anger heating her cheeks with a flush, her antagonistic response enflaming his own.

'Yes,' she bit out from between clenched teeth.

'Undo your shirt,' he commanded, his voice guttural, the jump from hypothetical to real, to *happening*, lightning fast, dumping adrenaline and dopamine into her system, landing in the pulse points across her body.

He stepped back from her as if giving her space to do his bidding, his eyes heated and heavy on her body, waiting, impatient for her to reveal herself to him. His voyeurism spiked her pulse as she fought the natural inclination to refuse, to deny him. But to deny him would be to deny herself, and to deny the truth of what they had just agreed on. Because he was right. She did want this. She wanted this more than anything else in the world right now.

With one hand, she undid the button of the oyster silk shirt between her breasts. Micha's eyes were glued to every single move she made, making her feel the lie. Making her feel like she was precious to him, wanted beyond reason. The latter, she could just about believe.

She thought she might have rebelled under his scrutiny, but instead, she *delighted* in it. One by one, she freed the buttons, the heavy silk material slipping open, revealing skin barely covered only by the thin lace of the ivory basque she'd worn.

Her breasts felt heavy, aching from where his gaze lingered, desperate for his touch, but he didn't move an inch. Was he holding himself back or was he that impervious to her?

No. He couldn't be. Everything in her roared in denial and the sudden need for proof that he wasn't.

She rolled her shoulders back, the loose silk that had been barely hanging on top of her body finally falling down her arms, pooling at her wrists. Not satisfied by the flush on the cut of his cheekbones, her fingers went to release the button of her trousers, before stepping out of them and shaking the shirt free.

Her pulse raced, her heart thudding in her chest as she stood there in her Louboutins and basque, needing him to react, needing to push him, just so that she could feel him push back. In the reflection of the glass behind Micha, she caught a glimpse of herself, standing there—proud, powerful and determined.

And more aroused than she had ever been in her *life*.

Oh god, she needed him to ease this want in her. She

couldn't bear it any more. But if this was his plan…to get her to undress, and to not follow through, she might never recover. The thought needled into her brain, getting stuck, but just when she might have buckled under the fear of it, he moved.

He closed the distance between them in a blink of an eye. His lips took hers—there was no other way to describe it— took them, possessed them. His tongue plunged deep, filling her mouth, tangling with her own, and it was *magnificent*.

He swallowed her pleasure-drenched gasp, as his hands grasped her shoulders and drew her powerfully against him. With just the basque and his shirt, there was nothing to stop her from feeling the contours of his chest, of the muscles he hid beneath well-cut suits and layers of false sophistication.

Moans turned into whimpers and she was all but begging by the time he had finished the kiss.

'What is it you want, Maria? Tell me.'

'You,' she confessed.

And his hands roamed from her shoulders. One to her breast and one shockingly, over her backside, his palm caressing the curve of one cheek, fingers grabbing at her flesh. Damp wet heat pooled between her thighs and she bit her lip to stop the pleading, begging words that would have fallen if they'd been allowed.

She looked to him and saw one brow raised in knowing, knowing what she wanted and what she wouldn't admit to.

He shaped her thigh with the palm of his hand and hooked her leg over his hip, pressing her back against the wall and inserting himself between her legs in a way that left no further room for doubt. She bit her lip and moaned when she felt the ridge of his arousal at the juncture of her thighs, unable to regret the slip when he pushed against her, rubbing the aching bundle of nerves until she was shivering with want.

* * *

Maria's gasp was the most erotic thing Micha Rufina had ever heard and he couldn't hold himself back any more. He slipped a hand between them, his hand covering her core, the heel of his palm pressing against her clitoris in slow lazy circles that were the direct opposite of the way his pulse was raging beyond his control.

She shifted under her pleasure as if torn between wanting it and wanting to escape it, unaware that the tease was as much for himself as it was for her. Unable to resist any longer, he slipped a finger beneath the clasp of her basque, beneath the line of the dampened silk panties into hot slick flesh.

This time it was he who groaned out loud.

A shudder rolled between them and he was uncaring where it started from, who it started from.

Cazzo.

He shook his head, giving up the internal argument he'd been having with himself, and dropped to his knees. His hands swept around her trembling thighs, and he could hardly believe that was where he found himself. After so many years, so much denial…

But just the scent of her need for him drove all thought from his head.

'Micha.' His name on her tongue was a plea, a prayer.

He tore apart the clasps of the basque and inch by inch revealed the perfection of her as he pulled her panties down her legs. His heart thundered, punching at his ribcage. He was a ravaging beast hell-bent only on her pleasure. He parted her with one hand and reached to palm her breast with the other, as he took her core in an open-mouthed kiss, sinking into heaven.

He growled into her hot wet heat and she bucked against

his mouth, as his tongue probed, plunged, filled and teased. Maria panted for air, as his palms claimed her backside, holding her to him as he devoured her with licks and sucks and nips and...

'Micha.' This time his name was a warning that he didn't need. He knew how close to orgasm she was. In part, because *he* was shockingly close to orgasm, and she hadn't even touched him. Her body, shaking and restless, her breath harsh and short, her hands clutching and grasping at his shoulders and his hair.

She was on the edge and he damn near loved it. *Loved* that she was as driven to the brink by him as she was. That she too was drowning under whatever this was.

'Micha, please,' she begged.

'No,' he said, against her clitoris, refusing to give her a quick release from this no matter how she whimpered, caught on the edge of an orgasm as sharp as it was sublime. He punished them by drawing out the painful pleasure that was killing them both.

'*Micha*,' she pleaded.

'No,' he said again, pressing his tongue against the small bundle of nerves and shaking his head as she shivered almost frantically now.

'Oh god,' she whispered, 'oh god.'

He lost count of her prayers, and instead indulged in the way her body readied itself for pleasure, the increase in heat, the dampness welling beneath his tongue, the way her legs tightened around him, the way that her cries became screams, and her breath got faster and faster, as he licked and nipped, and pressed and sucked, harder and harder, until everything stopped in a moment of shocked, tension-locked stillness... And then she collapsed against him in the ultimate surrender.

CHAPTER THREE

MARIA CAME BACK to herself, slowly. Breath by breath, her pulse thundering. Her body, almost painfully sensitive to everything around her, the light, the feel of the wall against her back, the neckline of her basque digging into the soft slopes of her breasts, and Micha. Between her legs, still, taking little sips from her that sent shock waves through her body again and again. Her hands were still fisted in his hair, her traitorous body doing its own thing, holding him to her.

She tried to think about what she'd done, but she couldn't because pleasure was still coursing through her body, carried thick and heavy in her bloodstream. She wasn't done, and she knew that Micha most definitely wasn't done. She'd felt the ridge of his arousal, through the superfine wool of his trousers. The powerful, steely length of him. And now she wanted *that*.

Micha Rufina had turned her into a sensual voracious monster and it didn't matter. Because after today, she would never see him again.

And rather than focusing on how that made her feel, she chose to focus on what that meant for her. On the fact that maybe, finally, she could take whatever she wanted from him. One final and only chance, to know what it was like, to explore everything she possibly could before never having to see him again.

It was liberating. It was freeing. She could do anything. She could *ask* for anything. Demand it. All the fantasies that he'd taunted her about. She could have them. This night. Oh, she knew he wouldn't deny her a single thing. Because he'd had fantasies too. She'd seen them in his eyes when he'd looked at her.

Her fingers flexed in his hair, before tugging him back. She looked down at him, at his mouth, glistening with her own desire. He licked his lower lip without taking his eyes from her and her heart pounded painfully in her chest.

He ran a thumb over the curve of his bottom lip, and drew himself from his knees to stand before her, forcing her to crane her head back to keep the eye contact that was driving her near wild with want.

'What?' she asked, trying to unearth the indefinable look in his gaze that was something like surprise. 'Did you think I'd leave now?'

'Yes,' he replied with the brutal honesty that had dominated their entire exchange that evening.

'I'm not leaving until this is well and truly done,' she said, the words landing like unexploded bombs between them.

'Are you sure, *cara*?' he asked, loosening the tie at his neck with two vicious yanks, her eyes hungering for the sight of a chest that had been impressive eleven years before but now would be incredible.

'Absolutely.'

'*Va bene*,' he replied, pulling his tie completely free with a snap.

Her fingers dug for purchase into the wall behind her as he freed his shirt buttons, reversing the way that she had stripped for him earlier. He tugged the shirt free of his belted waist, as his eyes roamed downward from her face to her chest, her legs, her feet. She was achingly conscious she was still wearing her Louboutins, and in her undone basque she felt carnal. Erotic. The way his skin flushed as his gaze devoured her, made her feel dizzyingly high.

He shucked the shirt from his shoulders, and kicked off his shoes, toeing off his socks, and stood before her, his hands tackling the black leather belt with a ruthless efficiency that cracked the air as he removed it from his trousers.

The ridge of his arousal proud and powerful against the fine wool material, nothing self-conscious about him, he eased the taut material apart by flicking the button and releasing the zip just a touch. He stood bearing her scrutiny as she had borne his, presumably understanding her fascination, her desire. Not only to take in the changes of eleven years, but to relish the impact, the power it had on her. The dips and curves of his body, ones that she wanted to mould with her hands and her mouth, the way she imagined wrapping herself around him. *Wanting* to.

She left the security of the wall and stalked towards him, his gaze on her hers, his hands fisting at his sides, the only sign he was as affected by her as she was him. Instead of coming face to face with him, she circled around behind him. And finally she let herself *indulge*—perhaps unaware that it was easier for her to do so when he couldn't see the sheer enjoyment she took from his body.

Her fingers moulded and pressed into his shoulders, her lips tracing the trap muscles down from his neck, and towards the juncture of his waist. Her hands explored the sides of his chest and around the front, feeling their way across his abdomen and the hollow lines between his hips and the lower abdominals. She encased him perfectly to feel how he responded to her and she felt the breath lock in his chest, despite his taunting arrogant confidence.

His shoulders tensed against her breasts and, as her hands dipped lower, as she palmed him boldly over his trousers, the rumble of the growl in his throat sent shivers down her spine, the way he fought with himself not to push back against her hand and the fact that he had even done so. But she wanted him to lose that fight. Like she had. She wanted him desperate and begging. Pleading for release.

So, she came around to face him and just like he had, she dropped to her knees.

A string of curses turned the air a shocking vivid blue as he tried to stop her. But it was too late. This was what she wanted. What she'd always wanted.

She flicked his hands away and instead, slowly pulled the zipper down, parting the sides of his trousers and guiding them from his hips. The black briefs, close to his skin, cupped every single part of him lovingly, leaving absolutely nothing to the imagination. She bit her lip, a last moment of hesitation—not doubt, never doubt—before she swept those from around his waist, down over the musculature of his backside, and letting the hard, throbbing steel of him free. She took him in her hand first, the soft velvet of his skin so deceptive of the restrained power she knew, she *knew*, was there.

She gripped him gently, but firmly, as she lowered her fist to the base of him, the guttural exhale teasing her own arousal back to life. His hand fell to her shoulder, anchoring him, when she felt the tiny tremors across his body begin, and so it was with a smile that she took him into her mouth, closing around the blunt tip of his penis, and humming her pleasure around the thick, heavy, hot feel of him.

'*Madonna mia.*'

And honestly, Maria couldn't tell whether she'd thought it

or he'd said it. He felt incredible in her mouth as she sucked and drew down on him. The power of what it did to him.

A hand fisted her hair, and she loved it—flexing and tightening, urging her on, or holding her back, it was a hardline into the wants and needs she'd never allow herself to voice.

His hips bucked, slowly at first, tentatively until she drove him ragged with teeth that gently and carefully scraped across the corona of his penis, her tongue testing the little nerve beneath it. The sound he made was unholy, sending fireworks across her skin and to her overly sensitised core.

More curses filled the air. *'Basta!'* he demanded, pulling away from her. It was small, but it was enough. But they both knew that he'd broken first. But she'd needed that, because he'd made her beg.

Oh, he was going to make her pay for that. It had taken absolutely everything in Micha to pull back from the brink of an orgasm that would have come far too hard and far too soon, and the sight of her still on her knees looking up at him, wide knowing eyes, was too damn much.

'Get up,' he ordered, turning his back, unable to keep looking at her like that and retain his control.

'Please,' she taunted from behind him and he cursed again, knowing that she'd stay right there until he said it.

On his lips, the word sounded feral, closer to a growl, but it was enough. He saw her rise to her feet in the reflection of the window. The low lighting of the penthouse office would have displayed them for all of Paris to see, if they hadn't been so far out of reach from any prying eyes.

But when he turned to find her standing in the middle of his office, barely covered by what remained of her basque, he thought for the first time that entire exchange that he'd seen a moment of vulnerability.

He nearly let loose the bitter laugh that filled his throat. She had no idea what she did to him. What he would do for her. What he had *done* for her. And before he could stop himself, he'd closed the distance between them and taken her in his arms and with his mouth. He'd swept her up against him, her thighs coming around his waist, ankles locking together, her hair tumbling around them in a cocoon.

'You don't want this, at any point,' he said between kisses that bruised and punished them equally, 'you stop. You say it. You tell me to stop,' he commanded.

'Like I'd have a problem with that,' she dismissed.

'This isn't a contest *cara*, I'm serious,' he said, flexing the grip on her thigh in warning.

He glared up at her, their dark gazes clashing and sparking, but she saw the moment the bravado fell away, and the tumble of tendrils shivered as she shook her head.

And that was all he needed before he walked them back towards the desk, placing her on the edge, and pushing everything from it onto the floor with a single sweep of his arm. She squeaked, starting in surprise, but he didn't care. He hungered for her. He always had. It had been too long and he knew that for as long as he lived, there would never be anyone like her for him. Never. She was it. She always had been. No matter how impossible it was and would always be. And if he was going to drown, then he would make sure that it would—for both of them—be *spectacular*.

Her hands reached for him before he could even take a breath, and he plucked his wallet from his pocket, retrieving the condom before tossing the wallet over his shoulder. He tore the foil packet open, her gaze hot and heavy on his every move, Maria biting her lip as he removed the condom and rolled the latex over his hardened length.

Her fingers shooed his hands away and she drew him to the cross-hatch of curls at the juncture of her legs, slowly guiding him between her folds, moaning in delight as she teased her clitoris with the head of his cock.

His fists flexed on the toned muscles of her thighs, spreading them wider, making more space for him. Her eyes opened straight onto his as she held him at her entrance. This was it. It was the furthest they had ever gone, back when they'd fooled around as teenagers barely understanding themselves, let alone another's body.

But things were different now. So very different, and without another thought, he slowly pushed into the hot wet welcoming heat of her, and *dio mio*, there were not enough words in the dictionary to describe this moment.

His head fell back, utterly surrendering to all that was sensation, that was Maria, that was what they could do together. Her shocked gasp expressed perfectly how stunned he was by this shared moment.

Micha swallowed. 'Should I—' He tried to engage his brain to offer to stop when Maria told him absolutely not to stop if he wanted to survive the night.

Micha wasn't sure he would survive either way at this point. Her heels pressed him deeper into her from where they were braced against the backs of his thighs. Her internal muscles seized his erection and if he wasn't careful, he'd start shaking very soon. Slowly, inch by glorious inch, he pushed deeper and deeper, her breathy little moans all the encouragement he needed, until she had taken him to the hilt.

And he had to move, or she'd know. She'd know how at her mercy he truly was, and he couldn't have that. So, he pulled back halfway before thrusting powerfully back into her, her nails gouging his back, and the cry of pleasure in his ear all that he needed to do it again and again.

'Oh god,' she whimpered as she spread her legs wider to accommodate him and he couldn't not look, his heart thumping powerfully when he saw how they were joined, how she took him, how much she wanted him. Sweat beaded his brow and tension coiled in his balls and in the base of his spine.

Madonna mia, she drove him insane with want.

With what felt like one fist squeezing his erection and another a vice around his heart, all he could do was make it so that she'd never forget him, make it so incredible that she'd never think of another man again without comparing them to him. If she was going to be written on his heart for the rest of his life, then she deserved the same.

Maria had never, *could* never, have imagined it would be like this. And while he drowned her in a pleasure so sensual, so *generous*, he could never know that it was her first time. That he was her one and only and always had been. She couldn't ever let him know that. Because if he did, he'd know the power he had over her. The lengths that she'd gone to, to preserve whatever dignity and power she had, would be all but destroyed. And she couldn't have that. But also, she couldn't *not* have this. Because this was…

He moved again, slowly pushing deeper into her, and the moan that fell from her lips was nothing short of erotic. Her head fell back and one hand palmed her breast as the other was around her backside, pulling her to the edge of the table, pulling her onto him.

On to him. *Oh god.* Her internal muscles flexed around the hardened length of his arousal.

There had been a moment at the very beginning where it had hurt, the sting of his intrusion, the unfamiliarity of it, that had locked her breath in her lungs and silenced her words. But so quickly it had transformed into something else, something softer, hotter, building into pleasure, to passion, building to a craving that she couldn't imagine, yet instinctively knew.

Her body reacted purely on instinct, her nails digging and grasping for him, for more, with him so deep within her, she wasn't sure where she ended and he began. And while a part of her thought that it shouldn't be like this with him, it shouldn't be this magical with a man who had all but broken her heart so long ago, a silent, more primal, more intuitive part of her had always known it would be like this.

He reached between them, his thumb pressing against her clitoris, pushed into applying pressure by the thrusts of his hips, the tilt of her pelvis, her body greedy for all that she could take from this one and only time she'd ever have with him. If she had to fit a lifetime of pleasure into this one moment, then damn it, she would.

'Lie back for me,' he ordered and, cheeks flushing at the command in his voice, the only one she'd allow him to give, she did. Her body shifted into the new position as he hooked one of her legs over his shoulder, the way that her heart pounded in time with each thrust of his hips as he slid even deeper into her reaching a part of her that simply imploded.

Out of nowhere, she was hit by an avalanche of pleasure. It slid over her, burying her, muting the world in a thick, hot blanket in the single space between heartbeats. Her body bucked and twisted as Micha found his release at the same time, the pulsing and clenching of their joined bodies prolonging a pleasure so intense it was near torturous.

She wanted to laugh, to cry, as if the pleasure had burst

through all the barriers that had been holding back her emotions for months, for *years*. But she didn't want any of that. She didn't want to feel those things. She just wanted… Oh, she didn't know any more. She bit her lip, trying to pull everything back before Micha could see.

He was braced over her, his head bent over her heaving chest, his own breaths powerful punches that she felt all over her body. The only thing that made this, any of this, okay was that he seemed as affected as her. That they had at least, finally, been equals, brought low by themselves, rather than each other.

His body heated hers as her skin began to cool, as realisation began to dawn and as doubts crept in. She needed to get away. She needed to regroup. She needed to get dressed, deeply discomforted by her vulnerability in her present state.

Micha leaned back up, away from her, his dark gaze searching hers, his eyes containing as many questions and as much confusion as she felt in that moment.

She opened her mouth to speak, but he took one final advantage of her and claimed her mouth with his. He didn't need to. They'd already shared what they were going to. But for some reason the kiss soothed just a little of the ragged hurt beginning to build. That he still wanted her, after everything. That he needed what she needed.

The kiss was raw, guttural, a tangle of teeth and tongue, of fisted hands and grasping fingers, and over far, far too soon.

'Stay there,' he said, as he gently left her body, pulling his trousers up over his hips and stalking over to a door at the back of the room.

Maria waited until he was gone, before lurching up off the table, and searching for her clothes. No way would she stay there waiting for him like one of his Parisian girls. She grasped her shirt from where she'd thrown it over a chair, found her trousers on the opposite side of the room. She was just about to put them on when Micha re-emerged into the room holding a small cloth in his hands.

'I should have known you wouldn't listen.'

Maria clenched her jaw, her gaze flicking to the cloth he'd brought for her. The touch, the care, the thought all more than she wanted to consider right now.

'Why would I start now?' she bit back, realising that the small room he'd been in must have been a bathroom. She clutched her clothes to her chest and passing him, she plucked the cloth from his hands, taking herself into the small en suite, ignoring what she thought might have been a growl.

Micha flexed and released his fists, frustrated that she wouldn't even let him care for her after what they'd shared. They didn't have to like each other for that, but she wouldn't even let him do that. Cristo, he'd taken her like an animal. He'd been as lost to Maria as his mother had been to the addiction that she'd spent her entire life fighting.

That's what made Maria such a risk. That she had, and always would, be the one thing that he could lose himself to. But Gio had been right. She wasn't meant for him. Not then. And certainly not now.

He stalked over to where his shirt had lain beneath hers and shrugged into it, doing up the buttons, one by one, re-claiming the cool, near icy-cold detachment he was known for. No one would have believed him capable of the kind of loss of control he'd just experienced with the granddaughter of his mentor and guide. But he'd always known, hadn't he?

He just wished to god he hadn't been so right.

Maria emerged from the bathroom behind him, not even a hair out of place. She looked as if she'd just conducted the most boring audit in the world, and he felt…

Wrecked.

'Maria—'

'This changes nothing. I still expect you to be out of here by the time the ink dries on my marriage certificate.'

Micha bit back a string of invectives that would have burned the entire building down, instead simply saying, 'Of course.'

There was so much he wanted to say, but nothing emerged from the steel band clamped around his heart. She didn't want to hear it and he didn't have the ability to say it.

She nodded once, more to herself, and brushed past him with barely a second glance, the ice-cold breeze rolling off her making him shiver. He tucked his shirt in to the waist of his trousers and pulled up the zip, turning to her, half outraged, half furious and beyond unimpressed.

'You're going to leave? Just like that?' he said, shocked enough to finally speak.

'Why not? You did,' she accused, and for the barest of moments, he thought he saw it. The sheer incandescent hurt that he sometimes thought she might be hiding. But then she blinked and it was gone, part of his imagination, a hangover from the young girl he'd once known.

'You know it wasn't that simple,' he replied.

'Seemed pretty cut and dry to me,' she said, reaching for the purse that had ended up by the door to the office. 'Which suited me just fine,' she said, adjusting the strap of her purse over her shoulder, near eviscerating him with her carelessness.

'What was this?' he asked. 'Really? Was it you just getting what you wanted?' he forced himself to ask, hating that weakness in him that needed to know.

'I got the only thing you were ever good for, Micha,' she bit out and stalked from his life leaving burn marks across his skin and soul.

Maria held it together, all the way down the corridor, in the lift she knew was covered by CCTV, and out onto the streets of Paris. She held it together while the chauffeur-driven car took her back to the private airfield where the Gallo Group's jet was ready for take-off. She waited until they were forty-one thousand feet in the air before going to the bathroom where no one could see or hear her, and shattering into a million pieces, knowing that she would never, not ever, be the same again.

CHAPTER FOUR

Three months later...

To say that Micha Rufina was pissed off was an under-statement of near epic proportions. The last place and per-son he ever thought he'd be, or *wanted* to be, on his way to see was Maria Gallo. And if he'd had a say in the matter, he'd have never laid eyes on her again as long as he lived. But no one could have predicted what had happened after Maria had left Paris that last, fateful night.

Not even Gio Gallo.

Antonio Gallo, despite his promise to his cousin Maria, had *not* divorced the wife he'd married six years ago for convenience and instead chosen to remain with Ivy for love. Meaning that he and Maria failed to meet the terms of Gio Gallo's will and less than two weeks after she had left Paris, the entirety of Gallo Group had passed into Micha's hands, setting off what the world's press had termed the biggest Italian bloodbath since the second Mafia wars of the 1980s.

Family had turned on family, threats both physical and legal had been made, retracted and made again. Stocks had plummeted and recovered, risen and tumbled in various dif-ferent ways until everyone realised that the world *hadn't* in fact collapsed under Micha's ruthless and—surprising to some—*expert* control.

Which was why Micha was absolutely furious that he

was now on his way to see Maria because one single client, one out of thousands spread out across the world, refused to continue to do business with Gallo Group unless *she* handled the renewed contract negotiations.

It had been on the tip of his tongue to tell the client that he could go and get incredibly creative with notions of self-pleasure, were it not for the fact that they were GG's biggest international client and if they lost that client, it could very well start a mass exodus that Gallo Group literally *wouldn't* survive. This one client would be the proverbial straw.

He checked his watch as his driver took the turn towards Sant'Arcangelo, and frowned. He lowered the screen between them and said, 'Why are we heading south?'

'We are going to Signora Gallo, *si*?'

'*Si*. Is she no longer in Arezzo with her mother?'

'Signora Gallo moved recently. It is the same distance timewise,' the driver said, misunderstanding the motivation behind his query.

'*Va bene*,' Micha replied, raising the screen again.

Why had she moved? And when?

Things had been so crazy in the last four months, but this was an alarming reminder that he could not afford to let things slip through his fingers. Like Maria, moving out of her parents' estate and to the middle of nowhere. He had known that she'd have been furious at losing the company, but he hadn't expected her to quit.

Even before the announcement that Micha would be returning to Rome headquarters to assume the position of company president and CEO, Maria had submitted her resignation.

And now this hermit-like move? It was the exact opposite of the fight he'd expected to have with her and he'd been left strangely bereft by it. There must be something else going on. He had approximately forty-five minutes left to arm himself with as much information as he could. But when he checked Maria's socials, there was resounding silence. No posts, no updates, nothing about her house move. Nothing since the day before Antonio informed her and the family of his decision to remain married to Ivy. Micha had checked Antonio's pages too, in case there was a reference to Maria by proxy, but nothing.

Which was why by the time he arrived at the small villa hugging the shoreline of Lake Trasimeno, he was as curious as he was frustrated, and in an even worse mood than he'd been when he disembarked Gallo Group's private jet.

Micha stepped out of the tinted-windowed car, slipping on his sunglasses and looking around at Maria Gallo's new abode. He surveyed the old farm-style villa, narrow and, unusually, all one storey. The stone walls were rough, but familiar, the light mortar making the terracotta and grey stones appear bright in the morning sunlight. But despite the evident age of the building, the roof was new, tiles gleaming, and the hints of modernisation were subtle but expensive. He could just about see the corner of a small green garden from where he stood, brushing up against the side of Lake Trasimeno.

What on earth was she doing out here? It wasn't exactly nowhere, but it wasn't the bustling, busy, swanky city address that he knew she'd loved so much. Because Maria thrived on busy, on the frenetic energy that surrounded her. It fed her and made her happy. This?

This looked a hell of a lot like exile and he didn't like it one bit.

But he didn't have to like it, he reminded himself. This was hers and it had nothing to do with him. All he was here for was to convince her to sweet-talk a client back into the

fold and then she could leave. Oh, he wasn't an imbecile—
he knew she'd make him work for it. Nor was he a complete
bastard. He'd give her a nice hefty commission for doing
it. But once that was done, they could go back to their re-
spective corners of Italy and never cross paths again as far
as he was concerned.

Liar, his inner voice taunted, reminding him of the sensual turmoil he'd been in ever since she'd left his office in
Paris three months previous.

Shifting his sunglasses on to his head only for the brief
moment he took to pinch the bridge of his nose, he attempted
to wrestle his wayward body back under his control.

It was no use denying it. He'd been tormented every single night with fantasies that had built on what they'd shared
that stolen night and spun them wildly into erotic fever
dreams. Each night he woke, bed sheets sweat soaked, heart
pounding, head aching and fiercely unsatisfied.

Maybe seeing her would purge her from his memory.
Show him that he had blown that moment far out of pro-
portion because of their history. That there was no reason
for him to still be lusting after a woman who thought him
little better than dirt beneath her high-heeled shoe.

And with that thought, determination imprinted on his
mind, he lowered his sunglasses to his eyes, turned and
went to knock on the door of Maria Gallo.

Maria eyed the red-soled heels and sighed before reluctantly
putting them away. She wouldn't be needing those now, or
any time soon for that matter. And she knew it was silly
to get so emotional about a shoe, but it wasn't really about
the shoe, was it?

She'd been unpacking box by box, day by day following
Ivy's suggestion when Maria told her about the move. She

knew that Ivy and Antonio felt truly awful about what happened. And Maria *loved* that Antonio had found true happiness with his wife. And having met Ivy, Maria couldn't blame him. The English woman was exactly the kind of person Maria would have picked for him. She was beautiful and smart and funny, and she made her cousin laugh. And Ivy had been utterly devastated that their happiness had cost Maria Gallo Group.

She *knew* that Antonio deserved that happiness. It was just that she hated that it had come at the cost of what *she* deserved but had never been deemed worthy of.

Gallo Group.

Her heart twisted and something that felt a lot like grief welled within her.

Maria's resignation hadn't been knee-jerk. It had been her only option. There was absolutely no way that she could have stayed at GG once it went to Micha. Not after what happened in Paris. And certainly not after the consequences of that night either.

Shaking off the thoughts that threatened to pull her in a thousand different directions, she pushed the storage box into the large cupboard containing the other clothes she'd not been able to part with. Clothes had meant so much to her over the years. They'd been her armour, her protectors while she'd worked at Gallo Group. They'd helped her to feel the confidence she'd faked until it felt a little less…fake.

But that part of her life was over now. She had lost Gallo Group. And the family that had never thought she was good enough for it in the first place, now held her solely responsible for the fact that it had slipped into the hands of…of…

Maria swallowed whatever feeling it was that thickened her throat. That was another unpacked box she'd brought with her from the move to this beautiful farm house on Lake Trasimeno, albeit an emotional one.

She looked out of the wall of glass that had been the true selling point of the recently renovated one-storey villa; the slash of placid blue reminding her of the calm that she was going to need. Especially now.

Micha. She should never have gone to see him. She should never have thought herself immune to him. But she had so desperately wanted him to see what he had abandoned all those years ago. She had so desperately wanted to see regret in his eyes. But all she'd seen was the ferocity of his want.

Her phone flashed with a message.

I'll be done in about ten mins and call you then? Ivy xx

Ivy had been a lifesaver. As unlikely as it seemed, Maria and Antonio's wife had formed a fast and firm friendship. And since Ivy and Antonio had returned from London and had spent the past few months in Antonio's Tuscan villa, Maria had seen more of them than anyone else.

And, if Maria was honest, she would need that friendship more than ever, because in six months' time it wouldn't just be her, she thought, sweeping a hand over her stomach. Especially since her father's reaction was less than understanding.

How could you be so stupid?

Who was it? Who did this to you.

And when she'd refused to tell him?

You're no better than a whore.

Maria swallowed, forcing herself to remember her father's last words. Because as much as they hurt, they also steeled her backbone. Made her determined. Determined never to be beholden to a man ever again.

Because for all her apparent independence, her managerial position at GG, her eye-watering—and wholly justifiable—salary and for all the power she'd *thought* she'd had, her father had still turned up at her mother's house and kicked her out of a home he hadn't lived in for over fifteen years.

And he could. Because, as he pointed out, *he* owned it.

She'd looked at the mother who had betrayed her secret and saw the guilt in her eyes, but the fear in them too when she glanced at the husband who hadn't been a husband for that same number of years. In that moment, Maria had realised that although they had lived in separate houses since Maria was eight years old, they only really saw each other at family events, where they played the image of a happy family, despite the fact that *the entire family* knew they were anything but, her mother had never really escaped her husband's rule or wallet. Her mother would *always* defer to her husband, even at the cost to her daughter.

So, in the space of six weeks, Maria lost her job, her family and her home. And no one had said a single thing.

The only thing that had kept her father quiet about her pregnancy was shame.

And what had kept *her* quiet? Fear. Maybe she was more like her mother than she cared to be. But could she really afford to be that way? Especially now?

Maria thought back to that day when Ivy found her red eyed and shocked and forced her to tell her what was going on. At first, Maria had thought the reason her period was two months late was down to stress. But one pregnancy test after another had told her differently.

She was going to be a mother. The realisation had filled Maria with so much emotion, and so many thoughts, she hadn't known where or how to begin sorting through them all.

In the meantime, she had sworn Ivy to secrecy, and she had only agreed because she—like Maria—knew that the first thing Antonio would do was to track Micha down and beat the living daylights out of him. But Ivy's agreement had come with a two-month time limit and that time was running out.

Butterflies fluttered in Maria's stomach and she once again soothed the slight swell of her abdomen.

At twelve weeks, she'd been told, the baby was now fully formed, and about the size of a lime. Her baby. Her and Micha's baby. And although it was probably hyperbole, she was convinced that they could feel everything, experience everything, vicariously. And *oh god*, she didn't want her child to grow up like she had, with a father who was mean and a mother who was a mouse. She wanted…more. She wanted love, security, confidence. She didn't want them to grow up fighting for their place in the world, but sure of it. She wanted…

She felt the tear roll down her cheek and swept it away. It didn't matter what she wanted, Maria thought determinedly, sweeping aside foolish hopes and dreams just as easily as her tears. She might have left Rome, she might have left Gallo Group, but she was still the practical, focused woman she had become. That didn't change just because she was going to be a mother. A single, unwed mother.

Zia Alessina had done it, after divorcing her husband to bring up Antonio on her own. And this was decades later. It was the twenty-first century. And although she firmly believed that she didn't need a piece of paper to make herself socially acceptable, she was devastated that her child might bear the burden of that decision.

This was the problem with her thoughts. Back and forth they swung, like a pendulum, hovering a bare millimetre over the biggest emotional box there was; the one with Micha Rufina's name scrawled on the side.

Oh, she *would* tell him—she'd never keep that secret either from her child or him. But she needed to make a plan first. She needed to make sure that she had security and her independence. Because if he found out that she was pregnant with his child... If he had even the slightest inkling... He'd come in and take over. Force them to do something inconceivably foolish like get married.

And then she'd *never* be free. And she just wanted so much to be free.

The thought rushed out of her on a sigh as she looked down at the large black bag of things she'd decided not to take with her into her future. Wasn't this part of her freedom? Not being weighed down with things that no longer served her? She probably should have done it before she moved, but there hadn't been time. She'd thrown everything she had into the back of cars as her father hurled abuse at her for bringing shame on the family.

She dragged the bag out of the spare room, down the corridor that opened into the large open-plan living, dining and kitchen area, and up to the front door. She'd throw this out and get rid of the bad energy of her thoughts at the same time. No more business suits that she didn't need, she decided as she put the bag down to open the door, no more thoughts of her father, she told herself as she unlocked the bolt at the top, pulling open the door, and no more...

Micha Rufina.

His hand raised to knock on the door, he was as surprised as Maria looked when she opened the door to find him standing there. But the last thing he expected was for her to slam it shut again.

He blinked.

Really? She was *that* childish.

He waited. And then waited some more, getting even more annoyed. And if things continued like this, he'd have a heart attack from sheer irritation.

'Maria, *per favore*, open the door,' he called. 'It's not like you can ignore me.'

Her silence objected to his statement.

'Maria?' He blew out a breath, ignoring the weight of the driver's gaze from within the air-conditioned blacked-out-windowed town car.

'Maria Aurora Guilia Gallo, open this door!' he yelled.

'I am not a child and you don't get to talk to me like I am one, just because you are now officially the boss of everything,' she fired back angrily through the door, in a—to his mind—very childish way.

'*Madonna mia*, Maria, open the damn door,' he said. The way the alliteration rolled around his mouth was familiar; tasting like affection, frustration and grief all at the same time. He was trying to parse his way through those feelings when she opened the door looking mutinous and absolutely glorious.

Dio, it was a punch to his chest that knocked the air from his lungs and he was thankful that he was at least wearing his sunglasses to hide behind.

Thick dark curls tumbled around her face, her cheeks flush with indignation, her eyes sparkling with fury and all he could think of was how she looked when she orgasmed and he forced himself to look away before he made a fool of himself.

'Why are you here?' she demanded, a large bin bag placed on the ground between them.

'I'd rather not have this conversation on the doorstep.'

'I'd rather not be having this conversation at all, but here we are,' she shot back.

He slipped his thumb and forefinger beneath the frame of his glasses and pinched his nose again. The tension headache that bracketed his temples was just getting worse and worse. He really didn't need this. He had very little time, maybe less than twenty-four hours to save the contract, and then get back to the rest of Gallo Group.

'I need to speak to you about the Peterson account.'

'Peterson? You need to… You're here because…' Her tongue swept out across her bottom lip before she pulled it beneath her teeth.

'What did you think I'd be here for?' Micha demanded, confused.

Maria huffed out a bitter laugh and honestly? He didn't know what was going on. Because she was the one who had quit after all. He'd have willingly continued to work with her because she was excellent at her job. And there was a small petty part of him that felt that Gallo Group might *not* have been in such a precarious position if she hadn't quit.

'Nothing. Absolutely nothing,' she said, answering his question, turning her back on him and disappearing into the house, leaving Micha to move the bag blocking the doorway so that he could follow her.

He walked into a large open-plan space that somehow managed to be both open and full of light, and yet cosy and calm. It was significantly different to the property she and her mother had lived in before Maria had left Rome.

That had been dark, cluttered with books, paintings and expensive trinkets. Old money, with no taste was how he'd once thought of it, when he'd been there for one of the family gatherings. He'd never visited it when he and Maria had…

He shut that thought down and followed her towards the

kitchen, letting her put the long marble-top island between them for distance and safety.

She avoided his gaze, fussing with coffee cups and the sleek machine that vibrated at an impossibly quiet hum. He watched her choose decaf and frowned. He was about to say something when she interrupted his train of thought.

'What did you do?' she said, her tone accusing but curious, as if in spite of herself.

'What do you mean?' he asked, confused.

'To Peterson. That account was safe, the client was happy. And you can't afford to lose Peterson right now.'

'Why do you think *I* did something?' he bit out, angry at the assumption that he had somehow messed up, and choosing to ignore the warning that he was already very much aware of.

'Because Peterson was happy. And now he's not.'

Micha rubbed his jaw. 'He wants you to handle the contract renewal.'

'I don't work there any more,' Maria said and he waved her statement aside with his hand.

She narrowed her gaze at him.

'What did you *do*?'

'It was an admin error,' he explained.

'What was?'

'Contracts used an outdated template, and Peterson thought I was trying to pull a fast one. He says the trust is broken and the only person he'll deal with is you.'

'An admin error? And management didn't think to check it?'

'In case you hadn't noticed, we've been a little busy in the last few months,' he bit out angrily.

'Poor you,' Maria bit back as she plonked his espresso before him, barely managing to keep the coffee in the cup.

As he took a sip, she shook her head.

'No.'

He had expected her to put up a fight. And he had come prepared. 'I—'

'No, Micha.'

'You haven't heard my offer yet.'

'It won't matter.'

'You'll be a consultant, and you'll get an on-signing bonus worth ten percent of the contract,' he explained.

'No,' she said again.

'Fine. I'll give you your job back with an increase in salary, and a promotion to senior vice-president.'

'No.'

'What?' he replied, genuinely shocked.

His offer was more than generous. It was so good it was almost bad business. And she would have known that. And she was still saying no? And even if it *wasn't* good enough, surely the risk to a company that was as good as her life-blood would be enough to get her on board.

'There is literally nothing that you could offer me that would make me come back to Gallo Group and work under you. It's yours. You handle it. And if that's all?'

Micha frowned, bracing against the punch of her words. He thought that she'd play hardball. That she'd take some convincing, but this flat-out refusal, this wasn't stubbornness. Because he knew what stubbornness looked like on her. This didn't even have the heat of outrage or anger. This was cold. This was...*numb*.

'If you've finished your coffee, I'd like you to leave.'

He clenched his jaw, stifling all the arguments and objections, the questions that thickened his throat. There was something going on here. She was definitely trying to get rid of him. But why?

Her mobile rang just as he was going to press his point, and she let it ring as she stared at him until he raised his hands in surrender.

'Va bene.'

She reached for her phone, and asked Antonio's wife to give her two minutes. He'd seen Ivy's name flash up on the screen.

Maria gestured for him to return to the door.

'You can see yourself out,' she said, turned her back on him and looked out through the large window that formed the back wall of the open-plan room.

He had been dismissed and he didn't like it one bit.

'Ivy... No, not at all. How are you doing?' he heard Maria ask in English.

Turning on his heel, he walked to the door. He wasn't going to beg her to come back. Yes, he needed her. But if Gallo Group had to continue without Peterson, he'd do that. But... it wasn't Peterson that had him curious now. It was Maria.

He closed the door behind him and stepped out into the sunshine.

Something wasn't right. He'd seen her furious, with him, he'd seen her grieving over Gio, he'd seen her pleasured and he'd seen her happy. He'd never seen her so...closed down. As if she was trying to hide something. But what?

Maria cast a look over her shoulder, her heart pounding in her chest and blood rushing in her ears.

'Are you okay?' Ivy asked, worried, after Maria had explained that Micha was there. 'How did he know where you are?'

'Someone must have told him,' Maria surmised.

'Maria, I'm not sure about this. I really think I need to tell Antonio,' Ivy wavered.

'Please don't,' Maria begged. 'Please. I just… I just need a little more time. And if Antonio found out, all hell would break loose.'

'Perhaps it *should* break loose.'

'Ivy!'

'Sorry. I just think that this is too much for you to be dealing with on your own.'

'It's a lot, I know, believe me. But I just need some time. I need a plan. I need…' Oh, she didn't really know what she needed.

Maria walked, unsettled, back through the house to the room where she'd been packing up her things. Her heart was still racing from having Micha here, in her home. He'd looked so…*good*. And so tired.

A part of her had felt victorious about the Peterson account. That Micha was struggling to hold Gallo Group together. And that was a mean part of her. But honestly, it had been a dream of hers for him to come begging at her door, to tell her that he needed her. To beg for her help. For weeks, months even, she'd fantasised about him doing just that.

So, how ironic was it that she'd had to say no? That she'd not even been able to take up his offer and prove just how vital she was to Gallo Group? Because she couldn't. Negotiations would take at least two months, and by then…by then she'd be showing. And she wasn't sure that even then she'd be ready…

She swept a protective hand over her abdomen. Very few people could have guessed that she was pregnant at this moment. Would the father of her child have been one of them?

'Ivy, if he finds out…' Maria shuddered at the thought, unable to even finish the sentence. 'I just need some time. And then, when I'm ready, I'll tell Micha.'

'Tell me what, *cara*?'

Maria spun round in shock, coming face to face with Micha.

'I saw you leave,' she whispered in horror.

'Well, I came back,' he said, grim faced and hard eyed. 'And now, I think it's time that you tell me exactly what's going on, whether you're ready or not.'

His gaze bored into hers, flicked down to where her hand was on her abdomen, and rose back up to hers, eyes widening, lips parting in shock.

'You're pregnant.'

CHAPTER FIVE

It was the nightmare that had haunted her for the last two months, come to life. Micha stood there, eyes wide, knowing, accusing, confusion, anger, and something she couldn't quite name, swirling in the rich gaze boring into her.

'Maria? Are you okay? Maria?'

Ivy's voice sounded so very distant.

'I have to go,' Maria whispered into the phone.

'If I don't hear from you in twenty minutes I'm telling Antonio,' Ivy warned.

Maria ended the call without taking her eyes off Micha.

'You're pregnant,' he said again. 'You're… We're…'

He looked as if he'd been sucker-punched.

'We used protection. We…' he trailed off again.

He looked, Maria thought, the way she probably had looked when she'd found out too. Shock, confusion, denial, *fear*. His eyes dropped again to her stomach and she wanted to put her hands there, to protect their child, not from *him*, but from what would now happen.

She braced herself for the question. For the hurt that would wash over her. For the accusations and denials. For the shouts and the recriminations. But instead, he turned on his heel and left.

What?

Her outraged gasp echoed in the empty room. He *left*?!

How *dare* he leave her again?

Fury had her chasing him back down the corridor.

'Where are you going?' she demanded, a blinding anger pouring through her veins at the thought that he would leave her, leave *them*.

She came into the living area and saw him yanking his tie loose with three firm pulls. He shucked out of his suit jacket and rolled up his sleeves, as if he was just about to get started, rather than depart. He anchored one hand on his hip, as the other flew to fist his thick, dark hair, apparently utterly ignorant of how the sight of him like that melted both her insides and her brain at the same time.

Maybe it was the pregnancy she thought. Maybe—

'Have you had the tests and the scans?' he asked, his question pulling her thoughts back to the room but not in a direction she had expected.

She swallowed before answering. 'Yes.'

He closed his eyes for a beat. 'Is everything…?' She thought she almost heard his breath shudder in his lungs, and she realised that he was worried.

'Everything is fine,' she rushed to reassure him.

He nodded, only opening his eyes after. Something in his gaze turned then. She suppressed the urge to shiver. There was a coldness there that she'd never once seen in him all those years ago. Age and experience had put that there, and for just a moment, she regretted it.

'And you answered all their questions? About the medical history?' he asked, bringing her back to the present.

On the surface his tone was polite, but there was something cold about the question. She ignored the warning signs, irritated instead by the implication that she would have already messed something up. Just like everyone had always expected of her. Just like she had done with GG.

'Of course I did,' she replied.

'Family history?'

'Yes, Micha. I gave them my family history too.'

'And mine?' he asked. 'What information did you give them about *my* family history?' he demanded, his tone morphing from polite to pointed in the space of a heartbeat. 'Would you have told them about my mother's gestational diabetes?'

Her thoughts crashed to a halt.

'I don't think that has any—' Maria hesitated.

'You don't *think*? Well, that's medically accurate, Maria.'

'I didn't know,' she confessed, shamefaced.

'You didn't *know* because you didn't *ask*, because you didn't tell me!' he shouted.

'I didn't tell you because I thought you would force me to marry you,' she shouted back.

'Oh, we *will* be getting married, Maria,' Micha declared with such supreme confidence it was maddening.

'Why do you think it is yours?' she struck out.

'Are you going to lie to me and tell me it's not?' he retorted.

'No,' she admitted reluctantly. She ground her teeth together, hating that he knew her so well. Hating that he knew she wouldn't resort to lies.

'Then such dramatics are unnecessary,' he said with infuriating cold-hearted logic. 'We will marry.'

'No, we won't.'

'Yes, we will,' he insisted.

Maria threw her hands up in the air and turned her back to him, just to get a moment's reprieve. He did this to her. Made her so feel so mad, so ungrounded…so *exposed*.

'How long have you known?' he asked from behind her.

And this time it was she who closed her eyes. He would

never forgive her for keeping something like this from him. She'd known it from the moment she'd decided she needed to.

'I needed time, Micha,' she tried to explain.

'How long?'

'One month.'

His shock was a gasped exhale.

'Were you…?' He seemed to brace himself against the question on the tip of his tongue. 'Were you waiting until… because you thought I would…?'

Realisation cut through her like a knife and she spun around to face him. 'No, Micha. No,' she rushed to reassure him. Whatever she felt about what had passed between them, whatever she thought about what he had done to her, she'd never have thought that he would try to convince her to terminate the pregnancy. Because while she didn't know the man he had become, she knew the boy he had been.

He might have spent the last eleven years in Paris doing god knows what, but that didn't mean she didn't know him, hadn't grown up with him, hadn't seen the way he was with his mother, with the people he considered his, family, friends. The people that Micha considered his were protected in a way that went almost beyond necessary.

But how could she explain that it was that very thing that she'd feared would stifle her? Would do more harm to her than anything else?

He looked deep into her eyes, searching for the truth in her words. His second shuddered exhale she felt down to her bones and that was when she felt truly sorry that she'd kept their pregnancy from him. Before it was so quickly masked, she saw the wound her secret had inflicted upon him. The doubts and insecurities she had forgotten in the years spent apart from him.

And for the first time a dust-covered memory floated free. Micha, aged sixteen, boyish and nervously charming, signs of the man he would become beneath his skin. Hints of the flirtation that would become something more in barely a few months' time, as they shared whispers of futures that they wanted. She'd told him about wanting to take over Gallo Group one day and he'd insisted she would. And when he'd haltingly confessed that he wanted a family, she'd told him she could see it, secretly hoping that perhaps it was something they could have together.

And here they were, nearly twelve years later and…

It was all so very wrong.

How had everything gone so wrong? Micha wondered, as he glared out the window at the placid lake, feeling anything but.

He was going to be a father.

Madonna mia.

He swept a hand through his hair in a way that he wanted to do with his life. He should have left, instead of coming into the living area and planting his feet. He needed time to marshal his thoughts. He felt it, the heady complex chaos of his thoughts filling his mind and stopping his tongue to a point of near silence.

There's no problem. It just takes Micha longer than most to connect his words to his thoughts, the doctor had said when Gio had dragged him there, wanting to make sure there was no 'problem' with the sixteen-year-old who would become his right-hand man. Most had thought that his monosyllabic tendencies were down to either limited intelligence or stubbornness, but Gio had known from the beginning that there was nothing unintelligent about him.

He just needed a little time, and a little encouragement to separate out his thoughts from his feelings.

But he didn't have time. Not now, he thought, pushing aside the familiar nauseating panic that threatened to clog his throat. He needed to think. And quickly. Because if he didn't get this right, he knew, he *knew*, Maria would wriggle out of his clasp and disappear. And he couldn't let that happen.

He was going to be a father.

He, who had never known anything but violence, fear and abandonment from his own. It was true that once, so long ago now he could almost think it unreal, he'd wanted a family. But that was before. Before he had learned that such things were not meant for a man like him.

Because no matter how far he climbed out of the gutter, it was still there: the dirt on his hands that meant he'd never be good enough. Certainly not for Maria Gallo. Only now, there was no choice in the matter.

She had known for a month and she hadn't told him? The realisation hit him like a freight train, dredging up the question from the deepest part of his soul. The part that had clung fiercely to a relationship that was long since gone.

'Would you have told me?' he demanded.

Maria looked at the floor.

'Yes. Eventually,' she said in surrender. 'I just wanted... time. Everything changed, Micha. Everything I thought I knew, everything I thought would be, it's all gone and this,' she said, sweeping a hand over a bump that was barely there, 'this happened and I just... I wanted time.'

He, of all people, understood and knew that feeling. He could appreciate the quiet desperation in her words. He really could. But they didn't have the luxury of time. And he didn't have the luxury of being nice.

'Well, that time is up,' he said, pulling out his phone and firing off a message to his assistant cancelling all meetings.

'What are you doing?' she asked, hooking her foot behind the ankle of her standing leg. She'd used to do that when she was younger, he remembered. When she was nervous. He dismissed the sight of it and went back to his emails.

'I'm cancelling all my meetings.'

'What about Peterson?' she asked, causing his head to snap up.

He blinked. Once. Twice.

Then he huffed out a bitter laugh, his eyes roaming the room, before coming back to her, in disbelief.

'Really? That's what you're worried about right now?' he demanded. Of course she would care more about Gallo Group than, oh, just a little something like telling him he was the father of an unborn child.

'Well, that's what brought you here,' she pressed. 'You said you needed me to handle the contract renewal.'

'It doesn't matter. I'll deal with it later,' he dismissed.

'You can't. He's GG's biggest client. If he goes, then the whole company will fall apart!' she exclaimed.

And he knew he shouldn't be surprised. He knew he shouldn't be angry that at this very moment in time, just when he was struggling with the fact that he was going to be a father, *she* was worrying about her family's damn company.

'This is very true,' he agreed. 'It's also something you didn't care one single iota about less than twenty minutes ago. And as you so rightly pointed out, Gallo Group is mine and I'll handle it in the way I see fit.'

She let out a growl of frustration that matched precisely how he felt. He locked his phone screen, slipping it back into his pocket, and watched as Maria did a very good impression of someone about to throw a tantrum. He imagined there would be only three seconds before she started tapping her foot on the floor in annoyance. That she did it in four seconds showed a surprising amount of restraint on her behalf. She huffed a long wave of thick black curls over her shoulder and his hand fisted from the memory of how it had once felt to hold those in his palm.

How she was still the most beautiful woman he'd ever seen was beyond him. He had spent *years* living in Paris, and had counted models as some of his companions. Was it because now he knew she was pregnant? Was he imagining the glow about her, or was that simply the heat of her anger? Did it really matter?

Certainly not now that she was carrying his child. Which brought him right back to the matter at hand. He'd checked his diary before messaging his assistant. And even if it hadn't been clear, he would have made it so.

'Will this weekend suffice?' he asked her, knowing that it would throw her. Knowing that it would confuse her. A small, mean part of him relished the fact that she might feel just a little of what he was currently struggling with.

'For what?'

'Our wedding.'

'Wedding? I can't marry you!' she cried, throwing her hands up in the air. 'What on earth would the family think? That I'm so desperate to get my hands on Gallo Group that I'd sell myself by marrying—'

Her words halted dramatically mid-sentence and midair, the temperature in the room dropping to freezing from his anger.

'What were you going to say, *cara*?' he demanded. 'That you were prostituting yourself? To someone like me? The

illegitimate bastard son of a whore who inherited everything they'd always wanted?'

'Micha, I—'

But he didn't want to hear it. Didn't want her to take back
her unthinking words. Because he needed to know, needed
to remember what she thought about him. He couldn't go
into this blindly and naively like he had before.

'I've been called worse. I don't care what they think,' he
dismissed.

'But *I* do,' she said, her eyes bright with indignation.

'And that's always been your problem, Maria. One that
I'm more than happy to exploit to my advantage.'

'What do you mean?' she asked.

'All I have to do is wait, Maria. Because it won't be long
until you start to show. And what do you think will happen
when news of an unwed Gallo heir gets out? No, I know you
better than that. So I know you'd rather marry me than drag
Gallo Group through the mud by such a scandal. You might
not work there any more, but you're a Gallo. You wouldn't
do anything to harm the company.'

'You bastard,' she bit out.

'Yes. That is quite literally true,' he admitted. 'Which
is why when I say that we will be marrying this weekend,
I mean it. So let me be very clear, *bella*. There is literally
nothing I won't do in order to ensure that my child grows
up legitimate. Nothing.'

She saw it. The absolute, uncompromising truth in his gaze.
When he got like this, he was a force to be reckoned with,
undeniable and unstoppable. It was both absolutely pig-
headed and infuriating, but once it had also been incredible.

He took a step closer to her, enough so that Maria could

smell the seductive hints of his aftershave and see the hard gold glittering in his eyes.

'I would become a hound of hell myself, *cara*, if it was necessary,' he vowed, and she believed him.

Tears pressed at the backs of her eyes, but she would not, could not, let them fall. Not in front of him. What she did behind closed doors was her business, but she couldn't show this man a single hint of her vulnerability.

He was right. She *did* care what her family thought. She did care how news of her pregnancy would shake the very foundations of Gallo Group—a company that prided itself on traditional family values. A family that prided itself on them, even though not a single one of Gio's children had ever entered into a happy, successful marriage.

But she also cared that at one point in her life he was the only man she thought she might be able to have this future with: a child, a husband. He had always been the shadowy face in her fantasies. But the hatred, the anger that she saw in his gaze right now? Oh god, it was the nightmare that had come from a beautiful daydream. But she couldn't dwell on that right now.

'So other than your ego, is there a single reason that you can provide that would stop us from getting married? Stop me from providing the kind of security that *our child* would need?' he asked.

'I have my own money, Micha,' she reminded him.

It devastated her, the way he made it sound as if it were nothing but selfishness to refuse his proposal—and what proposal? *Demand* more like.

But she didn't want her child to grow up the way that he had, with the scars that he had. Oh, he might hide them well these days, but once he'd been vulnerable enough for her to catch a glimpse of them. He'd never once blamed his mother, never once treated her with anything but the respect she deserved. But Maria knew those scars were there. And she'd do anything to protect her child from those same wounds.

'This weekend?' Maria asked, hating the weakness in her voice.

'What would you gain by waiting?'

She opened her mouth, but he pressed on, regardless.

'You've already had two months. And what has that brought you? Other than a house in the middle of nowhere?' he remarked, looking around him as if the place that she had hoped would be her salvation, her sanctuary, was lacking in some way.

She wanted to argue. She wanted to rail against him, against his accusations. She wanted to pound her fists against that powerful, broad chest of his. And he looked at her as if he knew it. As if he could so easily read her every desire. Just like he had looked at her the night she'd visited him in Paris.

'Mmm?' he prodded, as if he were actually waiting for an answer.

It had brought her nothing but the mirage of time. She'd not gotten anywhere other than where she'd been when she first arrived. She'd barely even been able to unpack. As if she too knew that she wouldn't be here long.

Because in truth, she'd always known. She'd go back to him. She'd go back to him because no matter what she felt, she couldn't, *wouldn't*, keep his child from him, nor keep her child from its father. Because no matter what passed between them, she knew that he would expend his last breath making sure that his child had whatever it needed.

And that was a man she'd marry.

As if sensing her surrender, he pulled his hands out of his pockets and rocked back on his heels.

'Registry office,' she bargained.

'No.'

'What?' her head snapped up.

'No; it's a one-syllable, very common word,' he defined unnecessarily.

'Micha.'

'If you think that you will start your life as my bride, come into my home as my wife, if you think you're going to stand by my side at the very least until our child is of legal, adult age, having had some secret, out-of-the-way wedding with no photos or family as if we are *ashamed*, then you are very wrong.'

She flinched, seeing it how he'd seen it and regretting her request instantly. 'I didn't mean it like that,' she whispered.

'Then what did you mean? Every single Gallo that has married in the last twenty years, with the exception of Antonio, has had the centre spread in *Hello Magazine*.'

'Oh, and you think you can organise that in less than four working days, do you?' she shot back, instead of answering his question.

'You would do well not to underestimate me, Maria,' he warned and she heeded.

'Nor you, me, Micha,' she said, feeling the hot scouring heat of anger crawling up her spine. She was tired of his threats, and if she was being honest, was a little bit hurt too. 'You think you can come in here and make demands that upend my life and that I have no say? What about after the wedding, huh? What about *after* you've put your ring on my finger and claimed me in front of the world?' *Like some trophy*, she mentally added. 'You'll go back to work running the company you know should be mine, while I stay at home and play wife and mother?'

'Play?' he asked, an arched eyebrow raised in a challenge.

'You know what I mean,' she dismissed.

'No, I don't,' he said, leaning back from the breakfast bar. 'The Maria I knew would never have kept such a secret to herself.'

'The Maria you knew grew up after you left,' she shot back, wishing his gaze wasn't so unfathomable. 'She stopped making assumptions long ago, so yes. Before I even consider agreeing to your proposal, I want to know what marriage looks like to you.'

She saw the muscle flex in his jaw, knew that his silence was not mutinous, nor malicious. He was struggling to formulate his words in that way that he sometimes did when his emotions became too much. The realisation, a knowing left over from a time when they had been close, when she had thought that perhaps they loved each other, hit her hard and took her own frantic pulse rate down a little. Because this wasn't easy for him. And somehow that made it less painful for her.

'I will not have our child growing up like you—watching your mother stand in silence while her husband flaunts his affairs for all and sundry,' he announced, the verbal blow striking a bullseye. It had been that silence, that mute acceptance of the most awful carelessness that had driven Maria almost entirely through her life, determined never to be that person, never to let another person turn her into a *statue*, with no other purpose than to stand there and look pretty.

'Nor shall it grow up like me,' he continued, cutting into her thoughts, and stopping himself before he could describe a childhood that she already knew. It had never been a secret that his mother had been forced to sell herself on the streets after his father abandoned them the day Micha was born. Perhaps, she thought for the first time, it should have been. Perhaps his shame would have been easier to bear—

not that she believed for even a second that he *should* have been ashamed.

How on earth were they—two broken people—supposed to raise something so pure, so innocent and so utterly dependent on them? When they hated each other.

But you don't. You don't hate him.

She pushed her inner voice down where she couldn't hear it any more.

'What did you mean about my mother?' she asked, wanting to know, needing him to be clear.

He frowned, the slash of his brow dark over his eyes.

'Affairs?' she forced herself to ask.

It was clear that Micha wanted a traditional marriage, but...

'There will be no affairs, Maria.'

His words reverberated in the room with his vehemence.

'I—'

'So that there is no confusion, after our marriage you, and our child, will come to live with me. We will live together until our child is eighteen. We will appear united and very much in love to every single person that knows us. Family, colleagues, the journalists that swarm this family like wasps, even the parents of our child's friends. The entire world will envy our marriage, Maria. So there will be no affairs. And before you can rage in accusation that I would have any different role in this marriage, I will never share my bed with another woman while my ring is on your finger.'

Maria scoffed.

'I'm not a savage, Maria. I can control myself.'

'For eighteen years?'

'Yes.'

There was no compromise in his response. No room for her to question or doubt. He meant every word he said.

Her phone on the countertop vibrated, causing it to jump a little across the smooth marble.

And yet Micha didn't take his eyes off her.

The phone continued to ring, completely ignorant of the battle of wills that was happening around it.

This marriage? This *kind* of marriage? It was everything she'd never wanted for herself. Everything she'd spent her entire life trying to avoid. But for her child? For the security, the legitimacy, the protection, he could offer them? There wasn't even a single moment's hesitation.

She nodded in agreement.

'Okay,' he said, his gaze flicking across to her phone. He picked it up and swiped the screen to accept the call, as if he had the damn right.

'Ivy? What are you and your husband doing on Saturday?' he asked and just like that, Maria's life changed *again*.

CHAPTER SIX

You need to get down here right now.

MICHA LOOKED AT the message Ivy Gallo had sent him less than ten minutes ago and checked the location share on the map. He was less than fifty metres away from the shop they were in, but he forced himself to stop. To breathe. To *think*.

It had been four days since he had left Maria's rented cottage near Lake Trasimeno and with only two days before the wedding he still hadn't wrapped his head around *her*. His assistant had kept him updated on her movements, Maria seeming to prefer to communicate with Eduardo rather than him—something he was both thankful and slightly resentful over.

Eduardo had informed him that Maria had checked into the hotel La Tormalina last night but her belongings and personal effects were still at the lake house. It wasn't that he'd expected her to magically uproot her life and integrate it into his, he told himself. That would be an outrageous assumption for anyone to make, he recognised, even as the twist of dissatisfaction tightened in his gut.

But he couldn't help but feel that it was symbolic of her holding back. Of her not realising the situation that she was in. They were in. He wouldn't, couldn't accept half measures in this. He'd been young when he learned that lesson and he'd learned it hard. But it was a lesson that had dragged him from the streets to the dizzying heights of control of one of the world's largest conglomerates.

At seven years old, he'd not had the luxury of time to adjust. He'd known that if he hadn't acted immediately, the next man his mother sold herself to might just kill her. That was the day he'd met Gio Gallo and his life had changed. It wasn't luck. It was because Micha had made a decision. It was because he had decided to go all in that Micha had picked the richest mark, the person he could steal the most from. And honestly, for a moment there he'd thought he'd got away with it. But Gio had been too clever for him. The Italian businessman had let him escape, but only so far. Micha hadn't even imagined that the man had followed him all the way back to where he lived.

And while it wasn't in the way he'd expected, Micha's life *had* changed that day. Gio had plucked him and his mother from the slums they'd barely been able to afford, and given them housing, given Micha an education, given first his mother work and then, when he'd been old enough, Micha had worked for Gio too; whatever the older man said, whatever he wanted, Micha made it happen.

And in just two days' time it would change again.

When Maria became his wife.

Micha followed the location arrow on the map on the screen of his cellphone until he was right on top of it. Looking up at the boutique Ivy had brought him to, he winced. Mentally cursing, he blew out a reluctant breath of air and braced himself.

The bell chimed as he crossed the threshold, but no one rushed to greet him and he soon discovered why as he ventured further into the bridal store.

'Absolutely not.'

The sounds of a somewhat heated argument came from somewhere in the back, he guessed, because he couldn't see past the rows and rows of dresses in various shades of white and increasing states of bouffant.

'But Ms Gallo, the designer assured me—'

'As the designer isn't here, I'm having considerable trouble wondering how on earth she could have assured you that I look anything other than absolutely hideous!' he heard Maria insist.

If the shop assistant knew what was good for her, she should probably give up the argument. Maria had never been one to back down from a fight, ever.

And just like that, a childhood memory flashed into his mind. About two years after Gio had 'adopted' him, in an attempt to civilise the hellion that he'd been, Micha had been sent to the same school as Antonio and Maria. They'd been inseparable back then. Not that it had stopped some opportunistic kids trying to bully him. The day he'd been about to prove exactly why it was futile to do so, Maria—half a head smaller than both him and the wannabe bully—pushed her way in between them and threated what amounted to grievous bodily harm if the kid didn't stop.

He rubbed his jaw, fighting the smile that threatened to crack across his features from the memory.

'The style of dress perhaps—' the shop assistant pressed on, heedless of Maria's ire.

'Is terrible? Awful? Makes me look like my grandmother? Ivy, you can see it, can't you?'

'Well…'

'Oh, you're so *English*, Ivy. Too polite to say anything negative,' Maria dismissed as Micha drew closer to the dressing area. Between peach-coloured draped silk, he caught glimpses of a raised dais, and several mirrors.

The assistant was helping Maria out of something puffy and white as Ivy turned, her eyes widening to see him, both in relief and warning.

Few knew that he and Ivy had met several years ago when Gio Gallo had sent him to try to bribe her into divorcing Antonio, thereby leaving Antonio free to marry Maria as Gio intended. Ivy had earned both his and Gio's respect when she had turned down a life-changing amount of money, instead choosing to stand beside the husband of a convenient marriage that soon proved to be so much more. And that respect had developed into like, forging a strange unspoken understanding and respect between him and Ivy. In some ways, Micha felt that she had seen him in a light that Antonio and Maria would never, because she wasn't tarnished by the Gallo family prejudice.

'Help,' Ivy mouthed and he couldn't stop the smile that came to his lips—the moment of humour easing something of the stress and tension that had held him taut for the last four days.

'It's not funny!' she mouthed again and he bit his lip to stop the laughter in his chest.

It wasn't. It really wasn't. But there was something painfully familiar about Maria's frustration over something as simple as a wedding dress.

Behind Ivy, the assistant had manoeuvred Maria into another bright white dress that made him wince. The low-cut neckline created more cleavage than he'd even thought possible for Maria, then puffed out beneath her breasts in a way that reminded him of a Victorian milk maid, creating an uncomfortable discord between the competing images of purity and impropriety. The shocking bright white made Maria look almost sick in the harsh lighting and he wasn't in the least surprised when Maria fisted her hands at her sides and let out a cry of frustration.

Which was nothing compared to the cry of alarm she made when she caught sight of him standing there.

Maria's heart dropped to the floor the moment she caught Micha standing on the brink of the dressing area.

Oh god, what was he doing here?

'You're not supposed to see me in my wedding dress!' she cried pulling her arms around her waist as if she could protect herself from his gaze.

She *hated* that he was seeing her like this. *Hated* that he was seeing her look so *hideous.*

Especially when he looked… She scrunched her eyes together, but the image of him standing there in that damn near perfect suit made him look like a model, harsh cheekbones, broad shouldered, thin hipped and that waistcoat that she remembered far too well.

'Don't worry about bad luck, *cara*, because there is no way that you'll be marrying me wearing *that,*' he assured her.

And she hated that she agreed with him too. At least, she thought, slowly prising her eyes open, he wasn't planning to punish her by forcing her to wear something as hideous as this in two days' time.

Two days.

We have very little time for alterations, Ms Gallo, so we will need to find something that fits as close to your size as possible.

Maria knew that. And she intensely disliked being difficult, she would *never* normally be so demanding. But this was important. It was her wedding dress. And while it might not be the day she'd ever imagined for herself, it was *vital* that her dress be perfect.

Because of what *they* would say, what *they* would think. Her parents. Her family. The Gallos.

Clothes were armour. And she needed armour. She needed to be as protected as possible when she stood before every single member of the Gallo family and married Micha. Because no matter how many times she had proved herself worthy, had worked harder than any other family member, longer than any other employee, gone above and far beyond whatever anyone else had ever done at Gallo Group, it had never been enough.

Not for her grandfather, who deemed her inferior because of her gender, *unworthy* of inheriting a company she could run better than anyone. Not for her parents, who had shown her nothing but irritation and disappointment for not being their much-needed *male* heir; the only way they thought they could have pleased Gio Gallo. And not Micha, who had left the first chance he could get.

Oh, she could hear the snide whispers and barely concealed critiques.

Pregnant. Desperate. Coerced.

Or worse.

That she'd got her hands on Gallo Group the only way she'd ever be capable of getting it, by trapping Micha with a pregnancy. Because she 'wasn't good enough' to earn it. But she *had* been. She'd been better than all of them. Even Micha. But in the end none of that would matter, because now they'd all think that she'd manipulated all this to get what she didn't deserve.

'Could you give us a moment?' Micha asked both the assistant and Ivy.

Ivy shot her a glance in the mirror and Maria nodded, not wanting to argue the point—certain that she didn't want Ivy to hear what Micha was about to say. Maria waited, breath locked in her lungs until they were alone.

She felt…vulnerable, exposed and she didn't like it.

'What did you tell her?' he asked as he started pacing the dais in a slow circle.

'Ivy? You mean, after you invited her to a wedding on the day that she knew you'd discovered that I was pregnant? I don't think even the most gullible would have believed that it was true love, Micha.'

He sighed, impatient with her answer.

'I told her that you were ridiculously happy. That it was the best news you'd ever heard,' she said, her angry whisper the opposite of her words. 'I told her that you confessed that you'd always loved me, ever since…' And she couldn't do it. Couldn't bring herself to touch on the precious, tender, painful past they shared. 'And that…you'd only ever imagined a future with me in it and…that you wanted to marry me and make me and our child happy.' Her explanation stuttered out past hurts and long-forgotten dreams and heartache that felt fresh even to this day. *God*, how she wished the story she'd spun around their betrothal was true. Tears pressed against the backs of her eyes and she turned away, biting her lip until the sting of pain pushed back the emotional rollercoaster her pregnancy had pushed her into.

'Va bene.'

She closed her eyes, hoping to compose herself, pressing a hand against the tight neckline that was making it hard for her to breathe.

'Take that off. It's making me uncomfortable,' he ordered.

She scoffed. 'Making *you* uncomfortable? *You* don't have to wear it.'

'Neither do you,' he pointed out with infuriating rationality. 'So, take it off.'

'I *can't*. You sent away the assistant,' she threw at him accusingly.

He glared at her before closing the distance between them in long, powerful strides. She watched him in the reflection of the mirror as he came behind her on the raised dais, gently kicking the wide expanse of the skirts out of the way so that he could get close enough to where the zip was concealed by a row of one hundred satin-covered buttons.

She felt the heat of him across the bare skin of her shoulder blades, inhaled the scent of leather and spice, something *tempting*. Her heart pounded against her ribcage, her body craving his expert touch, aflame with need that whipped up like an unexpected tornado that touched down over them, keeping them in the eye of a storm that had not exhausted itself three months ago.

He stared down at the zip that would set her free. Breath caught in her lungs, pressing her chest deeper against the neckline that was so confining. And for a heartbeat his gaze flickered between her back and her chest in the mirror in front of her and she wanted to… She wanted to…

Surrender.

She was a madness in his blood. How could it be that he had not satiated his desire already? How could it be that even as he fought and railed against what he'd been forced to do—what he'd forced her into, marriage—that *still* he wanted her? Self-recrimination was powerful, harsh and swift.

He found the tab at the top of the zip and yanked it free, stepping away from the dais before he could do what he really wanted to do. Which was rip the dress from her body and take her like the animal he truly was beneath all outward signs of sophistication.

He gritted his teeth and shoved his fisted hands into his

pockets as he focused solely on the dresses around him—anything other than where Maria was navigating her way out of that monstrosity and into a satin dressing gown that did nothing to hide the perfection of her body.

Cazzo.

But damn, it was better than the look in her eyes just before…the glistening of her eyes, the tremble of the lip she'd tried to hide from him. He hated that she did that, kept what she was feeling from him. But he understood it. After all, couldn't he say the same?

They didn't trust each other. How could they? But they would need to. If they were going to get through this, they would have to do it together.

'Why did you let her put you in that thing?' he asked, genuinely curious and a little surprised that she *had* let the assistant put her in that dress.

There was a moment's hesitation.

'She is trying to make me look…slimmer.'

Slimmer? He opened his mouth to object, until he realised what she was saying. She was trying to hide her pregnancy. Their pregnancy.

'Are you ashamed?' he asked, spinning round to confront her, struggling with the anger that was so quick to ignite. He couldn't, wouldn't, allow her to be ashamed of their child…of *him*.

He saw the clench of her teeth, the little flutter of the muscle at her jaw, the way her body straightened as if ready to fight, *always* ready to fight.

'I am not, and never will be, ashamed of my child,' she said with a blaze of glory that made him both proud and instantly relieved. 'And I will do everything in my power to protect our child from whatever snide comments and meanness comes their way, from whatever quarter; family, friend or foe. But,' she said, her shoulders threatening to slump, 'I would just like to avoid, if possible, any nasty speculation on our wedding day.'

And when she turned her back to him to reach for a glass of water, he remembered how much she'd always dreamed of a huge white wedding, a church full of her friends and family, of the perfect dress. He saw how that in some small way she was trying to keep hold of that fantasy. And he understood that. He knew how mean the Gallos could be. They were like a pack of hyenas when they got it in their minds. But she was one of them. And she had chosen them.

She will always choose them.

Gio's voice echoed in his mind as he scanned the rails of dresses that lined the walls of the dressing area. A cream silk confection caught his eye and he pulled the sleek-lined dress from the rack. Further down was another—a gently corseted dress with a sweetheart neckline, and one last one that was the complete opposite of either: lace detailed over the lightest gauze, with tiny little sparkling diamonds.

Just behind it, though, was a dress that stopped him in his tracks. The neckline dropped in a sweeping V into a wide belted waist, long draped material fell from slightly puffed shoulder sleeves into cuffs at the wrist and the skirt fell away in a swathe of oyster silk. It was soft, romantic, all the things Maria rejected, but had never managed to fully hide about herself. It was the dress he'd have chosen for her eleven years ago. But they weren't seventeen. Not any more. And too much had passed between then and now for them to go back.

Instead, he reached for the dress with the sparkling diamonds and placed all three on the back of an empty chair.

'One of these will do,' he said, forcing a boredom into his voice he knew she would view as a challenge. Far better for her to be angry than upset.

He checked his watch, trying to ignore the way a delicate blush pinked her cheeks.

'I have to go. You will be okay?'

'I was perfectly okay before you got here,' she growled like an angry kitten and he tried not to smile.

'You were about to let a woman convince you to wear a dress that made you look like a pornographic milk maid. You were *not* okay.'

'Get out!'

This time he couldn't hold it back. The laugh fell from his lips like sand slipping through his fingers, unstoppable and horrifyingly easy. It wasn't mean, there was nothing nasty in it, nothing tainted the air between them and he wasn't completely sure but he thought he saw her smile, a glitter in her eyes that wasn't sad, or hurt. But then the laughter quietened, leaving a silence between them that wasn't hot like it had been in Paris, or hurt like it had been earlier that week. It was something that was too close to what they'd had *before*.

He nodded once, to himself, as if putting a full stop on the exchange.

'I'll see you tomorrow night.'

'Tomorrow night?' she asked.

'*Si*, did you not check your emails? We have the rehearsal dinner.'

The pretty blush on her cheeks paled, leaving her looking wan under the harsh lighting. 'We *can't*,' she said, and just like that, they were back to where they always were. At loggerheads, with her ashamed to be with him and him never being good enough for her.

'We can and we will, *cara*,' he decreed, before turning on his heel and cursing whatever foolishness had made him think, even for a second, otherwise.

* * *

Maria watched him leave, wishing that they could have held onto that moment just a little bit longer. That brief reprieve from the constant anger and resentment that simmered between them. But it was hopeless. Too much time had gone, too much hurt. Gio had chosen Micha, Micha had chosen him and the only person Maria could choose was herself.

Then and now.

She looked over to the rack that Micha had chosen the three dresses from and, unable to help herself, crossed the room. One by one, she flicked through the dresses, hoping to find what had caught his eye—the dress he'd *not* chosen for her. She frowned as she passed glittering sparkles and lace, not thinking it would have been one of those until…

There. It was beautiful. Simple lines, the low V suiting her chest size, the soft, loose, but utterly elegant drapes of silk were romantic and would hide the small thickening of her waist without constriction.

'Oh, that's perfect!' Ivy cried from behind her. 'You must try it on,' she insisted.

Maria bit her lip and swallowed. 'No, I don't think so,' she replied, instinctively knowing that it *was* perfect and that she *should* try it on. But if he'd wanted to see her in it…

And since when did you start doing whatever the men in your life wanted you to do?

Since they won, Maria mentally replied.

She settled the dresses back on the rack, hoping that the dress would get lost in among the others, but knowing that she'd find it again in a heartbeat if she wanted to.

She shook herself out of the melancholy of the moment and turned to Ivy with a smile.

'The groom himself chose three dresses for me, so I suppose I should give those a go first, yes?'

Ivy nodded, but the concern was still bright in the light blue eyes that stared back at Maria. Forcing a little more effort into her smile, she rubbed Ivy's arm in reassurance and returned to the dais with one of the dresses Micha had chosen.

'You know that you don't have to do this if you don't want to,' Ivy said, her eyes firmly fixed on Maria, who concentrated on getting herself into the corseted dress with the sweetheart neckline.

Where was the assistant?

'Maria?'

The zip was nearly impossible to undo and she hadn't even got herself into it yet. Her fingers struggled with the tiny little piece of plastic, but everything was just so blurry she couldn't see. She wiped her eye with the back of her hand and was surprised when it came back wet.

'Maria,' Ivy said, much closer to her this time, putting her hands over where Maria's fingers clutched the zip. Ivy gently pushed the dress away and wrapped her arms around her tightly, as Maria's breath shuddered in her lungs. So slowly, so slightly, Maria felt herself gently rocked and soothed by her cousin's wife.

'Let's run away,' Ivy whispered into her ear, and Maria let out a bark of miserable laughter. 'Just you and me. Antonio will catch us up. Micha will never find us. You know what Antonio is like when he puts his mind to something. We'll all live together, and raise our children and have nothing but blue skies, laughter and all the love we need.'

Maria didn't think her heart could take the idyllic picture that a woman who had quickly become like a sister to her had painted. She wanted it so badly. But she knew she couldn't do it. Couldn't have it. Because when she imagined it, Micha was there. Not scowling or angry, or bitter. But smiling and happy and… That was nothing but a fantasy.

'Let me do this for you. Let me kidnap you,' Ivy begged. That the English librarian who was so very different from Maria would do that for her warmed some of the hurt and filled some of the fractures in her heart. She knew that Ivy felt guilty, that she and Antonio had fallen in love with each other. And that if they hadn't, then Antonio would have married her—as directed by Gio Gallo's last will and testament—and they would have inherited Gallo Group, and Antonio would have given it over to her entirely, having no personal or professional interest in running it himself.

'*Grazie*, Ivy. I believe you'd do it too,' Maria laughed sadly.

'I would,' she replied fiercely. 'You're not alone, Maria. You will never be alone again.'

But Maria thought that Ivy was wrong. It was clear that Ivy didn't realise that sometimes you could be lonelier in a marriage than you could ever be outside of one. And it was devastating to Maria to realise that despite all her intentions to avoid being like her parents—like her mother—she had ended up in exactly the same position.

Only, unlike her mother, Maria thought as she swept a hand over her abdomen, she wouldn't allow her child to become caught in the crossfire of such emotional neglect. She would do better, *be* better. She would, Maria realised, fight everyone and everything to ensure that her child grew up never feeling the sting of being deemed unworthy or inferior for any reason.

But that had to start with her, first. She had to find her armour again, she realised as she looked back to the rack of dresses.

'You're coming to the rehearsal dinner?' she asked Ivy as she swept the dress on the floor aside with her foot.

'Yes,' Ivy replied, unfazed by the sudden direction change of their conversation.

'Good. Where is the shop assistant?'

'Here, Signora Gallo,' the harried young woman replied rushing back into the changing room.

'I'm going to need a suit.'

'A suit?' the woman blinked.

'*Si*. A three-piece suit. In white,' Maria replied, unaware of the fierce glint, and sudden glow that made her features come alive.

CHAPTER SEVEN

MICHA REFUSED TO check his watch. He knew what the time was and Maria wasn't late. Not yet anyway. But unease swirled around him, making his body feel uncomfortable, his clothes feel too tight. The foyer of the central Rome hotel glistened elegantly in soft cream lighting, perfect to highlight the rich buttery marble flooring veined in black. But tension corded his shoulder muscles and he rolled his head to ease the ache, righting it before a couple entered from the bar area and caught sight of such weakness.

There could be none. Not tonight.

The entire Gallo clan had shown up. He wasn't surprised, but he was impressed. Whether it was their curiosity or their avarice that drove them, every single one of them wanted to see the new head of the Gallo Group and his fiancée, as if they were some spectator sport.

He hated it as much as he needed it, because he hadn't lied to Maria. He hadn't been exaggerating when he'd told her that everyone would believe in the veracity of this marriage. His child would grow up with nothing less.

Which was why he was doing this properly, the rehearsal dinner. Her family. His mother. Even now, his mother was sitting among them, and he didn't trust a single Gallo up there not to treat her the way she deserved to be treated: with respect, with honour.

He knew how they had seen him, let alone her. But not a single one of them knew what it was like to be desperate. To be so determined to put food in your child's belly that you'd sell yourself and your soul to do it.

Micha slowly and carefully uncurled the fist his hand had formed and smoothed his palm down the waistcoat of his black suit, pulling himself together. His mother had assured him that she would be fine, and he knew she would be. Rosa Rufina was made of stronger stuff than the Gallos could even imagine.

The old-fashioned circular doorway to the hotel began to move and he knew. He knew that she had arrived. He could feel it on his skin, in the way that his breath hitched and his heart pulled. He'd thought he was over that kind of stuff, but when Maria emerged into the foyer, he knew it had been nothing but a lie.

She was glorious.

Rich waves of espresso-coloured hair tumbled around her bare shoulders. The cream waistcoat dipped low, but not salaciously so, and perfectly matched the pressed wide-leg trousers. Her lips, a shocking slash of bright crimson, were a carnal focal point to an appearance that was expensive, confident, professional, powerful. All the things that he'd always admired about her.

And if he thought about the look of vulnerability that he'd seen in the bridal shop the day before, then he pushed that out of his mind as she closed the distance between them.

The click of her cream heels counted down the seconds until she joined him and when she did, she gave him a slow perusal from head to toe. Her blank response, presumably supposed to irritate him, only amused him. He knew what he looked like—he was neither arrogant, nor egotistical.

And he knew—the memory of that night in Paris coming to him in a flash—that she liked the way he looked.

'Did anyone cancel?' she asked.

It was the first thing out of her mouth. Not *Hello, how are you?* She wanted to know if anyone had the audacity to snub his demand that they attend this rehearsal dinner. She was probably calculating the impact on the stock prices if anyone had the temerity to do so.

Her nod of acknowledgement was only momentarily hesitant, betraying her surprise. He frowned, thrown by the 'tell'. She had clearly thought that a member of her family would refuse to come. Did she have someone particular in mind, or—

His chain of thought was cut off when she angled her head up to his and he fell into large brown eyes, wide and so dark as to be unfathomable. It was as if he were underwater, holding his breath—lost to this moment that he wanted to stay in—but starved for oxygen and sanity, he returned to reality, and held out his arm for her to take.

Together, they made their way up the grand red-carpeted spiral staircase to where the hotel had converted a ballroom into one of Rome's most sought-after restaurants. But instead of being led to a table there, the maître d' gestured for them to follow him round to the private room that Micha had secured for the rehearsal dinner.

Maria's eyes flicked to his, probably mentally calculating the amount of money that this would set him back. Again, always underestimating him, just like every other Gallo, and he stifled the spark of irritation that sprang to life.

Beyond the closed doors, the loud sound of voices pressed up against the wood.

Micha went to raise his hand to push them open, but stopped when Maria's fingers gripped his jacket sleeve.

'What is it?' he asked, as he noticed the tension in her body, the slight tightening around her lips.

'A united front, right? No matter what happens, no matter what…is *said*.'

'Maria—'

She shook her head to cut off his question and removed her hand from his arm, visibly gathering herself. And he couldn't quite work it out. This was her family. They were her people. The ones she had chosen over him, and probably would again, given half the chance. Stage fright. That's all it must have been, he thought as he pushed through the wooden doors, the raised voices of moments ago falling away into complete silence.

Maria's heart pounded in her ears. She hadn't realised that she would be so…*scared*. Instinctively her gaze sought out Antonio and Ivy, her lifelines this evening, and a warm breath shivered through her as she saw Ivy's obvious encouragement and Antonio's clear and slightly murderous glare at Micha. It was enough to soften the edges of the tension around her body and allowed her the first smile she'd had since she and Ivy had left the bridal shop the day before.

As for the rest of the room, a total of thirty-five Gallos were seated at a banquetstyle table and she doubted the place settings had been an accident. Her distant cousins and aunts and uncles—related to Gio through his siblings—were at the far end of the table. Closer to the head was Alessina Gallo, Antonio's mother and Gio's eldest, sitting beside the middle brother, Maria's Uncle Carlos. Their younger sister, who had been disowned by their father years before, was still only slowly making her way back into the family fold and had, according to Micha, politely declined. Her son Enzo and wife were also away, but would be there tomorrow. Her eyes rested on Rosa Rufina, the woman sitting at the left of the two seats at the head of the table where she and Micha would sit, and smiled.

It was instinctive. Maria hadn't seen Rosa for years, the realisation hitting her with something like guilt. Gio had moved both Micha and Rosa to Paris, and Maria had been so consumed with her own feelings that she had forgotten the woman who had always treated her with a gentle, reserved kindness. It was still there in the older woman's gaze when she met Maria's, a small smile gracing her lips, but an understanding shining in her eyes that Maria didn't think she'd get from her own family.

And then she looked to the couple that sat opposite Rosa. Her parents.

Her father refused to meet her gaze in what could only be the most obvious and blatant snub. The clenched jaw, the simmering anger—he'd have done better not to bother turning up. The shame of his disappointment burned her cheeks and her heart. Her mother's eyes flickered to hers and then back to her plate, her apathy more painful than her father's rejection.

Her fingers dug into the superfine black wool jacket over Micha's forearms, sacrificing all the hard work she'd done to put on her armour. It was nothing but a mirage. White knuckles would have betrayed her, and she was about to withdraw when his large hand covered hers. She wasn't entirely sure that he'd done it on purpose, but for a single breath his surprising act of kindness struck her dumb.

'Thank you all for coming,' Micha announced as he ushered her into the seat at the head of the table, before kissing his mother on the cheek and nodding at her father as if he wasn't being so painfully and obviously rude.

As waiters came round and filled glasses, Micha wel-

comed her family on behalf of him and his mother. Pro-
claiming how happy he was that Maria and he had found
each other. That he couldn't have ever imagined another
woman by his side and that tomorrow she would finally
make him an honest man.

She flinched when someone down the far end had the
audacity to scoff out loud.

He ignored it all. Instead, he was charming, not overly
so, and witty; perfectly pitched. Maria had never seen him
handle her family because his role had kept him primarily in Paris. She'd never really thought about how he would
manage them, because she'd been so angry and so hurt that
she'd refused to consider that he might actually be able to.
But also because until now, the only person who had been
able to wrangle the Gallos had been her grandfather.

God, she missed him. It was a strange thing. He might
have never considered her truly worthy in her own right
to take over Gallo Group, but he had still encouraged her,
given her a role in the family business that made use of
the skills other family members refused to acknowledge
or credit her with. Yes, there was resentment there that she
wasn't good enough for him, but he had been clear about
it, whereas everyone else pretended and smiled while ready
to stab her in the back.

As the first course was served, she watched Micha as he
interacted with her family, ignoring the obvious stares and
open curiosity around the table. She wanted to speak to Antonio and Ivy, she wanted to be anywhere else than here, but
she was trapped by her parents' stony silence.

At some point her father got up from the table without
even bothering to excuse himself. It was only when he didn't
come back that Maria began to notice—along with several
other members of the family.

Clenching her jaw, she excused herself.

In the quiet of the hallway outside the private dining room, she finally found the space to breathe. She hadn't realised how oppressive the sounds of the entire clan had been. Prising her eyes back open, she looked around for her father.

She heard him before she saw him.

'Yes, you needed to know… No, I want to continue our good relationship and thought you would be interested in who you are doing business with… Well, after, things will continue as they were.'

Business? Her father was talking business? Now?

'Papa,' she said as she rounded the corner, to find him ending the call and slipping his mobile phone into his pocket.

He looked at her with such disdain that she flinched, but she wasn't ready to back down. Not yet.

'It's my rehearsal dinner, Papa,' she pleaded.

'Rehearsal dinner? Isn't it a little too late for that?' he said, his gaze narrowing on her stomach. 'You should have kept your legs closed. You had one job, one!' he yelled, not bothering to keep his voice down. 'You were supposed to marry *well*. And instead you lay with that stray dog, Rufina.'

He might as well have slapped her. Her mouth fell open and she took a step back.

'We'll never be free of that bastard now. *Never.* And if you think for one moment that I'll be paying for this farce of a wedding—'

'That won't be necessary, Luca.'

Maria froze at the sound of Micha's voice from behind her.

Facing him, she saw the moment of shock in her father's eyes, and watched it turn to anger and defiance.

'I meant what I said,' her father snarled.

'So did I,' Micha responded. 'You won't be paying for a single part of this wedding.'

* * *

Micha took a step closer, enough to feel the warmth rising from Maria's body, the fluttering of her pulse at her jaw, from where she turned her head ever so slightly, to hear him berate her father.

'Luca, let me be very clear. I will never allow you to drip your poison into my family ever again. You may be present, you may observe, but you will never speak to Maria again unless she wishes it. You will not contact her, unless she wishes it. As for our child? Again, any contact will be on Maria's terms.'

'Or what, Rufina?'

'Luca, I will sever Gallo Group in half if I must just to get rid of you.'

'You wouldn't dare,' Luca said, stepping back in shock.

'Try me. I've gone head to head with your father. And trust me, you are not him.'

Maria's shocked inhale echoed between them, as Micha stared into the eyes of his future father-in-law. Oh, he wasn't naive. He knew that Maria's father would want to retaliate. He may even try. But Micha learned a long time ago that there was only one way to deal with a spoilt, talentless, insecure Gallo like Luca. And that was to knock him down hard and fast.

Luca clenched his jaw and glared back, anger reddening his cheeks unpleasantly. Eventually he pushed past his daughter and went back into the dining room.

Maria held herself taut for just a moment more before releasing her breath in a shudder.

And in that moment, he'd never hated a Gallo more. All the fight, all the defiance, the power and the determination that had pushed Maria to such dizzying heights at the Gallo Group had fled when confronted with her father's rejection. Something he understood in a way that Maria would probably never realise. Because he'd had that kind of relationship with Gio. Oh, he was their grandfather by blood, but for all of Gio's complicated and sometimes bigoted beliefs, the man had been like a father to him and he'd never wanted to let him down. Not once. And especially not when he'd been seventeen.

Hauling himself back to the present, Micha held out his arm for Maria to take, all the while wrestling with the fierce anger coursing through his veins, blocking out the sounds of spluttering outrage that Luca Gallo had left making. He led Maria back to the room where the rest of the Gallos waited, the whispers and gossip far too much for him to permit now that the lines had been drawn.

He showed Maria to her seat, and then bent to whisper to his mother that he was arranging a taxi to take her back to his home. He pulled out his phone and messaged his assistant to come and meet his mother and make the necessary arrangements. He didn't want her there for what he was about to do.

He felt Maria's questioning gaze on his, but he didn't have the time or the capacity at that precise moment to explain. All the words he wanted jumbled on his tongue, anger making him rash, and he couldn't afford to be either rash or incomprehensible.

Silence had fallen over the room as he pulled his mother's chair out for her and escorted her to the door where his assistant was already waiting. Maria's father returned to the room shortly after with a face that was both shocked and furious and Micha wanted to laugh. He hadn't seen anything yet.

He'd always known what the Gallos thought of him. He'd known that Gio had used the threat of leaving the family company to him as a whipping post for his family, a threat to keep them all in line. But they had grown even more greedy, their avarice increasing in line with the profit of Gallo Group. They were a monster, a cancer, and they had to be stopped.

It was one thing to turn on him, but to turn on her? On Maria? On one of their own?

How had Gio not stepped in to stop this kind of thing? Micha knew she'd had to work hard to get even the smallest amount of respect at Gallo Group, but this? The way that they picked on her, ignored her, treated her? Gio should have stopped it. Her father should have damn well done it, but he was the worst of them. And Antonio? What had he been doing all the time she had been treated like this? Fury bit into his soul and clung on.

He returned to the table, where, rather than taking his seat, he gripped the back of the chair and stared down the length of the table. He caught the concerned gaze that Antonio sent his fiancée's way, half rising from his chair, but Ivy pressed him back down and he felt a rush of affection for Antonio's English wife, a woman who had seemed to understand him more than the people in this room who had known him nearly his entire life. He waited until every single gaze in the room was on him, before starting.

'I understand some of you here may be under the impression that I was little more than Gio's thug,' he said with a shrug. 'I understand why, so there are no hard feelings. I also understand that it will have taken some time to acclimatise to the unexpected terms of Gio's last will and testament that installed me as the new CEO. So, I'm going to take this opportunity to clarify a few things.

'You have all grown a little too comfortable with the levels of disrespect and unprofessionalism. And that stops here. There will be no more whispers, snide comments, disparaging remarks and back stabbing. Neither professionally nor personally. Both you and Gallo Group are hovering on the brink of an abyss. If you continue down this path,' he warned, 'it is you, not me, that will lose everything. I don't care what you think of me, frankly, as long as you keep it to yourselves.

'But Maria?' he said, letting loose some of his anger into his tone. 'She is my fiancée and as of tomorrow, she will be my *wife*. And if any of you dare to treat her with anything less than the respect that she deserves as a member of your family, or mine, or professionally given the amount of revenue and work that she brought to Gallo Group—something that far outstrips the total combined income garnered by every single person at this table—then know this… You will be cut off. You will be removed from the board of governors, your shares will be dissolved and you will be banned from family events forthwith.'

Gasps of shock littered the table. Wide eyes stared back at him, and the moment the whispers started, he punched his fist into the table. The jump of cutlery and glass rippled out into surprised silence.

'And if anyone,' he pressed on, 'would like to know whether I have the authority to do this, please allow me to direct you to Alberto, the lawyer handling Gio Gallo's estate. You are welcome to try and challenge this, but I assure you, it will fail. Now, my fiancée and I have an early start in the morning, so you may all leave,' he said, gesturing to the door.

The moment that 'What?' and 'You've got to be joking' started, he punched the table again, and once again shocked the Gallos into silence.

Micha turned his attention to Luca, and locked eyes with

the man who would have to leave first if any of them were going to do as commanded.

Slowly, Luca pushed his chair back from the table, seething with anger and resentment, not even bothering to spare a glance at his daughter, who had sat through Micha's pronouncement, with her gaze straight ahead—the only person who hadn't flinched when he'd struck the table. And honestly, as her father left the room, slowly followed, one after the other, by the remaining family members, he didn't know whether to be impressed or concerned by her self-possession.

Maria forced herself to uncurl her fingers as she breathed through the pounding in her chest.

He'd stood up for her.

A part of her had soared when he'd done this…but another part? Why had it made her angry? Why had it made her embarrassed? She still felt the tinge of pink on her cheeks and she tried to swallow the emotional confusion she felt now sitting at the head of an abandoned table, save for Antonio and Ivy and Micha.

Antonio threw his napkin on the table and leaned back in his chair.

'Well, that was something.'

'Yes, it was. It was something that should have been said years ago, Antonio. And not by me now,' Micha bit out.

The tension at the table shimmered in the air, Maria not quite able or willing to meet either her cousin's or Ivy's gaze.

'I didn't know it had got that bad,' Antonio admitted. 'Why didn't you tell me?' her cousin asked her.

'She shouldn't have had to!' Micha yelled.

'I was working, Micha!' Antonio yelled back. 'I was

throwing everything I had into Alessina International. Where were you?'

'Gio sent me to—'

'Paris. Yeah, we know. And you can keep hiding behind that excuse all you like, Micha. But we all know that's exactly what it is. An excuse.

'Maria—' Antonio started and then stopped.

She wasn't sure why, because tears had clouded her vision and she couldn't look up, couldn't let them see. She'd never let them see how much she'd hurt. It was a weakness. A vulnerability that they would exploit. Even now, with these people she trusted more than anyone in the entire world—even Micha—she couldn't let them see.

You were supposed to marry well.

Now we'll never be free of that bastard.

We all know that's exactly what it is. An excuse.

She was vaguely aware of Antonio and Ivy excusing themselves from the room, Ivy with a gentle brush of her hand on Maria's shoulder, and Antonio stopping to whisper something in Micha's ear. But she couldn't move. She pulled and pulled, hoping that she could hold it together, hoping that she could hold herself together, but control was slipping through her fingers. She was slipping, and sliding and hurtling towards something and she couldn't stop it.

'Let it go.'

She shook her head, even as she fought to hold on, even as tears clung to her eyelashes.

'There's no one here,' Micha said gently. 'No one will see. No one will know.'

She clenched her jaw and shook her head again. *You're here,* she wanted to say. *You'll see. You'll know.*

'You're my family now. It's okay,' he whispered and as

if it were the key that she'd been waiting for her entire life, she let go.

She didn't know how long she cried for, but she came back to herself slowly, feeling more drained and wrecked than she'd ever felt before. She'd never done that. Never cried. Not like that. Not when her father failed to show up to her preschool dance recital. Not when her mother sat for dinner alone at night at a table set for two. Not when her father gave up pretence at home and moved out without bothering to say goodbye. Not even when Gio had passed. Because instead of mourning the grandfather that she had loved, despite their difficult relationship, she had been thrown into the family turmoil that bubbled and broiled at the complexities of the will.

But she had to pull herself together. She couldn't break. She couldn't do that to *her* child. Their child. She had to do better. Had to be better. As she gathered herself, she realised that she'd been in such a daze that she'd allowed Micha to do *everything*. Organise the dinner, arrange for the wedding, somehow magic up someone who had done all of this within days. And 'this' wasn't some quiet, out-of-the-way registry-office wedding. 'This' was a wedding in front of two hundred people, a priest and probably a significant number of journalists waiting outside.

It was time she did her part.

You're my family now.

Was she? She'd learned long ago that family meant different things to different people. As for what it meant to Micha, yes, he'd stood up for her tonight, but it was as much professional warning as personal. What it meant in the long run, only time would tell.

CHAPTER EIGHT

MICHA HAD NEARLY been late. For his own wedding. What a damn joke.

He'd been putting out fires that started last night. He'd expected Luca Gallo to retaliate, yes, but that quickly? He'd been surprised. Luca had a reputation as lazy, mean and selfish. It was distinctly possible that there were other family members involved, if not the whole damn lot of them. As it was, he'd only managed damage control. The rest, he'd leave for later.

For *after* the wedding.

Obviously, it had taken an obscene amount of money to gently nudge the wheels of church policy to move so quickly but as he knew the priest, knew the money would be used for good causes, Micha didn't begrudge it for one moment.

As he hastened along the ancient stone pathway to the side chapel of the church, he remembered what Antonio had said to him before leaving the restaurant last night.

She was broken after you left her. And if you do that to her again, they'll never find your body.

The threat had been laughable, but the information had near devastated him. The only way he'd got through those first few years in Paris was the white-knuckled grip he'd had on his belief that she'd have left him anyway. He couldn't have meant that much to her, because she would choose her family. A family that had never appreciated her. A family that had rejected her and still did. That's what had stung the most. That he didn't even stack up against *them*. But of course he hadn't.

He'd known at the time that Antonio would take Maria's side. He just hadn't realised that it would form a rift of resentment that even time couldn't breach.

She was broken after you left her.

Micha shook off his thoughts as he stepped into the cool, reverent interior of the church he had sneaked into when he was a child, seeking anything to assuage the ferocious summer heat. Because he'd not been able to go home. Because his father had still been there at the time, and would have given Micha a beating for sure.

And then later, after his father had left, he'd skulked in the shadows while his mother... He swallowed. There was something almost biblical about his feelings of his past and his future in that moment. Retaliation, redemption and in among it all Maria and their innocent child.

The priest's footsteps on the cool stone floor were soft.

'Micha.'

'Father.'

'It's good to see you,' Father Perosi greeted with a smile. 'Though it's been some time since your last confession.'

'I was away.'

'Mmm' was all he said in response to Micha's tenure in Paris. 'And now you are back. With a bride.'

Micha nodded, peering over his shoulder where he caught sight of filled pews.

'And in a hurry,' Father Perosi chided gently.

'Wasn't I always?'

'*Si*,' the older man said with a smile in his eyes. 'Ready?'

'Just like that? No questions about whether I'm sure, whether I'm committed?' Micha asked, only half teasing.

Father Perosi turned his considerably weighty gaze on him and Micha felt it pass beyond skin and bone until it felt as if he were gazing into Micha's very soul.

'You would not be here if you were neither sure nor committed.'

Micha nodded, knowing it as truth.

'And besides, I think you gave your heart to this woman a very long time ago.'

Micha clenched his jaw and acknowledged, reluctantly, that the priest he'd known since childhood was right. He *had* given Maria his heart a very long time ago. But she had let it go, abandoned it, *refused* it and now there was nothing but an empty space in his chest. Nothing to hope, nothing to want, nothing to hurt. Not again.

If she wasn't carrying their child, they wouldn't be here. So, while he was committed and sure about this marriage, he wasn't naive enough to think it was anything other than a way to protect their child's happiness. His happiness had never come into it.

Micha followed Father Perosi out of the small chapel into the main body of the church and towards the top of the aisle, ignoring the glares of the closest Gallos but landing on Antonio and the man beside him. Enzo Rossetti's mother—Gio's daughter—had been disowned by Gio years ago. But just before his death, Gio had reached out to Enzo and the two had become reacquainted. Micha had been only peripherally aware of the old man's attempts to meddle in the American Italian's life, as thankfully Gio had decided in this instance to do his own dirty work.

As such, Micha had only really encountered Enzo and his fiancée, Erin, a handful of times since Gio's passing. Especially since before he passed, Gio had made Enzo a member of the Gallo Group board. Undoubtedly the man was as flippant as his playboy reputation suggested, but there was something deeper there that warned Micha not to believe all that had been said about Antonio and Maria's cousin and respect the man's surprisingly good business sense.

Antonio, still clearly angry with him from the night before, glared at Micha, who turned his attention back to the proceedings.

There was no best man, and Maria had no bridesmaid. She'd have probably chosen Ivy and he wouldn't have minded, only it would have left him picking Antonio to stand behind him and while a certain amount of hostilities had subsided, given the détente reached over Micha and Ivy's surprising friendship, they were very far from the childhood friends they had once been.

Father Perosi gave him one last knowing look, and then nodded to the musical director, who managed to seamlessly blend the ongoing background music into the wedding march.

A split second before he was entirely ready, the wide wooden doors opened at the bottom of the aisle to reveal Maria standing in the open doorway and the breath left his lungs in a whoosh.

It was, he told himself later, because he had been expecting her to wear one of the dresses he'd selected in the bridal shop. Not that he was being autocratic and as much of a bastard as to insist that she should have worn one of them. It was just because he hadn't expected her to wear *that* dress.

The one that reminded him of when they'd been younger. The one that had conjured images of a future he'd told himself he'd never have. That made his pulse pound and his heart sore and soar at the same time. The one that made her look *incredible*.

Thick, dark, lazily curling hair framed her face and tumbled around her shoulders and down her back. Light touches of make-up left her natural beauty to shine all on its own, wide, large brown eyes locked on him, the plunging V neckline leading his gaze down to where she held a small bouquet of wildflowers, a miniature riot of colours that was both whimsical and fresh.

For a split second he remembered—a sunny afternoon, a feeling so powerful he thought his chest would burst, the gentle touch of fingers and lips, the warmth of sunshine from above and within, the sound of Maria's laugh and a hope for the impossible.

Then she faltered, ever so slightly, an infinitesimal pause in her stride, enough time for him only to blink and it was gone. Her hesitation, the memory, the past. It was all gone. And now a very different kind of future opened up before them. One that, he told himself, *had* to be enough.

Maria's pulse tripped and she just about managed to smooth it out without notice. She thought Micha might have caught the near wobble, but nothing had shown on his aggressively handsome face. Dark features stood out against the stark white of his dress shirt and bow tie. The light slid against the silk lapels every time Micha breathed and then got lost in the superfine black wool of his tuxedo.

High cheekbones, almost savagely sharp, and shadows beneath his eyes suggested a sleepless night. The clean shave to his jaw made him look both younger and leaner, *hungry*, *powerful*. Maria swallowed as she closed the distance between them, her gaze dropping to the sensual lips that had brought her so much pleasure. They opened then, just slightly, barely enough to draw breath, but she felt the rise of a flush on her cheeks, and flicked her gaze up to his where what she saw sent goosebumps scattering across her skin beneath the draping silk from her shoulders to her sleeves.

She watched as his gaze searched her from head to toe. Was he disappointed that she hadn't picked one of the dresses he had pulled for her? Was he angry that she'd found the one that he'd discarded?

Why was it that she could never tell with him? she cursed mentally. Why was he just so hard for her to read? He'd been so kind to her last night. After she'd finished crying, he'd walked her to the room he'd arranged for her and left her at the doorway. It had been naive, and supremely silly to hope that he might have stayed. Might have...

And he'd been gone before she could even ask about the wedding night. She'd been so intensely focused on putting one foot in front of the other, that if she wasn't careful, she'd end up like her mother. No. After today, after the marriage, she would find a way to claw back her independence. She had to. For herself and more importantly for her child.

She reached the top of the aisle and felt Micha's assessing gaze on her, as if he'd noticed a change in her demeanour. As the priest welcomed them, and the congregation, she held her soon-to-be husband's gaze. Looking, really looking this time. Not shying away or getting distracted by other things.

There were things she knew, the golden flecks in eyes so dark they almost looked black. The small flat mole just beneath his left eye, and the tiny silvery scar through his eyebrow on the right, where the hair didn't quite grow back as thickly. All these things were familiar, but she wanted more.

He held her gaze through her silent investigation, a raised eyebrow, rueful, challenging and open. As if he was saying, *Have at it, look* all *you want*. It was a dare, like when they'd been kids, and a strange wave of humour swept over them, pulled at the edges of his mouth, just as it drew on her heart. Her mouth wobbled, trying not to smile. And then it passed, just like the tide, leaving a long stretch of emptiness behind it. The smile fell from her lips and the humour from her heart.

She watched the little curve at the edge of his lip flatten, as a sense of weight, of heaviness settled between them. Seriousness. Something old and something responsible. As if she felt all the years since their childhood pass between them in just a few seconds.

And then she was hit by such an intense wave of longing. Oh, nothing like Paris, nothing as obvious as attraction. But for what they could have had. What it could have been. It could have been something beautiful between them. If he hadn't left her. If he hadn't chosen Gio over her, just like every other member of her family. They could have had *this*. And it could have been so wonderful. This time, the wave brought sadness and loss. An older grief, just as known, just as familiar, a sadness she'd never quite got over.

As the faint smell of incense and candle wax mixed with the wildflowers from her bouquet, and the priest pressed on with readings as familiar to her as the names of her family members, she saw it in his gaze too. The hurt, the anger, the sadness. The *loss*.

His naked emotions shocked her, but not enough to override the rising anger. He looked at her as if it were *her* fault. As if *she'd* done this to them. But she hadn't. *He* was the one who had left. *He* was the one who had disappeared off the face of the planet, so that she'd been alone with no one to count on but herself.

'Do you have the rings?'

The priest's question jerked her out of her thoughts, severing the strange, hypnotic moment that had locked them together, excluding everyone around them.

She turned to look at where Ivy and Antonio sat in the front pew—her stony-faced parents on the other side of the aisle. Everyone was either grim faced or fascinated, as if waiting to see if she would really go through with it.

Her gaze returned to Micha, who reached into his pocket and retrieved a small black velvet box without missing a beat. As if they hadn't just shared…*something*.

She just about stopped herself from pressing her hand to her stomach, to their child, to reassure them both that this was the right thing to do, that this would give them the protection and security they would desperately need if the Gallos decided to turn against them.

The priest continued with the ceremony, sharing words of commitment, of love, of honour, and she wondered whether she would ever have those things now. He despised her. That's what she'd seen in the emotions Micha kept locked away. He resented her for this. But it didn't matter, because she knew that he would love their child with the same fierceness and that was all she needed, she told herself as she repeated after the priest, 'I do.'

Micha had kept quiet, even for him, throughout the short reception that had followed. Well. The reception was short for him and Maria. By all accounts the Gallos were drinking the bar dry at his considerable expense.

'Do you not think they'll notice if we leave so early?'

It was the last thing she'd said to him, which was perhaps not that surprising given his response.

'Do you think a single one of them will actually care?'

The moment the car had pulled into the gated driveway of his villa, he'd flung the door to the car open and stepped out into the night. *Cristo*, he needed a drink. He'd not trusted himself or them to have one in front of the Gallos at the reception, and now…? Well, Maria was now a Rufina, he supposed. If she chose to take his name.

The thought pulled him up short, but he dismissed it as a problem for another day. Without waiting to see if she followed him, Micha marched up the stone steps to where the large front door was being held open by his housekeeper.

'Felicitazioni!' Benito proclaimed, ignoring both Micha's frown and the growl that would have scared a lesser man. But Benito had been with him for nearly eight years now, and had seen pretty much all there was to see.

What little was left of Micha's conscience forced his steps to slow and to at least ensure that Benito greeted his new wife—his *wife*—with the respect that her family clearly hadn't afforded her.

'Signora, welcome home,' Benito said.

The words struck Micha like an anvil, and for a single moment, his eyes connected with hers, took in the sight of her in a wedding dress, hovering on the threshold to his home, *her home*, before he let out another growl, stalked into his study and slammed the door behind him.

Of course, he should have known better than to think that Maria would leave him to his peace.

Less than five seconds later, she threw the door back open, only to come into the office and slam it behind her. It had taken more than he'd care to admit to stop himself from flinching from the sound of the door hurtling against its frame.

She stood there like one of the furies, her fists on her hips, glaring at him as if she had the right to be mad at *him*.

'Go to bed, Maria. It's too late for this.'

She opened her mouth and then closed it again. Before opening it and then closing it one more time.

'How…how dare you send me to bed like a *child*,' she whisper-hissed.

How dare he? *Cristo*, if she only knew that he was trying to spare her from the thoughts he was struggling to contain.

'*Va bene*. Out with it,' he commanded.

'You can't ignore me like this, Micha. You've been furious with me all afternoon. You didn't say a single thing to me through the wedding breakfast or reception.'

He shrugged off his tux jacket. 'And?' he said with his back to her.

'And?' she asked, eyebrow arched in surprise. 'So much for *everyone believing this marriage is real*,' she said.

He clenched his teeth together and turned, leaning back against the table.

'Don't do that.' She gestured angrily to where he perched and turned her back on him.

'Do what?' he demanded.

'Do *that*, lean back like *that*.'

'*Madonna mia*, Maria, this is my office, and I just need—'

'What? *What* is it that you need? *Tonight*. On your *wedding night*?' she demanded angrily.

'Space!' he shouted, swallowing immediately and regretting his outburst. It wasn't that he was angry. It was that it was uncontrolled, and she would know that and he was so tired of fighting her.

'Do you think I wanted this?' she accused.

'Do you think *I* did?' he fired back. 'Seriously Maria, do you think that I wanted this either? Me, whose mother had to sell her own body to put food in my mouth. Do you think that I would have ever, *ever*, wanted to force a woman to marry me?'

The shock on Maria's face would have stopped his words, if it hadn't been for the fact that the dam was well and truly burst and now everything was pouring out.

'Just the thought of it *horrifies* me, Maria. It fills me with the kind of self-hatred I wouldn't wish on anyone,' he growled, slashing his hand through the air between them.

'I *will* do everything in my power to protect you and our child, but damn it Maria, do you actually think I'm *enjoying* this? Contrary to what you and your family think, I'm not actually a monster and I do *not* enjoy forcing women against their will to do something they don't want to do. Of course, I appreciate that it would be hard, no, near on *impossible*, for you to credit that one day, *one day*, I might actually have wanted to be with someone who had chosen to be with me because they cared for me. And now, that is impossible.'

He shook his head and huffed out a bitter laugh.

'I could never bring myself to regret what happened in Paris,' he admitted, 'because I would *never* regret what led to the birth of our child. But by my word, I wish you'd never come to my office that night.'

For just a moment, he thought he might have seen a flash of hurt in her gaze, but he must have been imagining it. He stared into the fire that Benito had lit just before they'd arrived.

Maria stared at him, her aching heart bound by the confining silk of the wedding dress as she drew in breath after breath as if she'd run a marathon. She knew, in that moment, that she would never forget his words as long as she lived.

He was, just like her, trapped. Not by their child, but by this situation that had spun so wildly out of control. She wanted to cry just from the agony in his tone when the confession that he'd hated himself that much was wrenched from his soul. She could see it. Could see the torture pulling him from each side. The need to be a better parent, a better *man* than the bastard that had abandoned him and his mother, but the anathema of having forced her to marry him had damned him all the same.

And she was more than just complicit in that. She was integral. She had done that to him.

Guilt came thick and fast. *She* had done it to them when she'd gone to Paris determined to punish him. All she'd wanted was some kind of reckoning for her broken teenage heart, and instead, she'd doomed them both. But despite the shocking vehemence of his words, she couldn't leave it like this. She couldn't let him ignore her like her father, and she couldn't say nothing like her mother.

'But I did,' she said, finally coming back to his wish that she'd never come to his office that night in Paris. 'And I am carrying our child. And now, we're married. And I…' She hesitated, but pushed on. Because she needed to. Because their child needed her to. 'And I don't know where I'm supposed to go. I don't know where I'm sleeping. I don't know if you want—' Maria swallowed '—*expected* to share a bed. I don't know if we're going on a honeymoon. I don't know what I'm going to do when we come back from a honeymoon if we do go on one. I don't know *anything*, Micha, because you are not talking to me. And you need to talk to me. I can't…' The words caught in her throat.

He looked up at her then, his expression unreadable. He had given her his truth. It was the least she could do for him.

'I can't have a marriage like my parents,' she said, swallowing her shame and her hurt.

After a beat, he nodded slowly. He knew what she meant. Knew how much her parents' marriage had haunted her.

Her stay-at-home mother, who had nothing and no one to distract her from her husband's abandonment. Her uncaring and unfeeling father. *Cristo*, she'd told him enough of her childhood hurts back when they'd been teenagers and in love. Or thought they were in love. Could it really have been that easy back then? Could they have made a real go of it? If he hadn't left? If Gio hadn't sent him away?

If she'd gone after him?

'You were the one who wanted everyone to believe that this is a love match. I can work with that. But you need to help me. I can't keep running along behind you playing catch-up to whatever you deem I need to know when you think I need to know it. The wedding was one thing,' she conceded. But now that she was here, now that her mind had caught up, she couldn't sit back and let things happen to her. She hadn't before Paris and she shouldn't now. 'But the future is another. And I want to be partners,' she said defiantly.

She let him gaze at her. There was nothing left to hide, nothing to conceal. She'd meant every word she'd said.

Again, he nodded slowly. With the firelight on the planes of his face, handsome didn't even begin to describe the complexities of what he looked like to her. Familiar. Infuriating. Arousing. Angering. Powerful. Resentful.

'London.'

'London?' she repeated, bringing her out of the spell cast by the shadows of the fire.

'Our honeymoon. We're going to London. It would have been Hawaii, but your father had other ideas.'

'My father?' Maria asked, feeling her face scrunch in confusion.

'It seems that he is trying to get to me through Peterson,

which perhaps wouldn't have been possible if I'd been able to secure the contract with your help before now.'

She dismissed the light jab that she was—in some small way—to blame. In part because she knew it was true.

'Why would he do that?' she asked.

'I'm not quite sure,' he said, finally standing up away from the desk. 'But first we need to pay Peterson a visit and get him back in line. Or the Gallos will have much, much more to talk about than our wedding. They'll be sitting back and watching the end of Gallo Group altogether.'

'Okay,' she answered decisively. Gallo Group was where she felt strong. Where she knew what she was doing. 'Do you want me to arrange a meeting with him or do you think it would be better coming from you?' Maria asked.

'I think it would be even better coming from GG's chief financial officer.'

'Of course,' Maria said, nodding in agreement and looking away so he couldn't see the slight wince of hurt she felt at her offer being rejected. 'Is that Giovanni?'

'No.'

'Then who?'

'You.'

Maria frowned. 'What?'

'If you'll have it, of course. Giovanni will be on hand through whatever maternity leave you'd like to have, but he's more than happy to step aside.'

'I thought he wanted the job.'

'He did. Until he realised just how awful the Gallos can be,' Micha said, rubbing a hand over the back of his head.

'When did you decide this?' Maria asked through the thickening of her throat. She'd hate it if it had been last night, because of her father. She hated that he was the one to give her the position in the first place, but she'd meant

what she said. She and Micha needed to start working together, so it really didn't matter what his answer was.

'Before I found you in Trasimeno.'

The day she'd tried to kick him out before hearing what
he had to say because she was so worried about him finding out about the baby.

She pressed a hand to her mouth. Oh god, how had they
made a mess of so much?

He came to stand in front of her, something like acceptance in his eyes.

'Together.'

It was the echo of a promise they'd once made too many
years ago now to count. It was both hurt and heartfelt, and
she welcomed it as much as she could.

'Together.'

CHAPTER NINE

'AND THAT'S WHEN I told him he had a deal!' exclaimed Daniel Peterson.

He might not look it, dressed in an off-the-rack grey suit, a white-and-grey-striped shirt and a pink tie that aged him horribly, but Daniel Peterson was one of the richest men in Europe. It was, Maria realised, his own type of armour. He delighted in being underestimated and unfortunately Micha had committed less of a sin, and more the fulfilment of Daniel's often persecutory expectations, ones that told him he would constantly be undervalued and insignificant to younger and brighter men than him. Peterson's ego was often his downfall, but surprisingly enough, his intelligence was high enough to drag him back up again. It was just that most people didn't stick around long enough to find out that this was the case, until they had been dismissed by Daniel.

'Not bad, Daniel,' Maria offered, her smile wry, just the way the Englishman liked it. It hid the tiredness that was beginning to press against the backs of her eyes and she was fighting the urge to place a hand around her stomach. There was nothing there other than a bundle of cells, but she had walked into the restaurant at the top of the Shard feeling protective of those cells. As if she was being reminded that having both a career and motherhood was going to be difficult.

Micha had been content to let her take the lead. Something that surprised her. Oh yes, he'd said as much, but in Maria's experience, the men of Gallo Group often said one thing and did another. And this was, actually, the first time they'd worked together in the years since they'd both worked for her grandfather.

Unbidden, her gaze flicked between the two men. There was no contest. It had nothing to do with the fact that Peterson was nearly nine years her senior, or greying at the temples. Some would find that eminently attractive. But Micha?

She took a sip of her sparkling water.

It did nothing to wash away the taste of desire on her tongue. His jaw in dark shadow seemed arrogant rather than lazy, the high cheekbones sculpting the planes of his face in harsh lines, the furrowed brow only serving to draw attention rather than deter it.

Husband. Lover. Father of her child. Enemy.

Micha had been many things over the years, but she was finding it hard to pin down just what he was to her *now*.

She sighed.

'Ahh, is it that time already?' Daniel asked, misunderstanding her feelings. But she could work with this so she smiled and agreed that 'yes. The wining and dining is done, and now we talk business.'

'Okay,' he said, smoothing his fingers along the edge of the white-cloth-covered table.

The darkness of the night beyond the extremely thick windows, the subtle lighting and gentle hum of conversation, as well as the discreet positioning of the table, added to a feeling of seclusion; as if it were just the three of them.

'I heard there was a mistake during the contract negotiations,' Maria started, ignoring the slightest flinch from

Micha, without taking her eyes off Daniel. 'And I'd like to hear how you felt it came about.'

'We agreed verbally, to continue in the manner as before. And yet when we received the contract, key components had been changed.'

'What were you told?'

Daniel flicked his gaze to Micha before it returned to Maria.

'That it was a mistake with a new member of staff.'

'You didn't believe this?'

'What I didn't believe was that such an important contract for Gallo Group had been put under the charge of a member of staff so inexperienced as to make such mistakes. It shows a distinct lack of respect.'

'Mmm.'

Maria took another sip of her water, buying herself some time. She knew what had happened—Micha had told her as much—she just wanted to see how Daniel saw it. Needed to, in order to know whether the plan she had to rectify it would work.

'Mmm?' Daniel questioned.

'Yes. Mmm. I am thinking. I am also wondering if you know how many contracts GG was dealing with at that specific time, given the transition of power from my grandfather to the man he chose to follow in his footsteps.'

'If that had been the case, I might have been more understanding, but I'd heard rumours.'

Maria cut a glance to Micha, who, this time, was not just frowning, but positively scowling.

'Rumours that suggested that you, and not Mr Rufina, were Gio's intended heir.'

Maria silently cursed. It wasn't Micha who would be the downfall of this company, but whatever member of her family had a big mouth and seemed intent on letting the whole thing burn rather than trying to save it.

'But you are back. Wife and CFO. That could change things.'

She hoped to god that the dim lighting in the restaurant hid the blush of anger painting her cheeks. Of course, a man would see her marriage first. She opened her mouth to speak but Micha got there first.

'I think you'll find, Mr Peterson, that marriage to me comes a lot further down the list of Maria's priorities than Gallo Group.' Micha's voice was low, but cutting. But not to her. The cut was to him. To Peterson. The man who they had come here intending to woo. 'And if you don't see that, and don't want to continue with Gallo Group with Maria as CFO, secure in the knowledge that under her, your wealth will increase exponentially, then I'm not entirely sure that we want to do business with you,' he said, leaning back in his chair. 'Now, I understand your concern. Reading over a contract that differed to our verbal agreement must have been jarring. However, like Gio, I strongly believe in giving chances to staff, letting them try and letting them learn. And lessons were learned. The staff member is still in our employ and has not—in fact—made another mistake yet, despite working on multiple contracts simultaneously. You can be assured, he never will.

'Now the question moves to whether *I* want to work with someone who gets their—how do the English say?—knickers in a twist because a new hire used the wrong contract template. This speaks to me of someone *ungracious*.'

'Micha,' Maria cut in from across the table in warning. He had made his point. Rubbing Daniel's nose in it wouldn't help at all.

'Darling,' he bit back with a sinful smile.

She turned to Peterson. 'He is being defensive on my behalf.'

Daniel grinned. 'As he should, and very much as I'd hoped he would be. Maria, I hope you know me well enough to know that I am completely aware of your skills and your contribution to Gallo Group and would never dismiss you as "just a wife." I just wanted to see how that dynamic would play out. So, okay, you have me intrigued. I want to know what your new offer is.'

'Why should we make any changes to the original terms?' Maria asked, her words clear as a bell.

'Because I know how much you need me,' Daniel said.

'*Needed.* We have, of course, in the last few months been exploring other avenues,' Maria lied without compunction.

Daniel raised an eyebrow, willing to entertain the threat that Maria had dangled before him, like the stick instead of the carrot, and Micha didn't know whether to be impressed, or infuriated, but he was willing to see how this played out.

'I don't believe you,' the Englishman said slowly.

'That's irrelevant. We have been exploring a rebranding. Clearly there are people who have had some difficulties re-acting to the changing of the guard, which leaves us with two options. To hold fast, *or...*'

'We completely rebrand. Fresh blood, new contracts, new appearance,' Micha picked up seamlessly.

'You wouldn't. That's crazy,' Daniel said with a shake of his head.

'No, it's a gamble. And one that could very well pay off. There are quite a number of people out there who are getting tired of fusty old men making the same decisions over and over and over again,' Maria interjected.

'And some people are attracted to a little bit of crazy,'

Micha replied with an arrogant smirk, sure to exacerbate the rumours of his rebellious business sense.

'And the board?' Daniel asked pointedly.

'Will fall in line,' Maria replied with all the confidence that Micha didn't believe for a single second.

Peterson leaned back in his chair, his gaze flicking between Maria and Micha. A waiter approached, and veered swiftly away with a single flick of Peterson's hand.

'Mmm.' The sound was almost a growl. And almost approving. 'You work horribly well together. And I'd rather be on your side than against it.' With a nod, he stood from the table. 'I believe I have taken up enough of your honeymoon as it is.' Peterson cast a look between them. 'I will happily sign on the terms as originally agreed. But I leave you with a warning. Someone is stirring the pot. And you need to find out who, or there won't be a company for me to sign with.'

He left Maria and Micha in stunned silence with empty dessert plates in front of them, which the waiter came to take away as Maria struggled to catch up with what had just happened.

'He's right,' Micha said, his gaze heavy on her.

'About a traitor?'

Micha held her gaze. 'No. That we work well together.'

He meant it. He'd enjoyed working with her. They'd never done it before, their past a wedge between them like an iceberg, forcing them to only interact when necessary. Gio had been content to leave Paris and England under his purview, and Micha had left the financial discussions between his manager and Maria to get on with.

Oh, he'd known she was good, but seeing it in action, it was a rush. Firing his blood stream. Ignoring it, he signalled for the cheque, and led her out of the impressive London

Shard, which reached into the night sky above them as their car drew up to the pavement to pick them up. His hand hovered at the base of her spine as he guided her into the back of the car, his palm tingling. He flexed it open and closed before he slipped in beside her.

As the car wound its way through dark London streets he wondered whether they maintained their silence because of the driver, or because it was easier that way. They really only seemed to encounter difficulties when they spoke to each other.

There hadn't been a huge amount of speaking in Paris though. The swift lightning strike of arousal forked down into a simmering sea and he turned to look out of the window and away from her.

It didn't take long for the car to reach the apartment he kept in Notting Hill. While he'd been in Paris, it had made sense, especially with the amount of business that Gallo Group had with British clients. He hadn't been here for nearly eight months. The last time had been…the last time he'd seen Gio, he realised with a thud of his heart.

His feelings about the old man had always been complex. But above all, Gio had taught Micha nearly everything he knew. And Gio had appreciated what he hadn't taught him; what had been pure instinct for Micha. *You're like me, you know? And I like that.* But it hadn't been enough to make him worthy of the man's granddaughter.

As the car drew to a stop, Micha exited and held the door open for Maria, his hand waiting for hers. After a moment where he thought she might refuse, she accepted it and let him lead her up to the slick black-painted door, where he entered the pin on the keypad and ushered her over the threshold.

Maria blinked in the harsh lighting as they took the red-carpeted stairs all the way up to the third floor. A part of him wanted to see her expression as she took in his apartment. Of all of the places he'd lived, this was his. Not Gio's, not the Gallos'. He hadn't even tried to make his home in Italy—a place that had always marginalised him for his mixed European heritage. But here, in London, the melting pot of cultures and nationalities, he'd made it his home. At extreme expense of course.

It was an 'upside down' apartment, in that the door opened onto a hallway where a set of stairs would take you to the sitting room and open-plan kitchen on the floor above, while straight ahead the door was open onto a large bedroom suite and off to the left was a bathroom.

Without waiting for him, she took the stairs and came to a stop, forcing him to pause behind her where he could see the open-plan living area that had stunned her. He knew the feeling. It was precisely why he'd fallen in love with the building.

Glass fronted three whole sides of the room, London lit up against the night sky surrounding them almost entirely. A large U-shaped sofa faced, not the room, but the view beyond, making one feel as if they were at the very tip of the skyline looking out across the city in all its splendour.

'Would you like something to drink?' he asked.

'Herbal tea if you have it,' she said, unable to tear her gaze away from the sight. Two sides of the view had strips of decking, where there were large green plants in giant tubs, and chairs, and a table where he often liked to have his morning coffee, no matter the weather.

She went to the window, with her arms wrapped around herself as he made a cup of chamomile and himself a decaf espresso.

'You shouldn't have done that, you know.'

Her words carried easily across the room. It was a reprimand, but it had no sting to it. No heat.

'It was reckless to call Daniel out like that. His ego is as precious to him as his billions. It could have backfired terribly.'

'But it didn't. You saw to that,' he said, picking up their drinks and moving to the large sofa that was perhaps his most favourite possession oddly.

He placed the hot drinks down on the coffee table and sat.

She looked tired, he realised, and wondered how much she was hiding from him, whether the pregnancy was hitting her harder than she was letting on.

'My mother,' he started, swallowing his natural inclination *not* to talk, not to open himself up and be vulnerable with Maria, because of how much it had cost him when she'd cut him from her life before. 'She had terribly swollen ankles with me. And awful morning sickness.'

Maria heard the lifeline he was extending to her. She felt the hesitancy in him, but appreciated his effort. It wasn't as if either of them found it easy. Not after the decades of hurt and resentment that piled in between them.

'I'm actually not feeling too bad,' she offered him, turning back to the room and leaving the nightscape of London behind her. 'Tired, yes, but okay.'

She sat on one corner of the U-shaped sofa, absently rubbing her hand over the warm smooth leather beneath her palm. She didn't know why she found it soothing, but she'd been doing it ever since she found out she was pregnant.

'Do you have any appointments lined up? Scans or such?'

'They're scheduled for when I'm back.'

'Could I…?' He stopped, cleared his throat.

Instead of rushing him or filling in for him, she waited,

remembering this from years ago. Remembering how much he hated people doing that for him. And remembering how Gio was the only one who let him take his time apart from her. Did he miss him? Did Micha miss Gio the way that she missed Gio? Messily? With difficulty? Because he'd been a hard man to love, but also almost impossible not to.

'Could I come with you?'

'Yes. I would like that,' she said, hating that he'd had to ask, knowing how much that would have cost him. That that was how bad things were between them. They were married. They were going to be parents, for heaven's sake. They had to do better than this.

'If there's anything you need, Maria, just ask. Please.'

'I…'

'Yes?'

'I would like us to have a honeymoon.'

'We are—'

'Not one that involves work.'

He raised an eyebrow at her, accusingly. Yes, she found it *just as* ironic as he did that *she* was the one requesting that they take time off work. But maybe just maybe, away from everything they could find some equilibrium. She swept a hand unconsciously over her abdomen, the strange firmness there new and unusual, but full of just so much that she was almost terrified of messing things up. And she really didn't want that.

'Okay, a honeymoon,' he agreed, nodding.

'And… I want us to find a new home.'

This time his brows shot up into his hair line.

'Really?'

'Obviously I'm not expecting you to pay for it—'

'I can pay for it Maria,' he growled, interrupting her. 'What's wrong with my villa?'

'It's *yours*. Not *ours*. I feel like…' She'd felt like a fool, the night of her wedding. But she couldn't admit that to him. A silly bride, having expected more than a bed in a spare room. She swallowed. 'I feel like a guest.'

He frowned. 'I didn't mean for that.'

'I know,' she replied honestly. 'But… I think we need a fresh start. A new beginning. As equals as much as partners, and as confidants as much as—' She'd been about to say *lovers*. But they weren't lovers. He couldn't even bring himself to touch her. And she hated that she knew that. Tiny little tremors fissured out from the cracks in her heart. He hadn't touched her since the priest had them kiss to secure their vows. And that had been as cold as a fish.

'I will get my assistant to start looking once you give him a list of your requirements.'

'Our.'

He blinked at her.

'Our requirements. And I don't want your assistant to do it, I want to do it *together*.'

He bit his lip and nodded. '*Va bene*. Is there anything else?'

There was, but she was not at all sure either of them was ready for her request. Yet, if she didn't speak now, when would she? Would she become like her mother, sitting in silence waiting for her husband to suddenly start caring about her?

'You agreed that I wouldn't have a marriage like my parents.'

His eyes narrowed. He seemed almost preternaturally still.

'Yet that is what you gave me the night of our wedding,' she said, her insides trembling, worried about what she was asking for. Because that night was something she had absolutely no intention of repeating. Removing the gown herself, in an empty bedroom, all by herself, had been...devastating. She'd scrubbed at the tears that she'd kept silent, and burrowed into the bed beneath the duvet, red eyed and hollow hearted, all the way to dawn.

Micha might have demanded that they work together, but he had remained utterly removed from her in every other way. But she couldn't live like this. Couldn't bear to. She'd grown up in the shadow of her mother's silence, and her father's absence. It was the one thing, the *one* thing, she'd never wanted for herself. Oh, theirs wouldn't be a normal marriage. How could it be? But that didn't mean they couldn't have companionship, or...or... Her heart stumbled over itself.

'I... I don't know what you mean, what you're asking me for,' he said, slowly as if just as fearful of where this would go.

'I want more. More than just a marriage that looks good on the outside.'

'More,' he repeated dully.

Oh, for god's sake, she internally cried. *Why are you making me say it?*

'You want to share a bed?' he asked, his voice gravel and sending invisible shivers across her skin, which was nonsense, because she was pretty sure that he'd not lay a single finger on her in that way ever again.

'Yes.'

'Yes?'

'Yes,' she confirmed, with a raised eyebrow, daring him to ask for even more damn clarifications.

He opened his mouth and closed it again, and honestly if it wasn't for how insecure it made her feel, the entire thing would almost be funny. She'd not exactly ever thought herself to be in the position of negotiating billion-dollar deals one minute and then half of a marital bed the next. But here she was, doing precisely that.

'You said we'd work together. I want that. We're married. We're a team. And we're going to be parents, to our child, who will need us to be together.'

'Starting…?'

'Is there a reason it shouldn't be tonight?' she asked with a lot more bravado than she felt. She was beginning to regret her decision to confront him about it. Until she remembered the hollow ache in her chest only the night before.

'No?'

'Is that a question or an answer Micha, because honestly—'

'No, it's an answer.'

'As in no you won't let me share your bed? Micha, I swear you make things so unnecessarily—'

'Are you finished?' he asked, coming to his full height, holding his hand out for her to take.

Now she was the one with her mouth hanging open like a fish, which she promptly shut with a snap. She looked up at him, knowing that this was new for them. New territory, new dynamics.

This is what you wanted, right?

Wanted? No. Needed? Yes. ·

And she did need it. They both did.

She placed her hand in his, heart beating, and let him gently pull her up from the seat. They were closer than they'd been even at the church as they shared their vows. From here, she could see the little jagged line of silver through his right eyebrow and stupidly wanted to trace it with her thumb.

But couldn't. Couldn't because she had to claw to claim

only just a little. Because she got the sense that if she moved too quickly, or too far, he'd disappear from her like a mirage. The golden flecks in his eyes spun out like a snowstorm, making her wonder at all the words he was thinking that couldn't get past his ironclad control.

'Are you ready?' he asked, swiftly adding 'to sleep,' as if she needed the clarification.

She nodded, truthfully, as a wave of near exhaustion threatened to overwhelm her, and let him lead her back down the stairs to the bedroom.

She held herself back on the threshold, knowing she had no right to ask, but unable to move forward until she had.

'Have you…have you, with other women?' Oh god, why was she making such a hash of this?

'No. No one else has been in this bed, save me.'

Micha didn't know whether he'd needed to say it as much as she'd needed to hear it, but he felt some of the tension ease following his statement.

He'd expected her to scoff, or question him, but he realised that that expectation wasn't actually based on *this* Maria. But the Maria from before. The middle Maria, he was beginning to think of as the person he'd avoided for eleven years. The one that had, whenever they'd come into contact, bit and hissed like a cat. *This* Maria was different and different again to the young Maria he'd once known, and maybe he owed it to both them and their unborn child to get to know her.

'You can use the bathroom first if you'd like?' he offered, and she nodded and took her toiletries into the bathroom that was accessed from back out in the hall.

He stared at the bed almost resentfully. He'd planned to sleep on the sofa, obviously not enough of a bastard to make his pregnant wife unhappy. But she'd been unhappy the night of her wedding. His conscience twisted. Angry, furious, frustrated, all things he was very familiar with feeling over the last eleven years. But he'd not once felt *bad*.

Until now.

She'd had to ask for a damn honeymoon.

She'd felt like a stranger in his home, which—of course— she *would* have.

He was on the brink of really messing things up. He could feel it.

He imagined her washing her face, brushing her teeth, these deeply intimate moments of married life that others took for granted, and he just didn't know whether he was hiding in this room because he didn't want that, or because he wanted it so badly.

The door behind him pushed open, and her face glistened like dew, all make-up removed. She was wearing a little vest thing and a pair of silk black pants and she'd never looked more beautiful.

'I'll just…' he trailed off and backed out to the bathroom, the minty scent of her toothpaste in the air, the sink wet from where she'd run the taps.

He gripped the vanity, knuckles white, head bowed.

Get it together. Get it goddamn together.

Sharing a bed with Maria would be the sweetest of tortures. To be that close to her, her warmth, the smoothness of her skin. Not once had he forgotten the feel of her beneath his hands, on his tongue, around him.

She'd asked him for a real relationship, but in order for him to give that to her, he was going to have to let her in. But he wasn't sure he could do that. He'd barely survived the last time they'd broken up. Gio and the work he'd made

Micha do was the only thing that had pulled him through the days, weeks and months that followed his move to Paris.

Only, this time there wasn't even a choice. They were going to have a child.

I'll do whatever it takes.

His own words, delivered as a threat, come back to haunt him.

A short while later he returned to the bedroom to find Maria already under the covers, the night lamp on that side of the room already switched off.

He sat heavily on the opposite side of the bed.

'Is this okay?' she asked quietly. 'I don't know what side—'

'It's fine,' he hastily assured her, wincing when he realised he'd cut her off.

'Oh. Okay. Good night then.'

'Good night, Maria,' he said, as he slipped beneath the covers, the distance between them an insurmountable divide. The fear that, in the night, he might accidentally reach for her terrified him. His muscles locked, not even wanting to breathe loudly in case it disturbed her.

Long into the night and the early morning, he remained awake, planning the honeymoon she'd asked for as something to do. He would absolutely do what she wanted, the honeymoon, the new home, the fresh start…but he knew with a high degree of certainty that he'd lose his heart in the process.

Just like he had before.

CHAPTER TEN

MICHA HAD WATCHED Maria try to get comfortable in the private jet's seat for the last ten minutes.

'Do you want to swap?' he asked, finally.

'No, I don't think that would make much of a difference,' she admitted, still clearly uncomfortable.

He was guessing that it was her back, because she hadn't let him know what it was that she was finding uncomfortable and he fought the ridiculous—and frankly dangerous—desire to tell her to *use her words*.

She shot him a look from under her eyelashes. 'Are you going to tell me *now*, where we're going?' she asked.

He pursed his lips and shook his head. She sighed dramatically and he bit back a smile.

Their morning had proceeded as much as their night had. Going through the motions of getting ready for the day, while painfully conscious of each other, both aware it was strange and awkward and neither really knowing what to do about it except press on until it wasn't.

'Not even a hint?' Maria asked from across the cabin.

He opened his mouth to say it was somewhere she had always wanted to go, and then realised that she may have already been there. With someone else. His mouth shut with a snap. She frowned at him and then eventually looked out the window.

He'd been oddly pleased with his two-o'clock-in-the-morning idea of coming here. He'd dimmed the brightness of his phone screen so as not to wake her as he made the *incredibly* last minute booking, and notified the staff of the jet. All of whom would be handsomely recompensed for the change in itinerary.

But just the thought, the mere possibility, that she'd already come here with someone else was enough to sour his mood significantly. Which was nothing but a slightly bruised ego, he told himself sternly. He just had to get over it. And if she asked him about it? Reminded him that she'd once told him how much she wanted to come here? He'd lie and tell her it was just a happy accident.

They landed three hours later, Maria peering out of the small cabin windows to try and identify where they were from what little she could see.

'Oh!' she exclaimed as they were hit with a wall of heat the moment the flight attendant opened the door for them. Maria looked back at him, something like excitement and hope shining in her gaze.

'You didn't,' she accused.

'Well, as I'm not one hundred percent sure what you think I might have not done, I—'

'Oh,' she said again, with such sheer delight it left him speechless. He hadn't heard her sound like that since they were both teenagers.

If the palm trees planted around the lowslung building that formed Manera Airport hadn't given it away then Welcome to Al-Maghrib did it. The architectural design crisscrossing the front and sides of the building was impressive and eye-catching.

Maria was almost jumping up and down on the spot with excitement, in direct contrast to how she'd been on the plane and for the first time since last night, maybe longer, a thin thread of tension unspooled from deep within him. He'd done the right thing. Even if she had come here with someone else. As staff checked their passports and luggage, she raised onto her tiptoes and whispered in his ear.

'You remembered.'

'I don't know what you're talking about,' he denied.

'I don't believe you,' she said with the biggest smile. 'Thank you.'

He allowed a smile to pull at one corner of his mouth and she raised an eyebrow and pointed at him. 'I don't believe you,' she mouthed as she accepted her passport back from the administrator and went to peer through the window that looked out at the city of Marrakesh.

It wasn't long before they were on their way in a chauffeur driven car towards their destination. A lot of the main hotels on the strip were luxurious to the extreme, but Micha had wanted something more… His mind skated over the word *intimate* and chose *private* instead.

And the private villa, half an hour away from the city, on the grounds of what had once been a palace, had caught his eye immediately. It was modest in size, but absolutely outstanding in terms of amenities. Not only was there a bedroom suite, there was also a separate suite for massage and pampering treatments, a private pool, a personal chef, and twenty-four-hour waitstaff. No expense had been spared. Less than five hours after leaving London, Micha and Maria stepped out of the car and into paradise.

They both just stood there for a moment. The carved detail around the flat roof of the one-storey building filtered the setting sun's rays like a cut-out paper lantern, glowing a beautiful orange yellow, before the gaze was drawn to the sea.

Micha felt the breath sigh out of him, as if the tension

was beginning to leave his body just at the sight of it. He'd never come here. Never been able to, after how they'd left things. But now he was here with Maria it felt...*right*.

Maria couldn't help herself. From the moment they were welcomed into the villa, she just felt thrilled. The interior design was incredible, brass finishings, incredible detailed cut-outs in the panels that divided living areas, or shielded lamps, or the exquisite tiles in a bathroom that was near pornographic in its luxury. The bath was sunken into the floor, and little sconces held flickering flames already lit, the scent of rose in the air, and petals dancing on the water.

But beyond all of that was the fact that he'd remembered. And instead of trying to hide how that made her feel, she welcomed it, let it warm her like the ambient temperature around her, so much more pleasant than London had been.

'Dinner will be served in a short while out on the terrace,' the house staff member announced before disappearing magically.

'Where does he go?' Maria whispered to Micha when they were left on their own.

'There are hidden rooms in the walls,' he replied with such a dead tone that her gaze snapped up to his in shock, only to find laughter dancing in his eyes.

She smiled, tried to hide it behind her hand and then wondered why she should be so embarrassed.

He caught her hand just as she was about to pull it away.

'You don't have to do that. You don't have to hide your smile from me,' he said, his burnished gaze becoming serious.

She nodded, her heart leaping. She remembered. Remembered how he would look at her when she laughed. As if she were the most incredible thing he'd ever seen. He'd do and say silly things just to make her laugh. As if her plea-sure was his.

She swallowed, her heart turning in her chest. 'I'm going to get changed for dinner,' she said, slipping from the room before he could divine her thoughts.

When she had packed for the trip to London, she had thought it would just be a few nights there and that they'd return. She'd have to buy some clothes to get her through the stay here.

Twelve nights, he'd told her. Twelve nights in a North Af-rican palace. That's what it felt like. The grandeur was more than she'd ever seen as a Gallo. She sighed a little sadly at her clothing. It was unsuitable, either for Marrakesh or her feelings about what she wanted to look like. She sighed and opened the wardrobe to hang up her shirt before it crum-pled and gasped.

Her phone buzzed.

I hope you don't mind. I took the liberty of arranging some appropriate clothes for us. We can shop for more if none of these suit, I just wanted you to be comfortable.

From Micha, it was a veritable essay. But before she could ponder on how much easier it would be to talk to him over text message, her gaze was drawn to the beautiful clothes he'd arranged for her.

She loved them *all*. Colourful silks, all suiting her skin tone, hung in draped layers, soft easy clothes for lounging, all impeccable quality and incredible design—sleek, sophis-ticated, but just a little softer than perhaps she would have chosen for herself, and somehow more fitting. She wanted that softness.

When had she grown tired of the severe armour she'd

felt necessary to wear around the men in Gallo Group? How long had she stifled that softness in order not to appear weak? And how ironic, that this was what was going to set off an existential crisis for her—and not her pregnancy.

Or was this just hormones? Could she keep blaming her hormones for the swirling mess of confusion she felt when she looked at Micha?

Liar.

What?

Liar. You know it's not so confused any more.

She let the silk shirt fall from her hands. No, she couldn't lie to herself any more. She wasn't confused about how she felt about him. It was as if the closer she drew to him, he was becoming clearer and clearer, a lens adjusting until he was in focus.

Micha. The man who remembered where she'd always wanted to go. The man who, no matter what others had believed or how they had behaved, had never treated her business acumen with anything other than respect. Who had always stood up to the men in her family, honouring her grandfather's wishes, no matter what they were. The man who had set her on *fire* with a need so overwhelming and so incredible her body still reacted to just the thought of it. The man she had slept beside last night, who had given her everything she'd asked for. A man whose morals and character would make him the best father she could imagine for her child.

A soft knock on the door brought her out of her thoughts.

'There are drinks on the terrace for when you're ready,' Micha called through the door.

He had given her so much already. Could he give her even more? Could he give her the one thing she truly wanted? His heart?

Maria emerged from the bedroom suite just fifteen minutes later, dressed in a deep olive-green silk dress that floated down to her toes. After the flight, her ankles had felt a little swollen and she'd decided to leave her feet bare. The sleeveless dress draped down from shoulders and the dramatic V was perfect for her chest, which felt fuller than it had done before her pregnancy.

To the left of the secluded terrace was a small, but exquisite pool, brilliant white contrasting with rich deep blue tiles that made her heart happy to see. The terrace looked out over an incredible view—the slash of dusk touching the azure-blue horizon line of the sea was breathtaking. The mountains in the distance provided texture to the vista, and it wasn't that different to the Mediterranean view she loved so much. In fact, it reminded her of the little cottage she'd bought on Lake Trasimeno.

'You look beautiful, Maria.'

The words came from behind her and she let them settle about her before she turned to take him in. He, too, had changed from his travel clothes. The cream linen suit and pale blue shirt were about as relaxed as he permitted himself in the impeccable fashion he wore. And for the first time she wondered if they were the same in that. If they chose their clothes as armour against those who would take from them, or try to diminish them.

And suddenly she wanted to ask him. Ask him everything she'd been wondering about over the years. The little thoughts and questions she'd gathered and noted, that had become lists long enough to fill books.

'And you look very handsome,' she replied.

Micha blinked, the words reaching a part of him that he usually kept hidden. He wasn't stupid. He knew that he was attractive to most women, but handsome? From Maria? It felt like something shifted. He'd not been handsome to her back when they were younger—precisely because they had been younger. But they were adults now and everything was different in very small and very particular ways.

He gestured to the table set by the house staff, who had thankfully disappeared for the night. On pristine tablecloths had been placed a veritable feast of small plates containing food that looked incredible and smelled delicious. Only from the moment he'd spied Maria, his hunger for food had fled and been replaced by a desire that only she could satiate.

She came to the seat he held out for her and Micha caught the scent she wore, citrus, sweet, *soft*. That was what had surprised him about this Maria. The softness that didn't make her any less, but instead only made her seem *more*. More feminine, more powerful, more herself. As if she could finally be *all* the things that she wanted to be, rather than trying to force herself into the boxes that other people expected or needed from her.

'This looks wonderful,' she said appreciatively.

He had already removed any of the little plates that she couldn't have because of her pregnancy, and the chef had immediately presented him with a few alternatives. The plates were designed to be shared and he was happy to see her looking so eagerly at the food.

His mother had explained how ill she'd been with morning sickness. She hadn't had to say how useless his father had been at the time, and Micha had sworn that Maria would not be left to deal with anything like that on her own.

'There's so much here, I'm not sure we're going to eat even half of it,' she whispered.

There was a sweet, meaty tagine, stuffed fried sardines, *briwat*, the triangle pastries stuffed with cheese and meat, *zalook* with its stewed aubergine, tomatoes and spices, cous-cous and roasted vegetables, freshly cooked flatbreads and merguez sausages, and fresh tomato salads, with red onion and herbs.

'Eat whatever you want,' he said, placing a few things on her plate for her to start with, and then seeing to his own.

'You're still very considerate,' she said, her index finger running across the rim of the blue-and-white textured plate he'd just given her.

'I don't see why that would have changed,' he said with a small frown.

'You don't think that my family's obvious and inherent selfishness could have whittled that out of you, if you had been a man of lesser character? That working with them for so long wouldn't have rubbed off on you?' she asked, curious. 'Do you not think *I've* changed?' she asked, and instinctively he felt wary of where this was going.

He gave her question some thought.

'Yes, I think you did change. But it had nothing to do with the level of your character,' he said, finally raising his gaze to her. 'I think that your family gave you little choice. You were forced to fight for everything. But at least you know that you deserve everything you won.'

'You don't think you deserved what you have?'

'I would have absolutely none of this were it not for Gio,' he replied resolutely.

'I don't think that Gio is responsible for either your intelligence or your character.'

He clenched his jaw. 'I think that Gio's financial support gave me the luxury to be able to *use* my intelligence and maintain my character. There were many who grew up like me who didn't have that chance.'

Maria placed a hand on his forearm. 'I did not mean to

start an argument, I just… I sometimes think that perhaps you don't give yourself enough credit for what you achieved. He may not have offered you the company first in his will, but he wouldn't have offered it at all if he didn't think you could run it.'

He reached for the pale yellow wine in the cooler to pour himself a glass, stopping just before he did so.

'Go ahead,' Maria said. 'You can have a glass. Don't feel you need not drink just because I can't.'

'Just the one,' he said, pouring a glass and taking a mouthful before responding to her statement. 'I was the stick. Antonio was the carrot. He always was.'

If Antonio had done what he'd said he'd do and divorce his inconvenient bride from England, if he'd married Maria, if Maria hadn't come to see him… If Gio had never sent him away all those years ago.

'I don't think Gio saw it that way. I certainly didn't,' Maria pressed on, unaware of the direction of his thoughts. But her statement pulled him right back to the present.

'How do you see me?' he asked, feeling suddenly more vulnerable and exposed than he'd ever felt in his life. He knew how he saw himself. He knew that he'd forced her into this marriage, knew that he'd ordered her around and neglected her the night of their wedding, but only because he couldn't stand the idea of being so close to her and not touching her. Last night had been torture to him. And for a while he thought he'd understood what she'd wanted from him. But now, when she was looking at him like she was, he wasn't sure whether it was her desire he saw, or his own wishful thinking.

Maria bit her lip. She felt it, the precipice they were standing at. She'd felt it in Paris, but that had been different. That had been fuelled by anger and hurt and a very determined,

powerful kind of energy. This was different. Now, she felt…
curious, tentative, hopeful, wanting, nervous, vulnerable,
desperate not to be left again.

'How do I see you?' she said, repeating his question. And
wanted to stop fighting the instinct to hold herself back.
Hold her thoughts back, her feelings, in case they would be
rejected and spurned, like her father always had, ignored
like her mother always had, or not enough as she'd thought
had been the case with him.

'I see you as powerful, as commanding, and proud,' she
said, thinking of how he'd handled Peterson, who had notori-
ously cowed many members of her family. 'I see you as kind,
as thoughtful,' she continued, thinking of his mother and the
women in his life, which now included her. She remembered
all the little things he'd done for her, opening her door, holding her chair, thoughtless things to him, but utterly foreign to
some men out there. 'I see you as someone who is conscious
of the impact of their actions and deeds,' she said, knowing
that there were some out there who would have turned her
away if they'd discovered her pregnancy. 'I see you as someone who is loyal.' She thought of the man who steadfastly
clung to Gio's side long after he perhaps stopped deserving
such fierce fealty. 'And I see the boy in you that I once loved.'

All of her experiences crowded into her mind and heart,
jostling to remind her to be careful, to warn her against answering a question that was surely a trap. But she was so
tired of fighting everyone else that she no longer had the
energy or the inclination to fight herself.

'Do you think you could ever love the man?' Micha asked.

Her heart pounded in her chest.

'I think I could,' she lied. And it *was* a lie. Because, deep
down, she knew that she *already* loved him. That perhaps
she had never stopped.

He didn't move a muscle, but the golden glitter in his eyes exploded like fireworks. It was as if neither of them dared to breathe. And then slowly, ever so slowly, as if giving her every chance to stop him, to move away, to run, he stood from his chair and held his hand out for her to take.

This was the precipice. This was the moment. She would come back to this moment over the years, knowing how it had shaped her life, their lives. And she would never, ever regret what she did next.

She placed her hand in his and let him gently pull her to her feet. She was standing barely inches from him, close enough to feel the heat from his body, to see the little scar in his eyebrow, the mole on his cheek.

She was so caught up in her attention to him that she flinched when his hand cupped her cheek. He went to remove it, but she covered it with hers to keep it there. She leaned into the warmth of his palm, something in his touch that she'd never found anywhere else or in anyone else.

The scent of cedar, pepper and vanilla made her near dizzy with want for him. In Paris, she'd been almost out of her mind, out of her own body in some respects. Oh, she'd known what she was doing, but it felt as if she had been driven by the furies themselves.

This was different. This was slow, considered, grounded, rooted in something far deeper and stronger than the moment. She wasn't carried away—it wasn't thoughtless—but it was no less heady, no less intoxicating. If anything it felt *more*.

'Would you kiss me?' she asked.

Maria didn't know who was more surprised, Micha or herself.

But when the ghost of a smile traced his lips, she couldn't bring herself to regret it.

His gaze flicked between her mouth and her eyes, before he gently took her lips with his. It was a sampling. A tasting. A *testing*. And not even near enough to satiate her needs. Instead, it only inflamed her wants.

'Again?' she asked.

Once more, that ghost of a smile pulled at Micha's lips, but this time when he went to claim her mouth, she met him halfway, half open, and then, *then*, it happened.

That kiss that she'd only ever shared with him. The rush of *everything* she felt when he touched her. Tongues entwined, lips locked, her hand reached to his nape, gently fisting the hair gathered there, determined to hold him to her should he try to end the kiss that fed maddening amounts of magic into her blood.

His hand reached for her hip, fisting her dress in his palm, flexing and pulling her against him, her chest pressed to his, the muscles of his toned body, the growl in his throat travelling straight to her core as he began to lose that incredible control he had over himself.

'Again,' she sighed against his lips before he could even think of pulling away.

He pulled her against him and it wasn't enough to feel him between layers of clothes any more, just like it had never been enough to see him through layers of hurt and anger. She pulled at his shirt, tugging it from the waistband of his trousers, and he laughed a little and held her hand to stop her.

'Shall we take this inside? Can I finally find a bed to lay you on?'

The plea in his voice was as irrefutable as the want and need in his gaze, in his touch.

'God, yes, please,' she replied, and he picked her up in his arms and stalked through the villa and into a suite set for the perfect honeymoon.

CHAPTER ELEVEN

MICHA HOPED THAT Maria couldn't feel how his hands were shaking. *Shaking!* He wasn't some naive uncouth boy, but she made him feel like that, in the sense that she took him back through time, to how it *could* have been. *Would* have been if Gio hadn't sent him away and she'd not failed to come looking for him. He thrust those thoughts aside, ruthlessly. The past might have come to haunt him, but he couldn't bring that into this place. Not now, not here.

He laid Maria gently on the bed, her hair fanning out and around her shoulders, the olive-green silk dress cast in light and shade as it draped against the dips and hollows of her body, her breasts, her chest, her hips, her thighs… He couldn't stop looking. As if he couldn't quite believe she was here.

There'd been so much chaos in his mind in Paris, a little bit of confusion, a lot of surprise and a sense of completely overwhelming heady desire. But this? This felt different. This felt intentional, careful, considered and he was at peace with that. He was at peace with her. And that felt…more than it probably should.

Maria bit her lip, the nervous gesture bringing him back to the present. He didn't want her to feel a second's hesitation or doubt. Or was that actually true? Did he want her to think this through and still want to be here? With him? Wearing his ring? Carrying their child?

The thought melted the barriers he'd built around his heart, brick by brick in the days, weeks and months that had followed his first move to Paris all those years ago. As he'd waited for her to come to him. Because he could see now that they were here, she *had* eventually come to him. And that would have to be enough. Because he could no longer deny his feelings for her. Feelings that had never once gone away.

He picked up her hand and pressed a kiss to her palm, before coming to lie beside her on the bed, half content just to be there with her. He allowed himself the luxury of taking in the changes that the years had made. The lean lines her face had become, the startling light honeyed brown gaze watching him watch her.

'You have always been, and always will be, the most beautiful woman I ever know.'

Her mouth parted, as if in surprise at the softness of his words, but no sound came out. He gently pushed back a corkscrew curl from her forehead, and traced the curve of her cheek, the side of her neck, the hollow of her throat and across her collarbone.

Her body came alive beneath his, as if his touch were the strings of a puppeteer and he wanted to gather her to him and just *inhale* her. As if he could consume her, possess her, until they became one. He'd never wanted anyone like this. He'd been half terrified of his feelings eleven years ago, and was still half scared of them now. But he had to move past that fear if they were going to have any hope of the relationship he sometimes caught glimpses of in the deepest parts of his soul. A knowing of what they could be. Something so good and so pure, he wasn't sure he was worthy of it.

She looked at him then, something like sympathy in her gaze.

She raised her hand and mirrored the tour his fingers had taken, as she traced a fingertip over his hairline and skin. But her hand swept to his neck and pulled him towards her, and he swore he heard her whisper again, before his lips closed over hers.

He was hers to command.

Again and again and again he kissed her.

Chaste. Worshipful. Adoring. Enlightening.

Sighs not of surrender, but of yearning and want fell between them as he indulged them both, not in fast greedy grabs, but in easy, unhurried strokes and lingering tastes. Slowly, one by one, he unbuttoned her dress, slipping the silk tie around her waist and tossing it aside, even as it put erotic thoughts into his mind for the future. This, tonight, was something special. It was how that first time *should* have been between them.

He placed his hand over the silk of the skirt and stroked it up her legs, the satiny glide of the material over her smooth skin a delight to them both. Micha placed kisses to the stomach he bared to his gaze and touch and smiled as she squirmed in delight, breathy half laughs that were innocent and expectant, and lingering over the gentle swell of the child they had created together. Their eyes met as softness sank into something more. Something serious. As if they both knew how much this moment meant to the other, how important it was.

His hand rested over her abdomen, as her hand came up to cup his jaw, and he knew in that moment that he'd found it again. The heart he'd given her all those years ago, lost to him until now.

'Let me make love to you.'

To anyone else it would sound arrogant, commanding.

But he knew she'd understand it as a request, because she was the one who held all the power in this moment.

'Please,' she replied, and he dropped his head in relief and thanks, before slipping his hands beneath her to gather her to him. He buried his head in her, inhaling her scent, giving himself to her as she wrapped her arms around him, holding him to her. And in that instant, he surrendered to her and she let him. She took everything that he offered, unquestioning and without judgement.

His lips found her chest, her breasts, her mouth, her shoulder, his hands finding her hips, her curves, palming firm muscles and lithe grace, until they were both panting and desperate.

He released her only to reach towards the nightstand, when she stayed his hand. He looked at her questioningly.

'We don't need to use protection,' she said, her voice husky, eyes sparkling.

'Are you sure?' he hesitated.

She smiled, shyly. 'Yes.'

'I've been tested. You have nothing to worry about.'

'I know you would never put me at risk,' she said with a solemn gaze, before pulling him back to her and into a kiss that reached his very soul. The trust she was giving him, letting him into her in such a way, humbled him.

Maria looked into his gaze, so serious it was as if he were almost sad. And she felt it. A kind of grief for all they had been through, all the hurts and the years apart, all the painful ways they had been thrust into adulthood, the innocence that had once been between them long since lost.

She kissed him in a way hoping to heal, in a way that promised to do better, be better, for him, for their child, for herself. A kiss that started off slow, reverent, but stoked the fires of need until flames licked at her skin where he touched her. Restless with need, her legs shifted to make room for him, as he pressed open-mouthed kisses to her collarbone, her chest, as he palmed her breast and nipped at her nipple, licking, stroking, urging those flames higher.

Damp heat pooled between her legs, pulse points throbbing incessantly, needing his touch or tongue to soothe them. Need became sighs that fell from her lips, as her body undulated against him, desperate for friction, for release, for *him*.

'I could watch you forever,' he said, his gaze on hers as he parted her thighs with one hand, his fingers delving between her legs and finding her core. Her back arched away from the bed as he tested her readiness with his fingers, his thumb pressing gently, but firmly against her clitoris.

'Move for me?' he all but begged, and she understood that he wanted her to move against his thumb. That he wanted her to please herself. Heart thumping wildly in her chest, emotion thick in her throat, her entire body flushed, nipples tightening under his voyeurism as she moved against his hand, the moan of pleasure filling the air between them; hers, his, it didn't matter.

'Micha,' she begged.

'Not yet.'

'But I want you with me,' she all but pleaded.

'But I want this more,' he replied, forcing her to a pleasure that was near indecent.

Her gasps filled the room, the rose petals crushed beneath her, and his other hand came to rest across her abdomen, comforting, protective. Red slashes appeared on his cheeks as she drew closer and closer to an orgasm she half feared.

'Micha.'

Her hands reached for his, needing that connection, that

anchor, as if without it she might just fly away and lose herself completely. The orgasm built with a kind of slow intensity she'd never experienced, with a tide that started at her feet, creeping higher and higher up her body until she crested a wave so big she thought she might drown beneath the pleasure he brought her.

Her entire self was lost, boneless, weightless, thoughtless, lost not to nothingness but to him. Micha. Who held her and soothed her as she came back to herself in shivers and lightning strikes that threatened to change the very fabric of her being.

She opened her eyes to find his gaze on hers, wonder in his eyes…the same wonder that she felt. *Micha.* It was the gaze of a boy she'd not seen for eleven years and ridiculously she felt tears well in her eyes, and blinked, hoping to stop the flow before it started.

'*Mi amore,*' he said, but she wasn't ready. Wasn't ready to hear the rest of what he had to say. She felt so raw and vulnerable, she knew instinctively that he could break her, not with savage words or rejection, but with his love.

She took his hand and pressed a kiss to his palm. Used that same hand to draw him to her, and kissed away the hurt and the fear that she felt, willingly losing herself to him and his body. And if he knew what she was doing, he had the kindness not to stop her.

She moaned when she felt the steel-like press of his erection against her thigh. Ravenous and wanton, that's what he'd turned her into. She reached for him, palming the velvet length of him, her thumb tracing the small liquid bead at the head of his penis, and bit her lip in delicious expectation. He batted away her hand, and she growled in playful frustration. And when his lips found hers, she could trace the half smile on his mouth.

'Micha,' she whispered into his ear, letting her sighs tell him how much she wanted him. How much she wanted this.

He notched himself at her core, kissing her deeply. She felt the racing of his heart against hers, where their chests pressed against each other and it was as he whispered '*mi amore*' into her ear that he pushed into her slowly, surrounding her in such exquisite pleasure she wasn't sure where he ended and she began. Time lost all meaning as slow thrusts turned quick, powerful and deliciously hard. He filled her completely and left her almost never, as they spent hours and seconds and minutes discovering what it should have always been like between them. By the time another orgasm came for her, Micha was with her and when she fell, she was wrapped in his arms and they fell together.

Micha watched Maria sleep. She was completely still. No movement at all. Her head was on his outstretched arm and he didn't care that he was getting pins and needles. He wouldn't move her for the world. She was so peaceful like this. None of the energy that forced her so determinedly through the day. It was fascinating.

'Why are you staring at me?' she whispered, with her eyes still closed, and he jerked back a tiny bit in shock.

With a smile on her face she turned in to him, nuzzling closer, and his heart nearly careened right out of his chest.

'Don't stop,' she whispered, making herself comfortable. 'I like it.' And with that she went straight back to sleep and he held her like that all the way until the morning.

Over the next couple of days, Micha wondered whether he was living in a dream. Every morning, they would have breakfast out on the beautiful sun-drenched patio. The sounds of birds and the sight of the sea were an accompaniment to freshly squeezed orange juice, mint tea, his espresso—of course—*halwa dyal kouk*, a type of coconut cake that Maria couldn't get enough of, bread, olive oil, honey and other pastries filled with the flavours of orange and almond. The heat from the sunrise—Maria was an unconscionably early riser—was delicious. It crept slowly and seduced, relaxing muscles and sinking into weary bones. He tried to remember the last time he'd had a break like this. A holiday.

Never.

He'd been working so long and so hard, trying to outrun the poverty he'd grown up with and the insecurity he'd lived with daily.

After breakfast, Maria would speak to one of the house staff and they would be whisked away on a magical mystery tour. On the first day, they'd visited Medersa Ben Yousef, the fourteenth-century religious school that was full of the *zellij* tiling that he was beginning to really like, ancient cedar wood ceilings and breathtaking stucco work. On the second day they visited Souk Semmarine, where Maria deftly handled negotiations with several store owners to acquire intricately detailed carpets and cut-brass lanterns. The leather work was impeccable and she bought a wallet for Antonio, and Enzo—her newly acquainted cousin— and bracelets for Ivy and Erin, their wives. And when she smiled at him and asked if there was something he wanted to buy, he just shook his head and smiled. Because there, in the middle of a market in Marrakesh, with the scents wafting over him from the *ahba kedima*, the spice market, and the smell of coals, and hot leather from the *haddadine*, the blacksmith's alley, it hit Micha hard.

He had everything he needed. Everything he'd *ever* wanted.

And if there was a thought in the back of his head, an

alarm bell, that warned him it was too good to be true, then he ignored it.

On the third day, Maria took him to the Yves Saint Laurent Museum and the Jardin Majorelle, where he lived, where even Micha was awed by the incredible collection of art within such a beautiful setting. The design of the building was heavily formed by contrasting straight and curved lines, and radically different to where Saint Laurent had lived, where powerful colours sat perfectly with Moroccan architecture, and it made Micha realise that he'd not really thought of his home in such a way. But seeing Maria draw in all the colour, the inspiration, the architecture, seeing her come alive, he realised he wanted her to feel the same way about where they would live. He wanted to create that for her.

And at night? Well, never in his wildest dreams had he imagined anything so incredible. They spent hours rediscovering themselves and each other. He placed kisses on her belly, where their child was growing each day, and each night he slept with his hand possessively and comfortingly placed over them.

Maria beckoned him over from where she was bent at the waist, looking at a tray of jewellery that could cost less than their breakfast. He'd realised that for Maria, it wasn't the cost that mattered, but how beautiful she found it. She'd just as easily wear a dress from the market as one of YSL's haute couture pieces. As long as something about it caught her eye.

'What do you think of this?'

'I think you like it and that's all I need to know,' he replied, but cast a gaze over the handmade silver necklace. Rows and rows of tiny little beads, that rich blue of lapis lazuli. It *was* beautiful.

'Wise man,' the store owner said with a smile.

Micha inclined his head in recognition of the high praise. Maria slapped him playfully on the arm.

'Do you *like* it?' she pressed.

'Am I the one who will be wearing it?' he toyed.

'Yes. That and nothing else. In bed. All night long,' she replied, deadpan, and the store owner coughed in shock and Micha threw his head back and laughed.

By the time he stopped, he realised that she was looking at him in a strange way, and after buying the necklace he most definitely would *not* be wearing, they found a shaded table at an out-of-the-way cafe for Maria to rest the ankles that were, as predicted, getting a little swollen.

After ordering their drinks, a mint tea for her and an espresso for him, he asked her about it.

'It's just…been a while since I heard you laugh like that. Even when we were younger, you were always so serious.'

'And you were always trying to make me laugh,' he replied, the smile on his lips evident in his tone.

And then you weren't there to make me laugh.

'It's nice. I like it.'

'What?'

'Your laugh. It's nice. You should laugh more.'

'I will do whatever brings you joy,' he said, the words out of his mouth before he realised how vulnerable that could make him. But when he saw the look in her eyes, he couldn't bring himself to regret them. She looked as if he'd given her a gift far more precious than any stone, diamond or jewel in the whole of Marrakesh.

Is this what we could have? Is this what it could be like?

The question was in her gaze, so strong, so powerful, so in tune with what he was thinking that he wondered if it were even possible.

And, of course, *that* was when the universe decided to answer.

* * *

Maria's phone vibrated in her purse, the sound on silent. She wanted to ignore it. Unwilling to break the moment between them. It was so precious, these glimpses of what things could be like between them. Almost like when they had been younger, but better somehow. More mature.

But the phone didn't stop ringing, so she checked the screen and her heart thudded painfully in her chest.

Papa.

He never called. Which was why she knew, instinctively, whatever he was calling about couldn't be good.

She smiled up at Micha.

'Excuse me for a moment?'

'Of course,' he said, as she stood up and made her way towards the bathroom she knew Micha had believed had been her intended destination.

Out of sight from the table, she pulled the phone from her bag and answered.

'What do you want?' she asked without preamble.

'You need to come back,' her father commanded.

'Why?' she asked, instead of saying *No. It's my honeymoon, I don't want—*

'We're calling a no-confidence vote against Rufina.'

'What?' she asked, her world seesawing, as her mind scrabbled to keep up. 'We' being the family, the *board*. Any one of whom could call such a vote.

They were trying to oust Micha.

'Tomorrow. Be there. And if you vote with *us*, when he's gone we'll vote you in.'

The buzzing in her ears wasn't enough to drown out what her father was saying.

'He's my husband, Papa.'

'He's a trumped-up street thug who got my daughter pregnant and will ruin this company.'

'But we got Peterson on board,' she tried to explain.

'The paperwork hasn't been filed yet. That's why the vote is tomorrow.'

'Papa, this isn't right.'

'It doesn't have to be right. The company should be run by a Gallo. That Rufina is at the helm is unacceptable.'

'But I am?' she asked. 'Acceptable?'

'You're better than *him*,' her father spat. 'So, get back here for then, and cast your vote with us and we'll put you in as CEO.'

Maria clenched her jaw.

'It's everything you ever wanted,' her father dangled. 'Gallo Group will be yours.'

Maria stared unseeing at the cafe wall for long after the call ended.

What should she do? She had to tell him about the vote, but…

We'll put you in as CEO.

She started when Micha placed his hand on her arm.

'Is everything okay?' he asked, concern clear in his gaze.

'No, I don't think it is.'

Micha remained tight-lipped on the car journey back to the villa as she told him that a vote of no confidence was being called tomorrow.

He said nothing to her. Absolutely nothing. But he called his assistant to make arrangements for the jet to meet them at the airport and take them back to Rome immediately. She looked across the car to where Micha sat, grim faced and lock jawed staring out of the window. If she told him about her father's offer, it would only make things worse.

The car drew up to the villa and he got out, and although

he came round to her side of the car, and held the door open for her, his gaze roamed everywhere but on her.

She wanted to know what he was thinking. What he was feeling. And for the first time in her life, she *hated* Gallo Group. Hated what it did to her family. Hated how it made everyone and everything around her so desperate and selfish.

How it made *her* feel desperate and selfish.

Because she couldn't deny that a part of her saw how much she wanted it. For years it was all she'd wanted. The company. To show what she could do. To prove herself, to her family. To her father. To Gio. To *herself.*

But at what cost?

She followed Micha into the villa, and through to the living room, disconcerted when Micha turned to stare at her intently.

'What?' she asked.

'Did your father say anything else? When he told you about the no-confidence vote?'

Maria paused, her heart throbbing painfully in her chest.

'No,' she lied.

And then she saw it. The knowledge. The betrayal. And she wished to god that she could call her words back.

He shook his head, and turned away from her in disgust.

'Micha—'

'Do you really believe I'm so stupid as to not realise what he's offered you in exchange for your vote against me? There is no one in the company even remotely suitable for the president and CEO seat other than you. He's offered you the role.'

'And you think I'll take it? You think I'd choose *that* over *you*?' she demanded outraged.

'Of course I do! You did then.'

'What are you talking about?' Maria asked, confusion blooming in her heart and head.

'Eleven years ago, the day Gio told me he was sending me to Paris. When I came to see you. We were on the lawn, remember?'

No, she didn't remember. All she remembered was the shock and hurt of confusion. The agony that had threatened to swallow her whole after he'd left without a word. She—

I have to ask you something.

The smell of grass and the feel of the sun on her skin.

What would you do to become head of this company? If Gio offered it to you?

Anything. You know that.

Her stomach dropped, plummeting to the ground.

She stared up at him in confusion.

'You asked me that, without telling me what was going on?' she demanded, feeling a rush of anger. 'You asked me…without giving me the context,' she said slowly, realising what he'd done. 'You set me up to fail. Because there was no way I could answer that question properly without understanding why you were asking it! You didn't trust me. You didn't trust my feelings for you,' she threw at him, her heart breaking.

It hadn't been her. All this time, it wasn't something she'd done. It had been him. He'd always have left. Because he didn't trust her. He didn't think he was worthy of her.

'You've wanted this company almost since before you could walk. All you did was tell me the truth. You should take their offer,' Micha said, breaking her heart. 'It's what you've always wanted.'

'You,' she confessed, her throat raw around the word. 'You were what I always wanted. From the very beginning.

You are the only man I have ever wanted and…you are the only man I've ever been with.'

Standing so close, she could see the impact her words had on him. The realisation that she had been a virgin in Paris. His cheeks flushed and his eyes widened. He opened his mouth as if to speak, but she didn't want to hear it. *Couldn't.*

'But if you'd told me back then,' she pressed on, 'if you'd *trusted* me, trusted my feelings for you, if you'd explained what you were really asking me, then I would have answered differently. But you didn't. You didn't trust me then and you still don't trust me now. *That's* why you left me. It wasn't because I chose them, that's just an excuse,' she said, re-peating Antonio's accusation from the night before the wed-ding. 'One you've hidden behind for years.'

At her words, he shut down. As if all feeling had been shoved behind an impenetrable door.

'That's the way you see it? That I abandoned you?' he asked, his tone horribly level compared to the agony in hers.

'Yes!'

'And what did you do?'

'Nothing!' she cried, unable to call back the hurt that was spilling out of her. Why was he being so cruel? So harsh? So unfeeling!

'Exactly.'

Wait, what?

She stared at him in confusion.

'Maria, you have fought for absolutely everything in your life. You fought schoolyard bullies, you stood up to your grandfather before your uncles could even think to do such a thing. You worked harder and more determinedly at work, pushing back every single time they tried to discriminate and intimidate you.'

'Yes, I did,' she said with pride, as the distance between them grew smaller and smaller.

He was almost within touching distance now, her heart pounding in her chest, blood rushing in her ears. This argument had been brewing between them for *years* and it was finally here. *He* was finally here. His gaze was stormy, his breath seeming to punch the air between them. He was angry, she realised. Angrier than she'd ever seen him. This was nothing like the back-and-forth they'd had in Paris, where no matter how cutting or cruel, his impartiality had held him in check. But that was gone now. Here was the wild energy he'd had about him when he'd been younger. The passion that had drawn her, the drive.

He raised his hand to gently sweep aside a curling tendril from her face and tuck it behind her ear, the careful gesture seeming painfully at odds with the tension in the room.

'You fight everything Maria. So why didn't you fight for us?'

His words were a whisper, with the power of an atomic bomb.

The shock wave cut straight through her, through the years, through the hurts, through the feelings and agonies she'd experienced to the heart of something they'd never dared confront. The devastation of it was made somehow worse by the fact his words weren't a shout, weren't a ferocious demand, as if he had long ago surrendered to the belief that he wasn't worthy of such a thing. As if he'd already given up before she'd begun to see.

To see the part that she played in the past.

He searched her face as if finally, after eleven years, he saw what he needed to. The dawning realisation of what she had done.

Or not done.

'Why didn't you fight for me, Maria?' he asked.

Her soul shivered beneath his question. The truth emerging from the deepest, most sacred part of her childhood hurts. He deserved the truth as much as she deserved to say it.

'Because if I failed, if you still walked away, there would have been nothing left of me,' she confessed, her heart shattering into a thousand pieces.

He stared at her, as if understanding her pain, but that it didn't change a thing.

'So, who didn't trust who, Maria?'

Tears welled in her eyes, threatening to fall. Too much hurt and too much pain shimmered between them. He hadn't trusted her to love her, and she hadn't fought to prove that she did, because she'd been scared too. Hurt by his rejection of her, she'd built a steel wall around her so that nothing and no one could hurt her like that again. But if she'd tried…if she had reached out to him…

'I—'

'The car will take you to the airport,' he said interrupting her, ending the conversation.

'And what about you?'

'I need some time to think. I'll see you at the meeting.'

And with that, he stalked out of the room, but to Maria it felt as if he was stalking out of her life. Again.

CHAPTER TWELVE

KARL, HER DRIVER whenever she was in Rome, eyed her warily in the car's rear-view mirror.

'Shouldn't you be going in there, Ms G—I mean, Mrs—'

'Not yet,' Maria said, staring at the entrance to the Gallo Group Headquarters in Rome, through the blacked-out window of the town car.

She was watching them all arrive. Several generations of Gallo men, all dressed in impeccably tailored dark suits, with crisp white shirts and pinned ties. The family resemblance imprinted on similarly dark features.

Her phone vibrated with a message from Antonio.

I'm two minutes out.

She'd called him from the plane late last night, pouring her heart out to him in a way that she'd not been able to with Micha. Oh, she'd wanted to, but she hadn't trusted herself that night. She'd been too hurt. Too confused. Too…ashamed.

Antonio had threatened to get in the car and drive to her right then and there, but Maria wasn't even going to get into Italy for another four hours, so there'd have been no point. She'd wanted to know, needed to know, whether what Micha had said was right.

Antonio's voice had been regretful.

'I'd always known that it would have been hard for Micha to say no to Gio. And if Gio knew about you and Micha, of course he would have sent him away. And I…'

'What?'

'Well, I was so angry at how he'd hurt you, I refused to reach out to him.' The shame in her cousin's voice matched the one she felt in her heart.

'You think he's right then?' she asked, not because she needed him to tell her. She knew that Micha was right. 'That I…didn't fight for him?'

'I think we were all young. And,' he said hesitantly, 'I think you were hurt and trying to protect yourself. But I also don't think that he's entirely wrong, Maria. I'm not sure that, even with all the information available, you'd have been *able* to choose Micha. Yes, you were a fighter, even back then, but Maria…you were seventeen. Your father would have disowned you, Gio would have had to fire Micha, he would have lost every bit of financial security he had. It would have been…'

'Impossible,' Maria finished when Antonio trailed off.

Maria had looked out of the plane window, just as she was doing now from the car. It hurt to even think that she would have chosen the company back then. It seemed inconceivable, but realistically, could she have?

'Do you think Gio knew that? Do you think that's why Gio sent him away?' she had asked Antonio.

'If you're asking me whether Gio was somehow doing all this out of the kindness of his own heart? I can't tell you that. He was a very manipulative, business-focused, difficult man. But speak to Enzo about it one day, he might have a different story to tell.'

She watched the last members of the board enter the building and held her breath. She realised that she was waiting for Micha. But she hadn't seen him since she arrived, and didn't know if he had got here before her.

Her door opened and her cousin smiled down at her with a familiar grin.

'So. Are you ready to fight the family, Maria?' Antonio asked.

'I am ready to fight *for* my family,' she replied, taking his hand and stepping out of the car.

She should have felt a little bad about turning up at her favourite designer's studio last night at 11:00 p.m. Instead of going home from the airport, she'd called from the plane and explained what she wanted. Her friend had not disappointed.

She had on a black suit, with a few small adjustments. Instead of trying to diminish the way that her baby had increased in size, the tailored pantsuit fit her perfectly to show off her pregnancy. The waist rose a little higher than normal in order, almost, to proclaim it to the world. The white tucked-in shirt and loose tie made her look effortlessly cool and chic. And her black Louboutins made her feel powerful.

She was done hiding.

She and Antonio entered the lift that would take them to the boardroom, and he respected her need for silence as she gathered herself, preparing to give the speech that she'd spent all night on. She hadn't had much sleep, but she didn't need it. She was running on adrenaline and need. The need to do what she should have done eleven years ago.

When they arrived, they were ushered into the boardroom where around a table that sat twenty-four, only two chairs remained empty. Micha sat at the head of the table, his face utterly impassive, hiding his every thought from her.

While the gazes of her family ping-ponged between them, Antonio gestured her towards the seat at the direct opposite end of the table to her husband.

Antonio slipped into the seat beside her and she forced herself to take in, one by one, the faces of the men around the table. She felt Micha's gaze on her, but she needed to do this first.

Her uncles, her cousins, their sons. Three generations of Gallos and she was the only woman.

She saw expectation on their faces. A little resentment. But a huge amount of satisfaction. As if they'd all been waiting for this from the very moment of her grandfather's last breath. They were vultures and she hated every single one of them.

Her gaze rested on her father, who sat to her right. The man for whom neither she nor her mother had ever been good enough to capture his interest or attention, until now.

We'll put you in as CEO.

And he'd thought that would make her fall in line.

He hadn't ever really seen her, had he? He'd never realised what she had become in spite of him. Powerful, strong, dynamic and damn good at her job. She was so much more than just his daughter. She was a businesswoman. A wife. And a mother.

And it was time to protect her family.

'We are here to cast a vote of confidence for or against the current CEO of Gallo Group,' her father said to absolutely no one's surprise. 'I don't see a reason to delay. I shall start the vote. No confidence,' he said.

And one by one, up the length of the table, votes were cast.

No confidence, no confidence, no confidence.

And through every single vote, Maria held the gaze that Micha had locked on her. His expression, almost one of boredom and unchanging, until Antonio's vote.

Full confidence.

Micha didn't lift his eyes from hers, but he did blink. He hadn't expected that, Maria realised with a spike of sadness for the friendship they'd once had. For the Three Muske-teers that they'd once been.

But then it was her turn and every single set of eyes in the room looked to her in rabid expectation.

From a very young age, Micha had become adept at hiding his feelings and he doubted that anyone around the table would see anything more than a kind of lazy boredom. But beneath that outward display, was seething, gut-wrenching tension.

From the moment she'd left for the airport, he'd been reel-ing. For years he'd clung to the belief that she'd have done anything for Gallo Group. That she'd always have chosen it over him. But he realised in the silence left by her absence, that she'd been right. He *hadn't* given her a choice. Not re-ally. He'd not had the confidence to trust that she'd pick him, and selectively he had chosen to frame that choice in a way that had set her up to fail. Because then and even now, he'd not really ever felt that she'd pick him. And no, she hadn't fought for him, but he hadn't fought for her either. He'd sur-rendered to his fears and she'd deserved better than that.

Now, his eyes locked on the woman he'd given his heart away to more than eleven years ago and wished he could go back in time to fix it.

'Maria?' her father said. 'As CFO, how do you vote?'

'With my family,' she replied, and his heart flatlined.

From the corner of his eye, Micha saw the sickening smirk on her father's face. He opened his mouth to say something, but Maria cut him off.

'With Micha Rufina. My husband, the father of my child and the best CEO Gallo Group could have after Gio. With Micha Rufina,' she repeated before adding, 'the man I love.'

Gasps of shock and cries of frustration echoed out across the table at the same time as his heart soared back to life. He felt the pump of blood round his entire body and he would have sworn on a Bible that he'd heard his blood whoosh in his veins.

She loved him.

Beneath the table he fisted his hands to stop himself from sweeping everything aside and rushing over to her to take in his arms.

She could have had it. She could have had the whole of Gallo Group. She'd have been CEO. And she'd chosen him. As his brain tried to catch up to the instinctive reaction of his heart, Maria turned to look at the members of the board.

'None of you, not a single one, has brought in the revenue that Micha has over the last eleven years. He turned Paris around from a middle-of-the-road satellite post to the second-highest revenue earner to Rome. I don't know what poison my father has been dripping into your ears, but surely, *surely*, none of you would do anything as monumentally stupid as to remove the man who has consistently built and improved processes and revenue in ways that only financially benefit you?

'I mean, what would lack *more* confidence than making a decision that negatively impacted the price of your shares and your income?' she said, turning on her father. 'It almost reeks of sabotage, to make such a risky move when Gallo Group is still on such shaky ground following Gio's death. I mean…of course, if that *were* the case,' she said, her tone heavy on implication, just as Micha realised where she was going with this, 'then when all your shares dropped so shockingly low, there would really only be one person in this room with enough money to buy them off you before you lost any more money. And how very kind that person would be. To buy all of your shares from you,' she said, her tone turning whip sharp, 'at a knock-down price, in order to have complete ownership of Gallo Group.'

One by one, he watched the confused faces of Gallo Group's board realise what Maria was implying: that her father was purposefully sabotaging GG in order to engineer a buyout leaving him as the sole owner. And whether or not it was the truth, whether that had been his intention all along—which Micha believed probably was the case— Maria had just successfully managed to turn every single selfish one of them against him.

The shock and fury on the faces of the board rivalled only what he'd seen when they had been told that *he* would be the one stepping into the CEO position and he almost felt sorry for them. Almost.

And then he couldn't help himself. He laughed. Because in that moment, Maria really had shown herself to be worthy of running Gallo Group.

He stared at his wife. The pride, the joy, the genuine love he felt for her poured into his gaze and when she caught it, he thought that she'd understood. The flare of her eyes, the flush on her cheeks, the little hitch in her chest as her breath caught. He was almost sure that she'd felt his very thoughts.

'So,' Maria said, turning back to the faces around the table. 'Would you like to try this again? All in favour?'

One after the other, they raised their hands to cast their votes again, her father looking absolutely thunderous, his face an angry blotchy red.

Micha didn't spare a single person a second glance, even as they all voted in favour of him this time, with the sole exclusion of Maria's father, who desperately stuck to his guns. Micha didn't care. He didn't once take his eyes off Maria, not even as the rest of the board members filed out of the room, under harsh whispers and grumbles, utterly deflated and more than a little angry.

Throughout it all, he took in how glorious she was, truly

in her element, finally taking her position, whether in title or not, as head of the Gallo family. He wondered whether this was what Gio had been hoping for, or whether the old man would be turning in his grave. Micha liked to think that, somehow, he'd always known that this was the way it would be.

That if they could get over the deep hurts holding them back when they'd been younger, that *this* was how incredible it could be between him and Maria. That only through the trials and tribulations they'd been through in their time apart had they become strong enough to reach for what they wanted. Each other.

She dropped his gaze, only to speak in hushed tones to Antonio, who glanced in Micha's direction, eyes narrowed in assessment, before turning back to Maria, nodding and leaving the room. Maria closed the door behind him.

She turned to lean back against the door.

And for a moment they remained like that, staring at each other across the boardroom.

'Did you know?' she asked him.

He didn't bother pretending not to understand her. 'I had my suspicions that this was what your father was after. When did you realise that's what he was doing?'

She bit her lip. 'Last night. After speaking to Antonio. Enzo had given him a heads-up that my father had approached him for his vote. Enzo's position on the board might be new, but despite all accounts of him being some scandalous playboy, he is, in fact, a very shrewd businessman and was quick to realise what was going on.'

'He wasn't here today?'

'He couldn't come on such short notice, but he'd given permission for Antonio to vote for him in favour of you.'

It felt a little unusual to have the support of a stranger,

but although no one had known Enzo Rossetti that long, Maria's cousin seemed to have become a close friend to Antonio and Maria.

Maria closed the distance between them with a step.

'I didn't know,' he said, needing her to understand. 'I didn't know, in Paris, that you'd never been with anyone.'

'I wouldn't change a single thing about it,' Maria replied, truthfully, defiantly, her hand protecting her stomach.

'Maria, you deserved—'

'I wouldn't change a single thing,' she said again. 'It was perfect, it was us. It was the beginning of us,' she said, reaching for his hand as if unable to hold herself back from touching him.

'You are incredible,' Micha said, unashamed to offer his praise of her. No matter what happened between them now, not after their last exchange back in Morocco, he wanted her to know that. 'And I will happily step down as president and CEO,' he said honestly and truly. Nothing was worth more to him than her. Nothing. Not a job, not a company and certainly not his ego. He wanted her, in whatever way he could get her. Nothing else mattered.

The man I love.

She looked at him, and for a moment, he was reminded of how this all started, back in Paris, in a different head-quarters.

'I don't want it,' she replied easily.

'What? I—'

'No,' she said, interrupting him. 'I don't want it. I thought I did. I thought it would finally give me the acceptance I've been craving for an entire lifetime. That it would give me security and recognition. I thought that perhaps if I was CEO, finally, I'd be worthy of my father's attention. But I realised that being CEO wouldn't give me any of that. And

I don't want to be the kind of person that would do what he wanted me to do to get there.

'The only person that accepted me for who I was, was you,' she said, closing the distance between them. 'The only person that ever made me feel loved was you,' she said, tears adding a sheen to her eyes that stole his breath, and yanked on his heart. 'The only person I ever loved was you.'

Her words were like a puzzle piece, finally slotting into place after eleven years, like a thick heavy chain that had encased his heart, falling away and letting him breathe, letting his heart beat, true and strong for the first time in *forever*.

'You, Micha Rufina. I love you. You are all I ever wanted, and all I will ever need,' she said, looking up at him with the kind of love he thought he'd never see again in his lifetime.

'I love you,' she whispered again as she rose onto her tiptoes to press her lips gently, chastely, perfectly against his.

Maria wanted to give him this. She wanted him to know, whether he loved her or not, no matter what happened between them, she needed him to know that she loved him. That she'd fought for him and that she would always fight for him. Not because he was her husband, or because he was the father of her child, but because he deserved it.

She lowered back down onto her feet, staring up at him with all the hope in her chest and the love in her heart. She didn't need anything from him, but she needed him to understand that.

'You humble me, Maria,' he said, the emotion in the depths of his gaze filling her up, nearly consuming her whole. 'I am in awe of you. I am truly sorry that your family didn't see in you what I did. The amazing, incredible, talented, powerful, dynamic, quick-witted and strong-hearted woman you have become. I am lucky just to get to love you,' he whispered, as if shocked by the truth of his own words.

His hand came to cup her cheek and she couldn't help but lean into his palm. The safety he had always offered her, the protection.

'You are my family, Micha. And our child. That is all I'll ever need,' she vowed, the words more binding than their marriage certificate.

'I think Antonio might have something to say about that,' Micha teased and she smiled, and pressed a kiss against the palm of his hand, before turning back to look up at him.

'I love you,' he said, this time with no trace of tease or humour. His love was serious, grounded, a decade in the making, just as hers was. It was serious in a way that only those who had known what it was to be unloved could feel. Serious in the tears that rose to press against the backs of her eyes as something in her shifted, healed and became new and fresh and precious.

He kissed her then, the first of many that had no questions, only answers, only security, only love.

'What do we do now?' she asked, against his lips.

'Well, right now, I'm taking my wife back to my apartment and making love to her all night long.'

'Lucky wife,' she replied with a smile.

'Lucky husband,' he said, smiling down at her, the flames of his desire flickering in his gaze.

'And then?' Maria asked.

'Well, then we get to spend the rest of our lives together, happily…'

'Ever…' she added.

'After,' he concluded with a kiss that they both remembered for many years to come.

EPILOGUE

THE SUN SHONE down on the garden and glinted off the clear flat surface of Lake Trasimeno beyond. Micha's sunglasses would have shaded his gaze, but his eyes were closed, and he was content to listen to the sounds around him. The breeze playing in the leaves of the trees and the birds calling to each other, nothing but the sounds of summer and serene—

'Elletra Valentina Rufina Gallo, I swear to god, if you don't come back here and clean up your mess, I will ground you for the rest of the summer.'

His wife's angry voice travelled out of the villa and down to where he was in the garden.

'Mama! That is *not* fair,' replied their daughter, just as angry. It probably shouldn't have come as a surprise that she had become as much of a fighter as her mother. And while neither parent would have it any other way, it had made—and would continue to make—things both interesting and *loud*.

'Papa,' Emilio whispered.

'*Sì?*' Micha whispered back.

'Should I go and help?' Emilio asked. Their fourteen-year-old son was the softest of all of them, so earnest and so quiet, it sometimes made Micha ache just to watch how careful he was with other people.

'No, that's not necessary. It's Elletra's mess and she needs to clean it up,' Micha replied, not unkindly, but firmly.

'But I don't want her to be grounded all summer. And the others will be here soon,' he said, his voice concerned.

'Is she really going to be grounded?' Elisabetta, their youngest at twelve, piped up from behind Micha where she was making daisy chains.

Micha turned to take in the light halo of rich curls on her head.

'Not if she cleans her room,' he said, reaching to sweep her up into his arms and tickle her sides, sending her into a riot of giggles as Emilio looked on, wanting to join in, but struggling with being the young man he was feeling his way into. Micha pulled him into the fray and the three of them were a jumble of limbs and laughs and kisses.

'You started without me,' Maria complained as she collapsed onto the ground to join them, Elisabetta climbing from Micha onto her mother, her long limbs angular and pointy as Micha took an elbow to the gut that made both Maria and Emilio laugh.

'Where's Elletra?' Elisabetta asked.

'Tidying her room,' Maria growled gently.

Emilio rolled away and Micha propped himself up on one arm, taking in his beautiful wife. Not one day had gone by where he hadn't realised how lucky he was. They'd spent too much time apart, he'd missed out on too much and he'd vowed that he would never miss another moment as long as they lived. He loved her with the kind of adoration that he thought might have lessened with time, but instead it had only grown.

'Don't look at me like that in front of the kids,' Maria whispered as she planted a frustratingly chaste kiss against his lips.

'Why not?' he asked. 'I want another.'

Maria's eyes widened with shock, her gasp a punch of air against his mouth.

'What?' Maria said, becoming very still.

'Yes, Antonio and Ivy have four, Erin and Enzo also have four. We need another.'

'It's not a competition, Micha,' she said, slapping him on the arm.

'I know that. I just… I want four,' he said with a careless shrug.

'Our first just put three more grey hairs on my head. Are you sure you want another? Now?' Maria demanded.

'You're so sexy when you're pregnant, *mi amore*,' he whispered, reaching his hand out to stroke across her stomach.

'Sweet talk will get you nowhere, Micha,' she warned.

The sound of a car on the gravel drive at the front of the house made the kids scatter, running full pelt to greet their cousins. Whether it was Enzo's brood or Antonio's, it didn't matter. The cousins ranging in age from six to sixteen had nicknamed themselves the Musketeers.

'Okay. How about *dirty* talk?' he asked, cutting off the squeal of her laughing shock with a kiss that told her he was deadly serious.

Micha pulled Maria over him and stared up at his incredible wife. Her capacity to laugh and to love had always inspired him, and he loved her with a fierceness that surprised him even now. He swept back the curtain of curls that had fallen across her face.

'You *are* serious,' she realised with a half smile that distracted him for a moment.

'Absolutely.'

Maria let out an exasperated sigh that kind of surprised him. Of course, this would absolutely be her decision and he would never want her to do something she didn't want to do. But the thing about the love he felt for her and their children, it was exponential. It never ran out. It just kept increasing and it never filled him completely or stopped because there was just more and more space until it filled everything around them. He'd not quite ever imagined it that way, but it was how it worked for him, for her, for their family. The one they had created despite the difficult personalities in the Gallo clan.

After his marriage to Maria and the challenge her father had tried to mount with Gallo Group, he and Antonio had sat down together, without their wives, and talked properly for the first time since he'd been sent to Paris.

He'd realised in the course of that conversation that he hadn't just lost Maria, but he'd also lost Antonio, who had been acting in defence of Maria. Misunderstandings and miscommunications, furthered by Gio's agenda to see the two cousins together, had kept them apart and it had taken a while to get back into the firm friendship they'd once had as youngsters. And Enzo and Erin had soon become part of their group.

'Of course if you don't want to—'

His words stopped when she slapped him a little harder than necessary on the arm.

'What was that for?' he asked, rubbing his arm.

'You are so *impatient*,' she complained.

What? She wasn't making sense.

'You just had to wait a few hours,' she insisted cryptically.

'For what?' he asked confused.

'And then it would have been a surprise.'

'What would have been a surprise, Maria? Honestly, you—'

This time he cut his own words off as he realised that she

was grinning and that her eyes were dancing, glittering in the sun light just like the lake behind them.

Goosebumps broke out across his skin as he realised what she was saying.

'You're pregnant,' he said, lurching upwards and taking her with him so that she sat in his lap. 'We're pregnant!' he yelled.

'You're pregnant?' was echoed by several voices at the same time, as children and adults came to join them on the grass.

Everyone was there, the two other families having arrived one after the other.

Ivy and Erin, arm in arm, looked as if they were going to burst with excitement. Enzo and Antonio, each holding more children than probably safe, looked utterly delighted, but Micha had eyes only for his wife.

'You're pregnant,' he whispered, framing her face with his hands, knowing that she was the most precious thing in the world to him in that moment.

'I am.'

'I love you,' he said. 'I always have and I always will. Only you. For the rest of my life.'

'You are my home, Micha Rufina. My home, my heart, my hope and my soulmate. I will choose you every day, over and over and over again. You will *always* be my choice.'

And Micha knew it as a truth that kept them together through the hard times, the stressful times, the worrying times, but also the best of times. He was her choice, and she was his heart for the rest of their very happy lives.

* * * * *

If you were captivated by
Their Boardroom Baby,
then be sure to check out the previous instalments
in the Filthy Rich Italians trilogy,
Inconveniently Wed *and* The Rossetti Ring Requirement.
And why not enjoy these other stories by Pippa Roscoe!

His Jet-Set Nights with the Innocent
In Bed with Her Billionaire Bodyguard
Twin Consequences of That Night
Greek's Temporary "I Do"
Forbidden Until Midnight

Available now!

HEIR OF
SCANDAL

MILLIE ADAMS

MILLS & BOON

CHAPTER ONE

HATRED WAS SUCH a fascinating sensation. It had a taste: metallic and acrid. A feeling: a heavy weight that sat at the center of her chest and made her heart beat differently. It had a scent: whiskey, spiced cologne and old leather.

At least, for Heather Gray it did.

Because hatred smelled exactly like her stepbrother, Romeo Accardi. God, she wanted nothing more than to wrap her hands around his throat and squeeze until…

If he were dead she'd never feel this way again. The idea nearly took her own breath away.

It was maybe poor taste for her to ponder his death while his father lay dying in the room upstairs. But he hadn't been sympathetic to her when her mother had passed last year and now Giuseppe was close to following his beloved wife to the afterlife and she could still hardly get a whiff of emotion from him.

Just that same spiced cologne, which for her would always create a red haze of rage.

It had always been this way.

From the moment she and her mother had darkened the door of the Accardi mansion, when her mother had been nothing but a housekeeper and Heather had been a twelve-year-old girl, awkward and uncertain, thrust into a world she didn't understand.

Because right away Giuseppe had gone out of his way to give more help than they'd ever gotten before.

Where do you plan to have the child get her education?

At the public school down the road.

Nonsense, she shall go to the same school my son attends. Fairfield is sure to give her the sort of future she deserves.

I could never afford it...

It is part of your compensation, Miss Gray.

And so Heather had gone to Fairfield, with all of the rich kids, a daisy among the hothouse flowers.

It had been a trial by fire, a strange fire she had never seen before. When her mom had taken the job at the Accardi home it had been a chance for them to try something different, to be somewhere different.

After a childhood spent in New York City, living in an apartment the size of a closet while her mother cleaned houses on the Upper East Side, her mother had longed to give her something else. A taste of another place. Of another life. Perhaps her mom just wanted a different life, and Heather couldn't fault her for that.

She'd heard about the opening through the gossip network with other cleaners—a wealthy Italian looking for a housekeeper for his property in the Italian Alps, but also for potential travel to other homes he kept around the world. The salary seemed so generous that it almost felt like a scam. Perhaps human trafficking.

Her mother had taken the risk.

The job came with a house on the estate, and for the first time in her life Heather had her own bedroom.

She was still sad to leave New York. For all that they'd had very little, the city itself had a heartbeat, and it had resonated inside of Heather every time she walked to school, whenever she went to the bodega to get snacks, to find something to eat if her mother was working late.

The space and quiet of the Italian estate was deafening to her. It felt frightening. Yawning. Stranger still was the way Giuseppe Accardi treated her and her mother like they were people. He made eye contact. He spoke directly to her, not around her. Not as if she were an ornament or a pebble sitting in the middle of the floor that didn't belong.

They arrived in the summer, before school term at Fairfield started. And he had told Heather that she was allowed to use the pool.

That was the first time she saw him.

The man who would become her stepbrother.

Romeo Accardi.

Two years older than her, and already built like a man. In hindsight, she could see that wasn't strictly true, but at the time she had been…

Dazed by him.

He was six feet tall, shirtless and muscled, standing by the pool, his black hair slicked away from his face, a pair of dark glasses covering his eyes. He was the most beautiful human being that Heather had ever seen. And her mother had worked for celebrities.

She had seen her share of beautiful humans, both on the silver screen and at her mother's cleaning jobs for the rich and lovely.

She had seen her share of glamour and glory. Somehow, even at fourteen, Romeo Accardi supplanted them all.

But everything his father was, he was not.

The first time he looked at her, he was not struck dumb as she had been when she laid eyes on him. Rather, his lip curled into a sneer.

"Who are you?"

"I… Heather. My mom works here."

"Are you meant to be at the pool?"

"Your father said that I could."

He had lowered his sunglasses, looking at her with deep disdain. "I see."

Then he had left. As if sharing the same air as her was anathema. That had set the tone.

Things did not improve after that. In fact, they only got worse when her mother began a romantic relationship with Giuseppe.

Worse still when they got married.

It wasn't a clean start to a relationship. Carla Accardi, Giuseppe's wife, had always been a distant presence in the house. At least from Heather's perspective. The beautiful, statuesque socialite hadn't been cold; she'd simply been the way that employers usually were.

When the relationship had started between Heather's mother and Romeo's father, he had been insistent his romantic relationship with his wife was long over. At least that was what he said later.

It had been confusing for thirteen-year-old Heather, whose life had been improved in almost every way by her mother's relationship with Giuseppe.

And yet she had known that the way it had all come about was…wrong. She also had no control over any of it. Which, to this day, was the most important angle on that, she felt.

As an adult, she didn't think her mother was responsible for the dissolution of the Accardi marriage. The truth was, there had to be issues. Many of them, in order for infidelity to have been able to get a foothold. And Giuseppe wasn't a serial adulterer. He had married Lisa Gray and they had stayed together until death did them part after Lisa suffered a heart attack two years ago.

In the end, Heather saw them as a love story. An imperfect one perhaps, but over the years it had become clear that they were meant for each other. At least, it was clear to her.

One thing she could be certain of was that Romeo had never gained any perspective on the situation. As a result, Heather had never gained any perspective on him.

When his father and her mother had married, his disdain and distance had turned into outright cruelty. He blamed her mother for his own mother's unhappiness, and he hated Heather.

Popular and adored by all of their classmates, he had made her life a living hell at school. And then he had proceeded to make it hell at home as well. When he was in residence, that was. Often, he was with Carla. But when he was around he never hesitated to make his dislike of their family situation known.

Their warfare was as covert as possible, of course. Heather would never complain and risk ruining her mother's happiness. She had never really understood why Romeo bothered to hide his disdain, but while they were never friendly to each other in any situation, they were civil—mainly—in front of their parents.

If it had changed when they were adults, Heather would've been happy to revise her opinion of him. Like her, he had been young and at the mercy of the adults in their lives. But he had never changed. He had never grown any kinder, or seemed to gain any deeper understanding of the complexity surrounding his parents' marriage or anything of the kind.

He had been just the worst. Responsible for making her life miserable.

As if her rumination had conjured him, Romeo strode into the library where Heather was sitting staring at her computer. She felt him before she saw him. That low, vibrating frequency that always resonated in her chest when he was near. And then she looked up.

He was wearing a resplendently cut navy blue suit, his dark hair pushed off of his forehead, his jaw as sharp as broken glass. The artful stubble that covered it was like a tease. As were his full lips, which looked mobile, like they might smile easily and beautifully. The truth was, they did. For other people.

Never for Heather.

That had been one of the most damaging things about Romeo back when they'd been teenagers.

He liked everyone. To know him was to long to be in his orbit. He was like the sun, creating warmth and light wherever he went.

She was the only exception.

He hated her. And when he looked at her it was like being thrown into a snowdrift.

Freezing.

But it was only one of the most damaging things about Romeo.

The other was that he was and forever, irrevocably her first experience with physical attraction.

And nothing, not the vitriol that existed between

them, not the resentment that grew daily inside of her, not years or wisdom or maturity could do anything to dampen her response to him.

Hatred had a taste, a scent, a bone-deep feeling.

So, alas, did desire.

And for her the two things were intertwined in such a way that she didn't know how to separate them. She was sick.

Thankfully, after his father died they would have no further connection to each other.

What a horrible thought. That her only route to freedom was losing Giuseppe.

Giuseppe had been the only father figure Heather had ever had. He was her father.

But he had grown so frail and gray in the years since his wife had died. He had never really recovered from it. He'd gotten a cancer diagnosis afterward and hadn't seemed to have any fight in him at all. She hated to see him like this. She wanted him to be reunited with his wife. She had to believe that was what awaited him.

She wasn't looking forward to losing him. It was just that…

Finally having that last tie severed to Romeo would be a gift.

"How is he?" Sometimes if they kept the conversation limited to his father, they could make it through without having a fight.

"That eager to collect your inheritance?"

Well. Apparently that would be the case today.

"Yes, Romeo, of course that's why I'm asking about the well-being of my father."

"He is my father, Heather, not yours."

"He is my father in every way that matters. But thank you for taking this opportunity to stay in character. If we didn't have a villain in the play then this horrendous walk along the road of grief would be unbearable."

"I have never minded being the villain in your play, as you know."

"Yes. I do. You didn't answer my question."

"He's dying," Romeo said. "And nothing has on that score."

"I'll go and see him in a moment."

"What are you doing in here?"

"Sitting here counting my future riches," she said, smiling blandly at him. In truth, she had been catching up on work. She was a freelance editor contracted with several publishers, and she had a backlog of manuscripts to read and copy to write. But she had stopped trying to convince him of her goodness a long time ago.

She could remember clearly when the straw had broken her back. That very last straw. He had been on the verge of graduation, and she had been in her second year of high school. Part of his senior prank had been to get everyone in the entire school to act like she was invisible. They spent the whole day looking through her, not speaking a single word to her. Bumping into her, spilling drinks on her shoes.

Only her friend Vera had spoken to her. Well, and a handful of teachers. But even a couple of teachers had engaged in the behavior. Thus was the power of Romeo Accardi. Who had managed to frame it all as a brilliant joke, while giving her a look that told her he knew it was astronomically cruel. That it would poke at all of the insecurities inside of her. The way that she feared she would never be accepted.

That was when she had stopped. The high road had no longer been an option. Smiling at him to try to prove that she was worthy of…of something. That had ended that day.

Ever since, she had decided to give as good as she had gotten. She didn't have his power, she didn't have his influence, but in their private war she fired off as many shots as he did.

"I assume you'll be staying for the will reading after?"

She studied his face. He was beautiful. But he was empty. How could he say this, with that tone, concerning the death of his own father?

"Yes. Because it's what he wants." There was no point antagonizing him. She enjoyed it, yes, but this wasn't a game. She was about to be an orphan. And yes, she was twenty-seven, so it wasn't as if she was an orphaned child, but for the first twelve years of her life it had been her and her mother against the world. And then there had been Giuseppe. Without him, without her mom, she wouldn't be the person that she was. And whatever Romeo thought about who she was, she knew that she was a good person.

A strong one, an ambitious one. A good friend, good at her job.

Someday maybe she would actually finish writing a book, instead of just editing other people's stories. And when she did it would be because of not only the education that Giuseppe had helped her get, but also because of the confidence his love and support had instilled in her.

"What does surprise me, Heather, is that you have not found a rich man to pay your way the way that your mother did. Finding a fool like my father should be easy enough for you—you still have him convinced you're a fragile girl who needs protecting. I bet a great many men would line up for the privilege of...protecting you."

She was fed up with him. She snapped her computer shut, and stood, holding it underneath her arm. "I've been busy. Living my life. But you know, my mom didn't marry your dad until she was thirty-five. So I have time."

"Your mother pulled off a rare feat by gaining trophy-wife status in her thirties. I wouldn't count on your charms to such a great degree."

"And what about you? Why are you here, Romeo? You have your own billions with your investment firm, and I assume you want nothing to do with your father's company. It's going to fall out of the family's hands. Publicly traded and with someone else as CEO, I assume you and I will end up with stock options. You don't need to be here for that. Are you waiting to see if you inherit this house that you hate? Are you waiting to see the last breath of a man you despise..."

"I love my father," he said. "If I despised him then all of this would be easier. Why do you think I come to holidays? Why do you think I stayed engaged in this family in any regard? You think it's because I hate him?"

That was much more complex a thought than she wanted to give Romeo credit for. She wanted him to remain the one-dimensional villain. Selfish and cruel simply because he was. She didn't want him to be someone with feelings as complicated as her own.

"I always thought it was to perform your abject disgust to all of us," she said, ignoring the revelation.

"No. I am his son. His only child. I deserved to be there. I deserved to have a place at the head of the table, just as I deserve to have my inheritance, just as I deserve to sit by my father as he takes his last breath because I am the one with the birthright to do so. You are nothing, Heather, and you never have been anything at all. He wanted your mother, and he got her. He destroyed our family in the name of satiating his lust, and then in order to save face he married his affair partner and tried to make it legitimate. If I hated him, I could've simply walked away. I could have turned my back on him and never looked at him again. I don't hate my father."

"But you hate me," she said.

"I don't see why I owe affection to a cuckoo in the nest who has spent the last fourteen years trying to supplant me."

"Maybe I just wanted a dad."

"Yours didn't want you. It didn't give you the right to mine."

Then he was the one to turn away. To leave her standing there, fuming.

She truly hated her stepbrother with all of her being.

She couldn't wait to be rid of him.

And yet she could.

Because the day she walked away from Romeo, never to see him again, was the day her family dissolved.

Then Heather would be alone in the world.

With nothing but the burning hatred she felt for Romeo remaining.

CHAPTER TWO

HATING HEATHER GRAY had become a habit.

He woke up in the morning, brushed his teeth, shaved, and he hated Heather Gray. It had been like that from the beginning.

For so long that he no longer questioned it.

He could remember the first time he'd seen her. She was sulky, insolent, the corners of her full mouth turned down. She had been a child that first time. And he had dismissed her as being unimportant, because she was.

If only he had realized that within the year she would be his stepsister. His problem.

Prior to his father destroying his mother the way that he had, he had ignored Heather when he passed her in the halls at Fairfield. But after the affair, after his mother and father had divorced, and Lisa and his father had married, it was different.

He resented her presence.

His father was enamored of her. It was clear.

His father had always wanted a daughter, and had never had one, and this was even better, because she was pathetic. She had needed saving, and his father wanted to do the saving. What better way to have someone look up at him with uncritical eyes, than to become their hero.

And it didn't matter, the ways in which he had failed Romeo and Carla. It didn't matter that he had been neglectful at best when Romeo had been a small child, wedded primarily to his business, and only later had he had any time for a wife and child. And at that point, the wife had been Lisa, and the child Heather.

In many ways, he had taken the concept of sibling rivalry with her a bit far. But he was not a man given to half measures. He never had been. His life had been his own, and then she had appeared.

He had resented her presence from the beginning, but worse was when she had become beautiful.

When her sulky mouth had become a temptation, when her body had begun to take the shape of a woman's.

She was all of the worst parts of having a sister, he assumed. And yet she wasn't his sister, and that made the entire situation abominable. It always had been.

He was surrounded by socialites who starved themselves for a living. He had always liked women in every shape, but there was a particular sort of lean, hungry look that was more popular within the circles he ran in, and Heather was an anomaly.

She wasn't polished. Even though they wore uniforms to Fairfield, she had managed to look…different. She had buttons on her backpack, and her plaid socks pulled up to her knees often had a safety pin clipped to them with things dangling from it. It was maddening and strange. Her brown hair was a curly tangle, never tamed, and she was…

Lush.

She had only grown more so.

Her hips were round, and he had thought more than once about what it would be like to grip hold of them as he drove into her. Her waist was nipped in, but there was a softness to her stomach that held his fascination. And then of course her breasts… A man could spend a lifetime on fantasies centering on her breasts.

He felt that at this point he very nearly had.

And what a thing to be thinking about as he stood in front of the door of his dying father's bedroom. His stepsister's breasts.

He couldn't wait to excise her from his life like the tumor that was currently killing his father.

He pushed the door open, and went to sit beside the bed.

"Romeo," his father said.

"Yes, Dad," he said softly in Italian. "I'm here."

He was angry at his father. He always would be. There had been a strange sort of pain that had come with Lisa's death two years ago that stilled his tongue now. She had died suddenly. She had been there, and then she had been gone.

It had been astonishingly painful, and to this day he couldn't quite articulate why. He had spent the better part of the last decade and a half hating her. For what she had done to hurt his mother, for what she had done to change his life. But she had been a lovely and loving person. She had, in some ways, been better for his father. His mother and father had a tumultuous relationship, and he could admit that there in the relative silence of his father's room. In his own mind.

Lisa and his father had never been tumultuous. There had been deep care between the two of them. He resented that too. That in many ways it was undeniable that life had been smoother for his father once he had made the decision to rid himself of his first wife.

But Romeo was the one who had to be there for his mother. Then and now. He was the one who'd had to pick up the pieces, and there were so many pieces.

"You have to take care of her," Giuseppe said, his voice thin.

"Who?"

He had been thinking of his mother, but he knew very well his father didn't care about her. He knew the answer before his father gave it.

"Heather. I need to know that she will be okay."

Of course he had no similar concerns for Romeo. Romeo had never had the option to be anything but okay. His father expected him to get on with things. To be hard. To be a man. And so he was. Self-sufficient and successful.

But what he loved about Heather was that she was soft. Bookish and in need of support.

At least that was how he saw her, but then, Giuseppe had a rescue complex, when he felt the person could be rescued. Which had left Romeo's mother on her own, and Heather and her mother well cared for.

Heather was much more canny than his father wanted to believe.

"I assume you're leaving her enough in the way of money to ensure that she's just fine."

"She needs protection. She is not from this world, and she never has been. She never fit in."

He had alienated her from any potential friendships at school. The only friend she'd had had been another girl who socialized on the periphery. He had been the most popular student, and he had wielded that social power against her.

The idea that his father would think that he would stand by and take care of her in his absence was ridiculous.

He might not be a high school bully anymore, and on some nights he could muster up a little bit of shame for his behavior then, but he was never going to take care of her.

"Father…"

Giuseppe's hand shot out, and he grabbed hold of Romeo's forearm. "You must take care of her. She's special. I love her as a daughter, and with her mother gone she will be alone in the world if she doesn't have you."

"No harm will come to her," Romeo said.

In the early days, he had fantasized about revenge. In fact, he had made her life difficult because what he had wanted was the ruin of her and her mother. He had wanted them to be unhappy in this world, miserable; he wanted it to be the cost of destroying his family.

He no longer wanted that. But he wanted nothing to do with her either.

"Promise me," his father said. "If she needs you, you will be there. Promise me that you will not abandon her. That you will maintain a connection."

He gritted his teeth, his lip curling. "I promise."

His father would be dead within the next couple of days, and he would never know what Romeo did or didn't do. He felt it was a kindness to lie to the old man now. Why give him cause for concern? But Romeo would not do the bidding of a ghost.

"Send her to me."

"Of course."

He stood, walking out of the room, anger burning in his chest.

He walked down the hall, and her bedroom door opened, and there she appeared, wearing a yellow dress that complemented her golden skin tone, the low neckline showing her curves off in a way that proved too compelling for him to ignore.

"He wants you," he said.

"Okay."

He should've just let her go on without him, but he felt compelled to follow her. He pushed the door open, and stood there as she went to his bedside and took his hand. "What is it, Papa?"

The smile on his father's face was a cold dagger pushed through his heart. And this was always and ever the problem. He could see how much more his father loved them. But in a few days this would be over, and he would go back to his life. He would go back to New York; he would take a lover for a night and blot out all of this. He worked, he played—the end. He was, in fact, an island. And the only real connection he had, the only real relationship he had to maintain, was the one with his mother. Because she needed him. She had no one else, not really.

"I love you, Heather. You are my daughter. This… this estate, I want to leave half of it to you. Because you are both my children. You…"

His anger rose up inside of him, but he said nothing.

"You don't have to do that," she said. "This estate is part of your family line."

"I will," he said. "I'm leaving it to both of you. Because I love you in equal measure."

That was like a sword straight through his chest. Perhaps it shouldn't be. This girl who had come into his life a mere fourteen years earlier mattered just as much to him as his own son. He had been right to hate her.

Always.

"I love you," Heather said.

She leaned in and kissed him on the cheek. And then he sat up. "I feel cold."

He lay back down, and then his breath left his body. While holding Heather's hand.

It was done. His father was gone.

And it wasn't him who had been holding onto him, but his stepsister.

Who would inherit half of the estate that had been in their bloodline for hundreds of years. She had successfully supplanted him. In every way that mattered.

He had known it would be like this. From the beginning.

CHAPTER THREE

The beginning

SHE'D NEVER SEEN a boy who was so tall. Or so angry.

She'd never seen anyone like him. Not at any of the other houses her mom had cleaned in the past. But then, this place was unlike any they had ever been at.

No one had ever given them a house before. Especially not one so nice as the one they were living in now, down at the bottom of the garden of the vast estate.

And certainly no one had ever given Heather permission to use the pool.

Her mom's new boss was lovely. One of the kindest people that Heather had ever met.

And this must be his son.

Romeo Accardi.

Giuseppe had spoken about him before. She knew his name; she had simply never seen him before. He had been away on an après ski vacation with his mother, and then had gone on to the Riviera with friends. She had wondered how in the world he kept up with his school.

"Romeo is quite like his mother. He always finds a way."

It made sense, right then, as she looked up at him.

She had never seen a boy that tall. A boy who was also a man. She couldn't explain that thought; she could only feel it. She waited for him to smile. She smiled, her very best, most aggressive smile. He lowered his sunglasses, and fixed her with an insolent glare. "Does your mother know that her child is loose about the premises?"

She felt like she had been cut in two with his words. With the sheer dismissiveness of them, the coldness. But also his beauty. How could anyone so beautiful exist? And how could something so beautiful be so…forbidding?

He was nothing like his father.

"I… I have permission to swim."

"It's a good thing I'm leaving then."

That was her first interaction with him.

It was a while before she had another.

Giuseppe had invited her to come into the house on the days when her mother was cleaning, and she often did. Perusing the library, or enjoying the food that the staff made for her from the kitchen. Yes, it was generous. Overly so, but she was also living in some sort of dream. Going from spending much of her day alone in an apartment in New York, walking to school and back by herself, to this.

"Have you thought about school?" Giuseppe asked.

"I've been enjoying the break," she said honestly, looking down at the tangerine she was holding, the one she had just taken out of the kitchen, as he'd given her permission to do.

"I think that you should go to the same school that Romeo attends. It is the best school in the vicinity."

"There's no way that my mother can afford that."

She already knew. That the gap separating her and Romeo Accardi was far too vast to cross. She knew. There were the people that owned these houses, and there were the people that cleaned them. And there was not enough elbow grease in the world to work yourself from the position she and her mother were in to the other. You could not start from where she did and become one of those illustrious creatures, and much of that inequality began with the education. When you were given access to the best of everything from the very beginning, how could anyone ever hope to catch up with you?

"I will pay the fees," he said.

"But why?"

He smiled. "You're smart to ask the question. There are a great many people in this world who do things for the wrong reasons. I like your mother very much. I've never met anyone quite like her. And I want to give her a gift. You are the most important thing to her. I know she'll appreciate it."

Her mother had. When he'd brought her into the room and told her how it would be, she'd been more than appreciative.

Before Heather knew it, she was being outfitted for school uniforms. The navy blue sweater with burgundy trim and plaid skirt, knee-high socks and loafers felt like something out of a television show to her. Which actually was more real than the private school kids that she had seen wandering around the Upper East Side. It was more likely for her to step into a movie than to join one of those groups.

Fairfield was in London, which put her a short plane

ride away from her mother. It was foreign and exciting all at once. She'd been sorry to leave the estate in some ways, but she felt…part of something new. Part of something she'd never imagined she could be, and that made her more excited than anything.

The old building was made of stone, and more of a palace than a school. The night before school started she stayed in Giuseppe's London town house with him and her mother. Romeo did not join them. He was taking a different plane, apparently.

That sort of casual reference to their riches still astonished her.

They were astronomically wealthy, she knew. You couldn't live the life that she did and not be aware of it. But to go from their estate—in a private plane—to a glorious town house that also belonged to this family. The a luxury car and the school that was right out of a fantasy novel truly underlined the reality.

That feeling of the wealth surrounding her, compared to her own lack, followed her into the building.

She thought she would just keep quiet, do nothing to expose herself—as one of the impoverished, and as an American. She found out quickly that she wasn't the only American. The first time she saw Romeo in the hall, she heard him saying at an elevated whisper, "She's the housekeeper's daughter."

And that was when it began to follow her, like a trail of whispers. She didn't belong. Romeo did his best to make sure that everyone treated her that way. He did not manage to drive a wedge between herself and the initial friends that she met on the day, her roommates, who treated her with kindness even though Romeo was doing his best to ensure that everyone else treated her like she was invisible.

Quite literally.

Sometimes she would speak to somebody, and they would ignore her entirely.

When they went home on break things were no better. Romeo treated her like a ghost that haunted his house. Like an insignificant thing, and she hated it. She ached to matter. To be more. To not be stuck as something lower and lesser simply because she'd been born without money.

She'd always been aware of it.

Her mother cleaned for rich people; how could she not be aware of it?

But existing half in that world and half out of it was a glorious, sharp pain she'd never imagined before.

During summer break, however, she noticed that something was different between her mom and Giuseppe. They weren't like a boss and an employee.

They seemed like…friends, perhaps.

Or maybe more.

Within a year, Romeo's parents were divorced, and Giuseppe and her mother were engaged.

At fifteen, Heather was elated. It made her *one of them*, in many ways. She was no longer the cleaner's daughter. She was Giuseppe Accardi's stepdaughter. But that made Romeo her stepbrother, and if she had hoped that it might spark some sort of familial relationship between them, or even a civil one, she was disappointed.

At the wedding, she had on the most beautiful dress. It was peach colored, and finer than anything she had ever hoped to own. And he had been there, lanky and glorious in a suit cut perfectly to his lean frame. He had grown since she had met him the previous year. His face more angular, even more perfect.

His mother was a great beauty. He had his father's olive skin, black hair and dark eyes, and his fashion model mother's bone structure, her insolent mouth and the same sharp gaze. The few times that she had met the former Mrs. Accardi, Heather had felt cut to pieces by her steely blue eyes. Mainly, she hadn't lived in the house. Evidence, as far as Heather was concerned, that she could see a lot of his mother in him now.

"They might dress you up," he said, looking her up and down, and then circling her slowly, like an elegant predator. "But you will always be the housekeeper's daughter. And you will certainly never be anything to me."

It was lucky for her that she was no stranger to snobbery. Even going to the school she had, back in New York, she had been bullied. Her mother was a cleaner. And while many other kids at the school were in the same situation that she was, the ones that weren't, who still felt insignificant, thought to make themselves feel superior by creating a pariah out of someone else.

The fact that Romeo couldn't leave her alone let her know that he had a vulnerability. If he was entirely sure of himself, he wouldn't come for her. Which was what gave her the strength to simply smile in return.

Her response to him that day at the wedding only made things worse.

Soon, their rivalry at the school became quite legendary among their peers. They were smart, of course.

Teachers were never the wiser, and therefore neither were their parents.

And then one thing happened that she had not seen coming at all. Her mother marrying Giuseppe really did increase her popularity. And soon it felt as if lines were drawn through their school. Who sided with Romeo, and who sided with Heather?

There were no high roads taken.

She wasn't the underdog anymore, and she refused to be treated like she was. She invited a group of friends to the house for a pool party over the summer—and given that their school was in another country, it was a weeklong affair. Having access to that sort of luxury was a dizzying drug. She had a lovely home to invite her friends back to, places for them to stay. And an indulgent stepfather who lived to make her happy, particularly since he couldn't seem to make his own son happy no matter what he did.

Heather was happy to step into the role. She'd never known her father. And Giuseppe was wonderful to her.

He wanted to spoil her, and Heather wanted to be spoiled.

The entire pool area was transformed for them. Cabana set up with lavish fruit trays, glorious flower displays, various grottoes for them to take pictures to put up on social media.

Everything was going well, until Romeo prowled to the pool area, wearing an open white shirt. At seventeen, his body was more muscular than it had been when she had first met him. She despised herself for noticing. She despised herself for still finding him beautiful at all, because certainly his behavior should have transformed him into precisely what he was. Someone who was dark and ugly on the inside. And yet he remained stubbornly beautiful.

"Good afternoon," he said, resting his forearms on the gate that separated the pool from the rest of the estate.

Her friends exchanged glances, and giggles. They knew that the official stance was that they hated Romeo, but they also weren't blind. The trouble with Romeo was that he was charming. He had a reputation for being an exceptionally good kisser, and she suspected more. Though, no one was foolish enough to breathe such a thing in front of her.

"What is it that you want?"

"Shocking, *cara*. I come to say hello and you greet me with venom."

"I don't think you find that shocking at all," she said, standing up from where she was on her lounge chair, wearing the bright pink bikini that she had just bought for the occasion. And that was when she saw it. His eyes flickered over her body, and his reaction wasn't neutral.

He had made a mistake. He had just made a mistake. He'd *noticed* her.

He noticed her body, the same way that she noticed his.

And he had let her see it.

He might hate her—she believed fully that he did—but he was not immune to her. And that was an incredibly interesting piece of information. She walked closer to him, not looking away from his gaze. "What is it exactly that you wish to offer?"

"Oh, I live to serve," he said, not breaking eye contact.

"Do you? Are you here to play the part of pool boy?"

"Oh no, *cara*, only one of us is from the servant class."

"What a pity that I will never serve you," she said.

His eyes flickered over her again. "Someday perhaps I will have you on your knees." He didn't say it loudly enough for anyone else to hear, only her. That first time he had looked at her that gaze had been lethal. Cutting. This cut her somewhere different. And didn't leave her feeling cold. Rather she felt altogether too warm.

"I think you should leave," she said.

He grinned. "If you need me to."

That left her questioning everything. Perhaps nothing that he'd said had been real, but all designed to antagonize her. But the interaction echoed inside of her.

Finally, in her senior year, she was free of him. He graduated, and went on to university, and was never at home, never at school. Being an Accardi—even if by marriage—had made her essentially the most popular girl in school. And the only regret that she had was that Romeo wasn't there to witness the ascent. And maybe that was because his absence was necessary. Without his influence, no one knew they were supposed to dislike her. They forgot. As if it had never happened.

For graduation, Giuseppe and her mom were allowing her to use their London estate for a party. The money and detail that had gone into it was extraordinary, and Heather distantly remembered the girl that she was, grateful for everything—even for a tangerine in the corner of the kitchen—and she wondered if she had lost herself somewhere. What was wrong with enjoying all of this? Surely nothing.

She did pause to feel gratitude, rather than entitlement. But the entitlement was what buoyed her, often. Because Romeo was so intent on acting like she didn't deserve it, radicalizing those around her into believing she didn't deserve it either, so she had begun to walk around with armor suggesting that she did.

But she had to remember that she wasn't one of them. Not really. Because that actually gave her an advantage over Romeo. It did. He had nothing at stake. He was cruel for the sake of it. She was fighting for a place in a life that she knew she deserved. Having Romeo away was almost enough to help her forget about him, honestly. She had actually gotten herself a date to the party. Which was something she never managed to do when Romeo was around.

She found herself obsessing about him in strange and irritating ways, and while she would never say she had a crush on him—you could not have a crush on somebody that you hated—she couldn't lie about the effects that he had on her body. She was eighteen now, and much more aware of why she couldn't take her eyes off his chest. Much more aware of what he might mean by having her on her knees. Making fun of her, no doubt, and yet it was a mental image she couldn't quite get out of her head.

He was sexy; that was the problem. And there was no denying that. Every girl thought so. It was only that he wasn't a vile, cruel monster to every girl. Only to her.

I guess that makes you special.

Well, that was the most twisted thought she'd ever had. But it didn't matter. She was with Damien tonight, and she fully intended to lose her virginity, which was a ridiculous albatross to be carrying around her neck out of high school and into university.

All she needed was a little bit of liquid courage to loosen up. Which, with the intensity of the party, didn't take long. The music was loud, the mood electric, and she was pleasantly buzzed after the first hour, which Damien seemed to notice and appreciate as her nerves faded and she became looser and more affectionate.

Soon they were kissing on the couch, and if she thought of Romeo's sensual mouth as Damien kissed his way down her collarbone, it was only because it was a habit.

After a few moments of being on display, Damien took her hand and led her up the stairs, the two of them making their way into the bedroom.

As far as exorcising demons went, she felt like she was about to do it in a big way.

Until the door to the bedroom crashed open like an entire police brigade had broken it down.

"What is going on?"

She looked up from her position on the bed to see Romeo standing there, his black hair disheveled, his face fixed into a mask of fury, his hands clenched into fists.

"What are you doing here?" she asked.

"The better question is what the hell are you doing?" She thought he was talking to her until he crossed the room, grabbed Damien by the neck and pulled him up off the bed. "She's drunk," Romeo said.

"I'm not drunk," she slurred.

"You are," he said. "She can't consent to this—you get out of here before I call the police."

"I consented," she said.

"No," Romeo said. "You're being an idiot because

you're out of your head, and this party is a disaster. Clear everyone out."

"I have permission to have this party," she said.

"Because your mother is a fool and my father never tells you no. You need to be told no, Heather Gray. And I am telling you no now."

"You," she said, getting up off the bed, and trying to insert herself between Romeo and Damien, "are a nightmare. You can't tell me that you weren't doing far worse than this when you were in school, and now you want to come here and act like an authoritarian when you've never followed a rule in your entire life. You were probably snorting cocaine off of ski bunnies' asses when you were fifteen."

"What's good for me is not good for you."

"And since when do you care what's good for me?"

"Since this asshole was about to take you when you were drunk. I care about that."

"Romeo—"

"Get out," he growled at Damien, who did not argue. Romeo towered over him, and was broader and far more muscular. The man had filled out in the past several years, leaving the rangy boy behind. He was still devastatingly beautiful, with cheeks that could cut glass, but he could no longer be called pretty. And she especially wouldn't call him that now, while she was standing there with her heart pounding hard, with fury, with embarrassment. And then he walked out of the room, leaving her alone, shouting about how the party was over.

"You *can't*!" she yelled, trailing behind him.

"I can. I came here to sleep, and I'm not doing it with this bullshit going on."

"I've been planning this party," she said. "And you don't have the right—"

But it was too late; everyone was leaving. Everyone was listening to him like his was the only voice that mattered.

"*I hate you*," she said, standing in the middle of the now-empty town house.

"Of one thing you can always be certain, *cara*," he said, moving his face close to hers, so close that she could smell him, that spicy, masculine scent, so close that she could see the dark stubble on his jawline. So close she thought about reaching out and touching him, just for a second. "I hate you too."

CHAPTER FOUR

SOMETHING HAD BROKEN inside of him that day. When he had come to the town house, looking to sleep off some of his excess, and found his stepsister, drunk, crawling all over one of the biggest assholes he'd ever known in school.

And when said asshole had led his stepsister up the stairs, he had lost it entirely.

He knew that it was perhaps as hypocritical as she said that he was breaking up a party which was tame by his standards, but he hadn't been able to allow it. Heather Gray was a thorn in his side. And the thorn had only grown more acute as she had become more beautiful. They had been cruel to each other over the years, but after that, her behavior toward him became something like psychotic. And the twisted thing was it seemed to ignite a spark within him. Seemed to make him all the more interested in continuing the war that they'd been engaged in for years. Though they saw each other less frequently, it still happened on occasion that they would find themselves at his father's home in Italy at the same time.

Even their parents had to take notice of the rift, though they thought it was some form of sibling rivalry rather than the burning hatred that existed in them both. They traded barbs in front of both Lisa and Giuseppe, but were careful to walk the line.

In university, Heather traded her school uniform, and out-of-school bikinis, for something a bit more serious. Her red hair was often pinned up into a bun, her color palette ranging from black to darker black.

He would be lying if he said he didn't miss the color.

But she was clearly now obsessed with being taken seriously, in that way first-year university students often were.

Which was why he had thought—the first time—that perhaps some of her anger at him might've cooled. Until she walked by him in the hallway, and looked up at him, her green eyes catching him so hard that he froze.

Then she put her fingertip on his chest, dragged it right across the front of his cashmere sweater. "How nice to see you, brother dearest."

There was malice and promise in those words, and he would be damned if they didn't send a sharp signal of arousal straight down to his cock. The problem with Heather was that she took desire and added something more potent to it. It was the extreme distaste he had for her that seemed to add adrenaline to the attraction. What was forbidden to him? Nothing. Nothing but the stepsister he hated. He was a wealthy man, and doors flew open for him. But not her. Touching her would cause an avalanche of destruction. It was what made her compelling.

Over dinner she smiled at him sweetly. Later he cornered her. "And what is your game?"

"I don't have a game," she said, smiling sweetly at him.

He'd never once seen the look on her face before.

"I don't believe you."

She pouted. "What a terrible view you have of women."

"Only of you, *cara*."

For some reason that only made her smile more.

"You need to be nicer to Heather," his father said to him later when they were drinking cognac by the fire.

"Why exactly?" he asked, tapping his glass.

"Because I won't be around forever. You will have to take care of Heather and Lisa."

"Father, your money will take care of them well enough."

"Is that all you think I offer them?"

It was certainly why they had so happily broken up Giuseppe's marriage. Certainly why they had taken to all of this with such ease. Had his father been a poor man, it would never have happened. He knew that for certain. One of the truly difficult things was that Lisa was a kind woman. Caring and one who seemed to enjoy spending time with her husband, doting on her daughter. In spite of the frosty reception that Romeo had given her, Lisa had been persistently kind to him. But he was the one who'd had to be there for his mother. He was the one who had—

"Don't forget that I have to take care of your former wife."

"Romeo… You know I feel sorry for the timing of everything."

"Not so sorry that you didn't do exactly what you wanted to anyway."

By the time he was ready for bed he was furious. He walked into his room and stripped his jacket off, his tie, the rest of his clothes. He walked into the shower and stood blindly beneath the hot spray, then dried himself and walked back into the bedroom. He stopped. There was someone in his bed. He flicked the lights on, and there she was, the covers pulled up past her breasts, her copper hair spread out on the pillow.

His stepsister was naked in his bed.

"What are you playing at?" he asked, fury and desire creating a potent cocktail in his veins.

"'Wherefore art thou, Romeo?'" she asked, that same smile from earlier today playing across her lips.

Whatever she was doing, it was evil. It had nothing to do with wanting him; that was certain.

"Get out of here, you little slut," he snarled.

"I don't think that's what you want," she said, completely undeterred by his insult.

"It *is* what I want."

His heart was racing, his body hard, and the towel that was riding low on his hips was probably doing little to disguise the effect she had on him. But no matter how much he wanted her in that moment, he wanted her out of his room more.

She began to sit up, and in one fluid movement he went over to the bed, grabbed the edge of the blanket and pulled it around to the other side of her quickly, baring her body only for a moment without looking before he swaddled her, then grabbed the corners of the blanket and carried her, trapped inside, out into the hallway.

"Out," he said, dumping her onto the floor.

She was seething, her eyes shooting sparks from where she was lying, still trapped in the blanket. "Don't you want to take my virginity? Since you spoiled my attempts the last time?"

"You were drunk," he said, staring down at her in her glorious state. "And what you do with your virginity is none of my concern. Whatever trap this is, you're not going to catch me in it." And then it all became abundantly clear. He had always known what she was, from the beginning. It was only his attraction to her that had clouded things, for just a moment. He began to laugh. "You are trying to trap me, aren't you? It is not enough that your mother married my father—do you think that you can snare me in the same sort of fashion?"

Her face turned red.

"How *dare* you?"

"How dare *you*. But you did. Now there you are naked in the hallway, thwarted. Go to hell, Heather."

He shut the door violently on her and locked it. And then he went straight back into the shower and stood beneath the cold spray, cursing her name the entire time.

Heather was lost in a spiral of self-loathing. He had *rejected* her.

She had intended him to. Sort of. She pushed her fingers through her hair and pulled hard.

Everything was tangled up. She had gotten a little bit wine drunk and told her new friends in college all about her relationship with her stepbrother, and they had suggested that half the problem was that they wanted to bang each other. She denied it for a while, but then gave up. Because the truth was, he was beautiful. And she had never been immune. She also knew that he wasn't immune to her.

"You need to screw him," her roommate had said. "It's that simple. The two of you are drowning in all your unresolved sexual tension."

And the more she had thought about it, the more she had thought that perhaps she did. God knew that her attempts at dating were entirely thwarted because every time she kissed a man she remembered Romeo storming in like an avenging angel, and it never got any further because he had destroyed the idea of sex for her. She had gotten it into her head that at the very least she would shock him. That she would get some kind of advantage over him. And if they did have sex…maybe it would defuse everything between them. But he had dumped her out into the hall, and truly, she had realized that she had miscalculated anyway. Because the feelings had been far too intense. They had been so much more than she had anticipated. And now she was humiliated.

At least no one had seen her scrabbling back to her room with his blankets. It really was too bad that he was a billionaire, because her stealing his blankets might have been an inconvenience to him if he were a normal man. But alas, Romeo had everything he could possibly want.

Thankfully, she was heading back to school tomorrow. Thankfully, she probably wasn't going to have to face him again. They avoided each other well enough in the giant house.

Usually, the only time she had to see him was at family dinner, and as much as it pained her to skip one with her parents, she would just claim that she was tired and avoid tonight.

She would be heading back to school with her tail between her legs to an extent but...

She had certainly affected him.

Her attraction to him had always been so buffered by how much she hated him, and then she had been naked in his bed and he had walked in wearing only a towel, and nothing had been theoretical about that.

She had been so sure that she would have control over everything, because she was a woman and therefore more likely to keep her wits about her during sex.

She had lost her head completely. In that moment when he had walked over there and she had thought that he...

She let out a breath, and walked out of her room, needing lunch, and needing to sneak it back to her room as quickly as possible to minimize her chances of having to deal with Romeo.

And then suddenly, she found herself being maneuvered against the wall, and there he was, all six foot four inches of her outraged stepbrother, staring at her with fire emanating from his eyes.

He was so close she could feel the heat radiating from his body. So close she could smell his scent. Again.

She swallowed hard, and he lifted his hand and wrapped it around her neck, gently, but enough to let her know that he was dangerous. That he could do whatever he wanted right then. Whatever he wanted. Strangle her, kiss her, she wasn't sure that she would stop him either way. And the realization was terrifying. It all crystallized. That first moment he had ever spoken to her, and it had been like being sliced into, the second time when it had felt that much more intimate, that much deeper.

This time, she felt it between her legs. This time, it had formed perfectly into exactly what it had always promised to be. It was real, deep, adult desire mixed with resentment and rage cultivated over the course of years. She had no control. She had been wrong. She had played with this man, and she had only played herself. If he wanted to take her right there against the wall where anyone could walk by, she would let him. And that was the realization that finally made her move.

As soon as she did, he released his hold on her, proving that he had never held her so tightly as it felt like he had. "Don't play with me," he said.

She caught her breath. "Maybe we should call a truce."

"You would like that. We are not in school anymore, and I have no investments in this game. But if you think that ignoring you means that I no longer hate you, I wish you to comfort yourself with the fact that I still do. Forever."

"Same," she said.

She didn't stay for dinner. She made arrangements to change the flight plan for her father's private plane and left an hour later. With the inescapable, lowering realization that Romeo might have actually won.

CHAPTER FIVE

Now

HEATHER WAS EXHAUSTED from crying. It had been a devastating night. Losing Giuseppe had been inevitable, but she hadn't really been prepared for it. How could you prepare to lose a parent? She had now done it in two very different ways. Sudden and expected. She couldn't recommend either one.

The funeral had been planned and coordinated, and executed within a day. She and Romeo hadn't had to do anything.

Nothing but try to figure out how to go on with the pain of losing their father.

Whatever Romeo thought of her, of her mother, it didn't matter. Giuseppe was her father in every way that mattered. Losing him left a void she didn't think could ever be filled.

Losing him was losing her last connection to the Accardi name. To the illusion she'd ever been part of the family. For her it wasn't about assets.

She wasn't even sure when the will reading was happening and the specter of it was filling her with anxiety every time she took a breath. Giuseppe had said she got half the estate. Romeo wouldn't be happy. An understatement, and who knew what other surprises the will would have?

In the meantime, Heather had been fielding phone calls, managing things that she would have expected Romeo to do, but he was remote and even more unfriendly than ever.

She couldn't wait to be rid of him.

Dealing with him was the bane of her existence. The scourge of her life.

Every embarrassing, humiliating, terrible thing that had happened to her had him tangled up in it. She just… despised him.

Complicating her grief and turning it into an endless tangle of anger on top of everything else.

Things had changed in the years since that last, explosive confrontation between the two of them. They had changed the way they dealt with each other. She had gone back to university after that failed, utterly ill-advised seduction attempt, and thrown herself into her studies. She had changed the sort of people she hung around with. Had switched her major from hospitality to English, and begun pushing toward a career in teaching, which had then shifted to publishing. And which was currently freelance, which gave her an ample amount of freedom, freedom that she knew had only come from the relative privilege she had started out with.

She was the daughter of a cleaner. And the world had opened up to her when her mother had married a wealthy man. She had gotten lost in private school games for a while. She liked to think that she had found a piece of herself from before, and done good work integrating it with the woman that she had become, discarding some parts, clinging to others. She liked to think that she had become a better person. Though whenever she was around Romeo she didn't feel like a better person. And currently, she didn't feel better at all.

The doorbell rang, and she went to answer it, not waiting for a member of staff.

She knew the man at the door. Gray haired and serious, it was Marcus Santos, Giuseppe's attorney.

It was time. The clock was ticking. The will.

"Hello, Mr. Santos."

"I'm very sorry to hear about your father."

Heather nodded. "Me too."

"I've come to read the will. He left me strict instructions to do it as quickly as possible because he was worried that things would become acrimonious between yourself and…" His sentence trailed off, his eyes traveling to a place behind Heather. And she knew why. She felt Romeo's presence without having to turn around.

"My father's will?"

"Yes," Marcus said.

"He was afraid that there would be an uprising if it wasn't read immediately?"

"Yes, Mr. Accardi," Marcus said, never looking away from Romeo. "He was."

Normally, Heather would've enjoyed watching somebody stand up to Romeo, but her chest still felt like a hollow cavity. Enjoyment was a distant thought.

They went with the attorney into the dining room. They sat at the table, and he read out very plainly the terms of the will. Romeo's mother was to get a stipend, relatively limited, but certainly enough. And the rest was to be split evenly between Romeo and herself. Including Accardi Industries.

"That's outrageous," Romeo said. "Heather is not part of the day-to-day running of the company."

"This is not up for debate."

"She was an *English major*," Romeo said, with the same disdainful tone he might have used if he'd called her a garbage collector.

"These are the terms of the will," the lawyer said.

"You got your way," Romeo said.

"I don't want it," Heather said, seeing it as simply another chain tying her to him.

"Will you sign it over to me?"

"Yes," she said. "For the monetary value."

"Then it will be done."

It was a double-edged sword. Trading the Accardi legacy for money meant severing ties she valued but...

She wanted to be free of him. She *needed* to be free of him.

She wanted to have no association with him whatsoever, and being part owner in a company with him was not the way to do that. But she could feel his rage. She knew where it came from. It was because his father had seen them as equal. Because he had given her exactly what he had given to Romeo, and Romeo felt entitled to more. To everything.

"All of the assets are to be divided evenly."

"Good," said Romeo. "We will liquidate it all. Everything other than the company, and we will split it. You see to that. I don't want to see her again. Not after today."

"You think I want to see you?"

"It's hard to tell with you."

"Then let me make it explicit," she said, holding up her middle finger.

"Do I need to send a police escort to get one of you away from the property?" Marcus asked.

"*No*," Romeo said. "Leave us."

"Yes," Heather agreed, her pulse pounding. "Leave us."

Marcus did, even if grudgingly. He kept looking back like he might have to suddenly intervene in a fistfight.

Romeo moved to the double doors of the dining room and closed them in a fluid motion.

"It is settled," he said. "I'll buy you out. We liquidate everything. We are not family. The Accardi empire is mine. The Accardi name is mine. It isn't yours, and it never has been. My father is nothing more than a deluded, sentimental old man who believed that a gold digger—"

"My mother was not a gold digger, and you know it. Your mother is a gold digger, one who is being taken care of, even after your father's death. You could be angry that they had an affair. I can understand that, but the love story, in the end, was your father and my mother, and that is not ambiguous. Your mother is a selfish, awful woman who has spent years making sure that you don't get to enjoy your life because you have to do her bidding." She'd seen the way he acted whenever Carla called or texted. The way he responded to her marching orders, abandoned holidays and family dinners and meetings to go to her.

His eyes were like black holes, filled with fire and loathing. "How dare you! How dare you speak to me like this! Of such things, when you came in here with nothing and are leaving with everything all because your mother was a homewrecker."

"The home was already wrecked, Romeo, be realistic. My mother was not responsible for the state of your parents' marriage."

"It is a good thing I am no longer responsible for you."

"You never were. You've never been responsible for me. What you have been is a vengeful, diabolical, seething…" She realized then that she was moving closer to him, and he to her.

"And you are nothing but a brat. The moment that you had access to money and to wealth, what did you become? No better than me, so you cannot claim a high road where we are concerned. You are a grasping, manipulative…"

And then, suddenly they were so close they were sharing the same air.

"I hate you," she said.

"No more than I hate you." Then he wrapped his arm around her waist and brought her body up against his. "And we never have to see each other again. Not after today."

Adrenaline coursed through her, excitement lighting her up. She could feel a pulse beginning to beat between her legs.

It reminded her of that night in the hallway when he had grabbed her throat. Of the night before that when she had climbed into his bed and he had come out of the shower naked.

But this time there would be no consequences. No consequences because they never had to see each other again. There would be no holidays. No family summers, no more dinners.

She would be free of him once and for all. He lifted his hand and traced her cheek with his knuckles. "I can think of no more fitting goodbye," he said, his voice low.

"Yes," she said, her body feeling like a stranger's now. She was driven. A need, and not a lovely, romantic desire, but this toxic, utterly forbidden desire she had always felt for her stepbrother.

Part of being free of him would be to have this.

She knew it. She had always known it. Even though her attempt at seducing him had been half thought out, and all the way stupid all those years ago, it had come from a place of realizing that a powder keg packed this tightly would always be a risk. It had to explode.

It had to.

With them, it might be murder, or it would have to be sex.

She would take the sex.

He reached his hand back, and grabbed a fistful of her hair, drawing her head back, exposing her neck, and then he lowered his head and kissed her.

Right there, where her pulse was beating at the base of her throat.

She let out a raw, completely unhinged cry of pleasure.

She had expected that the first thing he would do was kiss her mouth, but no, he trailed hot, violent kisses up her neck until he reached her lips, and then he consumed her. His mouth bruising, his tongue taking no prisoners as he plunged deep into her mouth. She began to tear at his clothes, his tie, as he began to remove her clothes from her body.

"You will no longer have any power over me," he panted as he tore her shirt away from her body, then popped her bra open at the front, filling his hands with her breasts before lowering his head and licking her nipples, pressing her breasts together so that he could devote attention to both, then sucking her hard until it hurt. She didn't feel any sort of hesitation. She didn't feel any hint of virginal nerves. This was how she knew absolutely and completely that Romeo Accardi had broken her long ago. Because this was what she had always craved. The violence of it. The darkness.

Nothing else had ever been able to compare. Why would she want candlelight and roses when she could have this?

This man who despised her so much, shaking as he rubbed his thumbs over her slick, tight nipples. As he had to inhabit his own despised desire for her. As he surrendered to it. Yes, they were both consumed with the sickness they shared, and that made it something glorious.

She was disgusted with herself. And yet that guilt, the shame only made it hotter.

It only made it that much more intense. And they had been building on this intensity for more than a decade.

Every barb, every cruel comment, every moment where they had undermined one another, every time they had played with one another, it had been leading to this. The most twisted foreplay, and it had brought them here.

She popped the buttons off his shirt and pulled it

away from him. Finally she was touching this body. He had taunted her with it for years, and finally it was hers.

It was her turn to lick him, dragging her tongue over his nipples, over his muscles, his chest hair.

"You're starving for me," he said, his face set into a sneer.

She nodded, and began to work his belt free.

"I knew I would see you on your knees for me one day, Heather. And now here you are, begging. Starving for it, aren't you?"

Where was her pride?

It was gone. He would be the one begging later—she would be sure of it—but for now it was her turn, and she would accept it. She would revel in the humiliation, because it was hers and hers alone. Because this was their great and terrible shame, and so while they could dole it out to one another, they would also both have to live fully in the consequences of it.

She let him guide her down to her knees as he opened the closure on his pants. As he let his hard cock free, the sight of him, a sight she had only been teased with before, that night when he had been wearing a towel and she had seen that he was hard for her, made her mouth water.

"You always have so much to say. Perhaps you will find your mouth better occupied now."

He thrust his hips forward, pressing the head of his arousal to her lips, and she took him in greedily, the first taste of him on her tongue sending her off into a spiral. She choked on him, gladly. Took him in as deeply as possible as he thrust his hips in time with the movements, touching the back of her throat.

And then he pulled himself away from her, his hand shaking, for all her shame. Because she might be the one on her knees, but he was the one on edge. She wiped the tears off her cheeks and stood up slowly, unzipping her skirt and kicking it away, slipping her panties off and being careful not to catch the fine lace fabric on her high heel. She had on nothing but those shoes, and the long pearl necklace she put on this morning. She lifted the necklace up and caught it between her teeth, watching as color mounted in his face. All the muscles in his body tense, on red alert.

"You're begging to be fucked," he said.

"And you're begging to fuck me."

He growled, and closed the distance between them, lifting her up and laying her down across the long table. That site of all those family dinners. And here it was, this perfect mockery of the familial connection that they had never been able to feel. Only hatred, mingled with extreme desire. Extreme need. All of it playing out now, in the most decadent way. Then he pulled her up to the edge of the table, lowered himself to his knees and buried his face between her legs. It was not a slow seduction. He began to consume her. Like all the hunger, all the anger of the past decade had suddenly burst inside of him, leaving him feral. He pushed two fingers inside of her, the stretching feeling making her gasp as he thrust deep and hard, his tongue playing over her clit as he tormented her. As he pushed the desire up to unbearable heights in her body. Until her orgasm broke over her like a wave, and she cried out his name, leaving deep grooves in his shoulders with her nails.

And that was fitting. Because that was the way it

was between them. So much pain, so much need. The pleasure was blinding, though the cost seemed worth it. So very worth it.

"I need you," he ground out, climbing up onto the table, and kissing her mouth, letting her taste evidence of her own arousal as he hooked her leg up over his hip and thrust deep inside of her with no quarter.

This was not making love.

But she had never believed that they would.

The need was far too sharp, far too intense. He claimed her, the brutality of it beautiful, at least to her. She was lost in it. Everything they were. In everything happening. The glide of his cock inside of her, this closeness that felt far more like torture than intimacy of any kind.

And when she came again, it was like she had gone somewhere else. Years and years of pent-up need all folding in on itself and taking her somewhere beyond her body.

He gripped her hips, his hold bruising as he came hard, spilling himself deep inside of her, the hot pulsing setting off another aftershock in her own body.

It was like a storm had passed through, passed through them, passed through the room. It was like everything she had ever wanted, and ever feared, had come to pass all in one moment. It was done. They were done.

She could finally breathe again. It was like she had exorcised the demon that had been inside of her for the last thirteen years. And now it was gone. Everything was gone. She could go on with her life; she could go on.

"I'm going to pack my things," she said, sitting up on the table, still naked, resting on her forearms.

He was already up, pushing his black hair back into place, looking remote and untouchable, as though he hadn't just been inside of her.

"No need to hurry."

"There is," she said. "There's no need for us to see each other again."

His eyes locked on hers. "No. There isn't."

She wondered then, what she was supposed to say. *Goodbye* felt like such a whimper after all that roar. Bland and meaningless. So she said nothing. She got dressed, while he stood there watching her as he had always done. With that vague air of distaste. That superiority.

He wasn't better than her. He had been a slave to the exact same feelings that she was. He wasn't better.

She wasn't great.

But at least it was finally over.

When she stepped outside she felt like she had been thrown back in time. To the first moment she had ever gone to the estate. She felt like a child. Confused, out of place. Like all those years hadn't happened. A sob rose in her throat. But then instead of giving in, she took a breath. And another. And another.

There had been life before all of this, before him.

There would be life after too.

CHAPTER SIX

HEATHER WAS HAVING so much time trouble concentrating on her work she was starting to worry that she was going to have to tell her author that she couldn't meet the time frame she had promised to get her notes back by.

She had felt so gray and awful ever since leaving the estate. And having all of the monetary things filtered through lawyers wasn't helping the way she had thought that it would. Because it felt impersonal and terrible, and she felt like she had been turned inside out. It was all evidence of just how much awfulness had passed between her and Romeo, and…

Her body couldn't forget. She kept herself awake all night, every night, reliving what had passed between them, and then in the morning she was exhausted, sick to her stomach.

The grief mixed with all of this was just too much to bear.

She was grateful that she was doing mainly remote work, but she also sort of wished that she did go into an office every day, because at least she would be forced to get dressed and interact with people. This was all virtual meetings and chats, and it made it far too easy for her to disguise that she was unraveling.

The missed deadlines would definitely betray her.

Her stomach lurched.

She just felt…

Not like herself. She was an orphan now. That was kind of a terrible realization. She knew that when you were an adult nobody thought of it that way, that's how it felt. Drifting and rootless.

She had thought that cutting ties with Romeo would feel like a triumph.

She had thought that maybe she would go on dates. Be a normal person.

Right after it had happened, when she was on an adrenaline high she had called Catherine, her roommate from college, and she had told her that she had finally gotten her stepbrother out of her system.

"Well, thank God," she said. "Now maybe you can have a functional relationship with a nice man who doesn't want to degrade you while he has sex with you."

Catherine had been joking, but then it had forced Heather to reflect on the fact that she and Romeo had gotten a fair amount of pleasure out of degrading each other. And then that had sent her into a spiral where she had spent the entire night replaying what had happened. The most intense, soul-searing moment of her entire life.

Why were things so complicated with him? It didn't make any sense. It should just be nothing. Especially after all that.

She put her glasses back on and tried to focus on her reading, and her stomach turned.

She felt so nauseous and gross this morning. For a while she had been blaming that on her lack of sleep. She always felt gross when she didn't sleep. But it felt more pronounced now, out of the vague nausea territory and into something a lot more…frightening.

She took a breath, and stood up, trying to stretch and ease the unsettled feeling in her stomach.

A message popped up on her computer, not in her office interface, but from Catherine.

You've been very quiet, and I'm starting to think I need to send someone after you.

I'm fine.

Are you?

Feeling a little bit sick today, actually. But I've been feeling rough the last month and a ½.

It's to be expected, I guess.

I guess.

Suddenly, she felt like she was about to lose her breakfast, such as it was, and she ran into the bathroom, where she cast up her coffee and biscotti.

She went back to her messages.

A little bit worse off than I thought, since I'm vomiting up my coffee, which I need to survive.

There was a long time between that message and a response.

I feel like this is a stupid question, but there's no chance that you're pregnant?

Heather stared at the message. And stared and stared.

There had never before in her entire life been a chance that she could be pregnant. Everything that had happened had cast such a haze over her that she hadn't been thinking clearly. She had been so busy cataloging how fuzzy her brain was that she hadn't thought at all about her cycle. She also hadn't thought about…

They hadn't used a condom.

She had felt so raw, so exposed, so stripped bare by the entire thing that she hadn't given that enough thought. Hadn't done anything in the aftermath to prevent pregnancy.

"Oh my God," she said. Out loud into the silence of the room.

Are you pregnant?

The question flashed up on the screen, and then her phone rang. She picked it up. "I don't know," Heather said, because she knew exactly what Catherine was about to do, and that was ask the same question again, but this time verbally.

"You need to get a test."

"It can't be… We only did it the one time."

"Surely you paid better attention in health class than that. Your education was really expensive."

"I know," Heather snapped. "But it's just… That can't be. I'm never supposed to have to deal with that man again."

"Did you use a condom when you had sex with that man?"

"No," she said.

"Heather…"

"I know."

"You can still… I know it's not ideal, and I know it's nothing that you would've planned, but you don't have to be connected to him if you don't want to be."

She sat with that, for a very long moment. And Catherine just let her. In the silence, in the reality of it all.

"I can't not tell him," she said.

"Why not? He's awful to you."

"I know that. I know that, but his father was so wonderful to me. He changed my entire life. And…" She swallowed hard. "My mom was a single mom. It was us against the world, and I'm alone."

"You're not alone. You have me."

"I know that. I'm extraordinarily grateful for it. But the truth is, I was just sitting here feeling so incredibly sad. My mother worked so hard in order to support us, and I don't even have to worry about that. I'm working because I choose to. My stepfather just…died and made me a multimillionaire, which isn't even fair. But it's the way that it is. It's what happened. I don't have any excuse for not taking care of the child, and if it wasn't Romeo it would be straightforward. I would just keep the baby and never tell the father. But he's going to know."

"You don't even know yet," Catherine said. "Have somebody go get you a pregnancy test. You're rich."

"I don't even have to be rich to do that—there are apps for that."

"Well. Send somebody."

So she did. And she waited. And waited. She and Catherine were messaging now instead of talking on the phone, as she paced around waiting for the test. Reality and denial were warring inside of her. It couldn't be possible. The odds of her getting pregnant after one sexual encounter seemed so…

Like fate.

No. She refused to believe that anything like fate was wrapped up in Romeo Accardi. Yes, it had been inevitable that they were going to do that. But inevitable that they were going to find themselves together forever?

No.

Then on top of that she had to contend with the fact that she might become a mother. That didn't scare her. That would actually make her happy. If it weren't for Romeo. He was the wild card. He was the problem.

The doorbell rang and she nearly jumped out of her skin. She buzzed the courier up to her floor, and they left the package outside. She waited for them to leave, then opened it up and took hold of the bag. With shaking hands she discarded the bag onto the floor, and began to unwrap the test on her way into the bathroom, leaving a trail of trash behind her. She read the instructions carefully—she had never even seen one of these out of the box in person before—and followed those instructions as carefully as possible. It seemed like a cruel thing that it took minutes for the test to reveal the answer. Both too short and too long.

But the two lines were inevitable. Undeniable.

She was pregnant with Romeo's baby.

Her stepbrother.

The man who hated her more than he hated just about anything else in the entire world.

That man.

She put her hand on her stomach. She was pregnant with his baby. Pregnant with his baby. It seemed laughable. It seemed ridiculous.

She called Catherine.

"It was positive."

"Do you want to change your mind? Because I will fly there immediately. I'll give you whatever you need. I'll help you."

"I'm not changing my mind. If there's one thing I've never been it's afraid of him. I'm not scared of him now. It's just…exhausting."

"Of course it is."

"You think I'm crazy."

"It's not up to me. You and he have some kind of connection that I can't understand. I've never met the guy, but I've seen pictures of him. I understand why you're attracted to him, but he's awful to you. I've never understood why you… You have feelings for him, Heather. That's always been obvious. He's half of what you talk about in any given conversation."

"My feelings for him are toxic and negative."

"I think you wish they were. Only that. Anyway, let me know how he reacts."

"I'm going to have to get on a plane. I can't tell him over the phone." Just thinking about it made her laugh. "I've never spoken to him on the phone. Of all the ridiculous things. But why would I? We don't like each other. We don't talk to each other. This is ridiculous."

"I agree. It's ridiculous. But you have to deal with him in the way that only you can."

So she did one of the first very rich person things she had ever done as a woman who'd gotten a substantial inheritance. She booked a charter on a private jet. And then she cried the entire way to Italy.

CHAPTER SEVEN

ROMEO WAS EXHAUSTED. Talking his mother down from her latest episode had been worse than any business negotiation he had dealt with. Sometimes he wondered if this was his life. Forever. Always flying across the world to where she was when she told him that she didn't want to live anymore. But what else could he do? She was his last remaining parent. His father had done terrible damage to her, and she had never recovered. She was always seeking to re-create that relationship with new men, new lovers, and it was never good. It was always toxic. And it was just…

On top of that he was still dealing with Heather. Still dividing up all of these assets to liquidate, working on the legal aspect of buying her out of his father's company. Her lawyers were being nitpicky with details, and he was about to…

He thought of her. Every night. And those thoughts left him hard and aching, and he couldn't even bring himself to go out and find another lover because she had haunted his libido in such a way that he couldn't exorcize the specter of her.

Every time he looked at another woman he saw her.

He had gone through bouts of this for a good portion

of the last decade. But never this strong. Now he knew what it was like. To taste her. To be inside of her.

He wanted to get drunk.

That was his singular goal as soon as he walked into his father's old home. Everything was boxed up, ready to sell. Except for what had been his father's office, and the bedroom that Romeo used. Also, that damned dining table was still sitting there. The scene of the crime.

He was filled with hate.

Right when he walked through the front door, he was confronted by his own personal ghost.

There she was, her hands clasped in front of her, her face white.

"What the hell are you doing here?"

"It's both of ours," she said.

"I'm well aware. But I thought that there was an implied agreement that I would handle all of this and you would simply take the money."

"There may have been that agreement. But things have changed."

"Why? Or did you decide you wanted more?"

Something sharp flashed in her eyes. "And what if I have? What if I decided that I want what's rightfully mine? To be part of this family, because I am. I am part of it. And you can resent me all you want, but your father saw me as a daughter. You've been trying to supplant me—"

"Don't do this. Not now. You never wanted to see me again, and yet here you are."

"Because things are complicated now," she said.

He saw tears in her eyes, the sloped set of her shoulders, the pale color in her face, and that was the first time he felt truly disquieted.

Because there was one thing that Heather had never shown him, and that was weakness. She was weak now—he could see it—but what he didn't know was why.

"What is it?"

"I've got to tell you something."

She sounded grave. Grave enough that he wondered if she was telling him that she had poisoned his father. Or something similar.

"What is it?"

"I…"

"Dear God, Heather, you have never had trouble telling me anything difficult. Hard truths are in fact your favorite thing to speak to me, so just go ahead and say it."

"I'm pregnant. With your baby, obviously."

It was like the world was crumbling and falling away. Pregnant? With his child? How could that be? How was it possible?

You know perfectly well how it's possible.

He had taken her like a rutting animal; he had taken no precautions whatsoever. He had assumed that she had taken some. Well, that was a lie. He hadn't assumed anything. He hadn't thought about it. Never in his life had he ever taken a woman without protection, and now not only had he done it, but he hadn't even been aware of it. He had been aware of nothing at the time other than his need to take her. Nothing other than the triumph of finally having her.

"It's impossible."

"I thought the same thing, but tests don't lie."

"You will be getting another test, one that I can see."

"Why would I lie about this? You would find out. I'm not an idiot. You're a very rich man, I know how paternity tests work. There's no way and no point to be lying about this, Romeo, none at all. I wanted to be free of you. This is the last thing that I want."

"Then why are you here at all? If you want to be free of me."

Panic was tearing through him, and he felt wounded; he felt the urge to wound her back, as he had always done. And in the back of his mind was the realization that this was going to send his mother to an extremely dark place. A child with the daughter of the woman who had caused her so much pain?

This was untenable.

It was unimaginable.

"I can raise the child by myself. But if I do that, you can't be involved at all. You can't claim them. You can't... There is no middle ground when it comes to this baby, Romeo. There can't be."

He stared at her, and he couldn't even begin to describe the feeling that was flooding him. The intense possessiveness, the anger. "I would never deny my own child."

His own distance from his father echoed inside of him now. The sense of rejection. He would never, ever consign a child to such a feeling. What a horrendous thought. What an evil thing to suggest.

"You know how we are," she said. Her teeth were chattering now, and she looked sick. "We spent years living to hurt each other. When we are left to our own devices the choices we make are poor. There have to be…protections. Rules. If you want to be in this child's life, we have to get married."

"You dare come in here and make demands of me? Prove correct the thing I thought about you all those years ago? You were trying to get me to impregnate you then, weren't you? I always suspected it."

"No," she said, vehemently. "And I don't need you to. I was left just as much as you. This has nothing to do with trying to get anything, but it has everything to do with being the child that was always on the outside. Think about it. This child would never truly belong if we didn't get married. I would marry someone else, give the child some siblings, and they would only be half of that family. You would do the same. Who would that child belong to? And what would happen to them? I know what it's like. I loved your father so much, Romeo, and you never accepted me. You made me feel like I was an outsider all of my life, and I will not allow it."

"Why do you think you're in a position to allow anything? One way or the other. Why do you think—"

"If you don't agree, then I will fight you with all of my resources, and I will paint a picture of you that isn't flattering at all."

"And what will that do to our child?"

"You have choices, Romeo, you just don't like them."

"What will a marriage look like between the two of us? We can't even be in the same room without wanting to kill each other."

"I know. It's terrible. An awful situation and a terrible idea. But from where I'm sitting we don't have another choice. We need to do what we must for this child."

"So for eighteen years you expect us to live in a prison cell with one another?"

The truth was, he would've demanded marriage. He would have. Because he would not allow any child of his to be born and stigmatized the way that she was. He had been part of that stigma. He knew it. He couldn't deny it. And he had seen how cruel the other children could be. Even when she had been the stepdaughter, they had whispered behind her back. She had friends, plenty of them.

But…

The trouble was, she was scratching the surface of the deep truth.

A child who was the product of a union between step-siblings who had a reputation for long hating each other was going to face extreme ostracization. And it would be only their fault. They would've created the situation. And so it was up to them to mitigate the damage. He had already lived thirteen years of hell where Heather was concerned. What were eighteen more years of it?

It nearly made him laugh. They both thought that they were going to be free.

And yet, when had he ever been free? He had been thinking about her constantly since that moment. He had been obsessed with her.

For so much longer even than the last month and a half.

"We will have to construct a narrative," he said. "One of romance."

"Why?"

"You're thinking about our child, and that I find admirable. In some ways. But what you're forgetting is the fact that you and I have a reputation for hating each other. It is well known. Particularly in the circles that I'm in. Not unknown in yours. If you want to nip gossip in the bud, then it must... There must be a story. It can't be that we hate-fucked on the dining room table."

Her face turned red, and he felt his own body go warm in response to mentioning what had happened between them.

"I guess. I guess you're right. And what will our marriage look like?"

"I don't know," he said, and nothing pained him more than admitting that he didn't have an instant, immediate plan. It was infuriating, in fact, but there was no roadmap for this. He was a man who was accustomed to control, but with her, he was always out of it.

With her, everything was always near destruction.

"We will have to draw up paperwork. Very clearly defined paperwork."

"It's almost as if you don't trust me."

"I don't. You spent years making my life miserable, Romeo. You deliberately hurt me from the moment that I first came into your life, and you can blame the fact that our parents had an affair. That hurt your mother, but you were mean to me from the moment that we met. Nothing more than a snob. The thing that you now realize you have to protect your child from is you."

Her words lanced him through the heart.

"You grew up without a father," he said. "And your pain is that of a stepchild. I understand that. My pain comes from growing up in a war zone. And having to deal with the consequences of the fallout when that war zone exploded. I have just come from talking my mother down off a ledge, quite literally. She is mentally fragile. And I am the only one that bears the burden of caring for her. If you marry me, then you will assume part of that burden."

He didn't know why he said that. Maybe because he wanted her to feel the weight of it. He knew that he could trust no one but himself with his mother's care.

No one knew the extent of it, but she'd begged him to never tell. Why give Giuseppe the satisfaction of knowing he'd hurt his ex-wife's mental health this way? Why tell anyone when it was something he could bear alone?

"I... I'm sorry. Though I doubt that your mother wants anything to do with me."

"She won't have a choice. You're going to be my wife. The mother of my child."

The words tasted acidic on his tongue. How could this be happening?

They both stood there, with unspoken truths pulsing between them. He could ask her to terminate. He could say that he didn't want anything to do with her and the child. Neither thing was a real option in his mind. He had lost his father. And this was a link to him in some ways. It was carrying on what had been ended.

Perhaps if his father hadn't only recently died he would make a different decision. He wouldn't feel so compelled to do this. But he did now. He did now.

"We will have our lawyers draw up paperwork for the marriage. Detailed prenuptial agreements, and conduct requirements."

"Oh, that sounds lovely."

"You and I both know that we can't be trusted."

She blinked. "No. I don't suppose we can be."

"Obviously now the sale of the estate will not go forward," he said.

She bit her lower lip.

"What?" he asked.

"I moved back to New York for my job. I don't see myself living here."

"We will split the time between the two, but this place is now the legacy of our child."

"Now that there's a baby we're not burning it to the ground anymore?"

He chuckled. "We lost that privilege."

"I don't understand any of this. It's like no matter how hard I try to get away from you there is a rope that keeps pulling me back."

"It might be a tripwire," he said.

They were silent for a long moment. "I didn't do this on purpose. The idea that I could've planned it… It's ridiculous."

The vulnerability in her words stopped him. Shamed him. He did tend to see her as a character. A viper spitting venom. A creature, rather than a whole human being. But here she was now, a woman pregnant with his baby. She was not simply…

He had built her up in his mind. His enemy, for all intents and purposes.

"What was the purpose of you coming into my room all those years ago?" It had always astonished him that she had done that.

"To seduce you," she said. "Only when I got there did I realize that I was in over my head."

"You wanted to seduce me? Even then?"

"You're not a fool, Romeo, you know what happened

between us to create this situation. Do you think that it just appeared there? It didn't. You know that."

"But even then…"

"I told my roommate Catherine about you. She said it sounded like we needed to work it out of our systems. I agreed then. Except I was a virgin and… Your anger was more comfortable than the other things that I felt."

"You were far too young to feel something like that."

He didn't know why he needed to resist that.

"I was eighteen. I knew what I wanted, but I didn't. It's different now. That's why it happened. I knew what I wanted."

"Some sexual experience taught you the extent of your feelings, I assume?"

She laughed and looked away from him. "No. Does that make you feel good, Romeo? You got my virginity after all."

Shock tore through him. It had never occurred to him that she could've possibly been a virgin, not with the way that they had attacked each other. Not with the intensity of the encounter. Or the skill with which she had tormented his body.

"Impossible."

"You are so arrogant," she said. "You think that you know me. You think that you know me better than I know myself? You think that you know me better than all the evidence around you. You just think that you know. Back then I was somehow grasping and greedy enough to try to seduce you, while also knowing that I had stolen your father from you. That I wouldn't need anything from you because I had so effectively cut my way into his affections that I would be getting the lion's share of the inheritance anyway. And now you think you know more about my body than I do? You bursting in and ruining what was supposed to be my first time actually caused emotional damage."

"I should've let that drunken frat boy have his way with you? I'm not the villain in that story—that clumsy, grasping bastard is the villain. I saved you."

"Why?"

"Because it was the decent thing to do. Because I wanted you for myself. Do you have any idea the manner of torture that you have meted out to me for the past ten-plus years? I have been in hell. You appeared and turned my entire life upside down, and then you had the audacity to be beautiful with it."

He was breathing heavily, his heart raging.

"And this is exactly why we have to make legal deals," she said, moving away from him. He could see the pupils in her eyes dilate, darken. She wanted him. Just as he wanted her. Even now. Even as they were facing down the prospect of having a child. Having to deal with each other for the rest of their lives because they would always be linked. Now, they would always be family. The thing that they were running from they had inadvertently run toward.

Or perhaps it hadn't been an accident. It was so difficult to say with her. Always.

"The truth is," she said quietly, "you don't know me. Maybe you have wanted me all this time, but that doesn't mean that you know me. I am a creation of your imagination, and very little else."

"And does that mean that you can accept that perhaps I'm the same to you?"

"You've been cruel to me."

"As you have been to me."

He let out a long, slow breath. "I will have the estate put back in order. Go back to New York, and get everything sorted that you need sorted. My lawyer will be in contact with yours and we will begin drawing up the prenuptial agreement. There will also be a separate contract regarding expected spousal behavior."

"Oh, how lovely."

"You of course are free to revise it and add what you would like."

"Fantastic."

"The final revision will be done in person. I will require your presence back here. You will live here primarily for the duration of the pregnancy, I assume that you can arrange remote work with limited time in the office?"

She looked filled with spite. "Yes. I can."

"Good. Let us start this off on the right foot, and not in opposition to one another."

"I'm happy to do that, but that doesn't mean letting you be in charge of everything."

"Of course not."

"You say that, but I don't trust you."

He tightened his jaw, looked at her. "Perhaps we must start trusting one another."

She met his eyes, the gold in them fiery. "Trust has to be earned."

CHAPTER EIGHT

THE FIRST COPY of the contract came through while Heather was in the middle of meeting with client to arrange her time away. She wasn't able to look at it until she was in a car headed back to her apartment. By the time she was upstairs in her room she was fuming. She forwarded the contract to her lawyer along with a screed of notes that she trusted her to turn into a coherent revision.

Then she called Romeo. A video call so that he could see the anger in her eyes, because why miss out on that opportunity?

But as ever, she wasn't prepared for the impact of him. Why was he still beautiful to her? After everything.

You're jumping headlong into a marriage with this man. What do you think that's going to look like?

That was the scary thing. It was difficult to say what a marriage to that man would look like. Very difficult indeed. And yet she didn't see another option.

"I assume that you got the paperwork?"

"This is patriarchal nonsense," she said.

"What exactly?"

"Well, particularly the control that you're asking to have over my sex life."

"If you're unfaithful to me I will take you for everything that you have," he said.

Rage flashed through her. "And you?"

"You're welcome to submit a return argument."

"So I have to live like a nun or I have you as my only option?"

He was wearing a black suit. His black tie was slightly loose, and his hair was disheveled. It made her wonder if he had been with someone else. Even now.

Thinking of him that way… It made her so angry. It also sent a shiver of desire through her body.

"The question I have for you," he said, his gaze meeting her directly through the camera lens, "is if you think we can live in close quarters without touching each other."

"I am willing to try. Also, expect my response soon." She hung up the call, and paced around her apartment before stripping off all her clothes and getting in the shower, turning it on cold. The thing was, she had suggested marriage thinking about the baby, and really not about them. In her head she had thought that maybe they could live separate lives, but have some kind of protection. Not be in real relationships with anyone else, maybe, but…

Maybe she had thought they could live like they always had. Like stepsiblings raising a baby together while he independently conducted his affairs and she worked on figuring out who else she could possibly have an affair with.

He was trying to claim ownership of her. But did that mean that he wanted her? And why did that make her feel special? And not outraged?

She sent her lawyer four more emails of suggested addendums after she got out of the shower, and then waited for the response.

It went on like that for six weeks. While she wrapped everything up in New York, went to the doctor to judge the viability of the pregnancy—why go through all this if there was no baby?—threw up daily and arranged to have her mail forwarded.

They hadn't spoken in that time. It was all lawyers, but he'd insisted they meet in person to go over the final draft.

He had asked that she meet him at his office in London, before they would go back to Italy together. She hadn't been to the office in years. Not since her stepfather was in charge. Romeo had acquired the company to function beneath his own luxury travel conglomerate six years earlier, with the blessing of his father. In preparation for the day when he would have ultimate ownership. She could actually understand why he was angry that she had been given half of the control.

Romeo had used his connections, his education and his personal knowledge of the industry to begin his own company that didn't work in direct competition with his father, but rather complemented it. He had started an airline, and later a multitude of cruise lines. From luxury yacht travel to large, affordable cruise ships. Meanwhile his father owned one of the largest hotel chains in the world. Now they were all under one umbrella, and Romeo was certainly more qualified to attend to any of that than she was.

She didn't even want it. There was a reason that she had ended up ditching her degree in publicity. She had decided that she wasn't going to pursue a place in the Accardi business empire.

She loved books. All kinds. When she'd been younger it had been escapism while she'd waited out long hours with her mother cleaning, and then when she'd been older it had made the situation with Romeo manageable, in a strange way. She read all kinds of books—horror, thrillers, romance, mysteries. It made her think of herself as a heroine and him as her antagonist; it made her feel brave.

Plus, she had her stepfather's money to keep her from penury, which she'd found was a big asset in publishing. It was a passion job, more than it was a job for the money.

It was also funny now, because she and Romeo were enmeshed. Deeper than her owning part of the company could ever make her.

She took the high-speed elevator up to the top floor, and didn't find Romeo in his office. She got a text directing her to the boardroom down the hall.

The room was completely private, no windows on the door. She swallowed hard, and then walked in.

There might not be any windows out into the office, but the entire exterior wall was glass, offering a view of the streets below. They were more than forty floors up, so she knew that while she had a view of the world, the world did not have a view of them.

Her heart felt like it was being squeeze by a giant fist.

He wasn't in there yet. She had a feeling that was by design. She sat down at the head of the table. That would make him angry.

She despised herself with a little thrill of adrenaline

that raced through her at the thought of making him angry. She got off on that. She was going to have to work on that, probably.

The door opened, and there he was. All in black, looking sharply pressed. His gaze flicked to where she sat, and then he walked down the length of the table, taking his seat completely opposite her.

He got out his briefcase, the sound of the locks being opened loud in the relatively quiet room. He took out a stack of papers and tapped the edges once on the edge of the table with a crack, and then slid them across toward her.

"This is where we're at," he said, indicating the contract.

He had left it deliberately out of her reach. She stood up and walked to the center of the table, suddenly aware that the V-neck on her shirt was quite low. When she bent down to grab the papers, she watched his gaze, noticed the way that he looked at her cleavage.

The power play aroused her, and she had not come here to be turned on.

But then, she supposed if she didn't want to be turned on she shouldn't consent to share the same air as Romeo.

She began to look down the prenuptial agreement. If either of them broke the stipulations of the agreement, the other one would be given full custody, and a sizable share of the other's assets. They had both agreed to that. They had both agreed that the shackles needed to be tight, because what made sense now might become difficult for them to abide by in the future.

But when she reached the part about marital conduct, she stopped. That had been the most contentious part.

Because what they had agreed was that either they had no control over each other's sexual conduct, or all of it. The current version of the contract said that all extramarital sexual encounters had to be consented to by those within the marriage. And that there would be consequences if the affair ever became public.

She looked up at him. "I think that this covers everything."

"I have added another page," he said.

"Have you?"

"Yes. For you and I to go over and make adjustments to." He took a pen out of his briefcase and clicked the top once.

She turned the page. There were addendums to what she had previously seen.

In the event that both parties decide to conduct a sexual relationship with each other then sex outside the marriage becomes unacceptable.

She looked up at him. "You think that's going to happen?"

"Keep reading."

Provided that the sexual relationship is satisfying to both parties. Wherein all kinks and desires should be catered to and orgasm shall be achieved by both.

Her face went hot. "All kinks?"

"Why take anything off the table before you've tried it?"

Was he trying to goad her? Make her run? Make her freak out?

Oh, please, asshole. We've been at this for too long.

Her heart was beating rapidly, her face hot, and she took her own pen out and made an amendment to kinks, and to the section about orgasms. She slid the paperwork across the table to him. His dark eyebrows raised high. "Two orgasms to every one of mine?"

She threw the pen down and leaned back in her chair. "Women are multi-orgasmic, Romeo. If you're not up to overachieving, certainly I can find someone who is."

"Oh, you misunderstand me. The only question is why stop at two?"

Her throat went tight. "I assume we'll be busy sometimes."

He looked back down. "I think you might want to leave some of these things on the table."

"I don't need you to *spank* me."

"Don't you? Sometimes it seems as if you're asking for punishment."

"Not interested," she said, her heart beating faster, her pulse beating rapidly at the base of her throat, calling her a liar. Oh no. She was lying. His eyes continued to meet hers as he pushed the contract back toward the center of the table. She went and retrieved it. She crossed out the part she had added about spankings, bondage and other forms of submission. But her pride wouldn't let her leave it at that.

And so she took it upon herself to add a new section.

She passed the paper back to the middle of the table. Made him stand up, and walk over to the center of the table, where she watched him closely, every line in his body, the way that the suit fitted him. He slid the paper back with him, back to his seat at the table. He read what she had written and looked up at her. "You want me to beg?"

She nodded. "Yes. I will require begging. For what you want."

His lips curved into a smile. "And praise."

"Seems fitting."

"I thought so. That is of course, if we decide to pursue a sexual relationship inside marriage."

"Yes," he said. "Inside marriage. That is precisely what the paperwork covers."

That hung heavily between them.

After they got married, if they were to touch each other then the agreement changed. Then it became all of these paragraphs, all of these amendments. Punishment and begging.

But if they didn't touch each other then they were free to pursue other parties.

But all of that was only when they were married. It wasn't now.

Crucially. It wasn't now.

He stood up, and began to walk toward her, loosening his tie as he did so, and then, shocking her entirely, he began to slowly lower himself to his knees in front of her. He put his hands on her thighs, and began to push her skirt up her hips.

Electricity struck her, like a wave. Her heart was pounding so hard she thought she might sit. Except…

She was hot. Dizzy. Desperate.

"Is this what you had in mind?"

She had on thigh-high pantyhose—because she couldn't stand full-on types; it wasn't because she was trying to be sexy—but he lowered his head and licked the place where the lace met her skin.

She gripped the edge of her chair, watching her stepbrother's face as his tongue glided over her skin.

She gasped when he reached up, gripped her panties and pulled them to the side, exposing her as he pressed her legs wider, and dragged his tongue through her slick folds. The light shone bright through that window, and she felt scalded by it. So connected to what was happening. To the fact that it was him between her legs. This was happening again.

But it was okay. Because they had paperwork, but they hadn't signed it yet. It was okay, because it was paperwork meant for after they got married, and they weren't married yet.

Later. Later they could practice keeping their hands off of each other. Later, they would focus entirely on their child. Later.

But right now she was desperate for him. Right now, he was pleasuring her with such intensity that she didn't think she would ever recover from it. He sucked her deep into his mouth as he pushed two fingers inside of her and brought her closer and closer to the edge. It was happening so embarrassingly fast. She couldn't have resisted him if she wanted to. It was like it was inevitable. When the wave crashed over her, she cried out his name. And when he looked up at her, there was a satisfied smile on his face. "There was one."

Then he lifted her up out of the chair, brought her down on the boardroom table. Funny that it was the second time she had had sex, and also the second time on a table. Well, maybe there would be something funny about it later. Right now, she was just desperate. Tearing at his clothes and trying to get his skin underneath her hands. She tore his tie off, tore his shirt open and pressed her palms against his ridged abdomen. He was unbuckling his pants, as quickly as possible, freeing himself and thrusting deep inside of her as he unbuttoned her shirt so that he could palm her breasts.

It was completely savage and lacking in finesse. It was wild and hard. It was wonderful.

She cried out his name right before he lost control, and the two of them went over the cliff together.

His forehead was pressed against hers. "There. You had two to my one. I'm already practicing keeping your commandments."

She couldn't believe it happened again. Except of course it had. If they could think about it, they wouldn't be in this place. If they could control themselves, they wouldn't have been here to begin with.

Now that they had acknowledged it, now that they'd done the paperwork, it seemed like there was no more restraint left.

She looked at the paperwork sitting there at his end of the table. They would sign that, and she had a feeling there was almost no point pretending that it wouldn't end up here again. But those amendments wouldn't matter. But maybe they…

Maybe she could find someone else. Maybe this was just the discovery of sex. As she lay there on the glossy boardroom table, with that place between her legs still throbbing, it felt entirely disingenuous. But she wanted to hope that it was possible. Wanted to believe that it could be true.

But then the obverse would also be true. He would have other women.

And just the thought of that made her feel violent.

"You look angry. Which is not unusual when you are around me, but it is unusual for a woman I've just thoroughly ravished."

"I'm just thinking about logistics," she said, getting up off the table and putting herself back in order as he did the same.

"Then I didn't do my job correctly."

"You did just fine. It's only that we find ourselves in an extraordinary situation."

"Is there any chance you'll ever speak to me like I'm a human being?"

The question, asked with such gravity and sincerity, shocked her. She met his gaze. "I…didn't think you wanted that."

"It isn't a matter of wanting—it seems that it would be a better way for us to be."

"We have a zero percent success rate not shagging each other's brains out when a table is near recently, and I'm not really sure what to do with that. So being human or not human is sort of the least of my worries right now."

"Understandable."

She had the sudden, disorienting thought that they had done absolutely everything backward. She hated him, down to the very marrow of her bones, but it didn't even come from a deeply realized place. She had sex with him, but she didn't really know him. They had negotiated this entire marriage on paper. She understood why they needed it. She had even been part of insisting on it. But they had always had something between them. Whether it was the baggage of what had happened in his parents' marriage, or the reality of their relationship because of their parents' marriage. Now the baby. She didn't know what it was like if they were just Heather and Romeo. She had no idea at all.

He looked…not softer now, but perhaps a little bit more human. His hair was a mess now, his tie loose…

"When I called you, you hadn't just had sex with another woman, had you?"

"Excuse me."

"Did you? Because you looked a lot like this."

"I haven't touched anyone since you and I were together. How could you think that I would?"

"I don't know you. And even more crucially, I have no reason to believe that what happened between us meant anything to you."

He moved over to the boardroom table again, and rested his knuckles on the top of it. He looked down at the surface of the table. And then up at her. "What happened between us was more than ten years in the making. What happened between us stole my ability to think critically. And I am not a man who— Of course you don't even know that. Because you think of me as someone who is driven by emotion, because when I'm around you it is nothing but sparks and anger, but that is not how I am in my life."

Well, that didn't fit her narrative and she didn't like it at all.

"How would I ever know that?" she sputtered.

"You wouldn't," he said. "You would never know. Just as I know nothing of you other than your petulance, your vindictiveness. Your…softness when you are naked. The way that you taste."

It made her want to kiss him. There had been no kissing this time. Funny how they fell upon each other with such ferocity, but didn't engage in any of the tenderness. Or perhaps not funny at all.

She moved to the end of the table, and grabbed hold of the nearest pen, signing the paperwork with a flourish. "This agreement suits me. I will honor it. Down to every last detail."

"I sense a caveat in there."

"I think that we need to get to know each other. I think that we should practice abstinence while we…get to know one another."

"Excellent. I propose we get to know one another after we announce the engagement."

With that, he walked back to his briefcase, and took out a ring box. He held his hand out, and she went and took it from him. She opened the box slowly, and examined the ring inside. "It was your mother's," he said.

The realization of that hit her square in the chest. "My mother's."

Of course she hadn't had it all this time, because Giuseppe had kept it. She hadn't even thought of it in the aftermath of his death. "Will you wear it?"

It felt like such a double-edged sword coming from him, because he had never warmed to her mother, and had never accepted the relationship between her and his father. And yet for her it held great significant meaning. For her, it mattered.

She took the ring out of the box and slipped it on. "Thank you," she said.

She decided that she was going to take it the way that it had meaning for her, rather than the way it had meeting for him.

He was silent for a moment. "Your mother was very kind to me," he said. "Almost unfailingly. When I was not kind in return."

There was something so heavy about the admission. An olive branch that she hadn't seen coming.

"She thought you were a very brilliant mind."

She had been kind to Romeo, but she had concerns about his strained relationship with Heather. But he was Giuseppe's son, and even if he was difficult, her mom had felt affection for him because she loved Giuseppe so much.

"Thank you," he said. He looked like he was about to say something else, when his phone rang and he grabbed it quickly. His brow creased as he answered. "Yes?"

He spoke in German, quickly and decisively, and she had no idea what he was saying. There was a placating edge to his tone.

When he hung up, he looked like a haunted man. "I am going to have to fly to Vienna to see my mother."

"Oh. Is she…unwell?"

"She often is. I told you, there've been mental health issues. Ongoing for years. I am going to have to tell her about our engagement, she is already in a bad place."

"Would it help if I went?"

He considered that for a moment. "I… I don't know."

"What if I went with you," she said, looking to offer an olive branch that was in a similar vein to the one that he had extended to her. If there was one thing that was true about them both, it was that they both loved their mothers. Very much. They both could relate to each other in that way.

"You can come with me if you like. I will…evaluate the situation and see if I want your intervention."

She nodded. "That's fair."

It felt strange, to come to an agreement with him. While the touch of his body still echoed inside of her. While all the lingering memories of every poisonous and terrible thing they had ever said to each other hung between them. While the knowledge that she was pregnant with his baby settled over her.

He packed everything up, and they walked out of the boardroom. She felt disoriented now, getting to the elevator. A wave of sadness washed over her as it began to descend. "I miss your dad," she said.

"So do I," he returned.

She looked at him out of the corner of her eye. Shock weighing heavy at the center of her stomach. "I didn't think that you…"

"You didn't think that I love my father?"

"You were angry at him. Most of the time."

"Yes. I was. He distanced himself from me."

"You distance yourself from him," she said. "You were so angry after the divorce and—"

"Yes. I was a teenager when it happened."

That realization rocked her. Because of course he was. He was a child. He reacted like a child. Most of the interactions that she had had with him that been toxic and soul searing and affecting had been when he was an angry teenage boy. She had also been a teenager, so she hadn't handled any of it all that well.

But the stunning, jarring revelation that any strained

relationship that had remained had probably been due in large part to Giuseppe letting a teenage boy's reaction to something dictate the whole rest of his relationship with his son was... It was painful.

"I think he believed that you hated him," she said. She felt honor bound to defend her stepfather.

"I'm sure he did. You were also completely uncritical of him, and I imagine that was a much more satisfying relationship."

"That isn't the only reason that he cared about me."

Romeo frowned. "Of course not. Of course it's not the only reason he cared about you, but you can see that it would be more rewarding to have a relationship with a child that thinks you're a superhero, versus a relationship with one who sees you as a man who could do nothing right. And for that, I carry fault. I am sorry my father and I did not get to mend that."

Of course, they hadn't been entirely estranged; she knew that. They had still seen each other at holidays, and he had often been there just to visit. But you could feel the strain in the relationship, and of course Romeo's relationship with Heather's mother had never been easy.

And now both of them were gone, which meant that all that was left was regret over what might've been. What could have potentially been if things had been different. If he had handled things differently. If his father had.

"I'm sorry," she said. "Of course you were a teenager. Of course that should've been handled differently."

"Family is complicated," he said.

Particularly theirs.

"Well, the hope is that we make ours a little less complicated."

"We're stepsiblings getting married and having a baby. I don't think there's anything less complicated about that."

"You don't already have a wife." She said that dryly, but she wondered if he'd be offended. Judging by the hollow laugh he gave in response, he wasn't.

"There is that."

They didn't continue the conversation until they got on his private plane. Which was of course the most luxurious aircraft she'd ever been on. But that was what he did.

"This is extraordinary. Did you design it?"

"I had a hand in it," he said.

"More than just a nepo baby."

"Thank you," he said, pouring himself a glass of Scotch. She was instantly envious that she could not do the same.

"Somehow I don't feel like you're actually thanking me."

"Maybe I am. Maybe you need to start taking what I say at face value."

"Maybe," she said.

"Here we are, almost getting along."

"Almost."

"I'm going to take you to my favorite hotel in Vienna, and I will leave you there while I speak to my mother. I need to tell her that you're having a baby. I need to tell her that we're getting married. I will have to get my read on the situation."

"I can't apologize to you for our parents having an affair."

He looked at her, his expression intense, a muscle ticking in his jaw. "I never expected you to."

"You blamed me for it, at least in part. Somewhere, deep inside of yourself, you did."

"I suppose. You were emblematic of what had changed. And again, I was a teenage boy. I don't…"

"You were," she said. "But later you were a grown man who continued to hate me."

"I did decide that you had tried to trap me when you were in my bed all those years ago."

"Is that really why you hated me?"

He took a long sip of his Scotch. He rested his arms on the soft leather chair he was sitting in, his legs wide. It was an obscenely masculine posture, and she regretted that she found it so attractive. She regretted that she found him so attractive. But then, that was the story of her life. Rage at Romeo, fantasize about Romeo, repeat. Forever.

"I was angry at myself. For wanting you. It's like I always knew that the consequences would be heavy. Here we are."

Was that true? Had there always been this between them? The potential for this life-altering event, had it always been somewhat inevitable?

"I hated you because you were mean to me," she said, looking out the window as the plane reached its soaring altitude.

"Now, I don't believe that. I was mean to you, but you felt something else too."

"Do you know why I was a virgin?"

"No. Because I don't know anything about you, not functionally."

"It's because you messed my sexuality up. I'm convinced of it. I trained myself to want this disdainful, awful man, who promised pain as much as he did pleasure, and I have never been able to figure out how to want someone else. Someone who's nice to me. Someone who wants my company. I want you. And that is a truly disturbing fact. I met you too soon. You shaped my sexuality, and I think you might've broken it."

She felt exposed by that, but then she'd given herself to him on a table, so what was exposing at this point?

He smiled. Slowly. "Feels good, though. Doesn't it?"

She laughed. "Yes. It does. That's how I got myself pregnant. Why are you being a a pain when I can't drink?"

"I am very sorry."

"Somehow I don't think so."

The two of them decided to do work for the rest of the flight, and didn't carry on a conversation, and when they arrived at the hotel in Vienna, she was delighted by how glorious it was. Heather had gotten used to luxury. It was part of being an Accardi. But that didn't mean she didn't find it delightful in about a hundred different ways whenever she got to experience it.

The old, historic building with its palatial interior was a sight to behold. And the penthouse room that they were in had fabulously Baroque furnishings. It was all over-the-top and utterly ostentatious, and she adored it. She walked into one of the bedrooms, and her breath was taken away by the sight of the blue canopy bed. "This place is fantastic."

"I'm glad you enjoy it," he said. "And now I have to go. I am sending a dress for you to wear to dinner to-night."

"When did you decide that?"

"During the plane ride. Tonight we will go out. Since we're doing things out of order. I thought we might want to go on our first date."

CHAPTER NINE

"WHAT IS IT that has you upset?" Romeo asked, when he arrived at his mother's bedside. It was never a good sign when she wasn't getting out of bed.

"I feel like I haven't had the chance to properly grieve your father. Because I don't hate him. I love him. He was the love of my life."

Romeo clenched the back of his teeth together. It was difficult when she was like this, because it wasn't true. He knew that. She had hated his father for more years than she had ever loved him. But now that he was dead she was wailing as if they had been lovers only yesterday.

He wanted to get back to Heather. And that was a strange thought indeed. She had been beautiful on the plane. And his body still echoed with the satisfaction of their earlier coupling.

He wanted her again. Tonight in that suite. And he knew that she wouldn't resist him. Of course she would.

She wanted this as badly as he did. They wanted each other equally.

"It just feels pointless going on. All of these years without him have been like wandering in a desert and there is no more purpose."

"I do have good news for you," he said.

She looked at him, her eyes filled with tears. "What is it?"

"You're going to be a grandmother."

Just like that, it was as if a light had turned on; the sun shone upon her. He got an adrenaline rush, a fiery, intense feeling that he only ever caught otherwise when he was closing a business deal. A sense of triumph. Of winning. He had found the magic combination to fixing her this time. This was how it always was. She was devastated. And only he could fix it.

He had fixed it. Now he just had to break the news to her that Heather was the mother.

Because of course his mom had hated Lisa more than just about anything. That she had been left for a housemaid, one who was inferior to her in every way, had been galling for her self-esteem, and he truly did believe that she had been heartbroken on top of it.

She had carried ill will for Lisa all these years.

It was one reason that Romeo had never been able to find a way to have a good relationship with his stepmother, even though, the truth was, she had been a kind woman.

Even though, he knew, his father had had a more peaceful life with Lisa that he ever would have with Carla.

"Yes. And I'm getting married."

"That is wonderful news," she said. "You must have a big fabulous wedding. And you should do green. I look wonderful in green, and the mother-of-the-bride dress will be stunning."

"Yes. Of course there will be a big wedding. One fit for our family."

"You will get married in Vienna, not in Italy."

"There is no reason we can't have the wedding in Vienna."

It was beautiful here. And it would make a fine venue for a wedding. He could see no reason that Heather would object to the idea. They had enough money to fly all the guests here. And besides, he owned an airline.

"And who is she?"

And this was where it would be difficult. "Heather. Gray."

The shock on his mother's face nearly blotted out the earlier win.

"I am sorry if you find that difficult. I found it surprising. But…"

"You love her?"

He didn't know what the right answer was here. Couldn't quite grasp what she was looking for.

"Of course I do. I wouldn't marry her if I didn't."

She nodded. "Of course. There is something about those women, I suppose. Something about them that is quite irresistible."

"I don't know about that. But in the grief over the last few years, Heather and I found ourselves bonding."

He was lying. But if it smoothed things over, then so be it. It wasn't a problem. It needed smoothing over. "I'm pleased about the baby," she said. "A darling little child, one that I can dress up and hold and… That is good news."

She was trying to rally; he could see it.

When she was happy, she was the loveliest woman in the world. The most fun. She could be a great mother.

She could also be the most cutting, vindictive person that Romeo had ever known, and it was difficult to know which version of her he was going to get.

But he had taken it on. Because no one else had.

She was his responsibility, because she didn't have anyone else. His reward was those happy moments.

"I would like to bring Heather by tomorrow for a visit. You two can discuss the wedding."

"I suppose she has changed since she was the housekeeper's daughter."

"Yes, Mother. It's been quite a few years since you've seen her."

"Tea. Yes. That will be good."

"Yes, it will."

His driver took him back to the hotel, and when he walked through the door of the room, he was greeted by Heather, standing there in the brilliant, emerald-green dress he had sent to the suite.

"You look beautiful," he said.

It was freeing, to say that. To simply admit that he found her to be stunning. To have there be no subtext, no other meaning or emotion behind the words.

She was beautiful.

Her cheeks turned pink, and the pleasure that he saw there on her face ignited something inside of him.

"Really?"

"Yes."

He held his arm out, and she took it, tentatively. Slowly.

"How was your conversation with your mother?"

"It was good. Overall. She's happy about the baby. I made arrangements for us to have a visit with her tomorrow."

"Good," she said. "That will be...good."

"She wants for us to have the wedding in Vienna."

"Oh. Well, that's fine, I suppose."

"Thank you. I know you probably barely remember her."

They got in the elevator, and rode it down to the lobby. They walked through the ornate, gold space, and through the gold revolving door out to the street, where his car waited for them.

He held the door open for her, then got into the driver's seat. Tonight, he preferred to be behind the wheel.

"Yes, I think I was away most of the time they were still married. And she was often gone."

"Yes. I do know that my parents had marital problems before your mother arrived. I told you, I lived in a war zone. And that is one thing that I won't accept for our child. Whatever differences we have, we cannot tear each other down in front of our children."

"I agree."

"And we can never make it our child's job to build this back up."

"I agree with that too. I suspect your father wanted you to build him back up, and as much as I love him, that's not fair."

He hadn't even been thinking of his father. But he supposed in a way that was true. He hadn't reached out, had never asked his father to do it, but the relationship with him hadn't mended because Romeo hadn't made amends with him. Hadn't taken back the things that he had said. Some of which had been cruel and unfair, but some of which had been true.

They'd had years of difficult conversations, the fall-out of the divorce working itself out over the course of years. And never as fully as Romeo might have wished.

"I think we both want to do better. And I'm sorry. I'm sorry that you had such a difficult relationship with him."

He looked at Heather out of the corner of his eye, where she was resting her elbow against the window, looking out at the city.

"He loved me in a way that my own father never did. I never even knew him. My mother marrying him gave me things that were so wonderful, but I never wanted to look at the cost of it. I just ignored that they had an affair. I really did. Because I didn't want either of them to be wrong. It changed my life in such good ways that I didn't want any of it to be wrong. And you had made everything so miserable for me at school."

"I am sorry about that," he said.

Now, with years of perspective, he couldn't fathom why he had done it. Except that he had been angry. At everything. And she had made him feel things that he didn't want to feel, and it had felt like a convenient target for all that rage.

It had felt like an easy thing.

He had really, truly wanted the easy thing.

The bandage for the wound that seemed to be festering there in his chest.

"Thank you," she said. "I lost myself there for a little while too. I got wrapped up in what it felt like to be one of you. To win. So a lot of the things that I did to you when I was in high school, that was all because I was angry, and I wanted to get back at you. Later, though I…"

"You wanted me."

"I did. It confused me. I also realized that it wasn't a new feeling. But again it was confusing because…"

"Because I wasn't nice to you," he said.

"No. You weren't."

"And you really couldn't want anyone but me?"

"No."

"Even that idiot that you almost had sex with at that house party?"

"Even him. I just wanted to not feel like something was wrong with me. Like I was different. Because I was so tired of feeling different. You made me feel so different. It's funny that you were so mad about that party. About me and that other guy, because you pushed me there. You're the one that made me feel like I needed to do something extreme to fix myself. So yes, I am sorry for some of the things, but you are no small part of my insecurity."

He tightened his hand on the steering wheel, looked straight ahead. "I'm sorry. That's inexcusable of me. I have been…a bad person."

"No. You did some bad things, I think. Or I don't know. You're not altogether bad though, is the thing. You really aren't. Which is part of the annoying thing about you. Part of the reason that I could never fully hate you, and it isn't just because you're gorgeous."

"What good thing have you ever seen me do?"

"You were always there for your father, even though your relationship wasn't easy. And you love your mother.

I have always understood that a lot of the reason you didn't like me was because you loved her so much."

"I suppose we do know each other, a little bit."

"A little bit."

He was still grappling with the things that she had said when they pulled the car up outside of the restaurant, and he gave the keys to the valet.

They were ushered into the small building into a private dining room, where it was luxurious and quiet.

"I asked the chef to prepare us a selection of his favorite things."

"Oh, that sounds lovely."

"I know that you and your mother moved to Italy from New York."

"Yes. We did."

"I never asked you what it was like to grow up there."

She rested her chin on the back of her hands, looking at him thoughtfully. "No. You didn't. But then, I never asked you about anything before I met you either. Or really anything that you were experiencing after we met."

"True."

"Well, I went back to New York. Because in many ways it always felt like my home. But also on a slightly pettier note, I wanted to know what it was like to live there when I was part of the other half. We grew up in a studio apartment. It was tiny, and my mom did her best to keep it clean. She worked on the Upper East Side. Sometimes in the summer I would ride the subway with her. And spend most of the day outside on the playgrounds there. Sometimes I would wander around the Met by myself. Or the natural history museum. Air-conditioned. Nice. During the school year I would get myself to school. And usually I would cook dinner so that she would have something when she got home. She didn't ask me to do that. But I wanted to. It was us against the world."

"And then my father put out a ridiculous ad for a housekeeper after he and my mother had a fight."

"What?"

"Did you not know that? It came about because of a fight that they had. My mother was constantly chasing cleaners away by nitpicking their work. And my father said the only way that we would be able to get someone new is by finding them outside the country. And that once he did, my mother was not permitted to engage with the new cleaner. He also said that he would have to pay more than handsomely for them to keep the job. That is how that job posting ended up being the way it was. So generous that of course your mother would never turn it down."

"He fell in love with her at first sight," Heather said, looking down at her hands.

Romeo was about to respond to that when the waiter came in with a charcuterie, an array of meat and cheese. A glass of wine for him, and sparkling water for Heather.

"Did he?" Romeo asked. And he found he wasn't as angry as he used to be.

"Yes. He wanted to give her everything. That was why he offered to send me to the private school. He wanted…he wanted her to notice him the way that he did her. But he wanted to be careful because he was her boss. My mother worked for a lot of rich men. She didn't have relationships with them. And she didn't trust them just because they were rich and men. She knew better than that. It wasn't like it was a pattern with her or anything like that."

"I don't really know what I thought. It feels…salacious on the surface."

"Yes. It does. But it wasn't."

He nodded slowly. "I did see that. In the fullness of time. That what they had was real. It didn't ease anything, though, because it only made me feel all that much more protective of my mother."

"Why wouldn't it? It's a tangle."

"It was never your fault, though."

"No," she said. "It wasn't."

He very nearly laughed.

Their main courses came out after that—perfectly seared steaks and buttered vegetables. And he was gratified to see that Heather was enjoying the food. When she had first come to tell him about the pregnancy she had looked pale and unwell.

Now she seemed much better.

Taking care of her was…satisfying.

He had always felt a strange sort of possessiveness over her. It had been, initially, that she was the woman he hated more than anyone else in all the world.

But now she was his. In a different way.

It made him want to do things differently. Behave differently.

To treat her differently.

"What was it like growing up in your house?"

"I told you. Contentious."

"You said war zone."

He nodded slowly. "They were not a good match. All they did was make each other miserable. My father was rich. My mother was beautiful, and volatile. He didn't know what he was getting into, but they married each other. Based on my math, I assume it's because she was pregnant with me. I was the reason. And therefore, I'm responsible."

"For what?"

"For keeping her happy. At least as happy as she can be, because all of her misery is because of me."

Heather tilted her head to the side. "That isn't true. It's not a fair perspective. You didn't choose to be born, but she chose to have you."

"She couldn't have seen ahead to the consequences."

"Perhaps not. But that doesn't negate her part in it. I could've easily felt that way about my mom. She raised me without any help at all. It was really hard, but she never made me feel like I was a burden. We were family."

"Family, to me, has always meant something differ-ent. It has always been something…to do. A challenge."

"I don't want that to be the case for our child."

"Neither do I."

"Did you always want children?"

He shook his head slowly. "To tell you the truth, I hadn't thought about it. In my experience, loving an-other person is exhausting."

"Your mother?"

"It's a terrible thing to say."

"Maybe. But it's not untrue."

There was nothing more shocking than feeling like maybe the one person who had ever understood this was Heather.

And she had always been there. Yet they had never spoken. Not about this. Not about anything.

They finished their meal, and got back in the car, headed back to the hotel.

As they walked through the lobby, and to the elevator, he looked down at her, and she looked up at him. The expression on her face was soft. Different than any other way she had ever looked at him before. There was understanding there.

Intimacy.

And that had certainly never passed between them before.

The elevator carried them to their floor, and they walked down the hall, to the suite.

He let them both in, and closed the door behind them.

She looked at him, with determination. Her eyes glittering as she stepped toward him, pressed her hands to his chest and stretched up on her toes to kiss him.

The kiss was soft, tentative at first, but began to increase, deepen.

She tilted her head to the side and parted her lips, sliding her tongue against his.

A shiver went through his body.

They'd had each other hard. They'd had each other mean. This was something else entirely.

There had been very little kissing. Consuming, yes, but no kissing.

He captured the back of her head with his hand, her hair like silk as it slid through his fingers, as he kissed her deeper, longer.

As he wrapped his arm around her and held her hard against his body.

She whimpered. Her fingers curling around the collar of his jacket as she clung to him.

As she deepened the kiss, and it went on and on.

The dress was beautiful. The dress existed so that he could take it off of her.

And this time, he would enjoy her. This time, it wouldn't be fast and hard.

This time, he would take his time.

He lowered the zipper on the dress slowly, watching as it fell away from her body, as it pooled on the floor at her feet.

She was wearing black heels, a black pair of lace panties and a see-through bra. Beautiful.

The way that her red hair contrasted with the dark lace, her pale skin, sent his libido into overdrive.

"You're beautiful," he said, remembering what she had said about giving her compliments. How many things had he said to her that were sharp? Like a cruel sword digging into her skin. He had caused so much pain.

He wanted to erase it now.

"Incredible," he said.

He closed the distance between them, wrapped his arms around her and kissed her neck, her shoulder. "Perfect."

She shivered in his arms, and he unhooked her bra, casting it onto the ground, exposing her glorious flesh, and reveling in the sight.

He kissed her collarbone, down to the plump curve of her breasts, down to her tight, pink nipple, which he drew into his mouth, sucking hard.

"Gorgeous," he said again.

He left praise all over her skin with each kiss, each scrape of his teeth over her delicate skin.

He was not a man who had relationships. He had been preoccupied all of his life with his feelings for her. Such a huge part of himself had always been consumed by the toxicity of what existed between himself and Heather. He had lovers. But there had never been intensity. He had never spent the night in bed with a woman.

He had never lost himself entirely in a kiss, in an orgasm, in a moment.

With her, he was entirely enraptured.

Entirely lost.

"Take me to bed," she whispered against his mouth, and so he picked her up, and carried her across the living area, back toward that blue canopy bed that had so taken her when they had first arrived.

He thought about everything he had put in their contract. Everything about punishments and domination. But this wasn't the moment for that.

This was the moment to lavish her.

And he had never wanted anything more. Then to make her feel good in that moment.

To undo some of the hurt that he had caused.

He had never done that before. Had never tried to heal anything in himself that was wounded. Had never tried to fix a hurt he'd caused.

Had never tried to take back something that he had said.

He was a man who held grudges. He had done so all of his life.

But he had never tried to repair anything. And each kiss over her skin was an attempt to repair a crack that he had put there.

"Now I want you naked," she said.

She scooted up the bed, resting her elbows against the pillows there. She looked at him, direct and strong. He moved away from her, and began to loosen his tie, unbuttoned his shirt.

"Completely naked. No more of this half-dressed nonsense."

He shrugged off his jacket, unbuttoned his shirt, cast it down to the floor.

And she looked at him, her eyes hungry as he removed every last article of clothing.

"Yes," she said, rising up onto her knees and moving toward the end of the bed. "You are the most beautiful man I've ever seen. I've never wanted another one. In spite of my best efforts."

"You don't need another one," he said.

"Maybe not."

She smiled, just slightly, and he wanted to taste it. So he did.

He got onto the bed, and she moved around him, lightly pushing on his chest and laying him on his back. She hovered over him, her red hair shrouding them both as she leaned in and pressed kisses to his chest.

Down farther. And farther still.

She wrapped her hand around his arousal, and squeezed hard, then licked him from base to tip with the flat of her tongue. He let his head fall back, his breath hissing through his teeth.

"Do you like that?" she asked.

"Yes."

"Do you want more?"

"Yes," he said.

She teased him. Brushed his skin with her hair,

nipped at the head of his cock, sucked him in deep and didn't hold him long enough.

She pushed him all the way to the edge, again and again.

He was shaking, sweating. It would've been easy to believe that he was the virgin, and not so recently her.

She bit his hipbone, and he groaned, overcome by his desire for her.

By his need for more.

She moved over him, straddling him, her slick heat glorious against his hardness, and she moved her hips, taking him in an inch, before letting him slip out, denying them both what they so desperately wanted. She did it over and over again, the sensation maddening. Driving him to his limit.

Pushing him to the edge.

"Beg," she said.

"Please," he said.

"My name," she said. "I know you've been with other women. How many?"

"I don't know."

"How many times did you think of me?"

He laughed, dark and humorless. There was nothing funny about any of this.

"Every time," he said.

"Then it is a privilege for you to be able to have me. Isn't it?"

"Yes," he ground out, his hands on her hips.

"Beg me," she said.

"Please, Heather," he said.

She rocked her hips back, and slid onto him, taking

him in slowly, letting her head fall back on a sigh when he was buried all the way inside of her.

And then, he could not wait any longer.

He reversed their positions, driving into her, desperate, starving. He kissed her. Deep and hard while he was buried inside of her. She moved her hands up over her head, and he gathered them in his palm, holding her wrists together as he continued to take her.

He was lost. In this, in her. He had never experienced anything like this before. Anything like her.

And as he growled out his satisfaction, she cried out her own, clenching tightly around him and sending him into another time and space.

And tomorrow he would be with her, sitting across from his mother.

He let out a hard breath that was nearly a laugh as he collapsed, taking hold of her face and kissing her, the endorphin release so strong it took him by surprise.

"What?" she asked, looking up at him.

"Nothing. It is only that you will be the only woman I've ever slept with to meet my mother."

"And that's funny?"

"It's only… Our relationship makes it mildly amusing, I suppose."

"I would prefer not to think about your other lovers," she said, burrowing into the covers.

"But if we stick to our agreement it's possible that both of us will have them," he said.

"Possible," she returned.

Jealousy and possessiveness gripped him.

He did not like the idea, of course. But the idea of binding them both to a traditional marriage when they

had never had any sort of relationship that wasn't antagonistic before the last week or so seemed foolish at best.

Hell, it had barely been a week of them getting along.

And ninety percent of it had been fucking. They did
quite well when it came to that.

"I feel that I have to warn you about my mother," he
said. "She is sometimes the most delightful and engaging person you've ever met. And other times…"

"I think you're forgetting that I *have* met your
mother."

"No, I'm not. But whatever aspects of her erratic nature you experienced back then, it is worse now."

"I'm an editor," she said. "Do you have any idea the
number of erratic personalities that I work with at a
given time? Writers are not the most mentally stable
people."

He chuckled. "Are they not?"

"No. Typically, they are emotional, often missing
deadlines, and then you have to try to manage their
stress all while dealing with yours, and trying to make
them feel like they're geniuses, while gently suggesting they fix the dreck that you received from them. It's
a tightrope. I'm good at walking it. You know, initially
I was going into publicity, and I thought that I would
use it in the hospitality business. But what I've discovered is that part of being an editor is engaging in cus-
tomer service."

"I hadn't thought of that."

"Of course not. I didn't get into the job for that. I
thought it would be reading, and helping shape stories,
and I am. I love it. But I also have to figure out which
stories are going to make money, and present that to a

team, make the case for it. I have to attend more meetings during the week than I would like, though I've been let off the hook from a few of them because of the time difference. A lot of the reading I do on my own time."

"I'm surprised, in many ways, that you didn't pursue work under the Accardi banner."

"Of course you are. Because you always thought that was what I wanted. I'm not going to say that I didn't get a lot out of suddenly becoming rich overnight. Of course I did. But it wasn't all quite the way that you thought."

"I see that now."

"Why did you end up getting into that business when you were so angry at your father?"

"I wanted to prove to him that given the same arena I could do better than he did. But I was valuable, perhaps."

"He was proud of you."

He didn't know what to say to that, so he didn't say anything. He had never talked about these things with anyone else. But no one had ever asked him these sorts of questions.

She was interesting. The way she spoke about her work. The way she wanted to know about his.

He had branded her as something frivolous. Pointless. Because it had been convenient for him to do so, and yet on some level he must've known there was more to her. More to her than he had wanted to see. Than he had wanted to acknowledge. But it felt so much simpler to cast everyone in black and white, as he did his level best to keep his mother from imploding. It was easier to see things the way that she did. The appropriate people as villains.

And certainly not…

He certainly couldn't afford to be anyone else's savior.

That night that he had stopped Heather's sexual encounter with that man, he had been filled with such a deep, profound sense of rage and possessiveness. It had been nearly overwhelming, and he had no more room in him for that. Anger was easy. Wanting to protect less so.

It had a cost. Such an intense cost.

"Don't worry about your mother," she said, kissing him on the shoulder. The simple affectionate gesture nearly took his breath away.

"Sadly, Heather," he said, lying on his back and staring at the ceiling. "I have been doing nothing but worrying about her for the last twenty years. I'm not going to stop just because you told me to."

"But what if you did?" she whispered.

And without giving it too much thought, he fell asleep with a woman beside him.

CHAPTER TEN

SHE WOULD BE lying if she said she wasn't nervous about meeting with Romeo's mom. She was obviously very important to him, and a huge part of their issues came from the fact that the divorce had hurt her so much. And Heather had been lumped up into the grouping of very bad things that had caused trauma.

She figured it was in her best interest to dress demurely so as not to draw attention to herself or bring up any feelings about her being some kind of seductress who had trapped Romeo into this. "I have trapped you into marriage, though," she said cheerfully as they got into his car and began to drive toward his mother's home.

"Have you?"

"Yes. The ultimatum that I issued you was quite firm."

"I truly hate to be the one to tell you this, but you effectively couldn't trap me if you wanted to. You might have inherited a sizable fortune from my father, which we split, but don't forget I was already in possession of my own."

That made her bristle. "What are you saying?"

"You don't have as much power over me as you think."

She gazed at the Austrian countryside, which was beautiful, particularly in comparison to how annoyed she felt just at the moment.

"But you agreed."

"Yes. Because I think it's the best thing. I don't think that our child should experience the difficulties that either of us did. And I think that it's best, for many reasons, for the two of us to be married. But if I had decided not to marry you, I would never have surrendered full custody just because you said that was my only option."

"That is really annoying."

"Why? Why does it matter, when you got your way?"

"It matters because…" Well, now she felt manipulated.

"You wanted to think that you got something on your own?"

"Maybe. Or like maybe I was compelling."

"You are compelling, Heather Gray. If you weren't, I wouldn't have gotten you pregnant in the first place."

That placated her slightly. But only slightly. At least she had some pull, she supposed.

His mother's house was beautiful. Palatial and situated on top of a mountain that overlooked the city.

"Beautiful," she said.

"It is," he replied. "You would think that she might find some peace here."

"She doesn't?"

"Peace is not really in my mother's wheelhouse."

Her stomach twisted with nerves, or maybe it was morning sickness. It was really hard to tell. She had been feeling better in general, but sometimes nausea hit her, and not necessarily always early in the day.

They were ushered in by one of his mother's employees, and through the entryway, into the dining room. It was set up beautifully for high tea, with tiered trays of desserts and delicate china all around.

"This is beautiful."

Heather said that just before his mother swept into the room, and the look of delight on her face at hearing it instantly alleviated some of Heather's worries.

"I'm glad that you think so," she said.

Carla Accardi was one of the most beautiful women in the world. This was a truth universally accepted by many fashion magazines, and age had not dimmed her beauty. Her dark hair was just as it had been the last time Heather had seen her. Long and falling in waves around her shoulders, not a single strand of silver to be seen, though that was probably the work of color artists.

She still had the slim frame required of a runway model back in the '90s, and as Heather remembered, looked elegant just standing there. She was wearing a floral robe in a highly saturated silk. It could have been a dress, it could've been only a robe, but she made it look like high-fashion either way.

"Lisa's daughter," she said, her dark eyes fixed like lasers on Heather.

"Yes."

"Your mother is dead now."

"Yes," Heather said.

There was no real compassion in the other woman's voice. But no venom either. It was an observation. And even though it felt unkind, Heather wasn't going to react to it. She had too much practice being bullied.

"Let's all have a seat," Carla said, smiling brightly.

Heather returns the smile. "Yes. Let's."

"You're pregnant," Carla said, in that same matter-of-fact tone. No indication as to whether or not she was pleased by the news.

"Yes. And Romeo and I are getting married. I know he told you already."

"I do hope that you have a prenuptial agreement."

"Yes," Romeo said. "We do. Of course. To protect the both of us."

"You obviously need more protection than she does," Carla said.

"Financially," Heather said, shrugging. "That is inarguably true."

Both Romeo and Carla looked at her.

"Well," she said. "It is. I'm not offended by that."

"Is he only marrying you because you're pregnant?" she asked.

The question was cutting. But again, nothing that had never been leveled at Heather before. By Romeo himself, in fact.

"Yes. We both think it would be better to avoid the messy situation that we found ourselves in growing up."

"I'm familiar with the mess," Carla said.

"I know," Heather responded. "I wasn't casting any blame. It must've hurt you very much, what happened between my mother and your husband. I know that it's ancient history now, and both of them are gone. But it doesn't change the fact that it's a painful history."

Heather wasn't being disingenuous. She might believe that Giuseppe and her mother were the love story, but it didn't mean there was no cost to it. As a kid, she had filtered that out. Because it had been inconvenient to think about it or dwell on it. Because it didn't feel beneficial. But as an adult, she could look at it with a little bit more complexity. Now that she was not looking at Romeo as an enemy, now that she was actually giving some space to how his relationship with his father had been damaged, and it was entirely on him, she was just…seeing it differently.

"I was very hurt by it," Carla said. "Thank you."

"I promise that I don't want to hurt your son in any way. And we're going to be the best parents possible for your grandchild. You're their only grandparent. The only one they have left. The only one they'll ever know. That's an incredibly special position."

It wasn't about placating her, or managing her, though she was well aware she was doing that, but it really was about the relationship. Romeo couldn't fix the relationship with his father. He was gone. Their child wouldn't have another grandparent.

"That is a very…kind thing to say," Carla said.

"It's true," Heather said.

"We're building a family. I think it can be a good thing."

"I would like to wear green to your wedding," Carla said.

"Of course you can," Heather replied.

"I prefer a Kelly green."

"You can wear whatever shade you want. And I will choose whatever shade I like for everything else." On that she was firm. His mother would not be taking over every aspect of the wedding.

Of course, maybe it didn't matter if the wedding was… Was it a sham wedding? They were getting married for the baby? They weren't in love—they…

They certainly had a sexual relationship. Right now. But all of their paperwork had all those contingencies, and if they had sex while they were married, the stakes of it all went up.

But it was the only marriage she would have.

She had never really dreamed of marriage, or having children. Because the way that Romeo had obsessed her, wrapped himself around her desires and her fantasies at such a young age, had kept her from doing so.

And now she was marrying him. Consigning herself to life with him while they raised their child—it was what they had both agreed on. But she couldn't see life after Romeo, because she had never been able to see life after Romeo. And in the one moment when she had thought she might have a life after him, she had cut her own fantasy short by finally snapping the thread that had stretched between them for all this time.

She'd crossed a line with him and couldn't go back. So as far as she was concerned, the marriage was real.

The marriage was *real*.

What she didn't know was how to ensure it was still about their child.

Because right now that was a distant hope, and Romeo was here now. She wanted him, she craved him, but she also knew they'd only been getting along for about forty-eight hours.

That thought echoed inside of her as she tried to finish her tea. But that left so many unanswered questions. If it was real, then what were her feelings toward him? And what was she going to do when they walked down the aisle with all that paperwork between them?

Was there a world where they could try to make something real out of all of this?

When they left, he walked around to her side of the car and pulled the door open. He looked at her for a long moment. "You did amazingly well."

She got into the car, and he shut the door, and she released a shuddering breath on a realization.

She had never really hated him at all.

The way that she handled his mother had been skillful on a level he had never seen before. Moreover, she had made it seem easy. He had expected some kind of blowup, but that hadn't occurred. Instead, Heather had seemed to know exactly what to say and what to do. And though his mother was…happy with the arrangement, at least for now, he knew better than anyone how quickly his mother's moods could change. But he was pleased to be in the middle of a good one now.

Everything was working out well right now. But he had never been more aware of exactly what was at stake. The ecosystem was fragile. Between him and Heather, everyone and his mother. The environment that they were bringing their child into had the potential to be volatile. He had never experienced family any other way.

The idea of Heather being with someone else filled him with a rage that he couldn't quantify, but that in and of itself told him that he had to change the way that he was thinking about her.

The way that he was thinking about their relationship.

They had been enemies. They had now been lovers. Perhaps there was some world where they could be friends. That might be the only way to guarantee that their child experienced some form of stability.

The way that she had dealt with Carla…

He had never seen anything like it.

He wanted to *always* have that.

Passion was what his parents'd had. For a time. Then it had become hatred. He'd experienced hatred with Heather, and he felt like it was a tightrope walk. Easy, so easy for them to end up right back there, and what would that mean for their child?

He intended to do what the adults in his life had never quite managed.

To put that child first.

When they left Vienna, they went back to the estate, and he manufactured business that needed to be done in London—even though he could've done it anywhere. While he was away he sent Heather a text.

Perhaps you could spend some time back in New York. It would probably be good for you to check in with your job. Attend some of those meetings you like so much.

What made you change your mind on that?

Our wedding is set for a month from now. I trust you.

There. He was being kind. Shortly she would interpret his actions as kindness. This was the problem. He didn't want to tell her that he thought they shouldn't be lovers and have her afraid that it was because of something she had done wrong. It was, in fact, because of something that she had done exceptionally well. It was because he had seen a potential that he now longed to make reality.

They'd never had a friendship. And the feelings that fueled the desire between them were inarguably founded on toxicity.

That wasn't good for anyone.

She did send him messages about the wedding, and he enjoyed her including him in the process. She did go to New York, and she kept him up-to-date on the various meetings that she had to attend, and the absolute author meltdown she had wrangled.

She called the lead publicist thirteen times. Like we can't see who's calling. She called everyone. And then whenever Caroline's assistant would answer, she would hang up.

What was she mad about?

She didn't get as many trade reviews as she thinks she should. She's mad at the whole publicity department.

There was a pause in their texting. Then she sent another:

What are you working on?

Her question surprised him. Developing a new route on the cruise line, and negotiating port contracts.

Cruise traffic is in such a state right now that you have to have rights to get your passengers dropped off right at the fork. I'm trying to make sure that our line has the most optimum placement.

Well, it's not author tantrums.

No. It isn't.

What he didn't expect was for her to arrive in London without announcement at the town house where she had her ill-fated graduation party all those years ago.

But there she was, glowing in the middle of the entryway when he got home, her body curvier than when she had left nearly a month ago, her smile unlike anything he had ever seen before. Had Heather ever smiled at him like this? No. Of course she hadn't. Because there had been nothing but bad blood between them for all that time. And now she was smiling at him. Like he was something wonderful.

It felt weighted. Like there was an expectation behind it. Because how could there be anything else? That meant that he had to keep them here. In this place, where it was only a smile. Where he could not fail her.

"I didn't expect you," he said.

She blinked, and then moved toward him. He moved slightly, and the kiss that had been intended for his mouth landed on his cheek. There was something all the more damning about that. All the more intense. He gritted his teeth and took a step back. "I need to speak with you, and I confess that I was putting it off."

"Oh?"

She looked afraid. Ready for battle, then, and why would she? It had always been a battle between them. There'd been so little time where they had been cordial. Where they had been anything like friends.

"Don't look at me like that. Like I'm going to bite you. I'm not."

"You look like it," she said. "And not in a fun way."

He nodded once. "Come and sit down."

"Should I remind you that the invitations to the wedding have already been sent out?"

"I don't need to be reminded of that. I'm not backing out of this. But I have been thinking about the future. About what our home will look like, will feel like for our child. What you said to my mother has been weighing on me heavily."

"What?"

"She is the last remaining grandparent. And whether we would have chosen it or not, the three of us are now family. We must make a family for our child. I love my mother very much. But she is not an easy woman. She never has been. I assume she will be difficult in the future as well. Even if she doesn't mean to be. I will always have to shoulder the responsibility of caring for her. But the way that you spoke with her, the way that you were with her, it made me... It made me realize what I truly want for our child."

"What?"

"Peace. For the adults in his or her life to put them first. As no one ever did with us. I know that you had a better experience with your father and mother in the household, but when your father left your mother, he didn't think of you. He didn't put you first. Your mother did, though. And you have greatly benefited from that. My father and my mother put their own feelings first. Always. And I have always borne the brunt of that. You and I are looking at eighteen years of attempting to create harmony, and we've had a couple of months where we have done well with each other. And you were away for a substantial portion of it."

"Please get to the point. You're an infamous, ruthless businessman, and you're talking around me like a car salesman. We both know that's not you."

"I don't want to hurt you. I don't want you to think it's anything you've done wrong. I have been cruel to you, I accept responsibility for that. This is not cruelty. But you and I need to set aside our attraction."

"What?"

"I have only ever seen passion go badly."

"My mother and your father loved each other very much. Until the end."

"They had a love story—that much is certain. But I believe that it was founded very much on my father's desire to rescue her. And in many ways, I feel that your mother wanted to rescue him. They did. But my parents... They married because of me. Because she was pregnant. They married because their passion drove them together. And it kept driving them. It was toxic. So were they."

"If it was so terrible then why were you mad when they got divorced?"

"Because it doesn't end—that's what I'm trying to tell you. It doesn't burn itself out. My mother never could let go of it. And I know there are other reasons for that. I know that it has to do with her depressive episodes, but it doesn't change the reality. Leaving my father, the dissolution of the marriage, it didn't fix anything. Not between the two of them, and not between us. I had to be my mother's savior, and that made me my father's adversary, and he couldn't pull himself out of that either because his feelings for her were so twisted up at that point. We can never be that for our child."

He could see the hurt in her eyes, the confusion. But she wouldn't always be hurt or confused. She wouldn't be.

"This is a trick. Of our imaginations, of our hormones. I want for us to de-escalate the feelings. This has been good, this last month. We've communicated. And it feels like a foundation. Fucking on tables is not the foundation for a happy life for a child. You and I could follow that until it burns us both out, but to what end? That isn't why we are getting married, and maybe if you hadn't gotten pregnant we could've explored that. But you did. And we must be in this together."

She took a breath, and there was a single break at the center of it. But it never became a sob. Her eyes remained dry. "You're right. Of course you are. Because we are asking each other to do something impossible. To know, without a shadow of a doubt, that this relationship that we're trying to build is going to last until our child is an adult. Everyone intends for that to be the case. Surely that was why your parents got married. And then they couldn't do it. They couldn't manage it."

"To be fair to them, I suppose they did make it into my adulthood."

"Close. But you still bore the weight of the consequences. And you lived in a war zone, as you said. And when we are at our worst..."

"When we are at our worst it's very bad."

"Yes. I agree with that."

It was so much harder now that she was here. Because he wanted her. Wanted to touch her. Wanted to hold her. Wanted to draw her against his body and feel her heart beating beneath his hand. To move his hands over her curves and make her his. Definitively.

But they would marry. And they would be tied together. She would be his. Just not in that way.

"I'm probably going to go back to the estate," she said. "I'm glad that I was able to stop and see you."

"You might as well spend the night here."

"It's only a two-hour flight to Italy. I'll just head there."

"You came here for me," he said, his voice rougher than intended.

She wanted him.

God knew he wanted her.

He was trying. Trying to make the right choice, and where Heather was concerned he had a low success rate with that. He wanted her to want him, even as he wanted some distance and sanity where she was concerned.

A small smile curved the corner of her lips. "No. Of course not. I just came here to talk about our friendship. I'm glad that I did. I'm glad that we are on the same page."

He knew that she was lying. But of course he was going to allow her to have the lie.

"I'll see you in Vienna. For the wedding."

"I have a dress."

"Good. I'm glad to hear it."

Need flooded his veins. She looked away from him, and her red hair slid over her shoulder, catching the lamplight, gold playing over the top of the fiery strands. He wanted to touch them. Wanted to touch her. He wouldn't let himself.

He had never been one for exercising discipline when it came to Heather. But he did it in so many other areas of his life. He hadn't become as successful as he was without it. He worked day and night, he catered to his mother, he had brief, satisfying relationships with women who knew that he was never going to get emotionally invested. Because he didn't have any more to give. He was going to have to find more for his child.

There could never be anything else. He needed something that he could draw more from, not something that would take from him. And truthfully, the relationship with Heather filled the well inside of him in ways that nothing else had.

He needed her. Needed her by his side more than he needed her underneath. He was simply going to have to remember that.

"After the wedding we could start talking about the nursery. Find out whether the baby is a boy or a girl. That will be nice."

"It will be."

She gave him a smile before she walked out of the room, out of the town house, and he paced over to the bar, grabbing a bottle of Scotch and pouring himself a measure of it. Then he walked up to the wall and smashed his elbow right through the Sheetrock. The pain was searing, and he looked at the white shirt he was wearing and saw that it was red with blood.

He let it run.

There was pain now. So that there could be peace later.

He was standing solid in that.

She had been mildly devastated by the conversation they'd had at the London house. She hadn't expected it. Yes, she had found it disquieting that he had suggested she leave, but she hadn't put a lot of extra thought into it. She had hoped that it was actually a good-faith gesture, which was how he had presented it. That he trusted her, so she could go and be in New York for a while if it suited her.

She hadn't expected for him to cut her off entirely. For their sexual relationship to end just like that.

Logically though, she had been thinking that they would end it at least for a while when they got married, until they got their footing and then…

She had known that they would never be able to resist each other, so obviously they would end up back in bed and then maybe he… Maybe he would begin to feel the same way that she did.

Her chest was sore. But she looked amazing. She had bought the most beautiful wedding dress that she had ever seen. A sweetheart neckline with crystals all over. It was short underneath, with a sheer overlay, glimmering with all of those glass beads. Her legs were visible when the light hit it just right.

And she had the most risqué bustier that she could find beneath it, along with a pair of panties that might as well not even be there for all that they were as substantial as cobwebs.

But that felt like where they were heading. It had been her fantasy, of a wedding night, of the way that things could be between them, and he had decisively ended it. She couldn't even argue with what he had said.

It was impossible to argue with. They were getting married because she was pregnant. Not because they wanted each other.

She stood there, looking at her reflection in the mirror for a long moment.

It had been four days since she had last seen him, and now it was the wedding day.

And she felt…sad.

Just a little bit sad.

But also determined that this was the right thing. Them getting married was the best thing.

"You look beautiful," Catherine said.

She turned to face her closest friend, and did her best to smile. Catherine didn't know all the details of everything that was happening with her and Romeo, and she was pretty skeptical of the fact that he had suddenly become a decent human being. In fact, she had called Heather sex addled on more than one occasion.

But now that she was here, at the wedding, she seemed to be a lot more accepting.

Or maybe she had just accepted that Heather was going to do what she had decided, and wasn't going to be deterred from it.

"Thank you for making me your maid of honor."

"You're my best friend," Heather said. "I thought about having a whole big bridal party, but all of those people... I don't really know them anymore. Mind you, we have a huge contingent from our years at Fairfield here. Because the absolute spectacle of the two of us getting married was too much to resist."

"I would say. I never got to see the two of you spark off of each other. You were obsessed with him."

She looked back at her own reflection. The largeness of her eyes, the color in her cheeks. "I'm still obsessed with him."

"That's good, since you're marrying him."

"I guess. I guess it's good. But we have to raise a child and not implode. We don't have a lot of practice with not imploding. We're...a whole storm."

"I'm glad that the sex is good," Catherine said, dryly.

Heather laughed. "That's not the only thing I meant."

"I know. But clearly the sex is good."

"It's all-consuming. Which concerns me."

She was hedging around the truth.

"He's gorgeous. So, I get it. Though I've had sex with some pretty gorgeous men who turned out to be disappointing."

"Nothing about Romeo is disappointing."

"I think you might just love him."

She stopped, and of course Catherine was going to say that, because she didn't know about the contract, about the agreement. She didn't know about the connective tissue of all the moments they'd spent together since then. That he had never professed to have any sort of emotional connection with her. Nothing other than a desire for friendship, which was why he was determined not to touch her.

"You think I love him?"

"You're marrying him. In a gorgeous white dress. You look like you're glowing. You're having his baby. You're obsessed with his body. What part of that doesn't sound like love to you?"

"Isn't love supposed to be soft and wonderful?"

"No," Catherine sighed. "Listen, I'm not an expert. I've had some relationships that have burned themselves out quickly, and I've had some that have lasted longer. I haven't found the love of my life. I certainly never wanted the same man for nearly fifteen years, and nothing, not the passage of time or the way that he treated me, or the way that I treated him, could change the way that I felt. So I mean, there's that. Mainly though, I think love is a lot like the rest of life. It changes with us. Moves with us. I think it can be comfortable. Something lived in and lovely. But sometimes it has teeth. Sometimes you leave bite marks all over it because you're trying so hard to hold on. I don't think love is any one thing. It's too big for that."

Her words echoed through Heather. And it was difficult for her to deny them.

It had been him. From the beginning.

When he had stood there by the pool looking at her over the top of his sunglasses like she was nothing, and he had suddenly become everything.

She had watched him go from a beautiful boy to a beautiful man. She had tried to want something else, and she had never quite managed it.

"I spent so many years not even liking him."

"Is it that simple? Did you not like him? Or were you just desperate for him, and it felt like dislike? Desperate for his attention while he was seducing other women, and in general being mean to you."

"I…"

Desperate for his attention. That resonated. It echoed inside of her. Yes, she had been desperate for his attention. Desperate for him to see her. She had tried to shape herself into the kind of girl that would interest him, that would catch his focus, and when all she could get was his disdain, she had learned to feed off of that.

"We're worse than I thought. Because you're right. I never hated him. At all. I wanted him desperately in whatever form that took. And I was willing to have it be hard. Mean."

Catherine reached out and squeezed Heather's arm. "You're just a girl."

"What does that mean?"

"Who among us hasn't been absolutely wretched for a gorgeous man? A man who captures us no matter how bad of an idea it is. It is definitive proof that you can't choose your sexuality. Because God knows I would've been done with men ages ago."

She was about to protest again. There was no way they could love each other because there was so much… anger there.

But there hadn't been. Not recently. He was the first person that she texted in the morning, and the last before she went to bed. He had been her first thought all day, every day for the last fifteen years.

She wished she could deny that it was love.

She wished she could write it off as obsession. As something temporary or shallow, but nothing with teeth that penetrated this deeply could ever be shallow.

Nothing that had lasted this long.

She couldn't think about other men. She couldn't want them. She cared what he thought about her, so much so that she'd been performing at him in a variety of ways for years. She'd been sick over him, so much so she'd hoped to never see him again and then had destroyed that plan by sleeping with him, getting pregnant with his baby.

And now she knew they could actually like each other too.

That she could enjoy his company instead of only feeling like her skin was too tight when she was near him.

"I love him," she whispered.

"Yes, you do," Catherine said. "It really is a good thing that you're marrying him."

"I suppose."

But he had said that they needed to continue to pursue the friendship part of things. But there would never be another man for her. Not ever. And she wasn't prepared to let him go off and be with other women. She wasn't... She wasn't only doing this for their child. She was doing this for her too. Because she wanted him. She didn't just want to be a vessel for this life inside of her. She didn't just want to be a mother. She wanted to be a whole woman. Who had love. It was one thing she had never begrudged her mother, not just because it had improved their circumstances, but because Heather had always known that her mother deserved that kind of happiness.

Romeo simply hadn't been raised by a woman who had allowed him that feeling. His mother had often been miserable, and she had made her son feel miserable when she did.

His emotional state was so tied to her that of course he saw it more simply.

If they were happy, and at peace, their child would be.

But life was too dynamic for that.

And they were already too complicated. But that wasn't something to run from.

"You don't look happy."

"I am," Heather said.

Because for the first time, everything made sense. For the first time, she made sense. For the first time, all of this felt right.

She wasn't going to let him run away from this.

She had to believe that she still had power. To change his mind. To make things shift.

Catherine handed Heather her bright pink bouquet, and she took hold of it and gave herself one last, purposeful look in the mirror before the two of them walked down to the chapel.

It was absolutely packed full of people, because who could resist coming to gawk at this?

Not many that had been invited, it turned out.

The whole thing looked like an elegant wonderland, with twisting branches woven together with fairy lights wound around them. Making an arbor for her to walk beneath as she made her way up the aisle. And there he was. Stern and stoic in his black suit, his black hair ruthlessly styled off of his forehead.

Romeo. Her stepbrother. The father of her baby. Her husband.

Hers. Inevitably. There was no escaping him, and she didn't even want to.

She wanted him. She wanted this. Forever. He took her hand, and looked at her. His gaze drifted down to her cleavage, and back up. And just like when they had been teenagers, she knew.

He had made a mistake.

He wanted her.

When they spoke their vows, her heart began to beat harder. Faster. She meant every word. This was no performance.

Standing there in front of all these people, in front of Catherine in her pink bridesmaid dress, and Carla in her kelly-green mother-of-the-bride gown. This was real for her. The only wedding she would ever have.

"You may now kiss the bride."

They hadn't discussed this beforehand. But there was no need to discuss it. She knew what she wanted.

She wrapped her arms around his neck and kissed him. Deep and long. With all the desire that she had inside her body. He captured the back of her head, his tongue sweeping over hers, clearly overcome just as she was. He wasn't going to stop this now. He wasn't going to stop.

No. He kissed her deep and long, the desire that was building inside of her aching and desperate, even in front of all these people.

This was what everyone had come to see, so they might as well see it. This need that existed between the two of them.

It was real.

And it was strong. No matter what he said.

He pulled away from her, his breathing hard, the color in his cheekbones dark red, suggesting pent-up desire.

Oh yes. He did want her.

She was going to get her wedding night. And what she had that. He wouldn't be able to have anyone else, not without consequences.

She loved him. That wasn't making her feelings soft.

She could try to be his friend. But she wanted to be his lover. His wife. His woman.

She wasn't going to give the man peace.

He was going to have to work for it.

On that she was determined.

CHAPTER ELEVEN

HE HAD SEEN the challenge in her eyes. But worse was the moment that he had first seen her coming up the aisle in her wedding dress.

Like a dream. All white satin and glimmering jewels.

The shape of her body tempting him. Calling to him.

He had never seen such a beautiful woman.

Never.

It had been that way from the beginning.

Yes, she had been young when she first arrived. And his feelings hadn't been like that. But once she had begun to develop into a woman, he had been… captivated.

When she had come toward him in that dress, he had been reminded of the day by the pool when they had both been in high school. When he had been unable to keep his eyes off of the glory of her curves. When he had been unable to do anything but stare at how beautiful she was. So beautiful.

But it wasn't only that; it was the feeling of possessiveness. She was his. His wife.

And the challenge as she leaned in to kiss him…

Now they were back in that hotel in Vienna, where they had stayed last time, and it was heavy with memories. Memories of the last time they had stayed here, and what they had done in the beds. On the floor. Against the wall.

They had done it. It should be over. He didn't want this. He didn't want this sharp, awful feeling riding him all the time. He wanted what they'd had when she was a continent away. But they couldn't be separated by a continent, because they had to raise a child together.

He needed a Scotch.

But his suit was choking him.

He went into his bedroom, and it would be his bedroom—they had discussed this ahead of time, because they had an agreement—and closed the door behind him. Then he went to the sideboard where there was a decanter of Scotch, and stood there staring at it as he undid the cuffs on his shirt, undid his tie. He unbuttoned his shirt and slid it off along with his jacket, letting them fall to the floor. And then he took the top off the decanter of Scotch, very aware that if this was how he was going to cope with his feelings for her, he was going to be drinking a lot more than he should.

And how would that make him an exemplary father?

He had no idea. He didn't have a plan. This was entirely fucked.

He was aware of that. He also had no answer to it.

He lifted up his glass, and brought it to his lips, just as he heard the sound of the door opening behind him. He froze. He didn't turn around.

He heard her footsteps, and then she was just behind him. She reached around and took hold of the glass, setting it in front of him on the sideboard before wrapping her arms around his midsection. Her palms flat against his stomach. Then she began to let her fingers drift, one moving up over his nipple, the other moving down to cup his raging hard-on.

"Heather," he said, his voice a warning.

"I know," she said. "If we do this, then this is how it is. If we do this, then we have to contend with all of it, don't we?" While she spoke she was stroking him, and it felt so good he couldn't bring himself to stop her.

He didn't want to stop her.

He was a fool.

"We could be friends, Romeo. We can have peace, but there's always going to be this. Always. And I've decided that I can't accept that. I cannot let you inside of another woman." She wrapped her fingers around his cock through the fabric of his pants. And squeezed. "It's mine," she said. "You are mine."

He turned around on a growl, gripping her face, holding it steady in his palm. "Is this what you want? Because let me warn you. If this is how you want to play it, it isn't going to be soft or nice. If this belongs to you," he said, putting her palm flat against him again, "you belong to me. All of you." He traced the line of her jaw, down the side of her neck, and palmed her breast. Squeezing. "Mine." Then he moved his hand between her legs, stroking her through the thin fabric of her gown, feeling her heat, feeling that she was damp. "And this is mine."

"Yes," she said, her throat tight. "That's the agreement that we have. And that's what I want. That's what I want."

"You're asking for everything we agreed to?"

"Everything," she said.

She took a step away from him, her hand behind her back as she unzipped her dress and let it fall to the floor in a shimmering puddle at her feet. He growled when he saw what she had on beneath. A white lace undergarment that held her breasts up on display, showed the shadow of her nipples beneath the lace. A pair of panties so small they covered nothing. Rather they only served as a tease.

"I bought this for you in New York. Before you told me that you wanted to be friends. At the very least, I thought you should have the chance to see it."

"You're playing with fire."

"I know. I have been. For all these years, and that became so very clear to me today. I want everything. I want you."

"Then you get everything."

His hands were shaking. "But don't think you won't pay a price for it. You have been begging me to be punished."

Arousal clouded her eyes. "I have been."

"Because you've been a brat from the moment I met you. And you know what happens to brats."

"They get what they deserve. You were going to let me off far too easily."

Those words ignited something in his veins.

With one hand he undid his belt and pulled it through the loops. Then he moved to her, wrapping his belt around her wrists and putting the end of it through the buckle, pulling tight, binding her, as he had promised her he would do in their contract. And what she had explicitly added back in.

"My bratty stepsister's finally ready for the punishment she deserves?"

"Yes," she said.

He grabbed the end of the belt and pulled her toward the bed, where he sat on the edge and laid her across his knee. He looked at the back of the bustier she was wearing, an intricate series of hooks and eyes keeping her body wrapped in all that lace. Nearly all of her gorgeous ass was exposed by her thong, and it made his mouth water. He squeezed her cheek, and then slapped it hard. She squeaked, and jumped.

"If you say stop, I'll stop."

"You don't think I can handle you?"

"I know you can, but I also know that your stubbornness gets you into trouble," he said, smacking her on her ass again.

"I want trouble."

And he wanted to do this for her, because she wanted it. And he relished that. That she trusted him like this. That she was happy to have her hands bound, happy to surrender not just her pleasure, but the perfect amount of pain. It made him feel powerful. But at the same time it made him feel like begging.

To have her like this always.

He left her skin gloriously red, and she was whimpering on his lap, trying to ride his thigh to get some satisfaction. He pushed his fingers through her folds and found her slick and wet. "You enjoyed that."

"So did you," she said, her hand moving to his cock.

"You are such a brat."

"And you want me," she said.

He lifted her from his lap, and pushed her up to the

edge of the bed, propped up on her knees, as he tugged her panties down to her mid-thigh. He looked at her, glistening and glorious, and leaned in, thrusting his tongue deep inside of her, tasting her desire.

She came instantly, trembling and shivering, and crying out his name.

His. All his.

Oh God, he might be sending them both to hell right now. But she was his. In a way that no one had ever been. In a way that nothing had ever been.

This was triumph like he had never known. And he would give her whatever she wanted in order to keep it. He stripped himself naked, and he pulled her into a sitting position so he could undo all the hooks and eyes on that bustier, letting it fall away, letting him see those gorgeous curves. Pale and pink, more generous now than they ever had been.

The evidence of her pregnancy aroused him much more than he would've ever imagined. The evidence that he had claimed her. That she was his.

He freed her hands. Set her loose.

"Lay down," she said.

It was his turn to obey. Because he had agreed to it.

He did not take orders from women. Not generally.

But there was enough power between them to exchange it. At least for now.

He lay on his back, and she moved over the top of him, biting down on his neck. "You will always belong to me."

He gripped her hair, pulling her down to him and kissing her deep, reveling in the feeling of her nipples brushing against his chest.

Then he released her, and let her kiss her way down his body. She teased him. Bringing him to the edge with her mouth again then again.

Taking him to the edge of himself. Places he had never been before.

He didn't give women control of anything. He didn't give anyone in his life control of anything. Because he always had to be the one.

Always.

But not here. Not with her.

She had him on the edge of exploding. And yet she wouldn't give him relief.

She could feel his mounting desire, and knew exactly when to pull back.

It was pleasure and pain unlike any he had ever known before. He pushed two fingers inside of her as she continued to lick him, and she moaned against his shaft, the vibrations sending sparks of desire through him.

"Let me have you," he growled. "Let me have this," he said, pushing his fingers deeper.

"Not yet," she said.

"I can't give you any more."

"I think you can."

She sucked the head of him into her mouth hard, and he almost lost control then and there. Almost came into her gorgeous mouth.

But the promise of taking her like he wanted to kept him from doing it.

She moved away from him, and lay down like a queen, her head propped up on the pillows, her back arched, her elbows resting on the mattress. "You can have me now. But only if you tell me exactly what I am."

He knew. He knew what he had to say, and he would say anything to get inside of her.

He moved to her, gripped the back of her head and took her mouth in a searing kiss. Then he thrust deep into her wet heat, the relief of being inside of her making him curse. "My wife," he said, the words dragged straight from the center of his chest.

"Yes," she said.

And then finally he was fucking her. Taking her.

It was everything he needed. Everything. And he cried out her name as desire overtook him. She said his in return as she dug her nails into his shoulders, as she gave herself over to her orgasm, her internal muscles milking every last drop out of him.

He had done it. He had surrendered. He had consigned them both to hell.

But they had both gone in together.

So they would have to figure out what this looked like. He had tried to make rules. They had broken them.

They were married, and they'd consummated. There was no going back. So now they would have to move forward with all of these broken shards.

There was only one answer. At least as far as he could see it. They had to exhaust this. Until it didn't have teeth. Until it didn't own or control them.

Until they could find a way to wear it into something comfortable. And perhaps at that point they would have fucked so much they would have the appetite for someone else.

You will never want anyone but her. You were cursed that day at the pool. And behold the aftereffects of that curse.

And yet, she was in his bed. So perhaps it was only a curse in part.

She snuggled up against him, her hand on his chest. "Mine," she said.

He felt like he couldn't breathe again, but this time he couldn't blame the tightness of his tie.

He had made his bed. And he would use it thoroughly.

CHAPTER TWELVE

THE NEXT MORNING Heather had the feeling she might be staring down wrath and retribution.

So it was a shock to wake up to find a tray of coffee and pastries on her nightstand. She was surprised that he didn't look angry. Standing there, gazing down at her, half dressed and gorgeous. Last night had been intense. And given the way things often were between them, that was saying something.

"Get dressed. We're leaving."

And here it was. The other shoe was about to drop. He was going to distance himself again. Become her forbidding stepbrother, rather than her passionate husband.

"I'm taking you on a honeymoon," he said.

She sat up quickly, letting her blankets fall away. "Excuse me?"

"I am taking you on a honeymoon. I did not stutter."

"You didn't. But that's not anything that we talked about."

"No. But things have changed."

"I have an ultrasound appointment next week."

"I'm aware. We discussed it. But we're going to go to the Bahamas for a few days. I have a private island there."

"Of course you do. Is that where you take other women?"

The look he gave her was long-suffering. "It is where other people often schedule luxury vacations, but it is mine, and I wish to use it, so I will."

Of course, luxury vacationing was literally his industry. And her first conclusion had been one that let her rest on jealousy. Because it was comfortable, honestly.

"When I think about you with other women it makes me feral," she said, slightly annoyed with herself that she had given him that much. But they were married now. Why should she be embarrassed? Why should she feel insecure? He was hers. The end.

"You're like me," he said, his tone grim.

"In what sense?"

"You already know."

She marinated on that while eating, and on the drive to the airfield. Then further on the plane. She was in love with him. She knew that. She didn't think that he did. Nor did she think that he returned the feelings. For as much as they felt in sync when it came to sex, when she talked to him she still felt like there was a wall up between them.

So whatever commonality he was assuming, she wasn't going to make the same assumption. Not when she could still feel that distance.

"What made you decide on this?" She decided to ask that rather than continuing to push at something he didn't seem to want to discuss.

"Things have changed. And you and I need to come to a firm agreement on how everything is going to work. When we're back in our lives at the estate, I imagine that will be the time. We have months before the baby is born."

"Are you taking me on a sex vacation?"

His dark eyes sharpened, a muscle in his square jaw leafing upward. "Yes. Do you have a problem with that?"

"Not at all. I just thought I would make sure of what my expectations were. You don't want to bring a knife to a gunfight."

"No indeed." He was silent for a moment.

"I hope you're prepared to do this. You're the one who put us in this situation."

"Oh, because I seduced you?" she asked.

"Yes."

"You folded like a house of cards. Your resistance was futile, and hollow, I might add. No wonder you had to stay away from me."

"We cannot be like this. Because here we are yet again, bringing knives and guns. When we should be endeavoring not to fight," he said.

"I'm actually not trying to fight you. But I am pointing out that if you want to cast blame, you're going to have to have a little bit of honesty. You didn't want to resist this."

"No. But I'm well aware of the potential cost," he said.

"You don't think that we're going to have so much sex this week that we can burn it out of our systems?"

"No. But perhaps it will be less…knife-like."

"What are you afraid of?" she asked.

He raised a dark brow. "I'm not afraid of anything. But I am wary. You and I have been adversaries far longer than we've been lovers. Somehow, we have to find a different way to be."

He wasn't wrong about that. It wasn't all about the baby anymore. It was about them. Their relationship mattered. For the sake of it. Not simply for the sake of somebody else.

"What if we were happy?" she said. "What if we had a lovely relationship, and great sex?"

He laughed, dry. "What a lofty and valiant goal. That is what I would like. But look at the state of the world."

"You're very cynical for a man born into money."

"Only because I know that money doesn't fix every problem. Because I know how toxic people can be with one another regardless."

When they touched down on his island, the first thing that captured her imagination was the blue. The ocean was so clear, so vivid. Even in the deepest parts, as they were descending she could see flying fish as they rose to the surface and glided up out of the water, and then as they moved over the shallows, she could see stingrays floating like underwater birds, slow and peaceful.

The sand was bright white and smooth, the nature pristine and undisturbed.

"The house is stocked for our arrival. All of our meals are prepared. No one will disturb us here."

"Oh."

She got off the plane, and he gestured to a waiting car. He drove them both away from the airfield, and to the center of the island, to the place with the highest elevation, which wasn't much on the relatively flat plain. But they could see over the trees, down to the beach. The house itself was all glass and stone, letting all the beauty of the island in, with no need for privacy, since they were the only inhabitants. The high ceilings had skylights, letting in the warmth from the sun, and probably offering fantastic views of the stars at night.

She drifted from the entryway into the kitchen, which had black stone slab countertops, with a large platter set in the center, filled with sliced and gloriously arranged tropical fruits. "There's no one here?"

"No." He turned and looked behind him, and they could both see the jet they had come in on taking off.

"We are the only people on the entire island."

She nodded, and dropped her purse down to the floor. Then she took off her shirt, her skirt and everything else.

"We don't need clothes then, I guess."

She knew she had him then.

His smile turned wolfish, and whatever reserve he'd been trying to keep was gone entirely now.

"I don't suppose we do."

The days passed in the loveliest haze. Time, status, reality had no meaning. There was no discussion about the future. No attempts at reasoning out what they had between them. They didn't talk about the past. They didn't talk about the future. They were in something like an eternal present, which was definitely different. And lovely in its way.

It also gave her even more of a chance to know him. Just as he was. Not just the difficult things in their past, the way that it related to her. Not the ways in which they had hurt each other and the why. But what he was interested in now. Though she found herself feeling curious about other things. She should let sleeping dogs lie. The sleeping dogs being his past physical relationships. But she felt raw about them. And this felt like a safe space. It wasn't the estate, where so many memories, so many unkind words that had been exchanged between them hung in the air. It wasn't his turf in London, or hers in New York. This was a liminal space where everything seemed just a little bit kinder. They were Adam and Eve here. Unburdened and unashamed.

She was lying out in the white sand, and he was walking out of the crystal clear water, naked. The water glistened on his body, his muscular chest, his thighs—thick and defined, and so sexy she was developing a new fetish. She wouldn't have said that she was into men's thighs. But now she was quite corrected.

"What kinds of relationships have you had?" she asked, staring at him from her lounging place in the sand.

He looked down at her and pushed dark hair off of his forehead, water droplets flowing down his forearm, through the valleys created by his muscles.

"I don't live in your head, Heather. You are going to have to give me some context."

"I was a virgin," she said. "And yes, some of it was that every time I considered having sex with a man, I imagined you bursting through the door and pulling him off of me. But then at a certain point I just imagined you. It kept me from ever having a sexual relationship. I feel slightly wounded that I didn't have the same impact on you."

He made a dismissive noise, and she bristled.

"Don't look at me like that," he said. "I have no desire to fight with you. By the time I noticed you as a woman, I was no virgin. I was seventeen. And so, I already had experience. Also, I determined that I was never going to touch you."

"You did a bad job at that."

"Yes, thank you. I am aware of that."

"What were your relationships like? Have you ever been in love? It's easy for you to know my history. But I don't know yours. That seems stunningly unfair."

"I'm sorry that it seems unjust to you." He was silent for a moment. And then he sat down beside her in the sand, his proximity taking away some of her irritation. Some of her anger. It was funny how it used to be the opposite. But now that she could touch him when she wanted to, she didn't feel quite so much negative energy around him. She felt close to him. Which was unexpected.

"I knew that I was never going to fall in love," he said. "And I was always very up-front with my lovers about that. I can have any woman I wanted. Except for you. And I think that might've tempered some of my activity. I might've been a monster otherwise. But there was always tension. The knowledge that there was a woman out there that I wanted more than the one that I was with."

Her stomach went tight. "But you knew you would never fall in love?"

"No. I know that I can't."

"Why not?" Her mouth was dry, her heart sore. Because she loved him. She did. She had. And he was telling her that he couldn't. This man who had captured so much of her for so many years was telling her he had always known he couldn't love. He wanted her. But just a bit more than all those other women. And she supposed that she should be thankful for that? That she should be flattered? But that wasn't the word. No.

Flattered was not the word. "Because I know how it looked on my mother. And I know... It has the capacity to be such a toxic thing. It simply isn't something I would ever willingly subject myself to. Or anyone else. I made a decision a long time ago that I was never going to put anyone through that."

"So they were meaningless to you."

He nodded. "Yes. They were." He looked at her directly. "You don't need to be jealous of women that I've already forgotten."

"How would you feel if I had a long list of ex-lovers?"

He practically bared his teeth. "I would want to hunt them down and kill them because they had seen you naked."

"Then don't begrudge me my own feelings of being feral over the women that have seen you."

"But no one has shared a bed with me all night. And no one has stayed on a private island with me. And certainly no one else has ever had my baby."

"I'm your wife," she said. Because she couldn't say that she loved him. She just knew she couldn't. Not after this. But she could remind him that she was his wife. That she mattered to him. That what they had was special. Unique. Not like what he had shared with anyone else.

"You are my wife. And it is not enough for us to satisfy each other for an evening. We have to make this work for a lifetime."

Yes. Forever. She didn't need to worry about it. She didn't need to push him. They had forever. He was right.

And one thing that she knew about herself and Romeo was that they could hang onto something for more years than most. They had already had this obsession for years. Surely they could continue defeat it. Cultivate it. School it into something better, nicer. "Yes," she said. "We have forever."

They had already made it this far. There was no telling how much further they would be able to make it.

But only if she gave him the time that he needed.

CHAPTER THIRTEEN

THEY HAD TO be back from the honeymoon far too soon for his liking. But by the time they arrived back at the estate, he had everything in order. In his mind. There, the days and nights had been all the same. They had rarely worn clothes, and if they had it had only been for the purpose of the joy in removing them. They had eaten when they felt like it, slept when they felt like it, fucked when they felt like it. It had been exactly what he had hoped for. A kind of fresh beginning that was desperately needed. Without the baggage they carried everywhere else. And so now they were back at the estate. And he knew exactly how to take all the things they had created on the honeymoon and make them work here. They could be friends by day. Lovers at night. And it would not be the sort of uncontained passion his parents had had. The turbulence that had marked his childhood.

No. This would be good.

He wouldn't even have to be as firm as he had imagined. Because everything with her was going so easily. Perhaps they were different people now. Perhaps this was much more feasible than he had originally thought. The sharpness might be worn away. A glorious possibility.

This was the first time he had felt entirely calm. Entirely in control. Today was the day they were finding out the sex of the baby. The doctor was coming to the estate, which meant that there was no need for the two of them to prepare to go out. He hadn't expected to feel nervous about this.

"You've seen the baby before?" he asked as she lay down in the bed, wearing her nightgown.

"Yes," she said.

"And everything looks good?"

"Yes. Everything so far has been completely normal."

"I should've been with you."

"We weren't… It's okay."

Except suddenly it felt like it wasn't, and he couldn't readily explain that. At the estate, they did have staff. At the estate, they did live in that glorious bubble of isolation. This house held memories. And for some reason they felt particularly heavy today. Even as the doctor arrived and shook his hand. She was the same doctor that Heather had seen in New York. She had very generously flown over, though he also had a feeling they were paying handsomely for the privilege.

He didn't care. Right then he felt like he would pay anything. As long as everything would go well.

As long as he could make sure that everything would be just fine. That Heather would be safe. That the baby would be safe. Things just felt heavy today.

He felt like something was clawing inside of his chest, trying to get out. An intensity that he had denied at every other point in his life, except at times when he had taken Heather to bed.

This thing that he had always thought lived inside of him.

The thing that had been confirmed when he had pulled that man off of Heather all those years ago and had nearly committed a murder over it.

He watched as all of the equipment was set up. He wasn't particularly interested in technology, or rather he never had been. Not medical technology. But suddenly, all of these things seemed unbearably important. Because they would measure the health of Heather's pregnancy. Of their child.

"Can you explain to me what everything here does?" he asked, moving in near to the doctor.

Heather laughed. "You're not doing any of it," she said.

"But I could," he said.

"You didn't go to medical school."

"I could figure it out."

"That is the most nonsensical masculine idiocy that I've ever heard. At least, since we negotiated our marriage contract."

He looked over at the doctor, who wasn't saying anything, but silently setting up equipment. "And we worked that out," he said.

"In," she responded noncommittally.

"Okay," the doctor said, turning and smiling. "Heather, this time we just do the Doppler on your stomach. I'm going to do a full anatomy scan, and make sure that everything is looking like it's on track."

"What if it's not?" Romeo asked.

"Wow," Heather said. "That's reassuring."

"What. It's a serious question. What if it isn't?"

"There are certain things that can be fixed now in utero," the doctor responded. "There are heart surgeons who can fix defects before the baby is born. And of course we look for other things. Things that aren't survivable. And we would advise you on the best medical decision, but of course ultimately it's up to you."

With the blankets in bed around her hips, and her nightgown pulled up over her expanding bump, Heather said nothing as the doctor put gel on her stomach and pressed the Doppler against her skin.

"Are you finding out the sex?"

"Yes," they both said.

But then he could think about nothing, because suddenly, there was the baby. And arm, and hand. A profile. He hadn't expected to be able to recognize anything. But he did. There was truly a child growing inside of her. That they had created in a moment of desperation. The kind of heated lust that he had never felt at any other time in his life. The kind he had never felt for anyone else.

And the end result was this. It was miraculous. It grabbed him by the throat and held him hard. She was measuring things. Organs, and though he couldn't ascertain what was normal, he recognized certain things. The child's brain. The heart, fluttering there. He had known that they were having a baby. Of course he had. It was why they had done all of this. It was why they were together. But he hadn't been able to imagine it. Concrete in a way it hadn't been when it had only been a due date. A rounding of her curves.

"And there," the doctor said. "Right there you can see. That is a baby boy."

"Everything looks good. I don't have any concerns

based on this ultrasound. And I would say that your due date is right on."

"Oh," Heather said. "We both know exactly when the baby was conceived."

"Not everyone does."

"Indeed not," Romeo said. He smiled, and tried to look filled with good humor, but there was something about this that was sitting like a weight on his chest. A son. He was having a son.

And look at how the relationship with his own father had been. Their father-and-son bond had been severed forever by Romeo's inability to come to grips with his feelings. His father had died without Romeo ever reconciling with him. He had never… He had never managed to fix it. Because the truth was, all the toxicity that he had seen between his parents lived inside of him. Either learned or inherited, he didn't know. Heather's mother had been…

It seemed as if she loved in a superior fashion. Certainly she had loved his father in a way that his father had not been able to love Carla. In a way that his father had not been able to love Romeo. And in a way Romeo had certainly never managed to demonstrate affection.

All he knew was great and terrible pain. All he knew was all-consuming, desperate, painful.

And what would he do with this boy? He would need every ounce of strength and willpower. He would need… He would need greatly to expand his emotional bandwidth, which currently felt all taken up.

"Are you okay?" Heather asked after she had gotten out of bed, the doctor still taking the equipment and preparing it for transport again.

"Yes. Did you want to go and shop for the nursery?"

"Yes," she said. "I very much do."

"There is a shop in town that sells lovely, locally made furniture. Perhaps we can go to the village."

"I would love that. It's been so long since I've actually left the estate and spent any time here."

She was looking at him like he was losing it, which was maybe fair. Maybe fair since he felt like he was coming apart inside. Even if there was no reason.

They took one of his father's classic cars down to the village, and Heather stroked the dashboard. "He loved this."

"He did," Romeo said, his throat tightening. God. He hadn't anticipated this. Hadn't anticipated that there would be such a host of regrets connected to his own father as he faced down this new iteration of a father-son relationship. What had he thought? Of course there was always going to be a chance that it would be a son. He hadn't thought that it would matter. Maybe it didn't. Maybe he would feel equally unable to parent a daughter. But this felt like the potential to be a mirror. And he didn't want to repeat the same steps that he had already walked with his father, only backward.

No. The very idea was punishing.

The village itself was charming. It always had been, though Romeo himself had never spent an immense amount of time there. His mother had always taken him with her when she had traveled. She had required him to be her emotional support, she had always said. Even when his parents had been married, when she had gone on location for photo shoots, she had always taken him. His youth had been nomadic, or it had been stagnant. Because when they were at the estate, generally, whatever was happening was between his parents. And not him.

He had only been cannon fodder.

He swallowed hard, trying to regain his focus. This was about his child. This was about Heather.

"Romeo, you don't seem okay," she said.

"I'm fine," he growled. He was searching the narrow streets for a place to park, and nearly cursing everything before finding a place near the store that he was looking for.

They got out, and walked down the old, crooked lane into a stone building that housed handmade furniture made by local artisans.

And Heather was immediately bright and cheery and looking at rocking chairs, cradles and cribs. Toy boxes. So he was trying to pull himself out of the funk that he found himself in, because she was enjoying this. She'd—

His phone rang.

His mother.

He sighed, trying to disperse the tension in his chest.

It didn't work.

Predictably.

"Yes?"

"You haven't called me," she said.

"I'm sorry. I've been busy. I was on honeymoon, and now Heather and I have just found out that we're having a son."

She did not congratulate him. Because she wasn't in the headspace. He had known that the minute he had seen her name on his phone, and he didn't even know why he was bothering to introduce it into the conversation.

"I need you to come back to Vienna."

"I can't," he said.

"Romeo," his mother said, her tone shocked. "I'm not feeling well. I'm afraid… What if I hurt myself?"

"Mother," he said. "You have a therapist. And I need you to follow the instructions that he's given you. If you really feel as if you're in danger, then you need to check yourself into the hospital. You know that I can't get there immediately anyway. But I'm shopping. For furniture for my child."

"The baby isn't even born yet."

"No, but he will be," Romeo said, a cold rage filling his chest. His mother. His fragile mother, who didn't do this on purpose, and he knew that. But suddenly everything just felt wrong. It felt angry. It felt awful.

Suddenly, everything felt like it was in danger of breaking apart.

Because his entire childhood had been fucked. And if he wasn't able to build walls around all of this, then it was only going to be the same. He wanted his mother to be in his son's life. But he would not allow his son to give endlessly to his grandmother. Not when she was supposed to give to him. And that's how it would be. If ever Romeo did not have the energy, she would try to bypass him and get his child. It was what she had done to him. When she couldn't get attention from his father she had…

"I love you," Romeo said. "You know that. But I have a family. And—"

"This is about your wife. Because of course you care about her more than you do me. Because of course, she's just like her mother and—"

"Mother," Romeo said. "This is only you trying to make a bad feeling inside of you worse. Because if you do that, then you know that you can get me on a plane."

"Are you accusing me of manipulating you?"

"Yes. Whether you're doing it on purpose or not. Heather and I will come visit you soon. But I need you to follow your plan. I need you to take care of yourself. Because I have to take care of my family."

Anger was threatening to tear a hole through his chest. He couldn't act on it. He couldn't treat his mother the way that his father did. That would be awful. It would be inexcusable. There would be no justification for it. None whatsoever.

Why did his feelings feel like they were going to choke him out?

He had to get a grip on them. He had to get a grip on himself. This was the kind of life he did not want his child living.

Whether it be from his mother, whether it be from him. Because it lived in him. It was threatening to get out now, to burn everything to the ground. To take everything that he had ever tried to do with his mother and render it useless.

Because part of him wanted to tell her to just do it already if she was going to.

It was years of anger and exhaustion, and he knew that he couldn't say that. He knew he couldn't.

"Call your doctor."

He hung up the phone, and looked across the store at Heather. As she began to make her way toward him as he picked up his phone and called his mother's therapist. "I need you to do a check-in on my mother. Please go to the house as quickly as you can. She's supposed to call you. But I don't necessarily trust that she will."

Heather frowned. As soon as he hung the phone up she spoke. "What's going on?"

"My mother is being my mother. Nothing out of the ordinary."

He was trying to make light of it. Trying not to let her see the dark mess that his soul was in.

"I have some favorites. But only if you like them."

"No. This is… You can choose."

He followed her through the store, with one goal in mind. To keep everything together. He had to keep everything together. This was what he had proposed. He and Heather would be friends. During the day. They would not give in to the toxic side of their relationship. They wouldn't surrender to it.

He repeated that. As she chose furniture and made arrangements to have it delivered. As they went and bought blankets. Baby clothes. As she handed him a tiny white onesie that seemed impossibly small. Didn't seem like it could possibly contain a real human. Much less one that he was going to have to take care of. But he was desperate. He was desperate for it to be night. Because he needed her. He needed to exhaust the demons inside of him. He needed to do something.

He needed to make sure that she never saw this. He needed to make sure that he was never his own mother. That he didn't vent his toxicity onto other people.

In the bedroom. That was where he could release this.

It was the only safe place.

CHAPTER FOURTEEN

SHE COULD SENSE the change in him. He was pretending that nothing was wrong, and it was baffling her. He had experienced a near personality switch after they had found out that the baby was going to be a boy, and then his mother had called him, and he had refused to give her any details about it. But he was obviously upset. But also not flying to Vienna.

She had the chef at the estate make them a celebratory meal. She was happy they were having a boy. She would've been happy with anything, of course, but it was the way that it felt more real now. The way that she felt like she could actually picture their child.

A little boy like Romeo.

It made her heart ache. She loved them both so much. She loved this vision of their future. But the distance between herself and her husband felt…awful.

That was the thing that scared her the most.

But he was becoming more withdrawn, and the later that it got, the more pronounced that became. He practically didn't speak during their meal. And when they were finished they began to walk toward the bedroom they were sharing, and as soon as the door closed, he kissed her. Hard and punishing. This was Romeo as he had been months ago. The man who had taken her like he was possessed.

This was how he had been on their wedding night. Something was wrong. This wasn't gentle.

This was something else. Possessive, intense. Angry.

"Romeo," she said.

"Heather," he responded, wrapping her hair around his hand and pulling her head back, kissing her neck, her throat, down to her collarbone.

She gasped. Because even though she felt like there was something wrong, she was a slave to this. A slave to him. To the intensity of the desire between them. It was too good.

He looked up at her, something haunted in his dark eyes, and then he grabbed the edges of her blouse and tore it open, exposing her breasts. She hadn't worn a bra today, because everything was ill fitting and she hadn't had a chance to get something more comfortable. And judging by the light in his eyes, he appreciated that.

"That's what I thought. I was staring at your breasts, trying to see if you had anything underneath. I thought that I saw your nipples get tight anytime I got near you. You want me," he said, desperation carving an edge into his voice.

"Of course I do. I've always wanted you."

"It's a sickness. For you just like it is for me."

She gripped his face, and stared into his eyes. "It's not a sickness. It's the best thing that's ever happened to me."

He growled, like a wounded beast, and pressed his hand between her shoulder blades, arching her back toward him and lowering his head so that he could suck a nipple deep into his mouth. It was nearly violent, the edge to his desire gloriously unhinged. And she was caught between the desire to soften it and to push them further. To reassure him, or to give him a place where he could have whatever he needed.

She realized it wasn't one or the other. It was like they had been trying to make it one or the other. All this time.

Their days were soft, their nights filled with passion. But she wanted to get back to their honeymoon. Where every moment had been both.

And he seemed desperate to draw all these lines.

She knew why. It was clear that everything with his parents was painful. Complicated. It was clear that it had created a situation where something about emotional intimacy terrified him. She didn't fully understand. But she wanted to. And if this was the doorway, then she had to let him open it like this. If this was what he needed, then she needed to let them have it. Needed to let it go all the way, because somehow she had a feeling that on the other side of it she would find that way to him. That perhaps this would demolish the wall just enough for her to climb over.

Or maybe she just wanted him. All of him. His good, his ugly. His hard and his soft. His rough and his tender. She certainly didn't want it from anyone else.

She was incapable of it. He forced her down onto her knees, and she trembled as he undid his belt. There was a place for making him beg. But there was a place for her to beg as well, and she knew that this was the moment.

"Please," she said. "Let me have you."

"You want this," he said, gripping himself at the base and bringing his hardness to her lips.

"Yes," she said. "I do."

"Even when I'm like this?"

"Especially when you're like this."

He pushed his way into her mouth, and began to thrust hard against the back of her throat. Every moment that they'd resisted was leading to this. Not to that first time, but to this moment.

He was pushing her. He was testing her, and she was going to pass. She was going to do more than pass. Because she didn't just tolerate this. She loved it. She wanted it all.

He wasn't too powerful for her. If anything, she was too powerful for him, and this moment was proving it.

Because he was at the end of himself, and he needed her. Needed her strength. Needed her touch.

She could be there for him. She would.

He pulled her mouth away, and brought her back up to her feet, kissing her, deep and hard and bruising. She gasped as he reached around and cupped her ass, squeezing her tight before turning her away from him, wrapping her hair around his hand again as he bent her over the bed. "Ask for it," he said.

"Please," she said. "Please take me."

He thrust into her from behind, one hand on her hip, the other holding her hair fast as he lost himself inside of her. As he pushed them both to the brink.

This was what he needed.

This was what they both needed.

He released her hair, reached around and gripped her chin, held her face and turned it back toward him as he leaned down to kiss her, violently as he continued to thrust inside of her. Like he was reminding himself of who he was with. As if he needed the reminder.

"Romeo," she said, saying his name because she knew that it would undo him. Because she knew that however much he was more powerful than her physically, she had a different power altogether.

He growled, leaned down and bit her shoulder as he thrust hard into her one last time, coming hard as he pushed her right over with him. He rested his forehead against her back, and she could feel the sweat on his brow. Could feel all of his intensity. All of his anger. Everything.

She turned, uncoupling with him and kissing him deep on his lips, moving her hands through his hair. "I love you," she whispered against his mouth.

His whole body shivered.

"I do," she whispered. "I love you. Do you know how much? That's why we can be friends. That's why we can be friends and we can be this. We can be both and everything."

He pressed his forehead against the curve of her neck. "My mother had another episode today."

"And you didn't fly to Vienna?"

"No. I didn't. Because today had to be about our child. Because everything has to be about our child."

"I don't agree," she said. "I'm glad that you did that. But I hope that you did it for you. Because you're allowed to live, Romeo. Your life matters apart from her. It just does. And you shouldn't be made to feel like you have to drop everything to give her whatever she needs."

"You understand. It's me. I'm not any different from her."

"You're very different from her. You are not fragile."

"No. I'm angry. So is she, and she has mental illness on top of it, so the way that she chooses to express it is different. The way that she is able to express it is different. But I am petty, and I am vindictive. Look at the way that I treated you all throughout school."

"We were young. And you were going through things."

"Yes. It's true. I was. But I don't know another way to be. And that is the honest truth. I do not know another way. And I know what it's like to be held hostage by someone whose emotions are… It's her. I did to my own father, after all."

"You were a teenage boy. We spoke about this already. Your father should've reconciled things between the two of you."

"Maybe. But I was also prepared to hold him at arm's length forever. Punishment. I cannot believe that version of myself. I will not be what my mother has been to our child. I will not be that to you. Every strong emotion I have turned sour. And I will not subject you to that."

"Maybe you should ask me what I want to be subjected to. Maybe you don't get to make all the decisions."

"It isn't about controlling you. It's about controlling myself. And I… You will fall out of love with me. This I guarantee you."

"No," she said. "I won't."

Pain tore at her chest. Because she wanted to stay with him forever. She really did. They had a whole agreement. And suddenly, the agreement didn't matter anymore. Because it wasn't about a set of ideal circumstances that they were creating for their baby. It was about what the two of them could have. And what he wasn't allowing because he was so afraid.

But she couldn't carry on like that. So she was going to have to make this into something he couldn't control. Because that's what he was trying to do. She understood now. He was just so afraid of the strength of all of this. So he was trying to separate things. His mother, her, their passion versus their friendship. And this reality of having a child was what had pushed him over the edge. It was what had made it all too much.

She could understand that. She could sympathize with him. But she couldn't enable it. She simply couldn't. Not when they could have everything. And if he was going to draw lines so that he could hide behind them, so that he could give them both the least of what they could have, then she wasn't going to be complicit in that.

Because what he didn't understand was that there were other ways to hurt people.

"I love you. I love you enough to try and take a risk now. I love... Romeo. We've been fighting this fight for so many years. Fighting to stay away from each other. And we lost that, didn't we? So now, I want to fight to have the most of what we can have. I think we were meant to be together. Maybe we're the love story. Have you ever thought of that? Maybe all of this happened so that you and I could be together. Maybe we're the happy ending."

"I believe that's true," he said. "We are a mess. Created by a mess. And I believe that we can do our best with it, but I can't—"

"You're afraid. Then I understand that. Your mother turned love into a weapon for years. She turned it into a task that you had to complete. And today you did something incredible. You chose a different path. It doesn't change how much you love her. If she tries to make you feel differently, then that's on her. It's not you. Your love is the same. Whether or not we call what we have love, it's the same. I love you, and I think that you love me. But I don't want to have friendship and sex. When I decided to marry you, I decided that I was doing it because I wanted you. In the beginning, it was about the baby. But that's just a story I was telling myself. In the end, it's about you and me. It's about our love story."

"You don't understand what you're asking for."

"I do. I'm asking for you. All of you. And what part of me has ever seemed like I couldn't handle all of you? It's been that way from the beginning. When we only knew how to hurt each other."

"Maybe that's all I ever know how to do. Maybe that's the most that it will ever be."

"No. I just don't believe it. I'm sorry. I know that it might make you feel better to think that this is all we have, because you want something to numb it, don't you? You want some kind of a break from all of this. But this is intense, I fear. Becoming parents. Being married. Being in love."

"And what exactly are you proposing?"

"The agreement is out the window. You're going to have to penalize me. I'll give you everything. Every penny that I have. But we will have to figure out how to coparent. Because I'm not scared anymore. What I'm scared of is us having only a little when we can have everything. That's what I'm scared of. And that's what I won't allow."

"You can't leave me," he said.

"I can. And if you love me, you'll follow me. But if you don't you let me go. And I will never keep you out of your child's life. I'm sorry for what I said when I first found out that I was pregnant. But I would never do that to you. Not now. Not now that I know you. But I know you well enough to take this risk. So I'm giving you one more chance. Do you think you can ever love me?"

She saw fear in his eyes. Real. Raw.

"No."

"Then I can't stay with you."

He said nothing while she packed her things and left. There was nothing to say. She had said it all. She wanted something that he did not have the ability to give, and he had no choice but to let her go. It was the only kind thing. It was the only thing he could do. She wanted to escape him, so he needed to let her do it. There was no other option.

But as soon as she was gone, he began the process of tearing everything apart. Absolutely everything. The bedroom, and then he went down the hall and went into the room he lived in so infrequently as a child.

And he began to dismantle that as well. There could be nothing left. None of these false promises. None of this…

The pain inside of him was like a living thing. It had teeth. Monstrous teeth.

He was undone. He was finished. Because if he didn't have Heather, what did he have?

It was like years' and years' worth of pain was pushing forward now. It was like all of the feelings that he had ever withheld from himself were crashing in on him now.

Years of it.

Why was his mother not like other mothers?

Why did his father care more about her, and then his new wife? His new stepdaughter? Why never him?

Why did he always have to work to have love? Why did he always have to give? Until he had nothing left. Nothing for his father, who he had shut out, and then there was her.

Then there was her.

He could remember when she had first appeared, and it was like a demon had risen up inside of him and told him that he had no choice but to deny her. He had to.

And then, when he was seventeen, it had become clear why.

Her beauty intoxicated him. His desire for her surpassed any desire he had ever felt for any other woman. And it made him mean. It made him want to lash out at her. It made him want to push her away.

Because she was the key to unlocking the door that he kept so carefully locked.

The one that kept him from being his father or his mother.

The one that kept him safe.

Always.

He gazed around the room, at all the destruction.

He had torn apart the bed. He had put holes in the wall.

He was like an animal. He had always known he would be.

Confirmed when he had first seen Heather with that other man.

Oh God. It had been confirmed then. Because he had

been tempted to rip that fool's head off. He was lucky that he hadn't.

So very lucky.

He had been fighting this all those years. That his feelings for her were too strong. That they were...

That they were in love. And for him that was toxic, and it always would be.

She wanted them to have everything? He couldn't have everything. He couldn't.

And how did she leave him? How dare she. When he had been trying to save her.

You were trying to save yourself.

Maybe.

But he feared the alternative would be to drown.

CHAPTER FIFTEEN

SHE DIDN'T GO to New York. Instead, she went to London. She went to Catherine.

"Oh, my friend," Catherine said, pulling her in for a hug.

"I'm pathetic," she said.

"You're not pathetic. Well. You are a little bit. Tell me what happened."

"I demanded his love. And when he refused to give it to me I left him. Because I believe that he does love me. And I'm sort of just playing chicken with his fear now."

"Well. It was strong of you."

"What if he doesn't love me? What if he doesn't come after me?"

Catherine sighed, and brought her into the kitchen, where she immediately began to heat up the electric kettle. "Oh, he will come after you, my dear. The question is only in what capacity he will do it. Because he is not a soft man. Which means he's going to chase you down."

"He didn't. He just let me leave."

"Well. That means he's more scared of you than you are of him."

"But I don't understand… I don't understand how. I don't understand why it's so scary to him."

"It's scary to you too. But also he's a man, so it's going to take him longer to get there."

"But I was brave."

"Because women are. Think of everything your mom went through, and she still fell in love with your stepdad. Not just because it was advantageous to her. She really fell in love with him. And think about what Romeo put you through, but you still have a greater understanding of what your actual feelings are than he does. Honestly. Men have greater physical strength, but we...we have stronger hearts. And we have to, because if we didn't, why would we keep falling in love with those creatures?"

"I'm being selfish. I could let them be comfortable. But then I wouldn't be. And I just don't think we can thrive that way. I really don't. I think it would explode eventually, and it would be a mystery as to why. But I see it now. I see it clearly. I know why. Because if he keeps building walls, I'm going to keep trying to push them down. And he will resist harder, and... We can't keep doing that."

"No. But of course the man is going to want to see his baby."

"Of course. And I want him to see his baby. I've never said otherwise. But...my mother lived for me. For years. I'm grateful. We were all happier when she began to live as a whole person. Well, except Romeo. All of this is such a sore subject for him, and I think it's difficult for him to talk about, or maybe even understand."

"You tried. And in the end, if that's the best you've got, then it's the best you've got. You tried."

It was a lovely sentiment. She thought about it while

she went to sleep in Catherine's guest room. But she didn't want to try and fail. She loved Romeo Accardi. With everything she had in her. And if after all this time, all this pain, all this pleasure, they couldn't find a way to call it what it was, then she had failed.

She was strong. And she would go on. She would be the best mother to her son.

But part of herself would be lost. The part of herself that had fallen in love with Romeo all those years ago.

He was going out of his mind. She wasn't there. He had gone all the way to New York to find her, had gone to her penthouse, and discovered that she wasn't there.

It made him want to tear apart her home, but even he had limits. It made him want to lash out, at everyone. And everything.

This was love for him, unchecked. Painful. This was him. The absolute truth of who he was. And he despised himself.

He stopped right where he was standing, in her living room. And for a heartbeat he was silent. He was still.

And instead of fighting the feeling, instead of lashing out at everything around him, he let it roll over him.

This feeling that he had been running from all of his life.

Love.

He could remember the first time he realized that love had a cost. The first time that in order to get his mother's attention he had to make her feel better. The first time he had heard his father say cruel things when his mother was in the middle of a meltdown. Oh, Giuseppe had not been able to be there for her. He had been cruel in her lowest moments, and that had always made everything feel complicated. Because sometimes Romeo felt that same cruelty, but he would never say it.

He believed in his heart that his father was a good man. But a complicated one. As his mother was a good woman, but a complicated one. And so it wasn't as easy as saying that love the way they expressed it wasn't real. It was the most real love that they were capable of with one another. And with him.

And what real love was Romeo capable of?

You have loved her without exhaustion for years.

Yes. His mother. He had always been willing to do what he had to in order to make her feel safe. Even if it compromised his own happiness. He had not been sacrificial with his father. But maybe it was because he judged him. Because he felt like his father should be able to handle what Romeo had taken on. And then there was Heather. It had always been her. She had always been the only one. The only one who had engaged more than just his body. But his heart.

And he had rewritten that. Had told himself that it was hatred. With the fire of a thousand suns, so that he wouldn't have to…live with the extraordinary, magical, devastating miracle of love.

He knew how strong love was. How complicated.

But when he looked back over the years with her, he didn't feel exhausted. He felt foolish. Because how could he have ever believed that he hated her? He felt small, because he had taken his own fear and fashioned it into a weapon used to keep her away.

But it hadn't worked. Maybe she was right.

There were all these complicated loves. But maybe

theirs wasn't. Maybe theirs was the one that was meant to be. Maybe theirs was the one that was stronger than anything else. Maybe theirs was the one that would actually heal, and not hurt.

Because God knew a life without her wouldn't do a damn thing to fix him. But he had to stop running. He had to stop fighting.

He had to stand there, and let in the light.

Eventually she would go back to New York. Eventually she was going to have to tell him where she was. But not right now. Right now she was happy to just live with her best friend and try to piece together some semblance of a routine. She could feel the baby move now. She was so happy about it. And so mad at Romeo that she couldn't share it with him.

She had gone grocery shopping so that she could cook tonight. Something to make her feel alive.

Someday she would inhabit her strength fully. It was not this day. The streetlights were beginning to come on, and she simply couldn't make herself walk faster as she approached Catherine's town house. And then, beneath the glow of the light, she saw a tall, imposing figure. All in black. A man that she would know anywhere. A man that she knew better than anyone else.

"'Wherefore art thou, Romeo?'"

He stepped into the light fully. "I haven't had any poison."

"I'm thankful for that." Her chest tightened. "Why are you here? Because if it's for your wounded pride, to enforce a document or to try and have your way I—"

"It's not. It's not I... I came for you. Not because we

signed papers. Not because of my pride. Because of my heart. It would've been so much easier if I could have believed that what my parents had wasn't love. The problem is, it was. My father loved me. My mother loves me. Their best version of love left me scarred. And the intensity of my own feelings…it terrified me. That if I ever love somebody I would hurt them, the same way that my parents hurt each other. That I would hurt a child the same way my mother hurt me. When I met you, it felt like it was confirmed. All of the feelings that we have traded back and forth, it seemed to confirm that. That I would be a danger to you. To me. I kept renegotiating the boundaries, because I wanted you. It isn't going away. It isn't going to change. So I surrender, Heather. To you. To this. To love. If this is how I die, then it's how I die. By loving you. And I would rather experience it that way than to live all the years ever without you."

She didn't have words. So she just stretched up on her toes and threw her arms around his neck, her grocery bags hitting him in the back. "I love you."

"I love you."

"It won't be the death of us," she whispered.

"How do you know?"

"Because it has kept us going all this time. Even when we called it something else. So let's have this now. Let's have each other. I love you. I love you so much it hurts. And I love that it does. Because it also brings me joy. And so do you."

"Heather… I'm not worthy of that."

"You never had to be. You simply had to be you. That's all it's ever been. It was you from the beginning. And you all the days after."

"And it will be us forever."

She stretched up on her toes and kissed him. She kissed him with all of the love in her body. "Do you know that love has a flavor?"

"What is it?"

"It's you."

EPILOGUE

THEIR LOVE WASN'T painful. It was beautiful. The pain had been in trying to keep it from flourishing. Growth that was being suppressed by fear. But once it was given free rein, it spread over everything. And it made their life beautiful.

Once he let go of the idea that he had to earn everything, even his relationship with his mother improved. And ten years later, as they brought their four children to visit their grandmother for Christmas, going to the house in Vienna felt light. Which was something Romeo would have said was impossible. But it turned out that nothing was truly impossible with love. Especially not the kind like he and Heather had.

They enjoyed a lovely Christmas dinner with Carla, and then went back to their favorite hotel, with all the kids in tow. Though they did complain about having to share a room, since the suite only contained two bedrooms.

"It will build character," Romeo said to his oldest son before he closed the doors and then went to the room where his wife was waiting.

"They're such menaces," she said.

"My favorite ones," he agreed.

He looked at her, and familiar desire stirred in his veins. It had never stopped. This. The profound, glorious ache that he felt for this woman.

This woman who he loved so softly and fiercely. And who he made love with with all the passion contained in his being.

"I have loved you for well over half my life."

"It's true," she said. "Though you would never have called that love back then."

"No. But I was a fool then."

"Were you?"

"Yes." He wrapped his arms around her. "I used to think that hating you had become a habit. But it was just being obsessed with you. Thinking about you. Wanting you."

"What do you think now?"

"Loving you is not a habit, Heather Accardi. It is who I am."

* * * * *

Did Heir of Scandal *leave you wanting more?*
Then you're certain to love these other
desire-fueled stories from Millie Adams!

Billionaire's Bride Bargain
His Highness's Diamond Decree
After-Hours Heir
Dragos's Broken Vows
Promoted to Boss's Wife

Available now!

MILLS & BOON ®

Coming next month

ENEMIES UNTIL AFTER HOURS
Natalie Anderson

Mia drew on a defensive smile and headed into Sante's office—leaving his door wide open behind her.

Trying to steady her heartbeat. The appalling thing was that increasingly her body responded with chaos to his proximity. It didn't seem to care that he was a heartless jerk who'd betrayed her brother, her body just wanted his near. So, she was ignoring her body. Controlling it.

'You've screwed up my scheduling.' He glared at her.

'Where?'

He jabbed a finger at the screen, and she was forced to round his desk to study it. Big mistake. There was nowhere near enough of a barrier between them and she desperately needed to calm her overexcited response.

'You've blocked out a significant portion of my day tomorrow.'

She leaned closer and he turned his head toward her, meaning his mouth was only inches from hers. It was *searingly* intimate. It would take nothing to lower hers and—

What the hell was she thinking? Why had the idea to kiss him popped into her head? She stared into his brown eyes for three seconds too long.

Continue reading

ENEMIES UNTIL AFTER HOURS
Natalie Anderson

Available next month
millsandboon.co.uk

COMING SOON!

We really hope you enjoyed reading this book.
If you're looking for more romance
be sure to head to the shops when
new books are available on

Thursday 26th February

To see which titles are coming soon, please visit
millsandboon.co.uk/nextmonth

MILLS & BOON

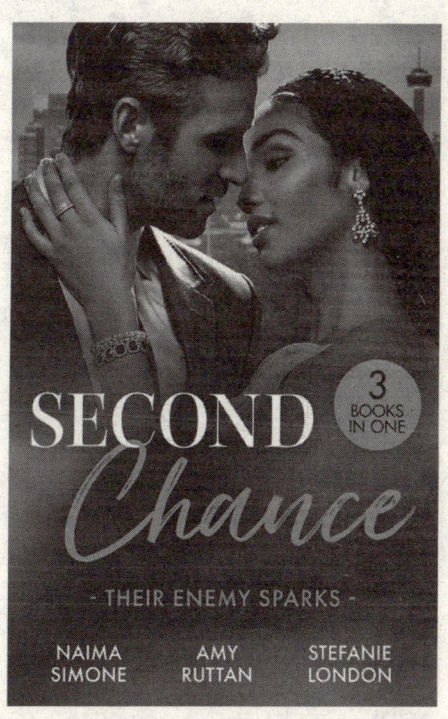

LET'S TALK

Romance

For exclusive extracts, competitions and special offers, find us online:

f MillsandBoon

X @MillsandBoon

⊙ @MillsandBoonUK

♪ @MillsandBoonUK

Get in touch on 01413 063 232